ELEPHANT
AND CASTLE

HANNAH LEDFORD

CITY OWL
PRESS

ELEPHANT AND CASTLE

CITY OWL PRESS
www.cityowlpress.com

Cover Design by Tina Moss LLC. All stock photos licensed appropriately.

Edited by Jessica Shearer.

For information on subsidiary rights, please contact the publisher at info@cityowlpress.com.

Print Edition ISBN: 978-1-64898-456-3

Digital Edition ISBN: 978-1-64898-455-6

Printed in the United States of America

For my mom and dad, who somehow always believed that "romance writer" was a viable career option.

And for John—you're the only reason I know anything about true love.

CHAPTER ONE

NORA SHRAPSAN SPUN in a slow circle on a street just south of the Thames. Not that she knew which direction was north or south or which way was to the river or to Buckingham Palace. Seven years ago, Nora had zipped through the streets of London like a local, hopping on red double-decker buses and hailing midnight cabs, emerging from the labyrinth of underground stations with the ease and confidence of someone who'd lived there for years, though it had only been one summer. Nora had found her way around the city without any problems when she was a teenager with few responsibilities and nowhere in particular to go, so she had foolishly assumed that she could just pick up right where she left off in her relationship with ye olde London Town. She had assumed that she —an expert traveler and experienced tour-book copy editor—could jump on the Tube with ease and get to where she was going.

She was wrong.

When she'd gotten off the Underground and pulled up the address on her phone, the little blue arrow kept spinning in circles, changing its mind about which way she should turn. If Nora didn't figure it out soon, she was going to be late for the first meeting with her new editor, and she was going to have moved all the way across the Atlantic just to get fired, which would really be a shame, honestly. She'd been preparing for months—

paperwork and visas, packing and parting words to friends. She had even broken up with her super-hot boyfriend, abandoning the comfort of upstate New York and regularly scheduled above-average sex. The breakup was a thrill for her mother, who always said that she shouldn't bother with Brandon anyway. Too pretty, too shallow. According to her mother, above-average sex wasn't worth the hassle of dating someone who made you watch Monday Night Football, but Nora was quick to point out that this was coming from a woman who wasn't getting laid at all.

"We're very comfortable together," Nora had explained to her mother again and again.

Kathleen Shrapsan, cancer survivor and member of the Binghamton City Council, did not take "comfortable" for an answer. They had the same conversation in perpetuity: "Brandon is very easy to look at," her mother would say. Even she couldn't deny it. "And he's nice to you. Heck, I feel comfortable with him too, but that doesn't mean he has any interest in marrying and impregnating you."

"Mom—"

"And you're too smart for him," her mother complained. Nora stopped arguing that a lot of men didn't care as much about *smart*.

"I want you to get married and have lots of babies and be happy, happy, happy, but I don't want you to do any of that with a man whose favorite book is *Sports Illustrated*. Also, not getting laid is a choice."

As usual, Nora knew her mother was right. Kathleen had been overjoyed when she heard the news about the London job, and she immediately waved off all the guilt Nora felt about abandoning her in-recovery matriarch. That was just a minuscule con in a long list of pros: no more football, no more dinners with finance bros, no more Brandon. With little regard for any of Nora's fears or concerns, her mother was praising the Lord that she wasn't going to just be *comfortable* anymore.

Even though her breakup was so fresh, and Nora kind-of-rudely told him two weeks before leaving the country, she was only partly concerned about the end of her relationship with Brandon and only slightly more concerned about the fact that she couldn't read a map. There was also the matter of the diary. A diary that had turned up while she was searching for her passport. A diary that was still sitting at the bottom of the overstuffed backpack slung over her shoulder, practically throbbing like it was a freaking tell-tale heart.

Nora decided she better just pick a direction and take her chances. She had done this before, after all; she'd trekked all over that city by herself or with her British boyfriend and his friends. She'd walked in the footsteps of The Beatles and Anne Boleyn and Idris Elba, probably. She shouldn't have a problem finding a company office in Southwark. She lifted her chin and marched down the sidewalk.

"Make a U-turn," her phone said. Nora wanted to fling it into oncoming traffic.

The diary had only started taunting her recently, and in fact she didn't even remember it existed until a few weeks ago when she'd opened an old shoe box, praying it wasn't going to be a smelly pair of Keds. Inside, there were old photographs, ticket stubs, a crinkled map, and a loose bunch of old tampons (not used, obviously). There was no passport, but underneath it all she found a diary with a pink, faux-leather cover that she recognized immediately. With her fingers touching the fake leather, Nora couldn't help abandoning the search for items that may have actually had some use to her as she prepared to move to a different country, and she took the little book over to the couch where she could sink into the cushions, crack it open, and remember for a second what it felt like to be nineteen. It was impossible not to memorize the words while studying the pages like an anthropologist who had uncovered a discovery that could unlock the secrets of a lost world.

London, June 5

Hugh keeps saying such romantic things, things that I don't know if I believe, but it's nice to hear them anyway. "I was perfectly content before I met you," he says, "but now I can't imagine what I'll ever do without you." He tells me he's sure I will ruin him. I know in my head that it's cheesy and he probably says stuff like this to every girl he dates, but I can't help feeling like it might be possible that he's falling in love with me too.

· · ·

London, June 29

Here's the honest truth. There is nothing like getting kissed by a British man in an elevator at three o'clock in the morning...

London, July 7

I have never slept with anyone before...well until now. I have roommates, and Hugh has roommates, so it's not like we get a lot of privacy, and even when I would stay over at his place just to cuddle, I still felt a little embarrassed at what Dev might be thinking. One morning I walked out, and Julian was over, and I think we both turned bright red. Dev eavesdropping on my love life is one thing, but Julian...he's so sophisticated and shy. So Hugh got a hotel room, and that's where we went. "I think maybe I'm a bad influence on you," he said. Maybe he's right. He's five years older, and he's a man, and I know very little about men. But I wanted it to happen all along. I wanted him to take me somewhere private. I wanted to kiss him all over, even if I was worried about looking like an idiot and not knowing what I was doing. When I was there with him, I didn't really worry about that at all.

Nora could admit that discovering this significant artifact may have had something to do with her breakup as well. Sure, she'd been preparing to leave the country, but long distance was a thing. She and Brandon could have tried that. She wasn't sure exactly how long she would be in London; they could get back together when she returned. But after reading those pages and remembering how she felt that summer, Nora thought maybe she had known Hugh Jeffries better than Brandon from just three wonderful British summer months. She knew she was probably being stupid and idealizing their whole relationship. For one, she had been so young and had never been abroad before, and she was already inclined to indulge in romantic notions. Then there was the man himself. Hugh was a musician. With an accent. And he wrote songs about her. How could you not be head over heels for someone who wrote songs about you? It really wasn't a fair fight.

If she had stayed, she would have grown up, and the rose-colored glasses would have come off. They would fight, and she would get bored, and he would get lazy and messy and forget her birthday after spending more time in the pub with his friends than making her happy. They had just never gotten to that part. A long time ago, she stopped fantasizing that Hugh Jeffries would show up on her doorstep and sweep her off her feet.

Still, Nora realized as she shuffled down the street—slightly frazzled and increasingly panicked—one part of her brain was looking for her office, but another part was disobediently searching for Hugh, as if she could imagine him into existence just by standing on a street in the city where he lived. You would think that someone who had finally gotten the chance at her dream job—or at least a lot closer to her dream job than sitting in a tiny office copy editing articles about beautiful places she would never get to visit—would have more important things to think about than men they'd been in love with when they were teenagers. She should be worrying about money, or how to actually do well in her new position, or the fact that she would only be freelance and the company could drop her contract and abandon her in the UK at the drop of a hat.

So no more NSFW British ex-boyfriend fantasies. She should probably wall the diary up behind a big stack of bricks and never look at it again. *Oh, wait. That was "The Cask of Amontillado."*

Nora was relieved to find that she had finally picked the right direction when her phone didn't command her to turn around again. With her eyes focused on the screen, she almost walked into a couple of well-dressed Londoners before she discovered the small office space with a big window and little yellow sign with purple lettering that read "99 Flamingo Publishing." Perhaps for the first time since exiting the Tube, Nora exhaled.

It was cozy inside—little desks blocked out at different angles, an office and a conference room in the back, and the sound of constant clacking as each person in the main room banged away on their keyboard. It wasn't exactly what she had imagined when she packed up her life and left America. She'd been picturing a big corporate office with elevators and a first floor Starbucks. This was kind of a rinky-dink operation, a one floor, very cramped, and very brown workplace situation. She knew publishing didn't have the budget it used to, and 99 Flamingo was only a very small imprint of a larger press, but this was still a surprise.

"Nora?" A woman at the front desk stood up and removed her glasses.

Nora did a double take, wondering if she should already be acquainted with this person. Surely the arrival of one American writer was of little significance to this place. "How did you know?"

The woman smiled warmly. "Well, we don't get a lot of people wandering in here, and we're expecting you." She reached out a hand for Nora to shake.

"I found the place," Nora said. It was an obvious statement, but she meant it more as an affirmation for herself than a conversation starter, as if she weren't a travel journalist with a terrible sense of direction.

"Give me a minute, and I'll take you back to Darcy," the woman said. "Also, I'm Jasmine. Did I mention that?"

Nora had forgotten how much she loved being surrounded by British accents, the way it made her feel as if she had stepped into a Jane Austen novel or a George Bernard Shaw play. It made her want to shout "hear, hear!" in raucous agreement whenever anyone said something exciting. She smiled to herself while she waited for Jasmine to introduce her to Darcy—of course her editor would be named Darcy. She wondered if it was a man or a woman. Perhaps it was a Mr. Darcy and her wildest *Pride and Prejudice* fantasies would play out in the little publishing office.

"Come on back, Shrapsan!" a smoky voice called from the back office, and Nora jumped. The other people in the main room kept their heads down with their eyes on their computer screens as she passed by them. *Friendly,* Nora thought sarcastically.

She popped her head around the corner and peeked inside the back office to see a mess of books and papers, maps and notes, ashtrays and takeout containers. Behind the desk was a beautiful woman in her mid-thirties with giant dark eyes and round cheeks. Her black hair was pulled back from her face, and her lips formed a displeased pout.

"Have a seat," Darcy said, and Nora quickly did as she was told. Jasmine slipped back out of the office, leaving Nora alone in a sea of publishing debris with her new boss. Actually, Darcy was just her editor, but Nora couldn't stop thinking the word "boss." She'd thought it so much that it didn't totally seem like a real word anymore until she saw Darcy. She appeared to embody the term, and despite the fact that she looked the opposite of Mr. Darcy in every way, she did exude his same sternness and derision. Nora had been practicing this moment in her mind, planning her first impression, but she didn't even get a chance to say hello before Darcy started going on in her raspy voice.

"Well, here you are then," she said, not looking up from the note she was writing on her desk. "They insisted on having an American do some research and writing for the project, though I find it unnecessary. We can easily write the book on our own city and every other place they throw at us."

"Right," Nora said. "Well, I suppose they just want multiple perspectives for the app."

Darcy scoffed. "Our perspectives are good enough, I think. But we do have a bit of ground to cover in a relatively short amount of time, so I'll want you writing and editing blurbs as quickly as possible. Am I correct that this will be your first time writing this kind of content?"

"Yes," Nora said quietly. She didn't know how to elaborate. She was pretty sure that she would be great at this. She'd been waiting for the chance for so long, but this woman was already making her doubt herself.

She tried to give herself a mini pep talk in her mind. *You can do this.* She could focus on her writing and publish incredible travel guides and forget that she was once again in the same city as the most beautiful man who had ever touched her. A man with stormy eyes and incredible fingers, the first man to ever give her an org—*Nope, get it together, Nora.*

"We'll check out the first place on the list together, go over what kind of details we're looking for," Darcy was saying. "That will be your training. It may be unusual, but I think it's important that you get a feel for the tone of the book." Nora nodded. "This isn't just a run-of-the-mill guide. It has personality and a special appeal for young, chic travelers. There's a restaurant in Kensington they want to include. A couple of new clubs in Piccadilly. A hotel in Marylebone. Those are going to get bigger write-ups in the book, but there will be even more content on the app. God knows

I'm too old to go to the clubs, but you can do that with Timothy. Did you meet everyone?"

"No, not yet," Nora stuttered.

"Timothy!" Darcy called, and a pencil-thin, dark-haired man appeared in the doorway almost immediately. He would have looked like a steampunk villain if only he'd been sporting an oddly manicured mustache. "This is Timothy. He does some writing, some IT, and whatever else," Darcy announced, as if that gave Nora all the information she would ever need to know about him.

"Hello, lovely, it's a great pleasure to make your acquaintance," Timothy said, running his hands through his hair. His accent wasn't as charming as she would have expected.

"That's enough," Darcy snapped, and Timothy was gone again. Nora felt terrified but also like she should be laughing her head off at the same time. It was not at all the nurturing mentorship she had been expecting with her new editor in her dream job. "Anyway," Darcy said, "about the museums…" She proceeded to talk about the project as if in bullet points, not pausing even when Nora tried to ask a question. Nora jostled the things in her backpack, searching for a pen as quickly as possible so she could take notes on everything Darcy was firing at her. Darcy wasn't even looking in her direction while she was talking—she was simultaneously typing an email on the computer. Nora tried to say something, but Darcy cut her off again. "You'll need to get to know some locals, as it helps to get some context about the different neighborhoods from their view. You want to get input from the kind of people that pass by these places every day as well. We're not just writing reviews or telling people about the latest events. We're telling a story. Though, you know, there will also be a lot of brochures to collect and facts to check."

"Ok, what do you think about—" Nora tried, but Darcy cut in again.

"I guess now is as good a time as any. Let's go."

"Go?"

"To the new restaurant. Training. Have you been paying attention?"

She mostly had been paying attention; there was just that one little part in the middle where she really zoned out. Maybe if she burned the diary, she could somehow stop her weird memory/fantasy life from taking over.

Darcy stood. "Come on then, let's get started."

———

When Nora was starting college, she wasn't quite sure what she wanted to do with her life. She loved studying English, but that wasn't really one of those majors that led to an easy, specific career path. She loved books and stories, but she didn't want to teach, which seemed to be the only thing that anyone expected you to do if you got a BA in Literature. She loved true crime and mysteries, but she didn't have the constitution to be a detective, and even the thought of blood made her queasy. When she found out about the study abroad program in London, it was the closest she had ever come to figuring out what she wanted as a career, because she wanted exactly that, to read Shakespeare and go to plays at the Globe Theatre, and take walking tours around beautiful, historic cities. How did one turn that exact thing into a job that paid you money?

Finally, her chance had come, which was perhaps a testament to the power of perseverance, or even more likely it was proof of the power of begging. The company where she'd been sitting at her cubicle for years had given her a shot in their most low-stakes writing position, and now that the job was hers, she was working hard not to let Darcy's persistent negative attitude depress her. In fact, as they sat in a dim restaurant that was going to get a tiny write-up in the book, Nora was beaming.

"Why are you making that face?" Darcy asked.

"What face?"

"That face like a puppy and a unicorn just had a baby, and it's going to carry you around the Froufrou Forest and grant you three wishes."

"I'm not sure what that means," Nora said.

"Stop smiling so damn much," Darcy barked. "This restaurant isn't even good. It would get one out of five smile emojis in the book."

"My soup isn't bad," Nora said.

"Who orders soup when it's thirty degrees out?"

"Is that hot? I don't know how to convert the temperature to Fahrenheit."

Darcy shook her head, as if embarrassed by Nora's stupidity or perhaps by the stupidity of all of America. "Aren't you dying? My whole body is covered in a layer of sweat. I look like a slimy sea lion."

Nora inspected Darcy for a moment, considering this comparison. "The only thing about you that reminds me of a sea lion," she said, "is your big, dark eyes."

Darcy snorted. "You're forgetting about my whiskers. Anyway, look at this chicken. It looks like my nan made this in 1976, and they've just defrosted it. It's actually wrinkled."

"Is that what you'll write in the review?"

"You're writing the review," Darcy said. "Though I don't really think this place deserves to take up space. This is why you can't trust anything you read on the internet. Now tell me the categories you need to cover in your 150 words."

Nora concentrated. "Year established. Convenience of the location. Atmosphere." Nora didn't mention that she had no idea about the convenience of location for anything, since she didn't know where anything was and would almost certainly get lost on her way anywhere.

"Yes, yes," Darcy said, "but none of that matters when the food is such shite. I'm at least going to try the pie. Excuse me!" Darcy raised a hand to flag down the waiter.

As Darcy bit into a slice of chocolate pie that she absolutely despised, Nora decided to steer the conversation away from the lacking quality of the restaurant. This "training" lunch was the perfect time to get to know Darcy a little better and to see if there was a way to break through to some kind of positive working relationship.

She could almost hear what her mother would say. Kathleen always seemed to understand what was at the heart of people immediately. She would recognize all of Darcy's little insecurities, the way she kept brushing her hair out of her face and gripping the table. She would say it was all a mask, that Darcy was really just scared of something, and she would probably know exactly what that something was, even if Nora hadn't quite put her finger on it. Her mother would know how to handle it too, how to talk to Darcy in a way that put her at ease or put her in her place, whatever was necessary in the moment. Nora just knew how to be nosy.

"So how long have you lived here?" she asked.

"Forever," Darcy said, shutting down any further inquiries. "Have you ever even been here before?"

Nora smiled. "I studied abroad here, and I fell in love with it. I took afternoon strolls through Regent's Park, I browsed record stores near Abbey Road, I went on the Eye at sunset. It's my favorite city in the world."

"The weather's terrible," Darcy said, but Nora could tell that she couldn't complain too much about her hometown. This was where Darcy had grown up, and while she could dislike almost anything, Nora was sure her boss couldn't hate London. "People are idiots too. Brexit? Come on."

Nora laughed. "The people I met here were wonderful."

"Oh gross." Darcy scrunched up her face.

"What?"

"You met a guy here, I can tell."

"What? How can you tell?" Nora looked around the room furtively.

"*The people I met here were wonderful.* Sigh. Wistful look. Memories stirring behind your blue eyes. I can read you like a book, Shrapsan. You batted those long eyelashes all over town, and you fell in love."

Nora stared. She must be so obvious, but she was also relieved. She'd been dying to talk to someone about Hugh, to say everything she'd been thinking for the past seventy-two hours—or maybe the past seven years—out loud, but now that she had the floor, Nora wasn't sure Darcy was the right person to talk to, and she didn't know where to start. It was so much more than a teenage romance to her, but how to explain it so that Darcy wouldn't think she was a dramatic weirdo? Maybe she shouldn't have decided to spill the beans to her boss in the first place. "He was my first love," Nora said. She cleared her throat.

Scenes from the life of nineteen-year-old, losing-her-virginity Nora kept playing in her mind. Make out sessions on Tower Bridge in the rain. White teeth glowing in black lights while they danced at Ministry of Sound. Steam wafting from hotel bathrooms, droplets of wine dotting the side of the bathtub.

"Well, that is serious," Darcy said, and Nora blinked hard, forcing herself back into the present.

"We met at the pub where he worked, and he was in a band. It sounds silly now, doesn't it?" She tried to shrug nonchalantly. "The first time he ever spoke to me, I could tell immediately there was just this *something* about him. He told me I couldn't handle my liquor and I'd be 'Oliver Twist' in no time. I didn't know what that meant, even though I love the musical.

"You Americans always fall for that Cockney bullocks," Darcy said. "A couple of rhymes, 'Oliver Twist' instead of 'pissed,' and you're completely charmed."

Nora laughed. "I totally was. I fell for it immediately. Even when I thought logically this guy is just charismatic and I shouldn't be so smitten, I couldn't help it. I was done for. And he was right that I couldn't hold my liquor."

"Wow, you're gullible." Darcy shook her head. "Seriously. How do you survive in this world?"

Nora was on a roll, and she ignored Darcy's comment. "I liked him, but I didn't take him that seriously. We always had an expiration date. I knew it would just be a summer fling. But then I got to know him… The band was actually amazing. I think it clouded my judgment." Nora looked off into the distance wistfully.

"So he gave you the struggling musician bit, and you ate it right up. You were probably throwing your panties on stage in no time." Darcy laughed at her own joke. "What was the band?"

Nora was still in another world, remembering all the things that Hugh had said to her, how much she'd wanted to believe him. When he'd told her he loved her. That had been real, right? That wasn't just some line to get in her pants. "Oh, it's not like you would have heard of them. They were just—the Pet Rockers," she said finally, and Darcy actually did a spit take. She had cider dribbling down her chin.

"You're fucking with me," Darcy said, suddenly alert and completely invested in the conversation.

"What?"

"You did not date a guy from the Pet Rockers. You're good, Shrapsan. I didn't think you had it in you to make up such a load."

Nora stared at her, eyebrows wrinkled. "What are you talking about? You know about a band called the Pet Rockers?"

Darcy was shaking her head. "I don't know whether to believe you or not. They are a relatively well-known local band, at least if you're into the music scene at all. They do shows all over the city. In fact, I have tickets to a special event they're doing just north of here."

"That's crazy," Nora said. "There's no way it's the same band, right? I mean, literally no one knew who they were when they used to play at the Goose and Cobbler."

Darcy stared at her as if trying to solve a puzzle. "No, that's it. You're not fooling me anymore. What's this bit you're doing? I don't get it," Darcy grumbled.

"What are you talking about?" Nora suddenly felt sick, and she wasn't sure if it was from the soup or some other kind of nausea.

"The show this weekend—*this* fucking weekend—is a special show at the Goose and Cobbler." Darcy tossed down her fork as if the sheer ridiculousness of this situation wouldn't allow her to hold it a second longer. Nora sat in stunned silence, but everything felt too loud. Her head was cloudy, as if she was just waking from a strange dream. Darcy was still saying something, but she couldn't quite make out the words. The diary in the bottom of her bag still seemed to be beating, and Nora couldn't hear anything else.

"You really aren't making this up, are you?" Darcy said, her voice finally breaking through. "I was going to have my roommate go with me, but she doesn't care about it anyway. I would much rather take you and see you reunite with your boyfriend."

Nora's mouth was hanging open. She'd been having the stupid debate in her head, ever since she found the diary, about whether or not to pop into the Goose and Cobbler for old-time's sake. She never thought Hugh would still be there, behind the bar, waiting for her. And she really never thought that his now semi-famous band would be playing a show in the very place where she had first laid eyes on him. She was trying to convince herself that there was no way any of this was possible—there was no actual way that she could set foot in the pub and fall in love with Hugh Jeffries all over again after seven years. But as Darcy sat there snapping her fingers in front of Nora's face to try to break her from her total state of shock, Nora realized the truth. There was no way in hell she was missing that show.

CHAPTER TWO

IF YOU WERE to ask Hugh Jeffries about his favorite things in the world, he would give you a straight and simple answer: music, pints, and soft cheeses. There were times throughout his life where he would have made slight adjustments to the list and its order. Music wouldn't have been first during the dark ages when he was uninspired and hated everything. There were always women that would move in and out of the top spot, though he usually kept that to himself. And Julian, his mate since middle grades, was hovering somewhere just out of sight of the top three. So when Marty brought him a pale ale and a plate of cheese while he strummed his guitar in the empty pub, Hugh was feeling quite pleased with the state of things.

"Bet you're quite pleased with the state of things, ain't yeh?" Marty said. That bastard still knew him too well.

"What do you mean?" Hugh asked.

"I mean your band is doing a sold-out show at the very best pub in all of London, and you're working on a new song—which always makes yeh 'appy, and you got a mighty fine plate of cheese right there."

Hugh snorted. The "very best pub in all of London" might have been considered more of a dive to some, and it looked almost exactly the same as it had when he had worked there. He could almost see the ghosts of him and his mates—their twenty-something bodies walking around like they owned the place, tapping kegs and washing pint glasses, setting up amps and mics, and putting out a stack of fliers directing people to a crappy website that played their best songs. He remembered how, even though Julian wasn't in the band, he had designed the fliers and passed them out every night. They'd tried so hard to get people to listen to the music, and somehow it had worked.

When their former boss, Marty, called and asked if the band would be willing to do a special show in their old stomping ground, even though they were "right-famous wankers now," something told Hugh to do it. He'd talked to the band and then called Julian and Dev and all the lads who had worked there in the old days, and said they had to make a night of it. It's not like they weren't still together quite often in some capacity, but it had been a long time since they'd all been in one place all night long, and what better spot to reunite than the pub where they came up singing "Penny Lane" after hours while mopping the floor? This was where it had all started.

"How'd you know it was a new song I was playing?" Hugh asked.

"Yeh think I don't know every song in the Pet Rocker's catalog by heart?" Marty scolded.

Hugh laughed, genuinely touched by his devotion. "You're right, Marty. I'm living my best life after all," Hugh said. He popped another cheesy cracker into his mouth.

Marty pulled a rag out of his back pocket and started wiping down the bar. It was a motion that Hugh had seen him do so many times that he once again had the sensation of being transported to a completely different era—an era in which Marty had a bit more hair on the top. "Your bird comin' out this weekend?" Marty asked.

Hugh shook his head. "Work." He shrugged. "She's seen plenty of shows though."

"Ah," Marty said. "But has she gotten a taste of that new song you're writing for her?"

Hugh strummed a little of the melody on the guitar. "Haven't had the chance to play it for her yet."

Marty abandoned the rag and looked at Hugh with wide eyes. "But yer still going to play it this weekend?"

"Why are you so interested?" Hugh said, looking up at the barman. He couldn't believe how excited Marty was for the sold-out show, but he also couldn't blame him for jumping at the chance to introduce new customers to the pub's charm.

"Well, I was only hoping that the Pet Rockers might release a brand-new original song at my pub on Saturday."

Hugh laughed. "No one cares that much about a new song. I don't think they care that much about any songs besides 'Lift.'"

Marty slapped the table. "But that's a great song, Hugh. One of the best, fer sure. Don't tell me you're sick of it? Soon you'll be like one of those artists who doesn't want to play the hits anymore even though their new songs are a bunch of weird shite."

Hugh shook his head. "Nah, I'm not sick of it. There's nothing like everybody in the crowd singing along." He smiled to himself for a moment, remembering the feeling of being on stage, the sound of the voices of the crowd filling up the room. *You're on the fourteenth floor...* That would never get old. He didn't think that song could *ever* get old for him. He absent-mindedly started strumming the chorus of "Lift."

"Oh yes, there yeh go." Marty grinned. "A classic."

It was a comfort to Hugh that Marty was still somehow just the same as he'd ever been. A stained shirt and a patchy beard, perhaps a bit grayer on his thinning head, but his heart was just as grand as it always was. "Have another pint, yeah?" Hugh asked, and Marty started pouring the draft.

"You set a date yet?" Marty asked from behind the bar.

"Not quite," Hugh said. "Not quite yet."

"Well, yeh better get a move on." Marty laughed. "And you better set up and do some kind of sound check, because I'm sure we don't have the kind of acoustics yer used to these days, and it's going to take some tinkering."

"But the cheese, Marty," Hugh said with a grin. "It's divine."

Hugh swung his guitar case through the door to the back of the pub, looking for signs of life. James was in the hallway with a stack of equipment, scratching his head.

"How's it going?" Hugh asked.

"Trying to remember how we fit all this stuff back here."

Hugh looked over the amps and mic stands and cases stacked on top of one another. He wasn't sure if the space had managed to get smaller or if James's drum kit had somehow grown in size. "Oh, that was half the fun of it," Hugh said. "Bloody game of Tetris every week."

Usually, the band would have squeezed in a sound check about an hour or so before the set, and it was what Hugh had expected at the Goose and Cobbler as well. But Marty was insistent that they come days early so they could see that everything worked properly and sounded right just in case he needed to rush out and buy a new speaker or wire or whatever it might be. Hugh loved how serious Marty was about it all. It was a royal treatment, the best they'd ever had, and certainly far better than when they'd played at the pub so long ago.

"Gimme a hand with the rest of this, yeah?" James said.

Hugh grabbed a drum and slid through the narrow hallways. Flashes of memory tugged at his mind—humming his way out the back door at the end of his shift (that happened many times), stumbling with his hand on the wall and puking in the supply closet (that only happened once), pressing a girl up against the closet door with his lips on her neck and his hands on her waist sliding lower…

It didn't take long for him to work up a sweat while helping James with the equipment. He slid off his jacket and threw it on the back of a chair, the same bloody chairs that had been there years ago. Nothing had changed much at all. The chipped wood, the little stage in the back, the uneven bar stools wobbling on their hind legs. It was like he could have been there yesterday.

When James went out to grab a bite before the soundcheck, Hugh stuck around the pub, fiddling on his guitar. Marty was in and out of the kitchen, so Hugh felt mostly alone. It was hard to imagine the place being full of people, though Marty said it would be far more crowded than when they used to play on the weekends. Looking out to the empty room, he could almost see another ghost as well—the ghost of a young woman smiling up at him, her frizzy brown hair moving in time to the beat of the music, her pink cheeks glowing. He had worked at the pub for years, and she'd only been there a single summer, but still the place was full of memories of her.

He had more time to kill before the rest of the band arrived to set up their increasing number of instruments and effects, so Hugh wandered around the neighborhood a bit. It gave him a feeling of déjà vu. He hadn't been in the area much in the last couple of years since he'd moved a bit north and hadn't been working at the pub. But there was a time when that little kilometer of Earth had been his whole world.

Tower Bridge was in the distance, its white spires arching across the Thames. On the other side of the river was the Tower of London and his favorite record shop. It all felt so familiar to him that he couldn't believe he literally hadn't set foot on Tower Bridge Road in ages.

The show on Saturday would be like most of the others—shows he did all around the city every week, shows he did at smaller venues out in the country as well. The set list and his guitar and the band would all be the same. But something felt different about this one; it felt important. He had played so many nights in that pub when people barely even listened, when no one gave a damn about the band, and they ate their suppers and chatted right through his set. He'd played to drunken shouting and bar fights and people snogging in the corners. Now, though, it was sold out. People were showing up there for the sole purpose of listening to his band. It was like magic.

James had always said that as much as he loved the Pet Rockers, the best thing about the band was picking up chicks. Girls loved hot drummers, according to him. Usually, he was right. But to Hugh, there was a lot more to it than that. It meant something to him that people actually gave a shit what he had to say up there.

Before, when he played at that pub, no one could have cared less, except for Marty, who paid as much attention as he could while manning the bar, and Julian, who was his biggest fan. The only other person who seemed to notice the music was just the girl who sat at the bar for nights on end watching his every move as he played. The girl whose ghost was still sitting in the pub waiting for him. She'd listened to him the whole time, from the very beginning—before he even knew her and well after. He'd written songs about that girl. He didn't often think about the fact that she was still out in the world somewhere, that though she was a ghost to him, she was still actually a flesh and blood person. Being at the pub made him realize it though. And now he was going back to that pub to play, and everyone was going to listen.

CHAPTER THREE

THE PUB LOOKED ALMOST EXACTLY the same as it had when they'd worked there. It was grimy, covered in a palimpsest of graffiti, and smelled like a bunch of folks with foot disease had wandered in and hung their shoes from the rafters. Julian had gotten used to that smell when he'd manned the bar, but he'd forgotten how potent it could be, especially on a hot summer day when it mingled with body odor and urine—how was it that the urine always seemed to evaporate and float into the air? It was terrible, but it made him feel nostalgic at the same time.

"There you are," Hugh called to him. Julian turned to hug his oldest friend in the world. He couldn't help being a little jealous of the way Hugh held himself in his black cut-off T-shirt and ripped jeans, forever looking the part of a rock star. Julian felt uptight and boring in comparison, even if he wasn't exactly either of those things. Compared to Hugh, beige trousers and a buttoned-up shirt seemed horribly uncool, but Julian's rock star best mate still had the ability to make him feel lighter somehow, as if Julian belonged.

"It's good to see you, mate," Hugh said. "I didn't know if you'd make it back to this old place."

"How could I miss this?" Julian gestured toward the small stage. "I feel like I should be behind the bar serving pints like old times. I've got a date tonight, so I can't stay for the whole set up, but I figured I'd hang around for the beginning bit."

"Oh right, the new lady friend." Hugh laughed. "You should bring her this weekend. I know the lads would love to chat with her."

"Show's all sold out, mate." Julian slapped his friend on the back. "People buy tickets to see you now; the place is going to be packed." Also, Julian wasn't sure that he was ready for this woman to meet his whole handsome bunch of friends. He certainly had more confidence now than when he was just a pimply "groupie" back in the day, but he still felt that sense of inferiority for not being one of the lads in the band.

"Ah, but I bet I could get you in." Hugh nudged him in the ribs. "I know a guy."

"I know a guy too," Julian said. "And the rest of his band is waving at him to get on stage for sound check."

Julian took a seat on one of the stools in the back and shook hands with Marty. Marty poured two glasses of Jameson and handed one to Julian, knocking back his own. The band started with a song Julian hadn't heard yet, one of their new ones. Then they did "Fire Away" and "Lakes and Rivers." Somehow they sounded just the same as they had seven or eight years ago when they'd just started performing and no one had ever heard of the Pet Rockers. They did a couple more new ones, and Julian bobbed his head to the beat, still impressed with the band's talent and Hugh's lyrics. Despite the fact that the band was a hot commodity, Julian hadn't actually seen them perform in a while. *Too long*, he thought. After a few more songs, just as Julian was glancing at his watch, a beat started that he instantly recognized—"Lift." It was a crowd favorite, so of course they had to play it. He shouldn't have been surprised to hear Hugh singing those words again, words written for a girl so long ago, a girl they never mentioned anymore.

Hugh belted this song so frequently that Julian wondered if he even thought about the lyrics anymore or remembered that they had any meaning. Julian never actually thought to ask. He never said, "Hey remember that American girl you were completely mad about, and how devastated you were when she left?" Hugh certainly didn't bring her up. He had moved on long ago, and since then he'd even had girls throwing their knickers at him while he was up on stage. Julian had never been a killer with the ladies like the guys in the band, but he *did* have a hot date tonight, and she seemed to quite like him for some reason. Hopefully he wouldn't turn everything to piss and get flustered like he usually did. He tried to imagine himself as Hugh—to embody that level of confidence and charisma.

He waved to his mate when the song ended. Hugh smiled and lifted one still hand in the air before plucking a few guitar strings and twisting one of the tuning knobs. It was like nothing had changed from all those years ago in the same pub.

The day was uncharacteristically hot, and the air felt oppressive underground. An automated voice echoed through the station, warning patrons of dehydration and heat strokes. Julian began to sweat, and he longed for those parts of the tunnel where the air seemed to flow. He helped a young girl get her giant suitcase onto the Tube car and filed in behind her. The doors closed, and Julian leaned casually against a pole, only to be jerked dramatically when the train started moving. He knew that was going to happen on the Underground, and yet he never held on tight enough. The automated voice rang out again, "This is the Northern line heading south toward Morden Station. The next stop is Monument." He glanced around the car, wanting to people-watch, but not wanting to make eye contact or engage with anyone. The girl with the suitcase smiled at him. For some reason, it was nice to receive a smile from a stranger. At least, it was nice when you were a man, and the smile was not in any way threatening. Julian grinned back at her before sliding onto a plastic seat.

He was looking forward to going home, having a cold shower, and daydreaming about Poppy, his new "lady friend." He had somehow managed, in the course of their multiple hours-long dates and an entire evening in bed together, not to mention the Trojan relationship to the Byzantine empire or his theories on dinosaurs with feathers or his Godzilla figurine collection or any of the nerdy stuff that made most women stare at him with their mouths open. That alone might not mean it was a full-blown love story, but it could be a start. There had once been a date where Julian had talked about Dungeons and Dragons for a full ten minutes and the girl had faked an emergency to get out as quickly as she could. He was a shite boyfriend, there was no denying it. But somehow, he was sure that Poppy would know everything about the Trojans and Byzantines, about dinosaurs and D&D; she wouldn't bat an eyelash if he went on about the existence of the multiverse for hours. She knew everything and always had an opinion. He was enjoying getting to know her, even if he wasn't yet sure where it would lead. Maybe they weren't head-over-heels for each other yet, but they had a lot in common. And how often did you fall head-over-heels for anyone?

He was replaying the events of their last evening together in his mind when the train stopped at the next station, and more people filed onto the car. He got up to let a pregnant woman take his seat. *So much more polite here than in America,* he thought. Someone had told him that once.

Somehow, his fantasies about Poppy started to morph and take a new shape until Poppy's face had changed, and in his mind, he saw a completely different woman he had known years before. He could picture her so vividly; it was almost as if she was there. She *was* right there, in fact. He saw her. On the train in the same car, next to an older man in a suit. She was sitting on the edge of a plastic seat, focused on the book in her lap. The train stopped again, and he did a double take, craning his neck around the people bustling between them.

He felt the same jolt in his body as when the train had started moving, except everything around him was still. He knew, logically, that he must be hallucinating—he was too tired from the night before, and this must be some strange doppelganger messing with his senses. He blinked his eyes a few times, but she was still there. She still looked like her. Somehow hearing Hugh sing the words to his hit song had messed with Julian's head, and he was imagining a girl from long ago just sitting right there on the Northern Line across from him. A teenager moved out of the way, and he spotted the woman again. Her body swayed with the movement of the Tube, her eyes went back and forth across the page, her hair floated on her shoulders.

No, that couldn't be her. He knew he was being ridiculous. But as the train slowed, she stood up as if to exit, and before he could stop himself, he was standing too and following a bustling blob of humans out of the car without even knowing where he was.

He stepped onto the platform, trying to weave through the crowd of people that separated them. *What station was this?* He looked for the sign and found that it was a few stops before he was supposed to get off. He should have just gotten back on the train like a normal person, but he didn't. Instead, he followed the flow of traffic, trying to catch up to the woman who was already darting for the exit and stepping out into the sunshine.

He kept following her. In fact, he couldn't seem to stop. He was laughing at himself internally as he remembered the woman–the real woman, not this imposter–skipping through Kensington Gardens, posing for intimate photos with the Peter Pan statue, and grabbing his arm and tugging him toward the little ice cream booth. Chocolate on her nose, marinara sauce on her collar, a colossal book in her bag that she insisted on hauling everywhere because she was supposed to be studying, not gallivanting around London. She made Julian and Hugh and the rest of the band get fast food in Waterloo Station and see an Agatha Christie play in the West End. He'd been all over the city with her and Hugh, and yet, it still seemed completely impossible that she could be here on the sidewalk in front of him.

He found her again at the street corner, about fifteen meters away. She had stopped there, looking up at the street sign as though she was lost. Her name was on repeat in his head; he was just a second away from saying it out loud. What if he called to her? What if she turned around and answered?

He shut his mouth and watched. As she turned her head to the left, he could see her face again. It had to be her. How could there be another woman in the world who moved just like that, with freckles on her cheeks in just the right places? If only he could hear her laugh, the bold exhale of joy that seemed to make an electric spark shoot all the way to his toes, he would know for sure.

She looked down at her phone, decided on a direction, and turned left to walk down the street until she was out of view. Julian was frozen on the spot, dumbfounded, almost tingling with excitement and terror, and feeling like a total wanker. Why wouldn't he have just approached her and said hello? How could someone he hadn't seen in so many years make him freeze up the same way she had the first time he'd met her, when she made him play some stupid American drinking game where he had to sit under the pub table staring at her feet when he lost all his cards?

He remembered taking her order the first time she'd ever been in the Goose and Cobbler, remembered how he'd been too shy to ask her anything but what she wanted to drink. She requested a beer recommendation and took offense when he offered something fruity. It was the first time he ever heard her laugh.

"Give me your very best lager," she'd said in a truly awful British accent.

"Who's that supposed to be then?" he asked.

"If I would have come in using that accent, you wouldn't have known the difference."

"I guarantee you I would have," he said, already charmed.

"Let's try it out on that guy," she'd said, pointing at Hugh. "You want to make a bet?"

He was smiling just thinking about her addressing Hugh with that phony British voice. Hugh had all the charm and bravado. Hugh hadn't missed the chance to talk to her as soon as he heard her laugh, and Julian had kicked himself for being nervous and quiet. He was still both of those things, but back then he'd been so young and even worse for it.

"Nora," Julian said, only to himself. After hearing Hugh play that song, his head had been filled with her. He hadn't thought of her in so long, and now she had just appeared right in front of him. Or someone very like her had appeared, anyway. He didn't know what to make of it. He turned on the spot and headed back to the Tube, ready to get home and stop chasing an old memory—to have a cold shower, just as he'd been planning.

Dev already had a pint waiting for Julian when he finally got to the pub that weekend. That was the nice thing about your oldest mates—they knew exactly what you liked, knew you were going to show up a little late and a lot disheveled, made all the more uncomfortable by the big crowd, and they were waiting with a pint and ready for a laugh.

Dev slapped Julian on the back and put the beer right in his hand without even speaking.

"You are a blessing," Julian said with a big smile.

"And you look terrible," Dev said. "I'll get all the ladies tonight. Although, wait a minute, Hugh said you've got a new bird now."

"Very new," Julian said. "And obviously way too good for the likes of me."

"Obviously," he agreed.

Before the band went on, Julian and Dev ragged on Marty and had a couple of shots, until things really started to feel like they had long ago when they'd all been young and trying to make ends meet on their pub wages. Julian could already feel the warmth from the alcohol spreading throughout his body, and his lips were starting to numb, which was always a good sign—or a bad sign, depending on how you were looking at it.

By the time the Pet Rockers got on the stage, Julian was half-drunk and quite happy. He and Dev were singing along to the songs they had heard hundreds of times, swaying back and forth and yelling out their praise. Sometimes Hugh smiled in their direction, and Julian wondered if he could see them there, standing in the crowd, holding up their glasses and toasting his success.

He and Dev chatted about work when the band took a break. Dev had just gotten a promotion at his firm, and he was bragging, as usual. Julian felt a hand on his arm, but he didn't turn. He assumed someone was just pushing past him in the crowded pub, trying to get closer to the little stage at the front.

"Julian?" a voice said. The hand was still on him, and so he turned toward the woman standing there.

"Oh my gosh. It is you, isn't it?" she said.

Even though he'd been thinking about her for days, imagining her and what she would look like now, Julian could not believe that Nora was standing there beside him. Her hair was longer than he remembered, and she was a little shapelier now, in a way that was completely adult and sexy. She looked natural, though, like she was exactly where she belonged. Perhaps she wasn't as sleek and put together as Poppy. Nora's hair was a bit frazzled, and she had on a dark lipstick that didn't quite suit her but also made him keep looking at her lips. Her round cheeks were flushed, and there was a line of sweat gleaming across her forehead.

"Nora?" Julian choked, and he didn't recognize his own voice. It *had* been her at the station, the woman he'd followed, not that he would mention it. He suddenly wished he hadn't had quite so much to drink already.

"I can't believe it," she said, and she flung herself forward to embrace him. Julian made brief eye contact with the stern woman standing right behind Nora. He had the feeling that this stranger could see right through him to all the desperation and turmoil bubbling inside of him as he held Nora in his arms. He tried to smile and act normally.

"I remember you," Dev chimed in as Nora released Julian. Dev pointed his finger at her accusingly. "Hugh's American girlfriend."

"Hi, Dev," Nora said.

Julian knew he should say something and stop standing there like an idiot. He felt hot suddenly, and he was sure he was sweating right through his shirt. "How—how are you? What are you doing here?" he asked finally.

She smiled. She looked genuinely happy to see him. She was excited about it. And there was something about the way the muscles in her neck tightened when she cocked her head to the side, the smooth skin that— dear God, he was staring at her neck like a complete tosser. "I'm here for work," she said. "Oh yes, and this is Darcy, my editor, so don't tell her any racy stories."

Darcy smiled up at him in a way that made him believe she truly knew all of his secrets, and he shook her hand nervously. Why did he feel like this woman could already sense everything about him and knew that he was having an internal meltdown at this very moment?

Then Darcy looked him over without bothering to hide it. "Julian is it?" she asked, though she didn't seem like she cared all that much about his name.

"I can't believe you're here," Nora said. "That you're actually hanging out in this pub, and that Hugh…" She trailed off looking toward the stage.

"This is a very unusual and special night that you're witnessing," Dev announced.

Julian was analyzing exactly how Nora had said Hugh's name. Was that longing he heard in her voice? Or was he imagining that? Why was he worrying about it? He didn't even know her anymore.

"What's work?" Julian asked. "I mean–how? I mean–what do you do?" He addressed his question to both Nora and Darcy, trying to avoid looking directly at either of them.

"Travel writing," Nora said. "We're working on a book about London. I really can't believe you're here. I mean, I can't believe I'm here and this is happening. I know I keep saying that, but it seems crazy, doesn't it?"

"Thank you so much for coming tonight." Hugh's voice rang out through the pub, echoing over their heads. He was back at the mic. Nora stopped talking and turned toward him, almost instinctively.

"How is he actually playing here tonight?" she said, smiling, watching him. She was in awe. There was no denying it.

"You have to go back and talk to him after the show," Dev said. "We'll take you back. He's going to freak out. Wouldn't be surprised if he fainted."

Julian thought that all Darcy needed was a bucket of popcorn and a fizzy drink the way she was taking all of this in, soaking up the drama.

"Too bad his fiancée didn't come," Dev said. "You could have met her too. Though I guess I don't know how fiancées feel about meeting past loves. What do you think, Julian?"

Julian was watching Nora's face, trying to read her again. "You look great," he said awkwardly. "It's good to see you."

"You too," she replied, though she wasn't looking at him. She was staring at the stage as Hugh started to play.

CHAPTER FOUR

FIANCÉE, Dev had said. Hugh had a woman in his life that he was going to marry. Nora couldn't really be surprised. As much as she'd indulged in romantic little fantasies, her logical side had supposed that the handsome, talented Hugh Jeffries would have a beautiful woman to love him dearly, and Nora was okay with that. Sure, it was a little disappointing, given the magic of how everything had just worked out for her to see him again, as if perhaps there was some kind of fate or all-knowing being that was pushing them back together after all. But reality had been there waiting to remind her that what she'd had with Hugh was long ago, and fate had turned out to be a bored Darcy (who certainly was not all-knowing, just pushy). Hugh was engaged, and Nora was going to be okay with it.

"I'm going to get another drink," she said, shaking her empty glass at Julian and Dev. It was strange how very much the same they looked, as if this was just another of the many nights they'd spent just like this, though the pub was never so crowded. Here they were again, listening to Hugh play. Here they were again, gazing up at Hugh as he strummed his guitar and flicked hair out of his face, his biceps firm as he gripped the microphone, his voice a low rumble that sent a tingling...

No. Nora was not going to think about that for another second. She held her mouth in a perfect, immovable smile as Dev and Julian nodded at her.

Julian, especially, was just as she remembered him, always so earnest in everything, the way he seemed like it actually mattered to him to see his best friend's old girlfriend. She knew that most people wouldn't care so much; they'd probably just say a polite hello and go back to their lives. But Julian was nice, just as he'd always been. He asked her questions and listened to the answers. He seemed like he wanted to talk to her, this pathetic single woman in England who was watching her engaged ex-boyfriend sing on stage at his rock concert. Julian seemed like he wanted to talk to her far more than he had seven years ago when he most likely avoided her out of sheer embarrassment at the way she snorted when she laughed and stuffed too many chips in her mouth. It made her feel a little better about the whole situation.

Not that she even really felt bad! That was silly. She didn't even know Hugh anymore, and really, she was happy for him. He should be getting married, because that's what people do when they are over thirty and in love. Still...another drink would be great.

Darcy followed her to the bar, and Nora ordered another round for both of them. She might be a little too tipsy for being at an event with her boss, but it was also an event where her ex-boyfriend's band was playing and she was going to talk to him again for the first time in seven years, so the lines of professionalism in this situation had already blurred quite a bit. People weren't so weird about alcohol in London, anyway. Teenagers went to bars and drank legally and had beers with their professors—at least they had when she'd been a student there.

"So, he's getting married," Darcy said.

Nora shrugged, trying to be nonchalant. "You picked up on that too, huh?"

"This night is getting interesting. I'm glad I brought you."

Nora sighed. "I'm glad you find me so entertaining." She handed Darcy the pint and took several gulps of her own. She'd been so caught up in seeing Julian and Dev—and then Hugh up on stage—she hadn't even realized that Hugh had started playing a different song. The first song he'd done after the break wasn't one she'd ever heard before. She liked it, at least the parts of it she'd been able to listen to when her head was spinning out of control. Now when Nora started focusing on the music again, she realized that the band was onto something different, something familiar, something that made her almost drop the full beer right out of her hand when she recognized what it was, a melody that was burned into her memory.

I'm on the fourteenth floor, waiting on the lift doors...

Hugh sang it out, and Nora looked around the pub. Everyone was singing along. The whole fucking crowd knew the words. The sheer volume of voices in a packed bar; that was such a huge thing. He had made it. This was what he had always wanted back when Marty was the only one in town who would let them do a set, when the band handed out CDs in the doorway. Nora realized that not only did people know Hugh's song by heart now, they knew the words to a song that was about her.

"What is wrong with you?" Darcy asked when Nora stopped moving. She was almost in a trance. Oh, God, Julian was looking at her. He was going to see the shock all over her face; he was going to know that she felt like she was on the brink of passing out.

He gave her a little pitying smile.

"This song is about me," she almost whispered to Darcy.

"What?" Darcy shouted. Nora didn't know if Darcy hadn't heard her over the singing or if she was just in shock too.

"This song is about me," Nora said again.

"Come off it!" Darcy yelled, and some people nearby turned to look at them.

Dev was laughing. He turned and pointed at Nora. "I remember when he wrote this. It was for you, wasn't it? Isn't that uncanny?"

Nora needed to sit down or put her head between her legs or eat a cracker or something. She downed most of her beer, but then she felt like she might puke. Brandon used to make fun of her constantly for being a slow drinker. "Stop savoring it," he would say. "It's just a beer at a party." If only he could see her chugging now.

"It must be strange to hear this again after so long," Julian said when she approached him again. Nora looked up at him and they locked eyes. It made her a little nervous, that long, direct eye contact. People didn't seem to look you in the eyes as much anymore, but there was Julian, baring his soul to her. Had he always been so tall? His hair was shorter, though still endearingly unmanageable, and he was still lanky, but his movements were controlled, more assertive than they'd been in the past. He turned away after a moment, as if the eye contact made him a little uncomfortable too.

"This is really about her?" Darcy said, giddy. "I think we should scrap everything we've written for the travel book and just put in this story. This is too good!"

Why don't you come on out, baby? I'm gonna show you 'round baby! Hugh sang, and the whole crowd sang along. Nora was starting to feel like she could breathe again, and suddenly she wanted to laugh. Here were all these people singing about her *in London*. They'd all been singing about her for who knows how long, and she'd had no clue. Her smile became real as Julian watched her.

She'd been so distracted by the fact that Hugh was singing this song and that everyone in the bar knew the words, it took her a while to realize she still remembered every line as well. She took a breath and let herself sing along to part of the bridge.

And we're running 'round lawless in the middle of the street
I'm shouting your name to everybody we meet
We're kissing on the lift and your lips are so sweet
Got your heels in your hand, walking 'round on bare feet...
I'm not much of a dancer, but I'm dancing with you
We're quiet in the hallway, the walls are all blue
Sneaking to the bedroom like you said we wouldn't do
But you can't get enough of me, like I'm something brand new

"It's a bit brilliant, right?" Julian said, looking around at the mob belting their hearts out. She nodded. It was brilliant. It didn't mean anything—definitely not that there was a cosmic force that had driven her to that bar to hear her first love crooning about her—but it was cool. She was totally cool.

"Make way, coming through," Dev shouted as he led Nora through the crowd. She was going backstage, if you could even call it that, to the little storage room where the band drank water after a set. Darcy and Julian were pacing behind her, everyone dying to see the weird reunion that was about to take place. Even though she'd just seen him onstage, Nora was still shocked to hear Hugh's normal talking voice echoing down the tiny hallway.

"I couldn't even hear myself over all of them. I don't think it's ever been quite like that before. Bloody amazing."

Nora looked back at Darcy wearily as Dev entered the room before her. She was stuck behind him, unable to see into the storage closet at all.

"Great show, mates," Dev said. There was some general merriment from the band before he continued. "Got a surprise for you, Hugh."

"I don't want it," Hugh laughed. "I'm terrified of any surprises from you."

"Think you're going to be interested in this one," Dev said, stepping aside.

Suddenly, Nora was there in the doorway, and she could see the whole band standing in the closet with their instruments. They were staring at her as she tried to take in the scene. Then she found Hugh's face, sweaty and shocked, blinking hard.

"Nora?" he said, clearly baffled. It reminded her of the part in *Grease* where the Pink Ladies shove Sandy in front of Danny Zuko for the first time, and Danny calls her name, his voice high and squeaky.

"Holy shit," Nora gasped even though she had, of course, already seen him on stage, heard his voice, and been perfectly aware that this was coming. "Hi Hugh."

Darcy nudged her from behind so that she was stepping further into the tiny room, only a couple of feet away from him. *Strike up a rousing chorus of "Summer Lovin'"*.

"What—what are you doing here? I don't even—" He handed his guitar to one of the guys in the band and moved toward her, wrapping her in his arms. "How is this possible?"

"I'm in London for work," she said, mostly into his chest, since she was still pressed against him.

He moved back but kept hold of her shoulders, examining her. "It's good to see you," he said, still amazed. Everyone was silently staring at them.

Nora couldn't believe how good he looked. His hair was still a little long, swept across his face so just a bit of it hung in his eyes. She could see the muscles flexing in his cut-off shirt and could feel the warmth of his large hands, a warmth that seemed to be shooting throughout her body. Against her will, images of the two of them, fingers intertwined, mouths pressed against body parts, flashed in her brain. She remembered how intensely he had grabbed her and kissed her, how he'd pressed her against the wall until she couldn't breathe but didn't mind it. She should not be thinking about kissing him.

"It's really good to see you. I never thought I would again."

"Me too," he said, his voice almost breaking.

Nora remembered that the band was still right there, watching every moment. She turned to look at all of them and gave a little wave. There was James and Will, and she forgot the other guy's name. Something with a C maybe? "Hi guys," she said shyly.

"Blimey," Darcy breathed from the hallway, where she was staring into the closet as if watching a tiny play. Julian was in the hall too, leaning against the wall, his eyes dark and unreadable.

"Nora," Hugh said again, as if he still couldn't believe that she was real, as if he just needed to speak her name aloud again to make sure that there hadn't been some kind of mistake, that he hadn't confused her with someone else.

"Yeah," she said. "It's me."

CHAPTER FIVE

IN SOME MIRACULOUS turn of events, Hugh found himself sitting in the pub past midnight with the first woman he had truly loved. After all the concertgoers left and Marty shut the place down to customers, they headed back out to the front to have a couple of drinks and a chat. The band was still there too, and Dev and Julian and the woman that had brought Nora to the show, Darcy something. Hugh wouldn't have noticed if any of them left, though. He couldn't stop looking at Nora, watching her every move, trying to determine if she was real.

Even as she was sitting there telling him about the book she was working on and the tiny flat she was leasing, he was having a hard time wrapping his head around the fact that she was talking to him in the same pub where they'd met.

"You're sure you aren't stalking me?" he said when she finished explaining how Darcy had gotten tickets to the show and insisted that she attend.

She may have blushed just a bit. "I know it's weird," she said. "In all honesty, I thought about you on the plane here and wondered what you were doing, but I absolutely never thought I would see you. I definitely never thought I would be listening to you play a song about me."

Suddenly, he wondered if *he* might be blushing. He hadn't even thought about the fact that she'd been there to hear that. She now knew that he was still publicly performing the song he'd written for her and that it was still the best Pet Rockers song, no matter what else he wrote. She'd been there listening as he was singing about kissing her. Hopefully, she didn't think it meant something romantic.

He knew that he should mention Rose. He should bring up the fact that he was engaged before Nora started thinking something was going to happen between them—that they could just pick up where they left off like a used candle that would take easily to a flame. He didn't know how to delicately drop it into the conversation though. He couldn't just come right out and say "I'm getting married" when it didn't have anything to do with what they were talking about. It would make it seem like he was worried about something happening or about Nora thinking that something was happening. He didn't want to imply that she must be pining for him.

"Dev says you're getting married," Nora said, and he felt a little relieved that he didn't have to tell her and also a little sad that she knew.

"I am," he said. "Don't know when yet."

"Well, congratulations." Nora smiled widely, but Hugh didn't know if it was genuine. "How did you meet her?"

He grinned back at her. He should have known she would dive right in with the questions. "Friend of a friend of a friend. All of us out one night. You know how it goes."

"You're a dream of a storyteller, Hugh," she said. "Magnificent details."

He shifted on his stool. He didn't really know if he should tell her the details. He didn't want to make Rose entirely real to her. He didn't want to talk about Rose at all. Rose was fierce and tireless, working long shifts to try to improve hospital efficiency across London while he was fiddling around on the guitar. She made him a better man. Nora may have been the first woman he ever loved, but Rose was the love of his life…wasn't she? He and Nora had never even at a chance at that. She'd left, and God, nothing had ever hurt that much before.

"Remember when I made you take me on that Jack the Ripper walking tour?" Nora asked suddenly.

Hugh thought for a moment. "That was a long time ago."

"You don't remember it?" Nora asked. "The kid who kept stepping on our heels and making ghost noises, and then he screamed and started crying when we went in that dungeon?"

"What made you think of that?" Hugh asked, not wanting to admit that he really couldn't remember it.

"Oh, I was just thinking about the tour. I might go back for the book and write something about it."

"I can't believe you're writing a book about London," Hugh said.

"Why's that?" Nora asked playfully.

"Aren't there enough of them already? The best stuff here is hundreds of years old. I think it's been covered." Hugh half-smiled, but as he watched Nora's face, he could see that she wasn't amused.

"There's always new stuff," she said. "The information just has to stay updated, or no one will want to buy our version."

He smiled at her. "You know what I *do* remember?" he said, desperate to make up for his last comment, desperate to have her grinning conspiratorially with him all over again.

"What do you remember, Mr. Jeffries?" she asked in the terrible mock British accent that always started to come out when she'd been drinking.

Before Hugh could stop himself, he was doing too much accidental remembering—remembering how she slid the strap of her bra over her shoulder in the hotel bathroom, how the steam from the shower fogged up the mirror before she drew a little heart on it with her pinky finger. They'd been so young and carefree, desperate for each other at every moment, like they could never get enough. He remembered splaying her across the bed, the taste of gin and mint leaves on her tongue, her wet hair spilling onto a pillow leaving a damp mark that wouldn't dry for hours. It took only seconds for him to wonder what it might be like to do it all over again and only a half second more for him to scold himself and clear his throat before knocking back the rest of his drink.

"The magician outside the hotel in Covent Garden," he said at last. "That was a very good day." It had been a good day, but also that memory felt safer, an innocent excursion where they'd both been fully clothed. He'd dug out every coin from his pocket to pay the magician to do another trick for Nora. She had a thing for magic, and it had been magical, truly. All fun, all the time. It was always easy with her.

"I remember," Nora said, her eyes shining.

It felt a little dangerous, the way she was looking at him, but he couldn't help wanting to see her again for another night, another drink, another chance to remember what it felt like to be twenty-four and invincible. The second Nora had left London, he'd been wondering what it might be like if she ever came back. And here she was. And here *he* was too, the person he was with her, a little reckless and irresponsible, uninhibited.

"I'm glad you're back in London," Hugh said, and he meant it.

CHAPTER SIX

THROUGHOUT THE EVENING, Julian had been trying to convince himself that he had been young and naive the last time he knew Nora, and all his stupid schoolboy fantasies had just been because she was pretty and paid attention to him, because she had laughed at his jokes on occasion, and because he could never really have her, which made her all the more enticing.

It wasn't working.

Instead, he found himself remembering the night she had started to draw a black mustache on his face while he was blasted on Hugh's sofa. Before she finished it, he jerked awake to find her hovering over him, her face so close to his, her forearms lightly pressed against his chest. Neither of them moved for a moment. She was too surprised she'd been caught red-handed; he was too uneasy at the sudden feeling that had welled up inside of him when he realized how close they were. Then she burst out laughing, and they wrestled over the marker as she tried to finish her masterpiece.

The next day, he'd woken up and touched the spot above his lip, wondering if he'd imagined it all. But then he heard Nora laughing again from across the room. She was watching him, triumphant about the crudely drawn black squiggle, even as she gulped water and nursed her hangover headache.

When Julian had watched her standing in the pub listening to Hugh sing, he could tell that she was experiencing a rush of very different memories. He recognized the way her face changed instantly when Dev mentioned Rose, even if she had tried to hide it. He couldn't help but notice the slight tension in her smile; it was just barely perceptible that it was forced, but you could see it if you looked hard enough. And Julian was looking very hard.

Hugh was a terrific man, his dearest friend since they were children, and he certainly deserved all of Nora's admiration. And yet, Julian couldn't help wishing that she would lose interest in him entirely and realize that Hugh had grown into some boring and unworthy hack (which wasn't true). Nora seemed to be glowing in Hugh's presence, and when they were all hanging about the pub after the show, Julian was keenly aware that Hugh wouldn't stop smiling like a goofy idiot, which of course just made him more endearing.

He was also keenly aware that he was alone at the bar nursing a drink and allowing himself occasional over-the-shoulder peeks at the beaming reunited couple. Then Darcy quite literally flopped onto the stool next to him.

"Too bad he's engaged," Darcy said, pulling Julian out of his brooding.

"Why's that?" he asked, unsure that he wanted to indulge in this conversation about Hugh's love life.

"They seem like they made a good match." Darcy raised her glass and gulped about half of it down.

"They were a great couple. Once, on a dare, they both took off their clothes and went streaking through this pub after close." Julian sat up suddenly. "I guess I'm not supposed to tell you that since you're Nora's boss. Don't mention I said anything." He looked down into his glass, ashamed at telling a story that might make Nora less-than-pleased with him.

"I didn't know streaking together was a thing that made for great relationships," Darcy said, unphased by her employee's nudity. "No wonder I'm single."

Julian smiled. It was true, if coupling involved streaking and shouting, fearlessly talking to strangers and yelling into the microphone between sets, then he was going to be out of luck. "Not the streaking so much," Julian said. "But they were both always up for a challenge, willing to take on anything."

"What'd you have to do?" Darcy asked.

"Pardon?"

"Didn't you have some kind of dare you had to do?" Darcy teased him. "That's the nature of the game, right?"

"No," Julian said. "Not me. I just stayed behind the bar and out of the way."

They sat in silence for a moment, and Julian glanced at Hugh and Nora again, the way they were laughing so easily together. "She was there when my dog died," he said for some unknown reason.

Darcy studied his face. "Nora?"

"Yeah. All my mates were like 'oh, so sorry about Ralphie, take care,' but she came to the vet's office and waited for me when I'd only known her a couple of months. It's probably stupid for a twenty-something-year-old man to be so broken up about a dog, but she didn't think so. She took me out for crepes afterward."

"Heartwarming," Darcy said sarcastically.

"I don't know why I'm even telling you this. I'm surprised I remember it."

"I'm kidding," Darcy said. "It sounds like Nora has the potential to be a decent person. I don't even know her. I just met her this week."

"What made you bring someone you barely know out tonight?" Julian asked.

"And miss this reunion?" Darcy pointed in the general direction of Hugh and Nora. "When she told me she dated this guy years ago and now he's doing a show in the same pub? I had to be there to see that. I have to admit, I feel bad for her that he's engaged though. I don't know if that's better or worse than married."

"What do you mean?"

"Well, if it's married, then that's it, right? I mean, unless he were a real skagger and going to start up some illicit affair. Engagement is different, though. It's like the deal isn't sealed. There's still some small glimmer of something there. An engagement could be broken in a heartbeat."

"There you're wrong, I think," Julian said. "Hugh's mad about Rose. He wouldn't just throw her over after an evening out with an ex." Julian felt less certain after the sentence left his mouth, but he tried to hold onto the conviction that this chance encounter wouldn't make too much of an impression on his best mate.

"Truth or dare?" Darcy asked suddenly.

"What?" Julian said, glancing over his shoulder at Nora again.

"Truth or dare. Just like old times."

"I told you I didn't play."

"Well, you can change that now. Pick one."

"Truth," Julian sighed.

"Okay, then." Darcy turned fully around on her stool and stared at Nora and Hugh. "You don't think there's any hope?" she asked.

Julian looked at the pair of them sitting there, completely oblivious to everyone else. Nora threw her head back and laughed, and Hugh's eyes followed her every movement.

"I don't think there's any hope," he said, but he wasn't sure what he was talking about anymore.

When the evening was over and the lot of them started to disperse, Hugh offered to escort Nora back to her flat.

She looked around while biting her lips where the lipstick had faded. "You're going the opposite direction," she said practically, and Julian wondered if she was worried about what it might be like to be alone with Hugh.

"Where are you staying?" Julian asked her.

"Not far from where I was last time I was in London, actually. Just down the road."

"Not far from me," he said. "I can walk you and Darcy back if you like."

"Darcy's feet are hurting and she's getting a cab immediately," Darcy said. "You want a taxi?"

Nora looked up at the sky, contemplating. "It is a beautiful night." She looked over at him. "I'm up for walking if you are, Julian. It'll be like old times."

Old times. That's what everyone kept saying. Julian didn't want it to be like old times.

The other lads grabbed a car, and Hugh prepared to take off in the opposite direction after making future plans for coffee with Nora. Julian stood to the side as the two of them awkwardly hugged goodbye.

"See ya soon," Hugh said into her hair.

It looked like Nora pulled away first. "Yeah," she said, but she seemed unsure.

"And then there were two," Nora said to Julian as they began ambling down the street in the warm night air.

"You always were great at maths." He grinned.

She rolled her eyes, but she was smirking. "Strange night," she said. "I feel as though I've traveled back in time."

Julian hiccupped, and she laughed at him. "And how do you feel about it?" he asked.

"Happy to see you," she said. "Tell me everything."

The alcohol helped, but there was also something about Nora's demeanor that put Julian at ease. She told him about breaking it off with her American boyfriend and how happy she was to be back in London. He told her about his teaching job and the book he was reading and a play he saw recently starring a very famous Harry Potter star. "He was quite impressive," Julian remarked.

"Oh, I don't doubt it. He's fantastic." The corner of Nora's mouth twitched up to the side.

"Would you date Daniel Radcliffe?" he asked her. "Or would it be too unpleasant because you could never see him as anything but Harry?"

"Ummmm..." Nora stared into the distance, thinking hard. Julian couldn't help staring at her throat again and found himself holding his breath. "I think I'd sleep with him once. Just to say I did it."

"Poor Dan," Julian said. "He seems a very pleasant fellow to me."

"You've convinced me then," Nora laughed. "I'll marry him."

"That took a right lot of convincing!"

"And you would definitely marry Emma Watson..."

"Be still, my heart!" Julian's laugh echoed down the street.

Nora playfully bumped him with her whole left side. Julian nudged her back across the sidewalk, his skin extremely aware of every part of them that touched. "You're over that American fellow then? Really?"

She shrugged. "I think breakups might be a lot easier when you put an entire ocean of distance between you and your ex, so you never run into each other at all. Maybe I should write a self-help book about it. That's some great advice."

"Oh, truly. I'm sure everyone has the means and ability to hop to a new country when they're through with a relationship."

"To be fair, the country-hop is what caused the split."

Julian glanced at her sideways. "You think you'd still be together if you were still in New York?"

"Sadly, yes. Thank God for this job and the swift kick in the butt that I needed. I guess the ocean thing worked for my breakup with Hugh too. I really am an expert."

"That one was also due to a country-hop," Julian said quietly.

"Yes, but here I am. Back again. With plenty of countries to escape to if a man should so much as ask me on a date." She beamed up at him, and Julian couldn't be sure what he was doing with his face or what expression he might be making. He was going for something casual and aloof but was sure he was missing the mark entirely.

"Well, cheers to a swift kick in the bum," he said.

Nora nodded. "I miss my mother though." She sighed.

Julian thought about this for a moment. "Will she come for a visit?"

"I think she will someday. But she hates traveling. Hates planes. Hates big cities. *Hates* exchanging money."

Julian looked around at the quiet street—the hodgepodge of brick buildings with their dark little windows, the occasional twinkling light in the distance, the seamless blend of diverse architectures. At least, they were probably diverse architectures; he didn't know much about buildings, but he couldn't imagine anyone hating London. "And yet," he said. "I bet she would bear it all for you."

Nora smiled at that, and suddenly the inside of his body felt like a pinball machine, different organs lighting up as a ball of delight bounced around his chest and stomach. When they reached Nora's flat, Julian thought of so many nights that had ended in just the same way, walking down the street together with the whole gang there—making sure Hugh's girlfriend got home safely.

"I think it's great that you're here working on the book," Julian said. "You're finally doing the thing you've really wanted."

Nora twisted her keys around in her hands. "Thank you," she said. "Hey, if you ever feel the need to check out a new club, you know where to find me. I've got to do it for work."

"Clubbing for work. What a life you lead. I'd certainly tag along." He realized that it was probably something he wouldn't do in any other circumstance. They exchanged numbers, and Julian gave Nora a hesitant hug and held open the door to her building. "Have a good night then." He almost saluted but, thankfully, stopped himself at the last second.

"Good night, Julian," she said.

He watched her through the glass as she walked toward the lift and pressed a button. He remembered once when they'd all been at the club together, the night Hugh had professed his love for Nora while they stood at the sink in the men's bathroom, and Julian had smiled at his best mate as much as he could. He'd clapped him on the back and gone out to stand awkwardly at the bar while the two of them kissed on the dance floor. He'd borne it all until the summer was over, and then she had disappeared.

CHAPTER SEVEN

IT WAS SOMETIMES two in the morning when Nora's mother called from New York. Kathleen Shrapsan didn't really care if her daughter was sound asleep across the Atlantic, she was going to talk to her whenever she damn well wanted to. Nora grumbled every time she rolled over in bed to answer the call, but she wasn't going to say no to a woman who was just starting to grow back any hair that looked remotely appealing and had only just experienced her very first blind date with a man she met online.

"A mother remembers when her daughter is devastated, so I will never forget Hugh Jeffries," Kathleen said after Nora updated her on the events of the evening. "You were so sad when you came back from London, and I didn't know how to fix it."

Nora sat on her bed eating Doritos from the downstairs bodega. She was settling in for a long, middle-of-the-night video call with her mother, who obviously needed to know about every moment that had occurred at the pub.

"Isn't it weird how even though people are no longer in your life, they still exist somewhere in the world and go on living and hanging out in London and becoming a little bit famous?" Nora asked.

"Well, you certainly think highly of yourself," her mother said. "Of course people go on living their lives without you, Nora. You shouldn't be so vain, especially considering how your hair looks right now."

Nora absently patted her wild bed-hair. "Everyone's incredibly vain, Mom. You literally just told me you were way hotter bald and with shriveled tits during chemo than the guy you went out with last night."

"I still have the shriveled tits, Nora. Sadly, they never had anything to do with the cancer. I actually think they're your fault...from the breastfeeding."

Nora licked the orange Doritos dust from her fingertips. "Well Hugh Jeffries lives. And he's still super handsome."

"And?" her mother said.

"And engaged obviously."

"You know even when you told me about him way back when, I actually thought that *he* was a little vain."

"What? You never told me that. Why?" She was about to put the chips away, but then Nora unrolled the top of the Doritos bag and dove back in. She watched her mother—who was still absolutely lovely with her slowly regrowing eyelashes and big, full lips—rubbing the top of her twelve-year-old Yorkipoo, Bebe's, head. Bebe was too cute for her own good, and actually, out of anyone mentioned, Bebe was absolutely the vainest of all.

"Just a feeling I got when you talked about him. He thought he was a great musician, and he didn't really seem to have any humility about how attractive he was. Didn't he tell you that he could have any girl he wanted, but he was picking you?"

"That was a joke," Nora said. She was a little surprised by her mother's blunt assessment, since Kathleen had never expressed this opinion of Hugh before, and it wasn't like she was one to shy away from giving an opinion. But her mother had never actually met Hugh, and she was cautious about making too many judgments about someone she didn't know—someone her daughter had been pining over for months. Maybe it was just hard to translate Hugh's sense of humor into anecdotes.

"Anyway, what's the fiancée like?" her mother asked.

"Wasn't there, so I don't know. He didn't really talk about her."

"That's probably not good."

"Why?"

"Because if I had just gotten engaged to the love of my life, I would want to talk about the person."

"To your ex-girlfriend?" Nora stared at the pixelated version of her mother on the computer screen. "He probably didn't want to rub it in my face, Mom. Poor, lame, unmarried Nora."

"You're in London living your dream, you weirdo. I don't think anyone can call you poor, lame Nora. Please don't tell me you're feeling sorry for yourself."

"I could never tell *you* that I'm feeling sorry for myself! You had fucking cancer!"

"I don't know what Fucking Cancer is, but that one sounds like it might be a lot more fun." Kathleen looked right at the camera and winked. "So now what? Are you going to see him again?"

Nora rolled her eyes like she was sixteen. "We're getting coffee."

"Be careful, Nora," Kathleen was wagging her finger at her webcam. "You don't want to get in over your head with an engaged man."

"Nothing would ever happen between us," Nora said, and she was sure that it was true. She was the type of person who believed in the girl-code and sisterhood and traveling pants and all that kind of stuff. She hated that little rumbly feeling she'd had in the pit of her stomach when Hugh hugged her. She hated that she'd daydreamed about kissing him ever since she'd found out that he was taken—before that really. Ever since that stupid diary. And then he'd offered to walk her home! *What did that mean?*

Nothing. It meant nothing, and there was nothing between them. She was definitely not going to mention any of that stuff to her mother, though. She was trying not to think about it at all.

"Focus on your work," her mother said. "That's what you're there for. I want to be able to read this book and find it interesting even though I'm never even planning on taking a trip to London."

"The book's going to make you want to visit," Nora said. "London's going to sound like magic."

"There are plenty of things that make me want to leave America, Nora, but fish and chips and portraits of old British dudes aren't going to do it for me."

Nora shrugged. "Suit yourself," she said, but she knew that Kathleen would come when she was feeling up to it. She knew they would look at so many portraits of old British dudes and eat all of the fish and chips. She knew that her mother would ask the Beefeaters at the Tower of London for every gruesome detail about Anne Boleyn's beheading.

"You've got Doritos in your hair," her mother said.

After their conversation, Nora couldn't fall back to sleep. Her mind was racing with images of Hugh singing on stage, the way he closed his eyes like he was experiencing so much emotion while he sang a song that he'd written about her.

Desperate for a distraction, she read and reread the first blurb she'd written for the book—an incredibly short piece about the restaurant she'd been to with Darcy. She wasn't quite living out her fantasy yet, but somehow she'd actually fought for the thing she really wanted. She allowed herself to be a little vain for a moment because she'd stood up for herself and gotten the job she felt she deserved. She'd *made* them give her a chance. Her mother was right—this was what she was in London for. This was the reason she'd left a recovering cancer-survivor back in New York, and she had to make that count for something.

Nora decided to spend her first days back in London as a real, full-blown tourist, getting reacquainted with the city so that she could be fully immersed in its whole vibe as she started writing. She went right up to the guards outside of Buckingham Palace and tried to make them laugh, just like people always did in the movies. "How do you get a squirrel's attention? Act like a nut. Why did the banana go to the doctor? Because it wasn't peeling well."

It didn't work, just like it never worked in the movies, and those soldiers that somehow managed to remain so incredibly stern even with those giant, feathery hats on their heads, looked right through her. She wondered if they remembered the jokes though. Maybe they took them home to their kids, and they giggled for hours while rolling around on the floor. Or maybe they thought she was a lunatic.

People were friendlier on her self-made tour of execution sites. What was it about a beheading that still could draw such a crowd? She'd been to the Tower of London on her last trip to the city, and she'd stood in the spot where Anne Boleyn lost her head. There was something incredible about that, about standing right in the spot where that very gruesome and famous piece of history had taken place, and feeling so deeply for the woman who had lost her life centuries ago. This time, she went to what was known as Execution Dock, which had been the largest port in the world at one point in history. Pirates who were found guilty of various crimes were also paraded to the spot and then hanged in front of a vast audience that had lined the street or even pulled up near the dock in a boat. Captain Kidd—the pirate who inspired *Treasure Island*—was executed at the site in 1701.

Nora was fascinated by the history and a little ashamed of her eagerness to view the gloomy spot near the water. It was part of some vast, barely real era that seemed so distant and obscure, and yet she could stand right there on the stony beach where it happened while also recalling hundreds of violent incidents that had taken place quite recently. She imagined writing up the place in the guidebook: a morbid site that will captivate any pirate-loving adventurer; there is not much to look at, and yet there is much to behold.

Or something like that.

She stopped at a pub near the site named after the most famous executed pirate and chatted with the bartender on his thoughts about being so near a place that had seen hundreds of years' worth of executions. "I don't think about it much," he said. "But I like the tourists." He grinned at her and asked where she was coming from, and they had a very pleasant conversation, though Nora was disappointed that it dealt so little with executions or murder. She traveled to Old Palace Yard after that, where she took pleasure in examining the face of King Richard I on his statue while also reading on her phone about the execution of Guy Fawkes, which had taken place in that same spot. She knew so little about the man that had apparently been behind the *V for Vendetta* mask and she might have gasped out loud while skimming the details of his being hanged, drawn, and quartered after the Gunpowder Plot. When she looked up what it meant to be "quartered" she may have even uttered a four-letter word into the wind and shivered. People around her rushed by without noticing the faces of Nora or King Richard. Perhaps they already knew what it was to be quartered, but they never thought of it while walking by.

At Smithfield, you wouldn't have even known about all of the people that were burned or hanged there if not for a few historical plaques. It actually looked rather cheery and lovely, particularly with the summer sun shining over the old bricks. Nora stood gazing at the stone arch commemorating William Wallace—the *Braveheart* guy—who was hanged, drawn, and quartered there at Smithfield in the year 1305. Yes, there seemed to be a distinct theme to Nora's day of tourism.

She had tea at a shop nearby, and the old woman who ran it chatted happily with Nora about the weather. When the woman asked what brought her to Smithfield, Nora answered truthfully that she was fascinated by violent executions, murders, and the macabre.

The woman turned to look her up and down again, perhaps a little surprised, but then she gave Nora a knowing smile. "A dark side," she said. She leaned in closer. "Well let me tell you something, dear," she said. "I've got quite a story that most people just don't talk about it as much anymore."

Nora watched as she started to tell her tale; it was as if this woman had been waiting a lifetime for someone to listen. She didn't even ask if Nora wanted to know, as if she knew instinctively that she'd found a kindred spirit. It was surprising sometimes how willing people were to talk about their darkest memories and deepest fears, especially with a stranger. It was easier to get it off your chest if you were practically anonymous, almost nobody at all to the person sitting across from you. Maybe it was why Nora had almost told the man next to her on the plane about Hugh. Maybe it was why this woman had just been waiting for Nora to walk into the tea shop and start talking about death.

"It was terrible. Thousands of people died. December of 1952."

"I don't think I've ever heard of it," Nora said. She took a bite of a perfect little tea cookie. Was this a British thing? Having a quiet conversation about mass destruction over a nice cup of tea? Nora was *so* on board with that.

The woman nodded. "The sky was black," she said. "Not just the sky… everything really. You could hardly see right in front of your face. It lasted days too, like something out of a horror film. Animals collapsed in the fields. Everything was closed up. Like a phantom had cast a dark shadow over the city."

"What was it?" Nora asked, her imagination captured by the sound of the woman's voice. She looked outside of the teashop window and pictured it—the unending blackness.

"Smog," she said. The little woman shrugged, as if this foggy monstrosity was just a simple head cold. "I think it was the worst environmental disaster in history, the deadliest. My father was ill afterward too, and for a while he couldn't seem to breathe right. But I remember when he came home that first night. He'd had to just leave the car in the street when he could no longer see where he was going.

"And my uncle already had a respiratory sickness and couldn't stop coughing. He had to stumble to the hospital in the darkness."

"That's awful," Nora said, more aware of the airflow in and out of her lungs. She thought then that the event did seem vaguely familiar. Maybe she'd heard something in a podcast, but it was entirely different to sit in this woman's shop, to hear the rising and falling of her voice, to see her eyes going hazy as she got lost in the memories.

"He made it," the woman said. "But the smog continued. I heard later that they found traces of it shut up in library books. So many people were sick."

"How did it stop?" Nora took a gulp from her lovely floral teacup.

"The weather changed, and it dissipated, but I'll never forget it. Not as juicy as a murder or an execution, but it's quite a story. London was always smoggy then, but that was something else entirely."

"And your father?"

"He recovered, thankfully." The woman patted Nora's hand. "More tea, dear?"

Nora nodded, realizing that despite the quiet horror of the story, she was glad to hear it, to connect with this woman in London who she never would have known, to have this moment with her. It was why she'd wanted this chance for so long—to experience something new, to find people and their stories, to bring this city to life in her writing with purpose and meaning.

"Thank you for telling me," Nora said, taking another sip from her fresh cup, still imagining a dark and smoggy sky out the window despite the bright yellow sun.

"Thank you for listening," the woman said.

CHAPTER EIGHT

TRAVEL, history, writing, a bit of murder when she was lucky, delicious meals, and interesting characters. It was everything she'd been dreaming of for years as she had tried and failed so many times to land this job. However, the well-established travel writers that had occasionally video-called the small office in upstate New York had warned her about the downsides of travel writing when she'd grilled them on all aspects of their lifestyles. Long hours, they said. Loneliness, homesickness, lower pay than people realize, difficulty focusing, and a blur of restaurants and hotels that swirl together under the pressure to meet a deadline.

By the end of the fifth day, she felt a twinge of the loneliness that the travel writers had warned her about. She was in her favorite city in the world, enjoying its rich stories and beautiful scenery, but at the same time, she was keenly aware that she was alone for all of it. She had no one to laugh with when the portrait of an old diplomat in a museum looked strikingly similar to Bill Clinton. No one to delight in shoveling mouthfuls of spicy Indian food into their faces with her. Her longest conversation had been with the old woman in the tea shop, and while she had treasured that woman's time and her unparalleled knowledge of tea flavors, the interaction between them was fleeting. Nora felt like a stranger, even to herself.

She was already feeling very lucky and relieved to be in the unusual situation of having a small publishing office nearby, to have Darcy, as surprising as that might be. While most writers were adrift, roaming around unfamiliar territories with only a notepad and pen, she was tethered to something, she had a place to go and write and share her ideas with other people. She was just a few days into her new job, and she was already realizing what a unique and important gift her office and Darcy would be.

"It has the potential to be an eclectic and enjoyable eatery, but as always, the most important thing is the food, and that's where *Larry's* is lacking." Darcy was quoting Nora's writing back to her, analyzing every phrase and sentence of the hundred-fifty-word piece.

"On one hand," Darcy said, "I like the 'as always' because it indicates a consistency of voice and style throughout the book. It has personality. But on the other hand, it seems a little too obvious. Of course the most important thing about a restaurant is the food. Why bother announcing it? Maybe say something more specific like 'the pie made me want to barf and the chips were sad and soggy.'"

"You want me to say that?" Nora asked.

"No, but I want you to get that sentiment across in a nicer way. I like the details and descriptions about the place though. I think it'll finish out nicely with a little more revision."

Nora didn't think she had ever worked so hard on a hundred-fifty words in her entire life. She'd combed through it, word by word, probably almost one-hundred-fifty times before she even handed it in to Darcy, but still all of her editor's comments had been incredibly helpful. Maybe Darcy could become a great mentor after all. It turned out that she did seem to be good at her job, even if her "bedside manner" wasn't the greatest. Nora was excited to go back and continue working on her piece, to change that one sentence until it was perfect. "Thanks, Darcy," she said.

"What else have you got for me?" Darcy said.

"Wh-what?" Nora froze, the pages of notes in her hand almost dropping to the ground.

"Surely you've visited other places and started writing them up?"

"Well, no, I've been working on this—"

"Nora," Darcy said, narrowing her eyes. "We have a deadline. We have so much to do. You cannot tell me you just spent several days just doing this."

Nora felt her stomach twist into the shape of a pretzel. "I thought this was just for me to get started. To get my feet wet, you know?"

"I know you're new to this," Darcy said. "But you gave the company writing samples, right? You had to use something to get hired. They expected you to jump in and do the work. We don't have time for handholding."

Nora tried to dip her head in a way that would allow her hair to cover her bright red face. She could feel the heat of it radiating from her cheeks. Darcy was right, of course. Nora had begged for her shot, but she'd also been a professional with a portfolio of writing samples and ideas. She was supposed to know what she was doing. "I'm so sorry," she said. "I will get right on them."

"I'm going to need twenty more of these, in near perfect condition, by the end of the week."

"Right," Nora said. "You got it." She was backing out of the office slowly, embarrassed that she had committed herself to focusing on a single piece of work and had tried really hard on those one-hundred-fifty words, but of course that wasn't enough. She had a million other things that needed to be done, and she was supposed to know how to do them herself. Yes, she needed to figure out the voice and style of the book, but other than that she needed to be independent. And she was not going to cry in Darcy's office.

"So how did your night end up after the show?" Darcy asked before Nora could escape. The door was opened. Nora's hand was on the knob. She was almost free to run to the bathroom to try to pull herself together.

"Oh, um fine," Nora said, almost choking. "What do you mean?"

"I mean that Julian is attractive if you're into that kind of thing, and he seemed very happy to walk you home."

"Julian?" Nora was having a difficult time following Darcy's train of thought. She was thinking of the twenty places she needed to visit in the next couple of days and trying not to sob. Anyway, had Darcy forgotten that Hugh was the one Nora was in love with? That is, Hugh was the one Nora *had been* in love with years ago. "He's very nice, but he's Hugh's best friend."

"So?"

"So we're just friends. We've always been friends, if you could even call it that. In fact, I asked if he might want to check out one of the clubs on the list with me when I do my research."

"You're taking him out to a club?"

Was that unprofessional? "It's just for work, obviously."

"And what about Hugh?" Darcy asked.

"What about him?"

"You're going to see him again?"

"Maybe," Nora said. Was Darcy trying to be her friend? Or was she only interested in making fun of Nora's drama? Either way, it wasn't helping her to focus on her work when her boss wanted to dish on the sad state of her love life. "It's all very boring. Julian is just Julian. Hugh is now engaged, and so we will have coffee and catch up, but there's nothing funky going on."

"You forget that I saw the two of you together, you and Hugh. You both had tunnel vision. The rest of the world was dead to you once you started talking to each other."

Nora gasped perhaps too dramatically. "Absolutely not! It was just exciting to see each other after so long, and that's all it was." Geez, Darcy was starting to sound like her mother. And if they were both exactly right, neither of them needed to know it.

"Well," Darcy said. "I guess we shall see what happens. Take Julian to the club. Take Hugh to the coffee shop down the street because we need to cover that one anyway. Terribly expensive, but I'll add it to your list."

Nora nodded, wondering again how her commitment to focusing on work was going to go when it would inadvertently involve Hugh. She was supposed to take notes on coffee and scones while chatting with the man she'd loved most in her life?

"Go on, go," Darcy said. "You've got a lot to do. They want the stuff for the companion app as quickly as possible."

Nora quickly turned to rush out of Darcy's office and get back to her revisions, but just as she did, the front office door opened, and she heard Darcy's assistant, Jasmine, greeting someone. "Who's that?" Nora asked, and Darcy shushed her. She stood up quickly and smoothed out her slacks before rushing out of her office without a word to Nora.

Darcy's voice changed drastically as she called, "Well, look who we have here" to the newcomer.

Nora couldn't help craning her neck to actually look at who they had there. From what she could tell, the person Darcy was addressing was a courier woman—a dark, fit messenger with long black hair who was removing her bicycle helmet as Darcy greeted her.

"Proofs from the Ireland book," the woman said, holding up a large manila envelope. "I don't usually pay attention to what I've got, but I know you've been waiting for this one."

"Delightful," Darcy replied pleasantly. "Thanks so much for bringing them over, Anika."

"Well, you know that's my job." Anika smiled. "Record time this round, I think."

Nora watched in awe as the same woman who had been lecturing her for the past half hour smiled shyly at this messenger woman.

"Well, I'll be off then," Anika said.

"Oh yes, of course. But ummm, thank you," Darcy stalled. "Oh wait, do you want to meet the newest member of our team? She's American." The words seemed to rush right out of Darcy with barely a sense for their order. Nora looked around, shocked that Darcy would admit that they were hosting some inexperienced American in their office.

"Oh, yes, who is it?" Anika stepped back into the shop.

Nora moved forward, stepped out of Darcy's office, and waved awkwardly, sure she must look ridiculous. "Hi, I'm the American," she said. "Nora." She looked around. The room felt tiny, and everyone in it was watching.

"Anika," Anika said, and the pair of them smiled and nodded at each other, unsure of what else to say as they were introduced in front of the rest of the team. *Why had Darcy forced this interaction?* Nora hadn't met most of the people in the room.

"You biked here?" Nora asked, and Darcy looked annoyed at her polite conversation.

"Yes, my bicycle's right out front. You're new to London?"

"Kind of," Nora said, and it was quiet again. She eyed Darcy suspiciously. Was this some kind of test? Were there certain questions Nora should be asking this woman?

"She's supposed to give us some fresh perspective." Darcy laughed without taking her eyes off Anika.

"Well, good luck with it then." Anika placed her helmet back on her head. "I should probably be off. Good to see you, Darcy. Take care, all."

"Nice to meet you." Nora smiled brightly. The whole thing had been incredibly odd, but Nora seemed to be the only one who had noticed Darcy's implication that the most important person for Nora to meet in the whole office besides Timothy had been the mail woman.

When a gruff Darcy returned to her office and sat back down in the chair, Nora couldn't help herself. "What was that all about?" she asked.

Darcy froze, blushing, before dabbing her face with a tissue. "Nothing. It was nothing."

Nora paused, unsure if she should push the subject, but admittedly it was in her nature to pry, and she wasn't going to make any exceptions for this uptight British boss. "It was definitely something," she said.

"All of you Americans are so nosy!" Darcy lamented, lifting her head and then smacking it back into her hands again.

"You nosy little American," Hugh had said to her when they had met. Unlike Darcy, he'd found it to be endearing. She'd asked him how many women he had slept with before he even knew her name. She'd pried about his songwriting and his relationship with his band. He told her whatever she wanted to know.

"Just curious maybe." Nora smiled at Darcy. She leaned back in her chair, a lot more comfortable now that she'd seen Darcy come out from her behind her desk, so to speak.

"I'm not discussing this with you," Darcy declared.

"I think it's only fair that you tell me what the deal is here," Nora said.

"You know all about me. You strategized my reunion with my ex-boyfriend. Tit-for-tat, Darcy."

"Shush." Darcy sat down in a huff. "Don't you tit-for-tat me. We'll talk about it later."

Nora shook her head back and forth as she left Darcy's office. She was sure she'd get to the bottom of it eventually, and it was nice to have something to think about other than Hugh Jeffries and the fact that she was apparently already crap at her job.

CHAPTER NINE

JULIAN HAD BEEN STARING at the fish and chips in front of him for about ten minutes without taking a bite. Poppy was telling a story about a time she went fishing with her father as a child. He was trying so hard to concentrate on what she was saying. She was absolutely beautiful and outgoing and actually interested in him, which definitely seemed like it must be some elaborate prank sometimes. Sure, she could be a little negative, like when she complained about her students and her headmaster and the shabby state of her school and the shabby state of her father, but who didn't complain once in a while?

"Aren't you hungry?" she asked him.

He had thought he was starving, but since the waiter had set the plate down in front of him, he hadn't taken a bite. *Has Poppy always vented this much about everything?* Julian thought to himself. He was seriously losing it. This girl was smart. She liked board games. She *always* won and sometimes got so competitive that it didn't feel exactly *fun* to play with her, but no one else ever wanted to play board games with him. Maybe they had just spent too much time together too quickly; almost every evening since their first date did seem like a bit much. He was the one being negative, and he knew why.

"I think I might just take it to go," he said.

"Is everything okay, Julian?" Poppy asked.

"Been a little out of it lately, haven't I?" He stared down at the pile of food.

Poppy smiled. "I'm not sure I even know you well enough to know what you're like when you're out of it."

"When I'm not out of it, I'm really charming and adventurous and cool," Julian said. "Just remember that at all times."

"Oh yes, you must be *really* out of it now then." She laughed and went back to eating her salad.

If Julian were to imagine a list of things that would create an ideal girlfriend, Poppy would be it. She was clever, confident, and gorgeous. They had a lot in common—teaching obviously—but also other interests like comic books and Backgammon. She was edgy, too, with an almost pixie haircut and a tattoo on her clavicle, always just peeking out of her V-neck tops. On their first date, Julian had tried not to stare at the black ink on her chest, though he had been dying to know what it was.

It was immediately clear from that first date that she was far too sophisticated for him, always so sure of what she was talking about, whether it was The Go Go's or Charles Dickens or Hinduism; there was never a question in her tone. He'd been positive she was going to realize any minute that he was in over his head and that she was far too good for him.

Truly, the only issue Julian had with their relationship was that Poppy hadn't mentioned her cat, and the first night they'd returned to her flat (he had already been clammy with nerves), it was a den of cat hair. He was allergic, but she had some Benadryl on hand. The cat's name was Linus, and he and Julian immediately hated each other. Julian was still mostly flabbergasted that she invited him up to her apartment at all, when he never would have asked, and he was even more baffled when she poured him a drink and took off her shirt. Linus was watching too, so Julian made sure to shut the door tightly when he and Poppy made their way to the bedroom. For a brief moment he wondered if cats could open doors, because they were incredibly conniving, if still lacking opposable thumbs.

Since then, he had worked hard to avoid Linus, partially because of a strong fear that he would accidentally kill the cat before their tenth date.

There was no precedent for that, but it did seem just like the kind of stupid, clumsy thing that would happen to him.

When he woke up in Poppy's bed after their first night together, his face was swollen and itchy, his nose a bit of a mess, and Julian was sure he was done for. He must have looked frightful, not at all the type of bloke Poppy would go for, but she simply kissed him and laughed, not even giving him enough time to be flustered about the splotchy patches across his chest. He left feeling buoyant and sure that he would see her again very soon, and satisfied in his knowledge that the tattoo had been a small, black rose.

And yet, besides the cat, Julian realized as he gripped his box with an entire untouched meal on their eighth date, there was some other issue in their relationship that he couldn't define. Poppy had everything from his made-up perfect-girlfriend list, but it was almost like there was something that wasn't even on the list, something he couldn't name and hadn't even been entirely aware of until he saw Nora. He wasn't sure if it was a quality, exactly, or if it was just a feeling, some feeling that he didn't yet have and couldn't find a way to fabricate.

"Let's go this way." Poppy pointed as they exited the restaurant.

She placed her hand on his elbow to guide him out onto the street, and right then Julian made a decision. He was not going to mess this up. Poppy was wonderful. She was smart and witty and funny and beautiful. He couldn't fuck about on this and send her an embarrassing text that was meant for his mum. There *was* precedent for that, even though it would be highly unlikely now that Mum was deceased.

He was going to be normal. He was going to open up. He was going to let down the walls that all the other women he had dated had been unwilling to scale or to topple. He was not going to make a pig's ear of this amazing thing. This was *good*. He would probably never even see Nora again, and even if he did, what did it matter? There wasn't anything between them, and he was happy. He didn't know why he kept thinking about her. It was ridiculous.

"Your place or mine?" Poppy asked.

"Uh, mine. Is that alright?" He needed to avoid Linus at all costs.

She nodded. He kissed her again, enjoying the warmth of her lips against his own. Whatever the missing thing was, he would find it eventually with Poppy. How could he not? If he kissed her enough, everything would right itself. If he kissed her enough, he would feel the unnamable feeling. He imagined that all his worries and insecurities could float away with each kiss, that with every touch of their lips he would find more and more of what he was looking for. He just had to try.

When Julian was a boy, he'd wanted to turn out just like his father. Perhaps this was a common thing for boys who had admirable fathers. They looked up to them; they wanted to emulate them until they, too, were good fathers with adoring sons. It hadn't quite turned out like that for Julian, however. While his father was gruff, confident, and often spontaneous, Julian was timid, lanky, and intellectual. He indulged in far too much deep reflection, which his father jovially mocked. "Stop reading and go outside," had been a common refrain from Julian's childhood.

However, since he'd finished university and his graduate coursework, Julian had found a little of the confidence that came so naturally to the man who had raised him. He'd started playing football with an adult league and built up some muscle. He'd found a career where he succeeded and received satisfaction. He'd become more comfortable being himself in a way that he'd never been before.

Still, his only lasting and meaningful relationships had grown from friendship, with the exception of Poppy, who had enough confidence for both of them. Julian didn't know how to be unabashedly himself with strangers—not in the way that his father was, or Hugh or Nora. He felt that he could only dole out bits of himself, little by little, trying so hard not to disappoint any expectations or let anyone see too much. Eventually they might get the full picture, might see what he was really like underneath all of that blushing and babbling, but it always took so much time.

Perhaps that was why he couldn't stop thinking about seeing Nora. Though his initial shock at being with her again had made him nervous and strange, by the end of that night at The Goose, he felt much the same way as he had so long ago; he felt like he could be completely at ease and she wouldn't judge his every idiotic phrase or movement. Why couldn't he just feel like that all the time?

"You're going to burn the toast, bozo," his father said, bringing him back to the present where they stood in his father's little kitchen making breakfast.

"I like it a little brown, thank you very much, sir."

"Well don't burn mine then." His father put the crispy pieces on a plate and started lathering them with margarine. "Any plans this fine evening?" he asked.

Julian thought for a moment. He had somewhat consistent, unspoken plans with Poppy, but he hadn't really told his father about her yet for some reason. Perhaps it was because he knew his father would be thrilled for him, and he didn't want him to be disappointed if nothing much came of the relationship. He seemed to recall his father smacking him across the head when he and Melody had broken up years earlier.

"Nothing too exciting," Julian said.

"You need to be out meeting women," his father said. "Or men. I don't much care. I just want you to be happy."

"Thank you for that," Julian said. It sounded a little sarcastic, but he meant it genuinely. He appreciated his father's concern.

As they sat down at the table, Julian's mobile went off, and he glanced at it. He wouldn't answer while he was having a meal with his father, but he just wanted to see what it might be about. It was a text from Nora—

"Want to check out the club with me tonight?"

Julian turned away from his father so whatever expression was on his face wouldn't be evident. He put the mobile on the counter and then sat down to eat. Of course he wanted to go to the club with her. But what would he say to Poppy? Did he need to explain it? It wasn't like they had firm plans. Or maybe he could just tell her the truth, that he was going out with a friend for the evening. Nora had always only been a friend, and even if she was back in town, she was still Hugh's first love, and he would never try to—he couldn't even finish the thought. Additionally, she probably wasn't even romantically interested in him anyway. *Why am I even thinking like this?* Once, sure, he'd had a harmless, meaningless crush on her. Now? Yes, she still made him laugh and feel comfortable in his own skin. But that meant that she would be a good friend, and that would be all there was to it. He liked Poppy. Nora was great, and it would be fun to hang out occasionally in a very platonic way, but he needed to dismiss any other thoughts of her from his head.

"Something wrong?" his father asked.

"No, why do you say that?" Julian could tell that his voice sounded abnormally high-pitched.

His father snorted. "Okay, don't tell me then. I'll figure it out soon enough."

"Figure what out? Nothing's wrong." Julian tried to change the subject. "Tell me about what happened with Michael at the shop."

Julian's mind wandered as his father discussed the latest gossip at the hardware shop. He remembered when Nora and his mates had all been together at the place one evening, waiting for Julian to finish up with his dad. They had roamed the aisles wielding hammers and wrenches. Nora put on a headlamp that his father kept in stock at the front. She'd looked adorable, even with that too-large piece of equipment on her head. She flicked the light on and pointed it in his direction, bouncing the beam around his body.

"What are you doing?" he asked.

"Putting you in the spotlight. What are you going to perform for us, Julian?"

"I'm not the performer."

"Well…" She paused. "You're going to be a teacher. That's kind of like a performance. How will you teach them about the Revolutionary War? What do you even call it here? You must tell them about the brave Americans who fought to get freedom from King George."

"I'll tell them how, to this very day, the Americans are devastated they aren't British subjects. I'll tell them how they still worship the queen."

"And her grandsons, don't forget that," Nora said. "I've always had a crush on the younger one."

Julian laughed incredulously. "I better get Hugh over here." He motioned as if to get Hugh's attention.

Nora batted his hand as she took off the helmet. "Shhh, don't tell him. He hates when I fawn over the royals."

Later that night, after the lot of them had put back the tools and left for supper, Julian's father had asked about the girl in the shop who was running around with all the lads. Julian didn't even realize that he'd seen her there.

"That's Hugh's girlfriend," he told his father.

"Oh really? She doesn't seem like Hugh's type."

"What do you mean?" Julian asked. "How do you know what Hugh's type is?"

"I don't really, I guess. But she seemed a bit too sweet for him. I thought he liked the wild girls. She seemed more like someone who you would be interested in."

For all of their differences, Julian couldn't believe how well his father understood him.

"What are you talking about? She's wild enough," Julian had said, pretending that he hadn't been daydreaming about her while brushing his teeth, while eating supper, while doing the wash.

"I suppose I don't know what I'm talking about," his dad had said with a wise smile.

———

Julian texted Poppy after breakfast.

"I'm meeting up with an old friend tonight, so I don't think I'll be 'round this evening. Tomorrow?"

He was sweating a bit when he saw that she was typing a response.

"Tomorrow is good." :)

That was all it took. Julian kept reminding himself that he hadn't lied, and she had responded positively. He should have known that Poppy would have enough confidence not to worry if they spent one night apart. She didn't even ask about the friend.

He promised himself he wouldn't spend too much time on his hair or wondering what to wear to the club. This was not even remotely in the realm of a date. It was so un-datelike, in fact, that it was work for Nora, which meant that she would be focused on her job the whole time, and it would not be romantic in the least.

Even so, Julian liked to imagine her thinking logically about how to rate and review the club. He liked to think about her passion for writing a piece about it in the book and how she would agonize over every phrase until it was exactly right. He'd lived in London his entire life, and he already wanted to buy ten copies of the book when it came out, because he knew how she lit up when she talked about it. The way she chewed on her pen when she was thinking was so incredibly… Bloody hell, why was he doing this again? He needed to stop.

They met at St. James square so they could walk together to find somewhere for a late dinner before going out. When he found her wandering aimlessly, waiting for him, he wished he could see inside her head and know exactly what she was thinking about as she peacefully paced back and forth. She looked beautiful, he thought. Objectively, of course. Anyone would have appreciated the effort she'd put in with her hair styled in soft, silky curls and her eyes highlighted by bright, sparkly colors.

"Thank God. I'm starving," she said when she saw him.

"Me too," he said, even though he didn't know if he could eat. His stomach felt like it was a wet towel being wrung out.

"I was not made for late dinner." She laughed.

They walked to a little place down the street and sat in a corner with dim lighting and a picture of a sleeping dog on the wall. Julian had never been there before, but he liked the atmosphere. There were cozy fabric booths and antique-looking dining sets. The bar was framed on the outer edge by white, twinkling lights.

"What will you get?" Nora asked him.

"I like the look of the pot pie," he said. "Are you allowed to drink on this excursion?"

"Well, I'm not going to drink here, because I want to keep a clear head for the club." She pushed her dark brown hair behind her ear and took a sip of water. "But, I mean, I have to try the drinks there, right? That's a pretty important aspect of reviewing the place."

"Don't tell me you have to try every signature cocktail," he deadpanned.

"Maybe not *every* one. But if we split the duties, it should be a breeze, right?"

"I'm surprised Darcy didn't want to join us for that," he said.

"Darcy has assigned all the clubs to me. She told me to buy a halter top and take care of it. She says her clubbing days are over, but to be honest, it's been a long time for me as well. I might be too old and out of touch for this." She put her head down on the table for a moment. "I'm afraid I don't know what's cool."

"I'm glad it's not just me. I haven't been to a club in ages."

She grinned up at him in her sequined top. "What a good sport you are then," she said.

They split an appetizer of cocktail shrimp, and it didn't take long for her to end up with a lump of red sauce dribbling down her chin. Julian tried not to laugh at her, but she didn't even mind it. She wiped it off with the back of her hand with a wide grin. "I bet it's going to be stuck in my teeth too. Everyone's going to feel sorry for you, sitting here with your disgusting date who doesn't know how to eat a meal like a lady."

"I can see their looks of pity now," Julian said. "The woman at the bar is a hair away from marching over with a wet nap just to put me out of my misery."

Nora laughed with a snort and quickly covered her nose. "Oh, God, it's getting worse, Julian. And I haven't even started drinking. You're in so much trouble."

"I'm going to ask for a bag to put over my head so I won't be seen with you."

Nora smirked and narrowed her eyes at him. "I always knew you were embarrassed by me," she said.

Julian wasn't sure if she meant it or if she was still joking, and he didn't know whether to laugh or try to explain. Embarrassed by her? He'd been enraptured, enamored, stupidly elated, but never embarrassed by her. "Do you really think I was?" he asked finally.

"Weren't you?" she said. "You were always so proper, so…"

"Boring?" he finished.

"No!" She laughed. "Sophisticated maybe. And I was…not. I assumed you found it appalling."

He stared at her, again unsure how to respond. He'd kept his distance, tried not to stay too close or get too caught up with her, and she'd thought him embarrassed. He shook his head.

"You were…" His eyes drifted over her face, her cheeks glowing in the candlelight. He didn't know how to complete the sentence but was thankfully saved by their meal.

"*Bon appétit*," the waiter said as he placed the plates before them.

They talked about old memories at dinner, about late nights at Hugh's flat, and Saturday afternoons at the pub. They reminisced about walks through Kensington and a trip to tour Windsor palace.

"You were all such great tour guides. I should give you credit in the book," Nora said.

"I don't even think we'd been half the places you convinced us to go."

"That's why it worked out. You showed me where the real locals hang out, and I took you to the tourist attractions you never would have visited otherwise."

"And watched Dev mock the Beefeaters." Julian laughed.

"Oh my gosh, I forgot about that!" Nora almost shouted.

They both smiled quietly, their eyes locked on one another. Julian still couldn't stop looking at her. "I think those excursions may have started my love of traveling." He cleared his throat, trying to remember to breathe normally. "Not that I was going anywhere then, but having that new perspective, getting a different outlook on the city. It was a similar experience when I was in Shanghai and Beijing. I was trying to step back and take everything in."

Nora's eyes went wide. "You were in China? I'd love to go there. That must have been so exciting."

Julian loved watching her light up when she talked about different countries she wanted to visit, like the world was one big adventure and it was out there waiting for her.

"It was. I taught English classes there briefly. It was a few years after we met."

Nora nodded as if she was piecing something together. "You seem different than you were then," she said. "The last time I was in London."

"What do you mean?" Julian's nervousness washed over him in an instant. Was he acting strangely? Did she not like him?

"I don't know," she continued. "You seem more—um—chill maybe. Like maybe you aren't embarrassed by me anymore." She grinned, daring him to contradict her again.

"I told you I wasn't—"

"And yet, you seemed to run the opposite direction when you saw me coming. Hugh's weirdo girlfriend."

"I never did," he said, surprised she'd given that much thought to his opinion of her. He had tried not to get too close, but he'd always felt that he was too obviously running toward her whenever possible. "Maybe I was just shy," he said.

"So you won't admit that I'm an embarrassing weirdo?"

"Well…" They laughed together again, and Julian felt a tightness in his chest like heartburn.

"I was awfully drunk, but I seem to recall you hiding in the bathroom the night we were streaking. You couldn't bear to be a part of that nonsense."

He grimaced. "I did not feel the need to witness Hugh's junk swinging around, thank you very much."

"Always so sensible," she said, locking her gaze on him again.

He looked away quickly, looked at the bar, at the exit, thought for a moment that he should flee. He wasn't feeling very sensible at all right now.

At the club, Nora solidified her embarrassing weirdo status. She was really a terrible dancer, limbs flailing all over the place against the rhythm.

She didn't care at all though, and Julian was thrilled with her wild ligaments. He couldn't dance either, but he wasn't quite so bold about showing off his lack of coordination.

They drank cocktails with names like "Punch up the Jam" and "Smells like Vodka Spirits." They were delicious, and Julian was already giving the place five stars or smiley faces or whatever Nora's rating system was.

"I didn't realize this place was nineties themed!" he yelled over a Britney Spears house mix.

"I forgot to mention that!" Nora called. "It might be the best place I've ever been!"

The music was fantastic, and throughout the evening Nora questioned him about what he thought of every detail—the drinks, the atmosphere. She even made him report back on the state of the men's loo.

"There are paintings of *My Little Pony* in the women's room," Nora informed him.

"It's *Paddington Bear* in the men's!"

"I love this place," she yelled, and they both went to the dance floor, fancy drinks in hand.

They spun around excitedly, and Julian was starting to feel a bit tipsy and dizzy, the dance floor a blur of colors and lights, a loud thrum beating in his chest. Then a Celine Dion ballad filled up the room, and everything seemed to slow into focus. Nora put her hands on his shoulders and started to sway back and forth with him. "Oh, I love this song," she said, and she loudly sang along.

"Are you drunk, Nora?" he asked her, laughing.

"Why would you say that?" she said. "I always belt Celine at the top of my lungs, no matter the circumstances or how many drinks I've had."

As the song continued, she wrapped her arms around his neck, and they kept dancing together. Julian felt warm—from the alcohol, from the dancing, or from the blush creeping over him from being so close to her— he wasn't sure. When Celine stopped singing, Nora looked up at him, her arms still enfolded around his shoulders, and sighed. Her face was glowing from sweat, and a bit of soggy hair was plastered to her forehead. Julian held his hands on her hips, and he was keenly aware of the warmth of her skin between his fingers. Only a few inches were between their lips;

it would have taken so little for him to bridge the distance. He could have just barely bent his head a little further. Her lipstick was smudged and faded as if she'd already been kissed. Perhaps, in another life, he really had leaned in and gone for it.

Then the song mix transitioned into "No Scrub," and Nora pulled away from the slow dance, spinning in a circle again. She took a sip from her drink, but it made that awful slurping sound when there's nothing left in the bottom. She shook the glass at him and jerked her head toward the bar. He followed her lead, and soon they were ordering a Macarena Margarita and an Mmmbop Mix. They took sips from their own drinks and then swapped.

"I like your Mmmbop better," Nora yelled.

"Well I happen to prefer the Macarena," Julian said. "Cheers!" They clinked their glasses together and headed back to the sweaty crowd in the middle of the dance floor. Julian watched as Nora shook her hips, her long hair flipping every which way. He moved less dramatically but still shook his arse with the best of them. He was reaching for Nora's hand to twirl her in a circle when a guy stepped between them and pressed himself against her backside. Julian didn't know how to react in such a situation. They weren't on a date. She was an attractive, single woman who might welcome the attentions of a good-looking man. Should he back away and leave her to dance with the guy? Or should he stay close by to protect her if she needed it? He couldn't see her face and had no idea how she was reacting. He should have considered the possibility that something like this would happen at a dance club.

In an instant, Nora took his hand and pulled him toward her, pushing the other guy out of the space between them. She held onto his neck again and pressed her full body against his, even closer than it had been before. "Thank you," she whispered in his ear. He felt goosebumps erupt down his whole left side, starting where her lips almost brushed his ear. "I wasn't quite in the mood for that this evening, and I don't think I could mention it in the book anyway."

"I wasn't sure what to do," he admitted. He placed his hand on her back and breathed in the sweet lavender soap and Nora-scent of her skin. They held each other like that for a moment, barely moving and breathless, until Julian hiccupped, and Nora pulled away laughing.

It seemed like they had only just arrived when the DJ announced last call, and Nora reached up to put her arm around him awkwardly. He was several inches taller than her.

"It's late. We've about closed the place down," she said. "Should we stumble out of here?"

"Is it required for work that you stay until close?" he asked.

"Nah, I think I have thoroughly assessed the situation." She moved her arm and nudged her shoulder into him.

"Share a cab?" he asked, and she nodded.

They walked out onto the sidewalk, and though they weren't touching any longer, Julian could feel some kind of static buzzing in the slim space between their bodies. He knew it hadn't been real, but for a couple of moments throughout the evening, he'd felt like they were so close, almost like it wouldn't be unexpected if he were to kiss her outside of her apartment building at 4:00 a.m. when he dropped her off, almost like she might lean into him and press her lips even harder into his timid kiss.

"Did you have a good time?" she asked as they sat in the back of the cab.

"Brilliant." He smiled.

"You said it's been a long time for you too, huh?" she said. "Going out to a place like that?"

"Oh yes, it's been years probably. Maybe for a mate's birthday a while back."

"Does Hugh still go to places like that at all?" she asked.

Julian blinked hard. He realized that the whole evening they'd barely spoken of Hugh. It was almost like the memory of her first love had disappeared, and it had just been the two of them, as if she'd never been with Hugh at all and none of that mattered anymore. It did matter though, and suddenly he wondered if Hugh might even be upset that he'd gone out with her like this, even if it didn't mean anything. He'd never even thought to mention it or ask permission.

"He doesn't really," he said finally. "Not since he met Rose."

"Rose," Nora repeated, but Julian couldn't sense her tone. It didn't seem to hold any jealousy or malice, just curiosity perhaps. "Do you like Rose?" she asked.

"I like her well enough," he said, souring on the topic but not wanting Nora to know how much he wished they could talk about anything else.

"They're good together?" she said, and Julian felt sick. He didn't want her to care about Rose or Hugh or their relationship. He wished so hard that she wouldn't think of it.

"What do you want to know?" he asked, as he accepted the fact that the perfect parts of the night, the parts where she pressed up against him and looked into his eyes like Hugh never existed, were long over.

"Tell me what she's like," Nora said. "Not because I'm jealous. Don't look at me like that. That's not what it is, Julian." He almost snorted. "I swear it's not! I'm just nosy. That's all. I've always been nosy, and a girl can't help it when it's her ex."

"If you say so," he said, teasing her. "Tell me what you're going to write about the club."

"You're changing the subject," she said. "And I'm going to let you because I don't want you to think I'm jealous of her or I still have feelings for him."

"You don't?" he asked, but then he wanted to take it back. If she said that she did have feelings for Hugh, he didn't want to know the truth, and if she said that she didn't, she could easily be lying, not wanting to admit her feelings to his best mate.

"I don't know," she said, which he supposed was probably the truest answer she could have given.

CHAPTER TEN

THE WEEK WAS a blur of restaurants, menu items, tea shops, and paintings. There'd been a Picasso exhibit at the National Gallery and an exquisite fashion focus at Victoria and Albert. Some of the content Nora was writing would be more immediately available on the 99 Flamingo Guide website, which held loads of supplemental tourism recommendations that were updated weekly. Some would be stockpiled for the release of the new app. It wouldn't be seeing her work *in print* yet, as she had always dreamed about, but she was still looking forward to seeing something that she had written on a website that actually had some traffic, unlike her poorly maintained blog. Actually, the website would probably get a lot more readers than a hard copy of the book, but Nora still couldn't wait to hold the thing in her hand. She had a notebook of meticulous notes about each of the places she had visited throughout the week, but she still had to refer to the pictures on her phone to remember which place was which. *This* was the one with the amazing tea sandwiches. *That* was the one with the stale scones.

She couldn't remember the last time she'd been in such a delicious frenzy of work and writing. The time of day held little meaning when she was up at random hours to organize her notes, write a new review, or FaceTime with her mother. Despite her mother's frequent calls and

Nora's delight in chatting with cashiers and waiters and bartenders and sommeliers, she still felt the creeping escalation of travel-writing loneliness. Sharing her witty observations with the stranger beside her at Picasso's "Fruit Dish, Bottle, and Violin" painting wasn't the same as sharing the whole experience with someone, and for that she envied the tourists who would read her work later, those who would make plans with their spouses and families and co-workers. Many of them would be in large groups to experience the things she had lived through alone.

Going to the club with Julian was her only exception. After a long day of meticulous editing, she hadn't expected to enjoy a night out quite so much, but as Nora worked for hours on her three hundred words about the nineties dance club, it was difficult to separate her clinical thoughts about the club—the cleanliness, the drinks, the music—from how much fun she'd had throughout the entire evening. She couldn't write about the music without thinking about Julian doing the running man or the sprinkler on the dance floor, just as she couldn't write about the drinks without thinking of the way they made her feel all bubbly inside or the way Julian's face had soured when he took a sip of one of the stronger concoctions. She was sure, despite her best efforts to remain objective, those memories were pouring into her review as well, the page overflowing with her sentimentality and nostalgia.

Julian. Nora was smiling to herself again. "This song is the bomb," he'd yelled in an American accent when "Say my Name" by Destiny's Child had pumped through the speakers. She'd been under the silly impression that the night might be awkward. She couldn't remember a time when it had been just the two of them for so long before, but it turned out that they might be friends. He'd told her about his teacher arch-nemesis and their adorable classroom-decorating feud. He'd made fun of the cocktail sauce dribbling down her chin and danced her away from the unwanted advances of a slimy guy at the club. And then...

One part of the night was a little too fuzzy, but Nora couldn't stop replaying the hazy images she could remember. She seemed to recall Julian wrapping his arms around her and pulling her close, then looking down into her eyes until her heart sped up. His soft breath was on her face; she could smell his neck. She didn't think she'd ever smelled his neck before, but it was sweet and musty at the same time—*why am I thinking about the scent of Julian's neck?* It was clearly ridiculous, and she must have been drunk or half-crazy, but it had almost seemed like—just for a quick, incomprehensible moment—it had almost seemed like he was going to kiss her. That wasn't the worst part though. The worst part—again, those drinks had far too much sugar and the lighting on the dance floor was probably distorting her memories—but the worst part was that she had really wanted to know what it would feel like if he did.

Nora was so concentrated on her *writing* (yes, writing, that was all) she almost didn't realize when it was time to head out for coffee with Hugh. In quite a miraculous turn of events, she had managed to focus on her work throughout the week and to avoid thinking about the fact that she would be seeing her first love again, this time just the two of them. Almost to the moment that she printed off her last article and handed the stack of writing off to Darcy, she had only barely imagined what this encounter would look like—what he would be wearing, how he would say her name, how he would spin a plastic straw around his coffee cup, mixing in too much sugar. Of course, the instant she walked out the door of the 99 Flamingo Publishing office, a nervous fear began to swirl around inside her until she thought she might either, one, puke on the sidewalk or, two, start running the other direction until she was keeled over gasping for breath (which probably wouldn't take that long considering how out of shape she was, though, hey, she had been doing a lot of walking lately. Maybe she could make it a mile).

Instead of doing either of those things, however, she kept walking so intently that people passing her might have noticed her look of determination. *Look at that powerful young woman. Must be a force to be reckoned with.* Her chin was in the air, her chest was out, her nose was bleeding. Oh shit, her nose was bleeding! She ducked into a storefront to grab some tissues out of her bag as drops of red blood spilled on the cement. This always seemed to happen at the worst times. She must have been rubbing her nose again, a nervous tick that she never seemed to recognize until it was too late. Once she had successfully mopped up the mess and checked herself in the shop window, she continued her walk, less confidently this time.

Perhaps what was so amazing about Hugh, what made him even more attractive than he had been seven years ago, was that he had actually done it. He had found success as a musician, despite the years of playing to indifferent crowds and cleaning the toilets in that filthy, delightful pub. Nora was inspired. If he could manage to do something so incredible as get a packed room full of people singing along with his every word, then surely she could write a decent travel review and get published in a guide book update.

As she waited at a crosswalk a couple blocks from the coffee shop, she accidentally found herself thinking about his lips again. Then, without warning, she saw Julian's face instead of Hugh's, Julian's bright eyes staring at her, his open mouth nearing her own.

Oh God, what is wrong with me?! There was no reason to be thinking that way about her ex-boyfriend's best friend. She just needed to get laid. That was absolutely what it was. She'd been used to consistent lovemaking with Brandon, very satisfactory lovemaking, and since she'd moved to London, there had been zilch going on in her pants. When Julian touched her, her body was just having a strong reaction to being held by a man like that, and her brain was trying to make sense of something that was clearly just a physical indication of her need for sex. It was the same reason that she'd just woken up a few days before in the midst of a very inappropriate dream about Hugh. She was not going to bother analyzing the fact that when the random stranger at the club molded himself against her body, she didn't have the same reaction whatsoever and immediately shrank away from him. She also would not be mentioning any of this to her mother.

By the time she finished that train of thought and determined she needed to find a new attractive British man to bang these inappropriate ideas out of her head, she noticed that it was starting to drizzle. She pulled out her umbrella, which was thankfully tucked at the bottom of her bag (underneath a pile of now-bloodied tissues—what did British people do with their trash in London?) and rushed toward the cafe a little faster, worrying that the rain was going to ruin her hair, and then worrying that she was concerned about how her hair looked in front of Hugh at all. *It's normal to want to look hot in front of your engaged ex-boyfriend, right?*

In the grand scheme of things, she and Hugh hadn't even been together that long. She'd been with Brandon longer. And yet, those few months, and the year or so afterward in which their relationship slowly faded away and evaporated over the giant ocean between them, had meant so much to Nora. She wished that she could feel like that about another man, but she hadn't since. What a waste for your love life to peak at the age of nineteen in one fantastic sparkler of a summer.

Through the large window in the front of the cafe, she could see Hugh sitting at a table. She didn't think it would be a stretch to say that he looked a little nervous, glancing back and forth, shaking his legs and rubbing his hands together. At first, he didn't see her, and she watched him sip from his espresso cup, locks of hair hanging in his deep brown eyes. She knew that chocolate color so well from memory. Then he looked up, and the lines around his eyes crinkled as a smile took over his face. She almost stopped in her tracks. How was she going to get through coffee while also behaving like a normal human? Coffee already made her jittery and gave her a stomachache. Why had she decided to indulge in two things that could make her jumpy and nauseous at the same time?

"Hiya, Nora!" Hugh said as she reached the table. Déjà vu swept over her. This exact scene had played out a million times before, except then he had kissed her hard on the mouth instead of giving her a peck on the cheek. "I almost ordered for you, but I didn't know if you'd want the same thing."

"You remember my order?" she asked.

"Vanilla-flavored iced coffee. Far too sweet for me. I don't know how you stand it."

"You dump around seven sugars into your cup," Nora said.

"But I don't go for all of that squirty cream."

Nora wondered if this was a sign. In movies, when a guy remembered a girl's drink order it meant something, right? Despite her attempts to fill the cracks in her foundation of logic, fantasy life kept creeping in.

She laid it all out in her head:

1. Hugh was getting married to another woman.

2. She would never even want him if he made a move on her. That would make him sleazy, and it would make her sleazy too.

3. It was fun to catch up with an old friend, but she needed to stop thinking like a jealous ex. Maybe Rose was as terrible and gross as she was in Nora's imagination, but still, that didn't change anything. Maybe Rose had a wart and bad teeth and no sense of humor at all…

"So how is it to be back in London?" Hugh asked, and Nora snapped out of her weird delusions.

"I love it," she said too enthusiastically. *Tone it down, girl.* "I mean, it's such a clean and beautiful city." *Cleanliness? How am I going to be a travel writer if my favorite thing about a city is cleanliness?*

"Not like New York," Hugh said. "I was there, actually, a couple years back. I thought to call or email you, but I didn't know if that might be a bit odd."

Nora was taken aback for a moment. Hugh Jeffries was so very British, with his strong accent and British Invasion haircut. It was hard to imagine him on her home turf in America, but he had been to New York City, and she hadn't known. She didn't necessarily expect that she would have suddenly had a tingle of intuition the moment that Hugh set foot on US soil. It just seemed like she should have been aware that he was nearby. Had he already been dating Rose then? Is that why he hadn't tried to see her? But she'd thought the same thing about trying to call him when she got to London, even as a single woman. She'd wavered for so long about whether to get in touch, but it happened anyway, and there they were, sitting together once again.

"You didn't like New York?" she asked, trying not to let her mind play out an entire storyline where he had called her and they'd seen each other in the city before there was even the idea of Rose, and somehow, they had ended up back at his hotel in the evening after having drinks downtown…

"Too many people all the time. London is just more spread out, ya know? And New York is just kind of grimy, I'm sorry to tell you."

"Thanks for breaking it to me." She smiled. "If you were going to live anywhere in the world, and you didn't have to worry about work or—you know—your *fans* or money or anything, where would it be?"

"London," he said. No hesitation. "What about you?"

"I think it's here for me too," she said, even though she actually loved New York—the little city upstate where she'd grown up *and* the Big Apple. And she loved Rome; she'd done a week there after studying in London. She loved California and Colorado; she wanted to go to Thailand and South Africa. There were so many places to explore in the world.

"Good answer," he said. "I'm not much of a traveler. Too bloody stressful."

Nora couldn't remember if she'd ever known that about him before. She couldn't imagine not wanting to see new places all the time. It was like an itch all over her body that could only be scratched with a new adventure.

"Anyway," he said, leaning in close to her. "Tell me all about everything that's happened to you since I last saw you. Start with getting on the plane when you left."

He looked at her intently, and she could smell his cologne. Was he wearing it for her? "I told you all the interesting parts after your show," she said. "Speaking of which, let's talk about that. You're kind of famous now."

"Not famous."

"Kind of," she said.

"Nora, Nora, Nora." His eyes looked her over. "I can't believe you're here. You look almost exactly the same as you did in my memory."

CHAPTER ELEVEN

HUGH WAS surprised at the nervousness that crept over him while waiting for Nora at the little cafe. He hadn't expected to feel quite that uneasy, and he couldn't help absently jiggling his leg up and down so fiercely that his knee went entirely out of control and banged into the underside of the table. He didn't want to admit to himself that he'd been thinking about her too much lately, that he'd been comparing her to Rose.

They were both beautiful, though perhaps Rose was attractive in the more classic, traditional way, with sleek blonde hair and nude lipstick, and Nora was, well, he didn't know how to describe it. She was a little disheveled most of the time—her clothes wrinkled, her tennis shoes separating from their soles—but she had big, excited eyes and dark, wild hair that made him want to run his fingers through it. Rose was often serious, but it was because she cared so fiercely about everyone. She took her work seriously, her friends, even Hugh and his music. Everyone else had seen it as a hobby, but Rose championed his art. She believed in him. It was kind of overwhelming actually, the beautiful weight of her expectations. She grounded his creative, sometimes chaotic mind, and he never wanted to disappoint her. Nora, on the other hand—her full, round cheeks always made her look happy. He'd never disappointed her, though. He supposed he'd never really had the chance. Their relationship was a breeze, a break from reality, a bright spot of fun and adventure that they'd both known would end.

But Nora still inspired him, even after only one reunion. Just a few days before meeting her for coffee, he'd been sitting on his bed thinking up a song when he realized it was all about Nora all over again. He sang absently while he played: *It's like I haven't seen you for one hundred years. But now that you're beside me, no one else is here. I could have gone without you for the rest of my life, but not tonight, not tonight...*

It was a shame that Rose had walked in right at that moment. "I haven't heard that before," she said, setting down a basket of folded laundry. "Is it new?"

"Ah, just something I'm playing around with," he said.

"Well keep going. I'll listen."

He absolutely did not want to continue, but he wasn't sure what to say. She could think it was about her, and while he didn't want to lie, it was just a song after all. He started to play again. *It's like I haven't held you for one hundred years. But now that I can touch you, the past is all right here. I could have gone without you for the rest of my life, but it wouldn't be right...*

"That's really it," he said when he stopped. "I mean, I don't have much, just messing about."

"It sounds lovely," she said. "But you held me only this morning, not one hundred years ago." She turned to open a door, so thankfully couldn't see his face. "I'm surprised you're already writing another love song. The one you played me last week was perfect."

Hugh took some comfort in the fact that the one from last week had actually been about his fiancée. He was a musician, though, and they had to draw inspiration where they could find it. He worried about Rose's feelings, but she didn't need to know what the song was about. It was just the same as when she'd asked about the origin of "Lift" when they'd first met. He'd told her it was just a song for a random girl from years ago, because why did she need to know more than that? It was mostly the truth, after all, and he couldn't account for every detail in the music; so many songs had hardly anything to do with his real life at all. Everything was fiction, an exaggeration. And yet, he also hadn't mentioned to Rose that he was going for coffee with Nora. He hadn't really bothered to mention that Nora existed except for when he said he saw an old friend at the pub. He'd seen loads of old friends that night, though the rest of them mattered much less in comparison.

In his defense, Hugh really did think that coffee would be entirely harmless. He enjoyed Nora's company, but anything between them had been so long ago, it was completely stale by this point. Yes, he'd imagined what it would be like if they could just have one night together, but he'd put that out of his head.

However, when he saw her approaching the little table by the window, the way she wove through the cafe making her way toward him, he wondered if perhaps he had miscalculated the number of years it would take to get over this girl. He'd stopped performing for a while after she left; he'd stopped wanting to go out, stopped talking to other women. His mates had shown up with bottles of whiskey and old records, trying to lighten his mood, but it had taken ages for him to get back to normal. There'd been no reason to think about how much she'd meant to him in a long time, but then, there she was.

"Hiya, Nora!" he said, and he pressed his lips to her soft cheek.

Hours passed without Hugh realizing that they hadn't moved from that table. He told her all about the band making their first album, about their songs being played on the radio and people starting to show up to see them play and then even buying some merchandise. He teased her about taking meticulous notes, but she swore they were for work—the coffee shop was on her list—and not because she was writing his autobiography.

They talked about her fighting for her job and deciding to come back to London, about her best friends in the world back in New York, about books. Nora was the most well-read person he knew, except for maybe Julian. She also had other ridiculous hobbies that he found entirely endearing, like roller skating and making homemade ice cream. Rose would never be caught dead doing either, but the thought of that made him almost laugh. Rose only saved her frivolity for him. She saved everything for him, all the pieces of herself she was too tough to show anyone else.

He couldn't get over the way Nora was the same but also…different. She was more aware of herself and certainly more hesitant with him. She bit her lip before she spoke and fiddled with her cloth napkin.

"The first time we went out you said it was a bloody awful idea," she said, mocking his British accent. It was still terrible.

And you said, "Oh my God, just chill, it'll be super fun." He mocked her American accent right back.

"I did not say that!" she cried. "I may have been young and ridiculous, but I never sounded like a Valley Girl."

"I don't know the difference!" He burst out laughing, and the people at the tables around them glanced in their direction, probably wondering how they could be so loudly enjoying themselves on a Friday afternoon. "I do remember I thought you were the strangest girl I'd ever met."

"What do you think now?" she asked. "Now that I'm older and so mature and worldly?"

Hugh smiled. "You are still definitely the strangest," he said.

"You flatter me." She grinned as if she knew that she was an entirely singular, special creature.

"You're not like other girls, are you?" he said.

She narrowed her eyes at that, as if put off by the compliment. "How many women do you know?" she asked.

Hugh backtracked, unsure of what she meant or where he had misstepped. "You certainly are strange, Nora Shrapsan," he said.

She looked down, a bit flushed, and took a sip of her drink. A rogue curl sprang from behind her ear and into her face as she lowered the cup. Hugh couldn't stop himself. He reached for it, holding it in his hand for a moment too long before pushing it away from her face.

She stared at him, unmoving. He thought she had perhaps stopped breathing; maybe he had as well. Again, his mind was flooded with stiff white sheets, bath towels on the floor, finding strands of hair on his pillow, a curtain of her hair hanging around them as she moved over his body, as he pressed his lips to her collarbone.

She was still holding her cup in her hands, still unmoving as her eyes searched his face. The way she looked at him went straight to his head. She'd always been impressed by him, and he'd always relished it. She'd thought him so mature when she was just nineteen, and no one in the world had ever thought him mature before. It was a powerful thing, to be adored like that.

"Sorry," he said, stuffing his hand back under the table. "Habit."

CHAPTER TWELVE

"I READ over everything while you were gone," Darcy said. Like a caricature of a Bond villain, she turned slowly in her office chair until she was facing Nora. Her arms were firmly crossed against her chest.

"Yes?" Nora said. She had not for a moment expected that Darcy—who was so often covered in a pile of projects, too busy to eat lunch or go to the bathroom—would read her pages so quickly. Nora had been hoping she would be able to slip out of the office for the weekend without any interactions with Darcy or even a hint of feedback. And yet, Darcy had called Nora into her office the second she'd returned from coffee with Hugh.

"Most of them were shite." Darcy scowled.

Nora deflated and fell into the chair across from her editor. "I'm afraid to ask," she said, trying to sound sarcastic. But she really was afraid.

"The research was great. I get that you know every fucking detail about the history of British tea, but they were just so...bland. Much like the Breakfast Blend that you tasted apparently."

"I—" Nora started, but she wasn't sure how to defend herself. *I worked so hard on them,* she wanted to say, but she didn't want to sound like a college student who'd gotten a bad grade on a paper. She was a professional. "How do I fix them?" she asked.

"They need some life, Nora," Darcy said. "Well, except this one. This one is brilliant." Nora craned to see the page that Darcy was holding. "You know I don't say that lightly. Make them all like this somehow, and we're back in business."

Nora saw a glimpse of the words on the page, words about pink drinks and Lauren Hill and strobe lights. "You know I don't do clubs," Darcy continued, "but you made this sound like something worthwhile. Not a history lesson. Not a heartless review of scones. Something with personality. Like a person wrote it."

"A person wrote all of them," Nora said.

"Well, this one's different," Darcy replied. "And if you want to keep working here, you'd better figure out how to do this again."

Nora took a deep breath. Once again, she was pleading with her eyeballs, begging them not to let any tears spill at work. "Could you give me something a little more concrete to work with?" she asked.

"I've made notes on the pages," Darcy sighed. "But it's about the essence, really. It has to sound like there is life in these places, that museums aren't just pillars and stones, the cafes aren't just teacups and scones." She paused. "I did *not* mean for that to rhyme, so disregard that as I give you writing advice. This job is a lot of work. It's not all glamor and good times, as I think you've been learning. It's hard and lonely. But even at the worst place imaginable, you have to infuse your writing with something more than just the place. You did that so well at the club. It was so different. So, like I said, whatever you did there, do that."

Nora was about to leave the office with her stack of marked up reviews when Darcy called her back.

"By the way," Darcy began, then hesitated.

"What?" Nora said. Surely she couldn't have messed up something else already.

"What was it like with your lover?" Darcy almost chirped, and Nora stared at her.

She felt like she'd just been beaten with a chair in a giant wrestling ring, and now the evil villain was asking her about her love life or lack-thereof. Nora just wanted to sit at her desk with her head in her hands trying to avoid Timothy's knowing glances. She did not want to stand in the doorway for a second longer while her editor acted kind of like a friend in a way that she couldn't comprehend. Darcy had just told her that her writing was "shite," and she was on the verge of losing her dream job. And now she wanted to chat about Nora's not-date with Hugh?

"Darcy, you're making a big deal out of nothing," Nora said, but she wasn't entirely sure it was true. Hugh was still charming and sexy—the way he said her name and put his chin in his hand and watched her. All the adorable mannerisms he'd had when they were dating were exactly the same. And when he looked at her... Unfortunately, that meant she couldn't help feeling some of the exact same things she had before, even if she didn't mean to.

"You're not getting off so easy," Darcy said. "Spill it."

"Remember when you said *I* was nosy?" Nora sat back down in the chair opposite her boss.

Darcy opened her mouth in mock shock and put a hand to her chest. "Who, me? Stop dawdling and tell me what happened."

Nora wanted to spill her guts. She wanted to sit down and analyze every detail of Hugh's body language with someone who really cared. The problem, though, was that she really didn't think that person was Darcy. *Tit for tat, Darcy.*

She took a breath. "Tell me about Anika," she said, hoping that bringing up the mail woman might distract Darcy from her mission of dissecting Nora's emotions.

Darcy almost did a spit take with her water. "What about Anika? Good Lord, you don't care to butt into people's lives, do you?"

Nora smiled. "Well, she works for the company, right? So I'm really only butting in to learn more about the company that I work for."

"She doesn't directly work for the company. We hire out for—"

"Okay, I don't actually care about that part," Nora said.

"I knew it!" Darcy pointed at her in triumph. Then she took a gulp of her drink.

"How about this?" Nora said. "I'll tell you every tiny detail after you *finally* tell me why you turn into a mushy alien version of yourself whenever Anika walks in the building. Do you like her? Do you two have a secret feud? Are you trying to butter her up and then steal her bicycle?"

Darcy pursed her lips with impatience. She was quiet for a moment, and Nora could see her breaking down. "Well played, Shrapsan," she said.

"Well?" Nora said. She could still get one small victory out of the bloody-nosed, almost-fired kind of day she was dealing with.

Darcy groaned. "You're lucky it's so bloody boring around here. I need some entertainment. The rest of these people have nothing interesting to tell me."

"You're a very supportive manager," Nora said.

"All right, if you must know, there was a night a few months back. It was before some holiday, and I'd sent the team home early—because I am a wonderful team leader. I knew I had to stay, though, because the company was sending over some pages to review. You know how they did that series of books about planning for specific trips? There was the honeymoon guide and the exotic hiking guide and the marathon guide…"

"Yes, I remember. That part isn't important, is it?"

Darcy scrunched up her face. "I stayed late to get the pages, and Anika was the one to deliver them, of course. It was her last stop of the night.

"I hadn't really thought much about her before. She brought stuff to us, and I signed for it when I needed to, and that was all there was to it. That night, though, it was just the two of us, and we got talking. Neither of us had anywhere to be, so we were chatting, and I had a bottle of wine here, and we ended up drinking the whole thing. Anika was interesting."

"High praise from you," Nora said.

Darcy ignored her. "She'd grown up on a farm in the country and raised sheep, but she moved to the city to follow her dream of…bicycling everywhere, I guess.

"Before I knew it, the wine was gone, and it was rather late. We got up and said goodbye, but then, before she walked out, we kissed."

"Juicy!" Nora said. She loved a good blossoming romance, and this was already taking her mind off of Darcy's criticism. "Then what happened?"

"She left. That was it. And now I see her when she's here, but neither of us ever mention what happened."

"Wait, wait, wait," Nora said, her hand braced against Darcy's desk. "Neither of you even mentioned it again? Tell me about the kiss. Was it awkward? Was she not into it, and then she peaced out, or did she kiss you back?"

Darcy rolled her eyes. "Why am I telling you this?" she sighed. "She kissed me back. I'm sure. It wasn't just a quick second. It was a real, two-way kiss."

"So you have a thing for her," Nora said.

"Yes."

"But you've never asked her out?"

"No."

"Well, why not? It seems like you both had a great evening, and she kissed you back. Is there some company rule against dating her or something?"

"Technically she's hired out from a courier company, so I don't think she's actually a 99 Flamingo employee, but I just haven't been able to do it. What if it was a fluke? We had one great kiss, but that doesn't mean she would want to date me."

Nora thought for a moment. "I guess you don't really know until you ask. If she says no, then at least you'll know. You'll have tried, and you can move on. And if she says yes, then it could be amazing."

Darcy sighed dramatically. "I don't think I can do it."

"Darcy–"

"It's easy for you. You just sail through everything—'la di da, life is great, I'm a happy American.' That's not how it works for the rest of us."

Nora wasn't sure how to respond. Surely Darcy didn't think that she didn't have any of her own problems. She had just had coffee with the man she'd loved most in her entire life, a man who was now untouchable. She was thousands of miles from her mother, whom she had abandoned while she was recovering from cancer. And to top it all off, Darcy had just told her that the articles she'd been pouring over for days weren't going to cut it. She opened her mouth but then shut it again. She didn't know what advice to give. Of course Darcy should tell Anika how she was feeling, but how could Nora say that when she would never ever tell Hugh...

But that was very different. Anika was probably single if they'd kissed like that.

"Well," Darcy said, clearly trying to shake off the fears and frustrations surrounding the night with Anika. "Now you know. Tell me about what happened with Hugh."

Nora told her about their conversation, how they'd talked of the band and Nora's assignments while steering clear of anything too personal. Nora told her how she'd been careful not to bring up anything that might lead to dangerous territory—no chatting about late nights at the Goose and Cobbler or any of the places that held meaning for them. No mention of the bench near Tower Bridge overlooking the Thames or the Sainsbury's on Queen Elizabeth Street, even though she couldn't imagine Hugh being sentimental about a little grocery market.

"Actually, it was just kind of like talking to a friend," Nora said, though she didn't advertise the fact that she could remember very clearly what it felt like to have this friend on top of her while his hand made its way up her inner thigh.

"And did he tell you about his plans for the wedding?" Darcy asked.

Nora was quiet for a moment, trying to decipher how the mention of Hugh's wedding made her feel, but she quickly gave up teasing out that emotion. "No," she replied. "He didn't."

"Hmm," Darcy said, as if it all meant something, as if Nora had offered her a puzzle that Darcy could put together, while Nora could not. "I'm not entirely sure why you want to go on being friends with him," Darcy added. "It's kind of odd."

"Because otherwise you're my only friend?"

Darcy snorted and shook her head. "Maybe Julian," she said.

Nora glanced over quickly, afraid that Darcy had figured it out somehow, her confusing thoughts about Julian or that she'd been imagining the smell of his neck, but Darcy was just typing on her computer, as usual.

"Maybe Julian," Nora said softly.

It didn't take long for Miss Darcy to return to her usual tough-boss self after her moment of vulnerability about Anika. She assigned Nora a new project in addition to her revisions, both with a quick deadline, which meant that Nora needed to get back to work as soon as possible. When she walked out of Darcy's office, Timothy spun in his chair and rolled himself into her path.

"Want some company at the restaurant you're writing up tonight?" he asked.

"Are you eavesdropping on my private conversations, Tim?" she asked. For Darcy's sake and her own, she wondered how much he had heard. They'd been quiet and closed the door for the personal parts, hadn't they? She didn't like the idea that he could possibly know anything about Hugh or even about Darcy's feelings for Anika.

"Of course not," he said. "There was an email out about current projects, and I saw your assignment. Like I said, I'd be happy to go with you. We could have a good time." He wiggled his eyebrows suggestively.

The truth was that Nora really didn't feel like sitting at some crowded new restaurant in the city alone, which was the only thing that led her to consider his offer for a second. She was so close to saying yes just so she wouldn't have to say she needed a table for one. Really, she would have liked to ask Julian, but the weird thoughts she'd been having about him since the club made her skeptical. Perhaps her earlier instincts had been correct—she needed to distance herself from Hugh and his whole group before things got really messy. And yet, she couldn't imagine not seeing Hugh again. She couldn't even imagine not seeing Julian. She shouldn't be deprived of having one good friend in the entire country just because he was besties with her ex and she'd had some strange, meaningless, completely out of the ordinary and purely physical feelings for him for one moment.

Then she remembered what Darcy had said about her articles. Whatever she'd done differently at the nineties club was what she needed to do for everything else she was writing. What had been different about that place? She'd had fun. It was nineties themed, which was freaking awesome. She'd been a little bit drunk. And...she'd been with Julian.

It didn't make any kind of sense, but *that* was the biggest difference she could come up with. She'd had Julian there to talk through her ideas and inspirations, to investigate the men's bathroom, to halfway scream song lyrics with her in the middle of the dance floor. Maybe if she were to invite him along on her next assignments, it would make a difference somehow. Maybe she could manage to find that "essence" that Darcy couldn't quite name, even if she knew when it was missing. For one single night, one single review, Julian had been there with her. That had to be it. She couldn't think of any other explanation. Darcy had said that review was brilliant, and that was what she needed to recreate over and over again.

This was her career. It was her dream. She had to try anything and everything, no matter how stupid, no matter if she had to beg Julian to tag along just so she could try to figure out how to be a better writer. She would ask him if he would go to dinner with her once so she could test her theory. Then she would also go out and try to get laid so she could forget about whatever weird thing happened in her stomach when he bent his face toward hers on the dance floor. She would get laid so she could also stop having sweaty dreams about Hugh, about his skin and eyelashes. After tonight, hot sex would be her priority, and then it wouldn't matter if she saw either of them anymore, because her needs would be fulfilled, and she'd have normal, acceptable dreams about clowns and people from high school that she hadn't seen in ten years.

She was scared, but at least she had a plan:

1. Nag Julian to join her for work outings so she could test her hypothesis about whether he mysteriously made her writing better.
2. Be super platonic friends with Hugh and get herself completely over him with no residual feelings or attractions whatsoever.
3. Have super-hot sex.

CHAPTER THIRTEEN

JULIAN CHECKED his mobile as he ambled to the Tube station closest to Poppy's flat. It had been another perfectly delightful afternoon with Poppy, and yet... *One voicemail from Nora Shrapsan.* His fingers were twitching as he tapped at the screen. He and Nora hadn't spoken since he'd dropped her off after the club—the club where drops of sweat had slid down the ridges of the vertebrae in her back as she danced. It was an image Julian had thought of many times, even though he tried desperately not to.

Nora rambled quite a lot in the voicemail. She needed help and was worrying about getting fired and all the places she needed to see in a matter of days. She was asking if he could possibly do her a huge favor. From her point of view, he was a teacher, so he had a summer break, right?

People always seemed to think that, but he had lesson plans and conferences and faculty workshops. He really could keep quite busy over the summer; it wasn't just a holiday even if there were no classes. He soon realized that he was arguing with a voicemail and replayed the last bit of what Nora had said.

"Would you be able to meet me at Elephant and Castle Station around six o'clock? I promise I will understand if not. We can make future plans that aren't so short notice and desperate, but just in case..."

Desperate. Julian's mind lingered on the word. It seemed to strike a note inside of him, to coincide so fully with the way he felt every time he thought about that line of glistening sweat gliding down her skin. He lost track of what she was saying all over and had to go back. "It's still work, obviously, but it could be fun," she said.

After he listened to the entirety of the three-minute message once again, he checked the time and sent her a single text.

"I'll be there."

He was at the station early, trying to busy himself by pretending to scroll through his mobile while secretly scanning the crowd for any sign of Nora. He was tucked off to the side of the stairs, an odd solitary figure in a sea of hurried people. Somehow she still managed to sneak up on him, and he almost jumped at the soft sound of her voice in his ear.

"I can't thank you enough for this," she said, squeezing his arm. He turned and took in the full picture of her—white dress, braid in her hair, bright pink lips. He forgot that he was supposed to talk. How was it that he'd ended up as her sidekick for her London adventures?

Finally he managed to find his voice. "I—well, you don't have to thank me. I'm glad to help."

She looked slightly unsure of herself for a moment, which was so uncharacteristically "Nora" that Julian started wondering what he was getting himself into. He hoped to God that she wouldn't just spend the evening peppering him with questions about Hugh. If there was any luck in the world, that would not be the reason that she asked for his help. Soon, the smile beamed across her face again.

"It turns out I couldn't get a table at the restaurant I need to visit tonight. They were all booked up, but I've already made a reservation for tomorrow." Nora turned suddenly and started marching down the platform as if expecting him to follow. Excited energy seemed to be radiating off her in waves.

"Oh." Julian tried to catch up, taking long strides so he was walking beside her. So what—"

"Tell me the truth. How do you feel about scary things?" Nora asked, but she didn't pause for him to tell her anything. "Hugh and I went on this Jack the Ripper walking tour years back, and it was something I was thinking about pitching to Darcy for the book, but then I found this Jack the Ripper haunted pub tour, and Darcy said I should see if it's worthwhile, and they happened to have two spots tonight." Her rambling was just the same as in her voicemail, and it took Julian a moment to sort through everything she'd just said. He smiled as he watched her finally take a breath.

"What?" she asked.

Why did he keep forgetting to speak? He was probably staring at her like an idiot again. "Haunted pub tour? How haunted are we talking?"

She shrugged. "If I had to guess, I would say about forty-five percent haunted, fifty-five percent drunken. One-hundred percent cheesy tourist attraction, but I can't help myself."

"I can accept those percentages." He nodded. "Where are we going?"

"Whitechapel, of course." She didn't even hesitate before pulling him further down the train platform, her thick braid flinging itself over her shoulder.

Julian was quite aware of the feeling of her fingers on his wrist, just as he was aware of the fact that he probably would have let her drag him anywhere, even to the site of an actual, on-going murder. A pub crawl was obviously a much better option, but in a gut-wrenching, terrifying moment, he realized he was sure he would have said yes to anything, and he could feel the weight of the knowledge lodging itself deep in his abdomen. He was absolutely bound for trouble.

The first pub was a spot where two of Jack's victims were said to have had their last drink before they met their untimely demise. Nora was gleeful as they ordered their pints and listened to tales of hauntings and horrors. Her eyes danced over the historic interior, walls covered in brightly colored designs, wooden stools that seemed like they could have been present in the 1800s, a large leather-upholstered couch in the middle of the room. When she turned to Julian, she let her full smile shine in his direction.

"One of the most haunted places in the whole of London," she almost squealed, bouncing on her stool.

"Do you really believe in ghosts?" Julian whispered.

"Not the ghosts so much, but it's fun to think about. I'm more fascinated by the crimes themselves, that something so evil truly exists in our world. I can't look away." She tucked a strand of hair that had come loose from her braid behind her ear.

"I do seem to recall you being captivated at the Tower of London when we all went together. You knew everything about Anne Boleyn."

She grinned. "You remember that? I have a special place in my heart for executions." Nora paused and made a face. "Maybe that's not the right way to say it. I just feel like I have to know every single detail. Maybe it's so I can avoid the same fate. Is that weird?"

"Yes." Julian laughed. "You have concerns about being beheaded?"

"No." She looked thoughtful before taking a big gulp of her drink. "But I suppose I could end up in a marriage with a man who tried to bend me to his will and have complete power over me." She shrugged as if this was a run-of-the-mill, everyday kind of fear and not something utterly terrifying.

"That's a grim view of marriage," Julian said, taking a long swig from his pint.

She gasped and smacked her palm to her head. "I sound like my mother!" she yelped. "One divorce, and that woman's a real cynic. But women have a lot they could be scared of. Anyway, that's not my usual view of marriage. I'm not a cynic, Julian. Just prepared."

She put a hand on his shoulder. "What about you?"

"What about me?" he asked, leaning toward her without realizing. Were they going to talk about his views on marriage?

"I bet you've never thought about being beheaded a day in your life," she said with a smirk. Then she ordered him another drink.

He couldn't tear his eyes from her as she rambled about Mary Jane Kelly and theories of who might have committed the crimes. "Was it a doctor? He did seem to have a particular medical knowledge or at least an inclination. Could it have been a noble?" He loved her odd mixture of a fascination with the macabre and her generally joyful demeanor. He thought she may have known more about the women and their murders than the tour guides, but she wasn't disappointed with the stories. She still listened intently to every word as they told their increasingly disturbing tales.

As they walked through the dark streets of Whitechapel, Nora's white dress seemed to glow in the moonlight. Occasionally she would wobble on the uneven cobblestones, and Julian would stick out an arm to steady her. When the skin of his hand touched her arm, he remembered holding her at the club, sweaty tendrils of her hair swept against his neck and collarbone, her mouth changing from purple to pink in the flashing lights.

"Thank you for catching me," Nora said. "I don't understand how you're managing to walk on this stone in the dark."

"You just happen to keep hitting the bad spots."

"It would be really hard to run away from Jack the Ripper in this situation."

"This isn't terrible," Julian said. "It's just slick from the rain." Julian glanced around the alley, the tour group was bunched up ahead of them, eager for their next violent tale and their next drink.

"When did it rain?" Nora asked.

"It's London. It has always just rained."

She threaded her arm through his. "I'm just going to hold on if that's okay. It's a beautiful street in the lantern light, isn't it?"

"It is. A shame to ruin the romantic setting with all this talk of the vicious things that happened here." Julian didn't know why he'd used the word "romantic." He could feel himself going pale.

"It's a shame unless you're entirely captivated by the murders."

"Admittedly, I wasn't. But being here does make it feel more real. It seems like they should have been able to figure it out."

She cocked her head at him in the darkness. "I've always thought the same thing. It's that on-the-tip-of-you're tongue feeling. The answer is so close."

———

By the third pub, the whole crowd was a bit tipsy and rowdy, gasping and shouting about the women who may have been lured to their deaths with grapes and the promise of a rich customer. Nora's face was glowing with a rosy shine from alcohol and from the night wind that swept around them in darkened alleyways as they made their way from one spot to the next. He didn't know if he should bring up everything she'd said in her voicemail or ask her why on earth she'd chosen him for this unordinary assignment. He thought she may want to talk about it though, especially if she was truly concerned about being fired.

"You said you were worried about your job," he mumbled quietly before bringing his glass to his lips.

"Right. You know, I should never leave voicemails. They are definitely not my best medium of communication. But a text didn't feel like enough to convince you to meet me."

He avoided telling her he was almost entirely certain a text would have worked just fine. An upside-down smiley face emoji would have been enough to get him to see her. "You really think you might be fired?"

"Darcy implied that if my blurbs don't improve, then I don't belong on the team. She's a tough woman, you know, but probably right. I thought I would be great at this. I've read so many travel guides and articles. I had to edit them for years, and now I just can't seem to find that *je nais se quois.*"

Julian scratched his head. "I don't believe that. You're so passionate about it. I know you must have had a lot to say about the club the other night. Even your observations while we were there were so great. Admittedly, I was a bit drunk, but still, you were very astute and insightful."

Nora bit her lip and looked up into his eyes. "The club...yeah. The club turned out okay."

He looked at her with a question on his face, but she didn't elaborate. "Some of Annie Chapman's organs were missing," a tour guide announced, and Nora turned away to give the story her rapt attention. "People have speculated that Jack the Ripper may have kept something from his victim as a kind of trophy."

"That's sick," Julian said.

Nora looked up at him with a sad and knowing face. She already knew all of it; she was aware of how dark and cruel the world could be, but she was still so bright and full of life. Julian wanted to take her hand and hold it in his. He glanced at her fingers but didn't move.

As the tour group broke up at the last little pub with Ripper drink deals, Nora took some time to sit at the bar and scribble in her notebook. "What'll you write about the tour?" Julian asked. "Do you plan to recommend it?"

"Oh absolutely," she said. "I think the guides may have taken a few liberties with their facts, but they were great storytellers, weren't they? I didn't even know about the guy who poisoned his victims. The fact that he worked in that pub is a great little tidbit. That really increases the spook factor." The thought of it gave her another idea, and she turned to write something else down. "I know you're a local and probably not into all the tourist stuff like this, but what were your impressions?"

"I never would have done this if it weren't for you," he said. "But I thought it was interesting. A bit over-the-top, sure, but you're right. The guides really sold those stories. I might have nightmares tonight."

"I am going to check the locks on my doors so many times. I will probably get up at three a.m. to check again, even though I know they're locked and bolted."

"I certainly won't be having an evening walk in the cemetery." Julian laughed.

"Why would you?" Nora said, aghast.

"There's one right outside my building. I cut through there on occasion. There's a nice little bench where I like to read."

"You hang out in a cemetery, Julian?"

"It's not that uncommon." He shrugged.

She grinned and scrunched up her nose. "For ghosts," she said.

He rubbed his chin. "I promise you, it's not weird."

She shook her head, as if letting that one slide for now. "Okay, tell me the truth then. Are you free for dinner tomorrow night or will you be too busy wandering your graveyard and performing séances?" She nudged him in the rib cage. "It's my treat...kind of."

Of course, he wouldn't say no, but Julian still hesitated. *What was going on here exactly?* Somehow, he and Nora had managed to make it through the whole evening without the mention of Hugh's name. He thought they'd enjoyed each other's company. And that night at the club, they'd been so close. He had been right on the brink of touching her lips with his. But he hadn't done it. He couldn't—not with Hugh and Poppy...

He didn't know why she'd asked him, of all people, to go with her. Maybe she was feeling insecure because of Hugh's engagement, and Julian was used to always being second choice to Hugh. But it felt like there was something else, something like friendship at the very least.

"I can make it for dinner tomorrow," he said. "I'll postpone my next séance until Thursday." Perhaps it was a self-destructive decision, but he was dating Poppy after all. He could be friends with Nora without any other kind of feelings getting in the way.

CHAPTER FOURTEEN

IT SHOULDN'T HAVE BOTHERED Hugh that he hadn't heard from Nora since they'd had coffee together. He kept glancing at his phone like a teenager, as if waiting for a sign from her, maybe an inside joke or a comment about squirty cream. There was something about artistic types like him that just craved a little drama and excitement, even while he knew that he was perfectly happy with Rose.

"You waiting for a call?" Rose asked as she put the kettle on. He didn't know how long he'd been sitting at the table, staring at the mobile in his hand, willing it to light up. It wasn't surprising that she'd noticed a change in his behavior. On most occasions, he had no idea where his mobile might be and had to resort to digging through sofa cushions or searching his guitar case.

"There's just a gig we might be on for in a few days, and I'm waiting to hear back." That wasn't a complete lie, at least. The band could be playing at The Vine over the weekend, but they were renovating the stage area and weren't sure if the place would be ready yet.

Rose turned toward the stove and murmured something to herself that he couldn't quite hear. "What was that?" he asked.

"I'm wondering if it's just me or if you're acting odd. You seem out of sorts."

"I'm afraid I'm in one of my moods, Rosey, but it's nothing to worry about." He flicked the hair out of his eyes and gave her a sheepish, apologetic smile.

"Does that mean you're getting a load of writing done, at least?" she asked.

"Maybe," he said. "Maybe I want a beautiful song to play for you at our wedding."

"You already have plenty of options for that." She placed a steaming mug of tea in front of him. "I quite enjoy being your muse."

At the word *muse,* he stared down at his phone again. Truthfully, the songs about Rose and the songs about Nora were probably equal in number. But the songs about Nora were about love *and* heartache, some that he never played anymore, even in private. Rose's share was all about love.

Rose leaned against his back, wrapping her arms around his neck and nuzzling her face into his hair. She fit there so naturally—she always had —like their bodies were made for each other. He sighed and relaxed into her. This was obviously where he belonged, and he'd be a damned fool to think otherwise.

But he'd always been a damned fool.

If Nora hadn't showed up at the pub the other night, her wild hair falling around her shoulders, would he still have a mind full of memories of her force-feeding him chicken nuggets in a filthy booth at the back of a chicken shop? Or skipping through the park with ice cream on the tip of her nose? Rolling on top of him all wrapped up in his white sheets?

He'd thought of Nora since she'd been gone. Often, at first. He'd thought of her since he'd fallen for Rose, sometimes remembering the way she gripped his hand or rubbed his chin. But would he have ever thought of her *this much* if she hadn't popped into that closet at the back of the pub with a wide smile and too much lipstick?

Rose put a hand on his shoulder and squeezed. "See ya round for dinner, yeah?" she said. "Maybe we should go out somewhere. I've been so busy, lately, we've hardly had a proper night out."

Hugh nodded. He loved nights out with Rose. It was like she always knew what he needed, whether it was to drink too much and laugh about something stupid James had said or map out a plan of next steps for the band. She knew the best places to go, and when he couldn't figure out what kind of mood he was in, she'd already figured it out. The Indian place with the amazing samosas or the pub down the road for some bangers and mash. She had the best intuition for those things, and she understood him. No one had ever figured him out quite like Rose.

But lately there'd been so much talk about the wedding, about actually picking a venue and putting it into motion. He was the one who'd proposed, so he should be keen to discuss the details. It was time to stop worrying about settling down and making a commitment. It was time to grow up.

After Rose left the room, Hugh picked up his mobile again. He hesitated a moment more before finally typing out a message to Nora and hitting send.

All it said was, "Hi." Innocent enough. He told himself it was to clear the air and set proper boundaries, to take that step towards growing up, but he still didn't know why he'd felt so compelled to do it.

CHAPTER FIFTEEN

ALL EVIDENCE and past behaviors would have, of course, suggested that it was her mother who kept making Nora's phone buzz with texts at five in the morning on a Saturday. Five o'clock meant it was midnight in New York, and it wasn't uncommon for her mother to stay up binging years-old shows before calling her daughter to ask questions about who was going to end up on the Iron Throne and how Walter White could be so cruel when he let that thing happen to Jesse. When Nora finally rolled over on her little bed and reached to the floor to pick up her phone, however, it was actually Darcy who'd sent seven messages demanding that Nora get out of bed and meet for a cup of tea.

Despite a brief inner torment, which included shutting her phone off and hiding under the covers before finally climbing out of bed three minutes later and throwing on jeans and a baseball cap, Nora did want to know what the hell her editor could want with her this early on a Saturday when she hadn't even given her anymore material to disparage. Darcy did not seem like the early riser, eager to start the day type. On any given day, Darcy trudged through the office with a giant travel mug and a sour look on her face. She worked later than anyone and hardly looked up from her computer, but she was never around bright and early.

Perhaps Nora shouldn't have been surprised that the Darcy squished into a corner table at the cafe was not at all the Darcy that Nora was expecting. She was totally disheveled, wearing some especially horrible idea of sweatpants and a stained T-shirt with her greasy hair hanging down in her face.

"Oh God, why did you do this to me?" she said as Nora approached.

"What are you talking about? Are you sick?" It was the only explanation that made any sense in Nora's brain as she tried to decipher the situation.

"She didn't even say anything."

"What?" Nora sat down, still entirely confused.

"I took your advice, and I sent a message to Anika. She didn't even bother to answer me." Darcy put her face in her hands and moaned.

Nora took a breath. Darcy wasn't deathly ill. Nora wasn't getting fired. It wasn't actually an apocalyptic event after all. It was heartbreak, which was perhaps the worst thing of all. "Oh, Darcy, I'm sorry. What did you say? What happened?" She leaned across the booth. This was definitely not the Darcy she had been expecting. It was hard to imagine anyone ever would have seen Darcy this way. Nora wouldn't have believed it if she wasn't witnessing it for herself.

Darcy lifted her head. "I just asked if she would want to get a coffee. I didn't say anything about the kissing or make it sound like a date or anything like that." She put her head back in her hands again.

Nora couldn't speak for a moment. The same Darcy who had told her that her writing was terrible and balked at her London love story was losing it over the fact that a woman hadn't texted her back. In a strange way, Nora felt a little better about the fact that she was only very slightly losing her shit about seeing Hugh. If Darcy could be this beat up about a text message, then maybe Nora could forgive herself a little for being so confused about hanging out with the man that she had once considered the great love of her life.

"Maybe she hasn't seen it yet. I can't imagine she just wouldn't say anything at all. She seems like a decent person."

"A decent person who doesn't want to speak to me, apparently." Darcy moaned again. "It was yesterday," she murmured. "Right after you left the office with your whole speech about going for it and knowing one way or the other. I decided to say 'fuck it' and give it a try. I thought she would at least say something. After what happened that night."

"Maybe she was really busy. Or she was sick. Or her cat was sick. Or her bicycle got a flat tire. What if she's stranded somewhere and her phone is dead? There could be a logical explanation," Nora said.

"Why does this always happen to me?" Darcy grumbled.

"What do you mean?"

"I get so lost in my head and nervous about everything until it all becomes more important than it is. I know it's just a stupid message, and I don't even know Anika that well. I don't know why I've let myself go on with this silly crush. I'm a complete idiot."

Nora couldn't help it when a little smile appeared on her face. She felt terrible that Darcy was so down and feeling rejected, but there was something surprisingly endearing about the whole thing. Or maybe it was just the lack of sleep.

"What?" Darcy snapped.

"I just can't help thinking..."

"Yes?"

"That this is just so very normal. It seems like exactly the kind of problem I talk about with my friends all the time. We all get caught up like this and let it get to us, even when we don't mean to." Nora had spent so many nights analyzing three-word texts from boys, but she never would have imagined Darcy to be that kind of person. Darcy was always interested in the drama but too above it all to take part or become emotional. Even at work, she simply brushed Tim off and turned up her chin when he started acting like a drama queen.

"Oh God, so you're saying that I'm just as pathetic as all of your friends?" She held her face in her hands again, only making her meltdown more over-the-top.

"Ummm yes? But that's not a bad thing. That's just, ya know, being human."

"Being human is terrible," Darcy said with a snort.

"Yeah."

"I honestly don't know if I've ever been rejected by someone before. But I never really tried..."

"Well, welcome to the club, I guess?"

"You've experienced this a lot?" Darcy squinted at Nora.

"Kind of? I mean not *a lot*, but it happens."

"And what do you do?"

"Darcy?" Nora's smile widened as Darcy looked at her skeptically.

"What?"

"Does this mean we're friends?"

"Don't go all loony on me," Darcy said, already rolling her eyes like her usual self. "I called you here because this is your fault."

"At least now you know," Nora said. She sank her chin into her hand and tried to stifle a yawn. She was *so* tired. "You can move on. Start dating other women."

"To be honest," Darcy said, suddenly more serious, "I don't usually let my real friends see this side of me."

Nora shook her head. "Disregarding the fact that you just very rudely said 'your *real* friends,' I think you should. It's kind of nice to be able to open up to people sometimes."

Darcy hung her head again, mostly ignoring Nora's piece of advice. "This really is terrible. Why do people do this?"

"Because it's kind of awesome when it finally works out." Nora gave her a small smile.

"And is it 'awesome' for you with Hugh Jeffries of the Pet Rockers?"

Nora chewed on her lip and looked away. Honestly, she hadn't gotten to the part where it was all worth it—all the heartbreak and rejection and pining for your first love. It had to pay off sometime, right? That's what people wrote songs about. "God bless the broken road" and all that shite. That's what Darcy would call it. A bunch of shite. Sometimes things were just hard without much payoff.

"It is decidedly not awesome," Nora said. "I need a muffin."

"I need a Bloody Mary," Darcy said.

"Do they do bottomless mimosas in England?" Nora asked.

They sat there for hours, Darcy drinking Bloody Marys and Nora opting for some orange juice because bottomless mimosas were not a thing at that particular establishment. Nora definitely would have docked points in a review. After getting past Darcy's moping and the shock of rejection, Nora found it to be actually kind of…fun. Darcy was laughing, and her face changed in a way that Nora adored.

"Is this what you do with your friends then?" Darcy asked.

"We did, yes. It's been a while now."

"Why's that?" Darcy took another sip and pushed wisps of greasy hair out of her face.

"Some of them moved away. Some are busy with kids. Some of us moved to London. Do you do stuff like this with your friends?"

"My friends would never get up this early," Darcy said, eating a bite of celery that was garnishing her drink. "They're mostly a bunch of night owls." She checked her phone. "I'm sure my roommate is still in bed."

"So you had to call me instead." Nora smirked.

"Well, like I said," Darcy teased, "it was all your fault."

Nora rolled her eyes, but she was smiling.

The restaurant where Nora was meeting Julian was fancier than she expected. There were *linen* tablecloths, which was already a bit out of her usual league. People wore suits. There were lit candles—real flames, not battery operated. Nora couldn't help thinking, as she sat alone waiting for Julian, the place was just a little bit too romantic. She kept reminding herself that this was a work event, and she shouldn't have any concerns about it feeling like a date even if the restaurant was playing soft, Italian music in the background and serving elaborately plated dishes to the tables around her.

"Wine," she said too quickly when the waiter asked for her drink order. She knew she was supposed to specify what type, but she was desperate to get a drink down her throat before Julian arrived. Suddenly, she saw him standing there in a dark gray blazer. Had he *dressed* for this occasion? She didn't look shabby either; she'd thrown on a cream-colored, lacy A-line dress, made an effort to tame her curls, and even put on red lipstick, which she was starting to think was a mistake. It was different from her usual flirty shades of pink or purple. They were noncommittal and casual. Red was hot, serious, and passionate.

"Hey," Julian said as he approached the table. Nora rose to meet him. "You look great. I didn't know how nice this place would be, so I hope this is okay." He sheepishly tugged at the edges of his blazer. There was something about it that was incredibly endearing, and Nora couldn't speak for a moment.

"I didn't know either," she said. "We seem to fit in, I think. They'll never suspect us."

They both sat down, and Julian leaned toward her conspiratorially. "I quite enjoy being undercover," he said. "They'll never know it was us reviewing their food."

Nora's breath caught in her throat, perhaps from his closeness or the way he was looking at her, but she gulped and managed to smile normally. Julian ordered a glass of wine as well, and they perused the menu. After they'd ordered—lobster tail and fancy pasta—Nora took in a mouthful of wine and started writing work notes about the place to reiterate the platonic nature of this dinner to herself once again. She'd joked with Julian about serial killers and cemeteries. Everything the night before had been perfectly normal, right up to the point that he hugged her before she got out of the cab, when she almost thought that he might have kissed her hair. And she accidentally smelled his neck again. And his arms felt so warm and strong. She'd forced herself to back out of the car so she'd have to stop touching him.

"Are you seeing anyone at the moment?" she asked before stuffing a chunk of warm bread into her mouth. It wasn't until she started chewing desperately that she realized how much she wanted to know the answer. She could tell that he hesitated, though she didn't know why. Why would he be reluctant to tell her? Perhaps the question was too private for this quiet British man, and he wanted to keep everything between them on the surface level. She was just a nosy American, after all.

"It's nothing serious," he said finally. "I've been seeing this teacher from another school. It's all very new, so I don't know yet what it might be."

"What's her name? I can give you some love advice if you want." As soon as the sentence passed her lips, Nora regretted it. Why had she said something so weird? And why did she feel a clump of sadness welling up in her chest at the thought of Julian dating someone, which meant that the only person who had a remote possibility of feeling like this evening was too date-like was her? Maybe it was just because Hugh was engaged, and here she was, all alone, without even a decent single man to ask to a romantic dinner. Julian was probably wishing he was with his girlfriend instead.

"What's your love advice?" Julian asked. His cheeks were a little red. He looked so good, but Nora scolded herself for thinking it.

"Oh, well, I meant more like if you had a specific issue, then maybe I could help you out. I don't really know why I said that though. I should definitely not be giving anyone love advice. Just ask Darcy."

"You gave her some bad advice?"

"Oh yeah. Well, I stand by the advice, I guess, but it didn't work out. So that was my fault. She's probably going to have to move to another country."

Julian grinned. "Another gem from the love guru."

Nora slouched in her chair. "What's the opposite of a love guru? I think I might be that."

"I've never had much luck myself," Julian said. "I can't figure out why Poppy likes me."

Oh, God, her name is Poppy? She is definitely really fucking cool and great in bed. Shit, why am I thinking about it? Poppy and Rose were probably both glorious people, and she needed to stop being jealous and instead become a confident, self-actualized woman who didn't need to bother worrying about her male friends and their chosen partners. Julian was wonderful, and she wasn't going to spoil their evening by feeling sorry for herself all night.

"Of course she likes you, Julian."

He stared at her again, almost like at the club when she thought that he might kiss her, even though that had clearly been a misguided interpretation. Still, she felt goosebumps pop up across her arms. He really had a way of just *looking* that made it feel like he was touching her, even when he was several feet away.

"Now you give me advice," she said. "I had coffee with Hugh, which was great. Do you think we can be friends, though? Or is that too much? I'm trying to imagine how I would feel about it if I were Rose. I'm sure he told her she has nothing to fear." Nora remembered the text she'd received from Hugh the day before. It had said "Hi." That was it. She'd responded in kind, but she couldn't figure out what it meant, if it had any meaning at all. Now she was analyzing one-word texts, which she would absolutely not admit to Darcy.

Julian looked off into the distance, as if he had entirely disappeared from the conversation for a moment. *What was he thinking about so intensely?*

"If you still have feelings for him, it might not be a good idea," Julian said finally. "I want you both to get on, but if there's a chance that something might happen between you..."

Nora looked down into the plate of lobster the waiter set before her. Maybe before she arrived in London, somewhere buried deep, she had thought there was still a chance, but she didn't want to hope for that. She definitely did not want to break up Hugh's relationship, even if she sometimes wished that she could be with him again, just to see what would happen.

"Let's talk about something else," she said. "Let's talk about global warming or abortion or something more comfortable. Enough with these hot-button issues."

He laughed, and a warm sensation eased throughout her body. "Finally, we can get to something neutral and easy," he said. "I've been dying to chat about immigration."

Nora wished she would have had a camera trained on Julian's face when the lights of the restaurant dimmed, and the music changed from Italian love songs to a dramatic orchestral theme. He looked at her with his mouth slightly open, as if *she* had been the one to do it. She hadn't, of course, but she knew what was happening, and surprising Julian was all the more exciting. How could they go from a tour of serial killer murder-spots to a plain, boring old dinner? This place was more than meets the eye, which was especially true since that was also their slogan.

A large velvet curtain hung in the back of the room, and as it slowly began to open, Julian mouthed to Nora, "What is happening?" with a look on his face that was somehow both gleeful and terrified. After last night's date—no *not date*—she couldn't imagine what he would be expecting this time, but when the Amazing Lorenzo stepped onto the stage, his shiny red bow tie glimmering in the dim light and his top hat tilted slightly to one side, Julian smiled at her in a way that made her intestines wiggle.

"I saw a poster of him in the foyer, but I thought it was just some quirky art," Julian said.

"I felt like it would be better as a surprise. Though, be warned, I have no clue if he's any good. This is a nice place, though, right? He has to be kind of good."

"He's a magician?"

"Good evening, ladies and gentlemen." Lorenzo's voice boomed from the stage. "What beautiful guests we have tonight."

"He's a magician." Nora leaned back in her seat, waiting to see how Lorenzo was going to start the show.

"What is that accent supposed to be?" Julian murmured. The Amazing Lorenzo was preparing for his first magic trick by talking about all the important objects he needed to have on hand every day as a magician. He spun his top hat in his hands before throwing it up and allowing it to land on his head. Then he showcased his deck of cards, shuffling a deck back and forth between his hands like a dealer in Vegas. Finally, he pulled lengths of ribbons from his sleeve, making them dance on the table in front of him.

"That's just good showmanship." Julian grinned.

Nora couldn't help watching Julian's face, waiting for his reaction at each moment. She was the one that was supposed to be writing about this place, deciding whether or not to recommend it to her readers, but she only seemed to be able to glance at Julian, always wondering what he was thinking and if he was enjoying the show.

The guy had dropped everything to come to this dinner for her, so Nora supposed it made sense that she wanted to make sure Julian enjoyed himself, but she couldn't explain why watching his face alight with a childlike fascination made her feel so happy.

The Amazing Lorenzo's booming voice seemed to be some kind of mix of Italian and Irish, which made very little sense, but somehow also made everything he said even more enjoyable, and Julian kept glancing at Nora with a smile, truly tickled by the whole experience.

"Ladies and gentleman, one of the very first rules of magic is that you should never reveal your secrets. But tonight I have a great many things to reveal to you…"

A bird came out of his hat and flew off-stage, a sword appeared from his sleeve, and then a bowling ball fell out of his jacket. Nora and Julian looked at each other with wide eyes, clapping until their hands hurt. "How do you find these things?" Julian whispered. "I didn't even know something like this existed in London."

"You just didn't know to look." Nora took another sip of her wine, pleased with the smokey taste that washed over her tongue.

For his next trick, the Amazing Lorenzo used the sword to cut his jacket in half, but then somehow made it whole once again. "This is my very favorite ensemble, so I'm always afraid to slice my coat in two," he said dramatically. "Thankfully, there is magic…" Was Nora detecting a hint of The Count from *Sesame Street* in his accent now? He whipped the remarkably undamaged jacket back around his shoulders, and everyone in the restaurant cheered.

Julian and Nora were fully enthralled by the time Amazing Lorenzo asked for a volunteer assistant. Nora had her head down over her notebook, her face ridiculously close to the page as she tried to take notes in near darkness. She barely registered that the bulky Lorenzo had managed to hop limberly off the stage until he came to be standing at their table.

"How are you two this evening?" he said to them, his accent somehow even stranger up close.

"Very well, thank you," Julian replied. Nora looked up quickly to see Lorenzo's magnificent form towering over them, a wide smile on his face.

"May I ask what you're writing about, miss?" he said, and Nora flipped her notebook closed.

"I–uh. It's a travel journal. I just wanted to remember that I came here."

"Ah, then we must make this night very unforgettable," Lorenzo said. "Perhaps you or your fine date would like to offer me some assistance."

"Oh, he's not–" Nora said, but then she wasn't sure why she was bothering to explain her relationship with Julian to a muscled magician.

Lorenzo caught her meaning though. "Oh, not a date?" he said into the microphone. Nora flinched as she heard the words reverberate throughout the room. "Then perhaps you could be my date for a moment to help me with some magic." He put out his hand, and Nora smiled tentatively. She'd been to magic shows before, but she'd certainly never been a magician's assistant. She'd also never seen such an attractive illusionist. It seemed to her that they were usually old and lanky with Timothy mustaches. She glanced back at Julian as Lorenzo led her up to the stage. Her hand seemed to disappear entirely into Lorenzo's massive palm, and Julian shrugged, an amused smile playing at his lips.

Her first task was to pick a card. *What a surprise.* It was easy enough to remember the Queen of Hearts, and Lorenzo had her write her name across the face of it with a marker while he turned away. "And what is your name? Please introduce yourself and show everyone your card," he said. Then he had her fold up the card into a tiny square. When she handed him the card, he held it up for everyone to see again, then unfolded one of the creases and ripped the card in half.

"Where are you from, Nora?" he asked.

Nora stood in the bright stage lights, trying to find Julian sitting at their table, but she could only see shadows of people in the distance. "New York," she said. People had heard of New York, even if they only knew about Manhattan.

"Ahhhh," the magician said. "My first date with an American." Lorenzo put her card in a paper bag and lit the whole thing on fire. After the audience "oohed" and "ahhed" while he doused the flames, he directed Nora to stand beside him, positioning her right next to him in the bright spotlight. "Okay, Miss Nora from New York," he said, winking at her. Was he flirting with her in that strange accent? Or was it all just part of the show? "Would you please take the suitcase on the ground and open it so that it is facing our audience for all to see?"

She did as he asked. He placed the burnt bag in the suitcase, then had her retrieve an orange from the table on stage. He kissed her hand after she handed it to him, before holding it up for the audience to see and then placing that in the suitcase as well. After he spun the suitcase toward him, closed it and locked it, he asked Nora if she would take the suitcase and stand at an appointed spot on the stage.

"Are you doing well over there, love?" he asked. "That suitcase is locked up tight, correct?"

"Yes," Nora said.

"Hold it up for everyone to see. Yes, just like that. Thank you very much."

Nora's arms were getting tired, even though there was hardly anything in the suitcase, so she lowered it slightly. She wondered what Julian was thinking, out there in the crowd, if his eyes were on her at this very moment.

"The problem is," Lorenzo said. "I had to tear and burn that card as part of my show, but I'm starting to regret it. I'd like to give you the card, Nora, as a souvenir for your travel journal." He walked toward her, and as he did, he kept his eyes locked on hers. Nora was pretty sure she was sweating under the lights and under his gaze. "Perhaps with a little magic I can resurrect that treasure," Lorenzo said. He swept back across the stage as if he was searching for something. He looked under the table, up his sleeve, under the curtain. Then he removed his hat and pulled out a perfect, round orange—the same one that was supposedly in the suitcase Nora was holding. He grabbed a knife from the table and sliced around the center of the orange until he pulled it apart to reveal the card inside, folded into a little square.

"Thank God for magic, so I can return this to you," he said, unfolding the card. He held it up for everyone to see the Queen of Hearts with Nora's name written across it. The one he had supposedly ripped and torched and locked in a suitcase. The audience went wild, and even Nora heard herself gasp. Of course, this was the obvious conclusion of the whole trick, but it still felt amazing to see it all play out successfully. He was certainly impressive. There was no denying it.

Lorenzo walked over to her and unlocked the suitcase. It fell open in her hands, empty. She looked up at him, truly amazed. She'd been standing right there the whole time. *How did he do that?* He took her hand again so they could both take a bow, then he wrapped his arms around her. "Thank you so much for your assistance, Nora. You've made it a truly magical night!" He held down the mic and whispered quickly in her ear, "Thank you. Truly." The accent was all Irish.

"Umm no problem," she whispered back. Lorenzo took her hand again to help her down the stairs, and just as he released it, he gave her fingers a little squeeze. He locked eyes with her again and smiled before he turned back to the stage.

As Nora made her way back to her table and the crowd whooped again, a brief flash of a thought popped into her head. Was this the number three on her to-do list? Could she have super-hot sex with a magician?

CHAPTER SIXTEEN

AT FIRST, Julian had loved the fact that the very large and very cheeky magician had chosen Nora to be his assistant. It was already a marvelous night—her face glowing in candlelight across the table from him, lobster butter dripping down her chin as she laughed at his jokes about his dad. Yes, she had mentioned Hugh, but it hadn't been for long. It didn't matter anyway. He and Nora were mates. They had a good time together. Everything was brilliant, and watching a nervous Nora walk about the stage was only making everything more enjoyable.

But then the magician started holding and kissing Nora's hands, and Julian started to sweat. He rubbed his palms against his pants legs and took a long drink of water. Lorenzo kept saying her name, imbuing it with meaning, which was fine. That didn't bother Julian. All those magicians did the same shows every night, and he'd probably perfected this with hundreds of women, mooning all over them, going on about the card he needed back so he could gift it to them as a reminder of this amazing occasion, all while some little prat sat back at the dinner table watching his bird get felt up by a magic bodybuilder. Julian didn't mind one bit. It was funny, really, the whole little sketch that had become part of the show, and the audience was loving it.

Nora kept looking toward him, and Julian wondered if she could see his face. He tried to unfurrow his brow so he would seem friendly and encouraging. He tried to smile, and he was doing quite a good job for the most part, especially when other patrons at the tables surrounding him glanced at him with a kind of pity as they watched the magician kiss Nora's hand. In fact, Julian was smiling so hard that his cheeks hurt. It was all part of the show; he could keep this up for ages.

It was idiotic to be jealous of the magician who was literally just up there doing his job, Julian was well aware, but he wasn't even sure that it was jealousy he was feeling. Perhaps just loss, though he wasn't entirely sure what he was losing.

Nora laughed and shrugged as she came back to their table. Decadent desserts were starting to be served now that the show was over, and the people at the tables around them clapped and smiled as she approached. She did a little curtsey and sat down. Her face was red from blushing or heat or both. She flopped into her chair and rested her chin in her hands, elbows on the table. "Well, that was interesting." She laughed.

"Quite the show," Julian said, trying to sound casual. "Do you know how he did it?"

She told him all details from her perspective, how, no, she couldn't make out how Lorenzo had done any of it, how the orange had been firm and real when she held it in her hand, not like any kind of trick fruit that was just for show. That had been her exact handwriting on the card he pulled out, and she had no clue how it had managed to come back from the dead after being torn and torched and locked away. She asked about Julian's point of view from the audience, about whether he had any insights into how it was done, which he did not.

"When he whispered in my ear his accent was all Irish, I think, so I don't know if he was trying to be Italian or if he just thinks that's how magicians should sound."

Julian laughed quietly, but Lorenzo's strange accent didn't seem as funny as it had twenty minutes earlier. He focused on trying to unclench the tight feeling in his chest. *Poppy, Poppy, Poppy.* He should think of her instead. The way she stroked his back and wrapped her entire body around his torso, the way she walked around brushing her teeth while also somehow chatting on her mobile, the way she wrinkled her nose at the mention of dessert.

"Oh my God, this dessert menu is amazing," Nora said. "Can we split one? You have to decide because I can't pick. Salted caramel cheesecake, double fudge brownies, peanut butter crème brûlée?" Julian locked eyes with her as she drooled over the different options. "What is it?" she asked him. "Is everything okay?"

He tried to shake off the fog that seemed to be hanging about his shoulders and go back to having a good time—before the magic. "Peanut butter crème brûlée?" he said. "That sounds very unusual."

"I've never had it before," Nora said. "Shall we be adventurous or play it safe?"

Their eyes locked again, and Julian wished he could grab her hand across the table, that he could rub his thumb across her lower lip and sweep his fingers across her face. *Stop it,* he scolded himself, but then he said, "Let's be adventurous."

Julian was starting to turn a bit pink as Nora moaned with pleasure after every bite of crème brûlée. "People are really going to wonder what the magician did to you now," he said as she inhaled another large bite.

She grinned with her mouth full. "No man and no magician has ever made me feel like this," she said after she swallowed.

Julian tugged at the collar of his shirt before picking up his fork again. "I'm enjoying it, but I don't think anyone has ever enjoyed a dessert as much as you," he teased.

She paused from devouring the peanut-buttery confection. "You think I'm embarrassing again, don't you?" She laughed, pointing a finger at him. "You said, 'Oh no, Nora, I never thought you were weird; I've always found you delightful.' But now the truth is clear! Admit it."

"I'm flattered that you think *I* could be embarrassed of anyone. I spend most of my time trying not to make a fool of myself."

Nora gasped. "Didn't you used to have a little mustache?" she asked suddenly.

"Oh, I see," Julian said. "I see how it is. Speaking of embarrassing, let's bring up Julian's old mustache. That's so kind of you."

Nora laughed until she snorted, and Julian joined in. "No, no," she said, trying to catch her breath, but then she dissolved into laughter again. "Do you want some more crème brûlée, Julian?" she asked as she went about snogging her spoon and moaning even more obnoxiously.

"You're repulsive," Julian said, which only egged her on.

They were laughing so hard, and Nora was still moaning so loudly that it took a moment for either of them to register the fact that Lorenzo had approached the table again, this time without the bow tie or top hat. Nora coughed and groped for a napkin when she noticed him, trying to get rid of the evidence of melted chocolate that was lingering on the corners of her mouth.

"Sounds like you're still having a good time," Lorenzo said. He was quieter now, and Nora was right. His accent now sounded like it had been distilled into something that was entirely Irish and natural. He was more casual as well, the top buttons of his white shirt undone, jacket missing entirely, though there were hints of the showman as he found an empty chair at another table, a little flourish as he whipped it around and sat down, uninvited, at their table.

"Um, hi Lorenzo," Nora said, glancing at Julian with a questioning look. "Nice to see you again."

"Oh," the magician said. "You can just call me Lachlan really." He stuck out a hand to Julian. "Nice to meet you mate." Julian shook the hand and smiled through his teeth but didn't say anything.

"This is Julian," Nora said.

"What'd you both think of the show?"

"It was a good bit," Julian responded without hesitation, wondering if he might be able to hurry this conversation along and get back to his evening with Nora. "I mean, I had never seen anything like that before. I have no idea how you did it."

"Right, well, I can't tell you that." Lachlan seemed a little nervous, as if he felt more natural and confident on the stage than sitting down for a chat, and his eyes were all for Nora. Maybe Lachlan was only nervous to be chatting with her. "You were a fantastic assistant," he said. "The crowd loved you."

"Oh, maybe I should do this professionally," Nora said. She glanced at Julian. "It seems I'm better at being a magician's assistant than I am at my real job."

"Right, there ya go, Nora," Lachlan said. "I'll have to snap you up then, before any other magicians come sniffing around."

Yes, it was clear, the beefy magician was flirting with Nora. Like Hugh, Lachlan had the charisma of a performer—though he was more subdued as he focused all of his attention on her.

"You two really aren't on a date?" Lachlan asked as if he suddenly remembered Julian's presence.

"Julian's a good friend," Nora said. "We're not—he's got a Poppy."

I've got a Poppy? As in, if I didn't have a Poppy I might actually have a chance? Julian was sure that wasn't the case, but the easiest way to reassure this magician that there was absolutely nothing going on between them was to make sure it was clear that Julian was attached to someone else. He suddenly wanted to sink under the tablecloth and pretend he didn't exist at all.

Lachlan smiled. "Well, in that case, Nora, ummm..." He fiddled with something in his palm for a moment before handing Nora a card. Julian stared at him curiously. Did this bloke just have a stack of cards that he handed out to beautiful women at magic shows?

Nora flipped the card between her fingers, inspecting it as Lachlan got up from the table. Julian peered over at her, but he didn't see anything on the small white paper. "It's blank." Nora blinked up at Lachlan, clearly confused.

He shuffled his feet for a moment, then ran a hand through his hair. "Invisible ink," he said before finally disappearing.

CHAPTER SEVENTEEN

"YOU'VE NEVER NEEDED a boy to help you do anything!" Nora's mother shouted. It was three o'clock in the morning, and Nora had turned the volume down on her computer so that she wouldn't wake the neighbors on either side of her tiny flat. "I don't understand why on earth you would think that having some guy around is going to improve your writing."

"I don't need him, except—well, I think it is actually helping. After the tour and then tonight after the magic show, I came home and wrote, and it all came so easily. I think these reviews might be just as good as the one that Darcy liked, the one where Julian was with me the first time. I know it sounds crazy, but—"

"Yes," her mother said simply. "It's crazy. Did you ever think it's just because *someone* is with you? What does it matter that it's Julian? Maybe you just need someone there to talk about your ideas."

Nora was quiet for a moment, pushing up the sleeves of her pajamas and brushing back her hair. "I've thought about it, but even when I wrote about a place where I was with Darcy, it wasn't nearly as good as this. Or even the coffee shop with—" Nora hesitated. She didn't mean to bring that up.

"What?"

Nora racked her brain for a way to cover her error. It was impossible to keep something from her mother. "With another colleague. Anyway, it didn't work. It only worked with Julian."

"Well, I'm glad you're feeling better about your writing, but I still think it's ridiculous. And you swear there's nothing going on between the two of you?"

Nora bit her lip. Of course, she couldn't stop the night at the club or the moment in the cab from popping into her head. Or the moment she saw him walk into the restaurant—his lopsided smile and fidgety fingers. "He has a girlfriend, actually, so no."

"And you're still in love with Hugh?"

"Mother."

"What? You don't want to talk about it? I worry about you, ya know."

"I worry about you and your breasts!" Nora shouted.

"I'm fine, Nora. Bebe is taking good care of me, aren't you, Bebe?"

Nora smiled as the Yorkipoo enthusiastically licked her mother's face. "Can I go to sleep now please?" Nora asked, her head drooping into her hands.

"Just be careful with your little heart," her mother said.

When Nora hung up, she rolled over and looked at her phone. Another message from Hugh that she hadn't responded to. There was a band, the Trash Can Bunnies, that had an upcoming show, and he said he had a feeling that she would love them because apparently he still remembered everything about her taste in music. He hadn't told her any of the details yet, and she'd been trying not to ask. In fact, she hadn't asked for six whole hours since he'd first sent the message.

Instead, she pulled out the blank card from Lachlan. *How did one read invisible ink, anyway?* According to the internet, it depended on the *kind* of invisible ink. Some suggestions for how to try to read it included a black light, a UV light, or just some method of heating the paper, though lighters and candles were discouraged considering the very real possibility of setting the thing on fire. Nora settled for trying to heat the card from the lamp by her bed. It did seem to work, though it was hard to make out the letters and numbers. She squinted over the little rectangle long enough to see that it said "The Amazing Lorenzo" and to decipher the cell number that was written there. A card that was written in invisible ink. Who was this guy?

It was nearing four in the morning, but she sent Lachlan a message anyway, unsure if she would still decide to do it once she'd had more sleep and some caffeine. She didn't expect it, but he responded almost immediately. "Hey, beautiful. It was lovely meeting you tonight." In a matter of minutes, he'd already asked her out for next weekend, and she'd said yes, though she didn't know what she was doing. She didn't know if she could imagine herself dating Lachlan, the phony-accented, over-the-top magician. But then again, she *could* imagine sleeping with him, so maybe that was why she'd agreed to go to dinner. Or maybe it was because her fingers were itching to type something to Hugh, and she thought this might be the only way to stop herself.

When she was nineteen, she wouldn't have hesitated to go out with a magician, to text Hugh back, to go streaking around a bar at midnight. Hugh seemed to have brought out that side of her, the side that said yes to wild adventures, the side that didn't try to keep her heart cradled carefully in her chest, sheltered from any possibility of heartache. She wasn't that same person anymore, though, and maybe Hugh wasn't either. Maybe sweepingly romantic love stories and kissing in rainstorms, cuddles in the back of the cab and dancing all night, maybe that was all just for teenagers and Taylor Swift (Nora's absolute queen). But Nora didn't live in a Taylor Swift song, unfortunately. She didn't even live in a Pet Rockers song anymore, even if they still played about her on stage. She needed to be practical, get her work done, and stop fantasizing about Hugh. She needed to stop acting like a nineteen-year-old girl.

The following week, Darcy read over Nora's revisions and new pages, the ones she'd written after being with Julian. Nora was still sure that they were much better, that somehow being with Julian had helped her writing despite her mother's incredulity. However, she was a little shocked to find that Darcy thought the same thing.

"What did you do?" Darcy asked. She was standing over Nora's desk in the office.

"Pardon?"

"What did you do to these pages? I mean, you obviously followed my advice on the revisions, but the new stuff is better somehow. Not perfect, by any means—I still have suggestions—but far more readable."

"I guess I'm going to have to take 'more readable' as great praise coming from you," Nora said. She was shrugging nonchalantly, but inwardly her muscles seemed to be relaxing with great relief. She hadn't totally fucked up again. Being with Julian had worked!

"What did you do differently this time?" Darcy asked again.

"Umm—" Nora paused. She was relatively sure that "I took an adorable man along to all of my work outings" wasn't the completely professional and sophisticated solution she should be offering to her editor. "I just paid careful attention to your notes and tried to give the reviews some heart and character," she said.

Darcy eyed her suspiciously. "Well good, then."

Instead of marching off, Darcy lingered, opening and then closing her mouth before finally leaning down and whispering to Nora. "I'm doing better, by the way, with the whole Anika thing. She never responded to me, but at least I tried, right? I can move on and stop letting these ridiculous fantasies take over my brain space."

Boy was she preaching to the choir on that one. Nora nodded. "That's great, Darcy. I'm sorry it didn't work out like you were hoping, though."

Darcy started to walk back to her office, but then she turned back to Nora once again. "I almost forgot. There's a music venue I want you to check out. I was thinking of going to see a band that's playing there anyway, but I thought maybe you could come along. It might be something to add to the book."

"That sounds like fun," Nora said, already secretly wondering if it would be weird for her to bring Julian along so that she could actually do a good job with her review. "When is it? What's the band?"

"Trash Can Bunnies?" Darcy said. "They've been getting some attention lately. It's up in Notting Hill, but we could go together."

"You've got to be joking," Nora said.

"What?"

"Hugh."

"Oh fuck, what is it now? He's a Pet Rocker, not a Trash Can Bunny."

"But he invited me to go see them. He said he thinks I'd like their stuff. Maybe it was a different show, though. I don't know if he'd be going up to Notting Hill."

"Bloody hell, you would think that within the whole fucking huge city of London that you could manage to avoid this guy. The Trash Can Bunnies next show is in Scotland as far as I know, so I don't think he was inviting you to that one. Maybe you won't even see him, Nora. It's going to be packed."

Just the thought of being in the same room with Hugh, even if that room happened to be full of hundreds of other people, made Nora start sweating. "Right, and he'll probably be with his fiancée anyway. No big deal." She wiped her forehead. How was this happening again? What if she saw him kissing Rose?

"I'm telling you, it will be easy not to run into him at all," Darcy assured her.

"I know. It's totally fine. I'm not worried."

"You look a bit worried," Darcy said.

"I'm super cool. It's okay."

"You're going barmy. I can tell."

Nora rolled her eyes. "I don't know what that means, but I'm good."

"You're—"

"Darcy!"

"Right, I have a lot to do. Stop fucking about. See you Saturday."

Nora sighed, but then she smiled to herself. Darcy had invited her to hang out. She grabbed her phone and sent a text:

> Nora: You asked me because we're best friends now, right?

> Darcy: No.

> Nora: I don't believe you. You want to hang out with me…

Darcy: You're fired.

It officially was not a lie when Nora had to cancel her date with Lachlan for the Trash Can Bunnies show. She was technically going to be working, even if working also meant drinking at a concert with her editor and possibly seeing her ex-boyfriend. Lachlan was bummed but still seemed eager to reschedule and see her again, so it wasn't as if she completely burned that bridge just for a stupid chance at laying eyes on Hugh Jeffries. Lachlan was The Amazing Lorenzo, after all, so he wasn't someone who would question her claim that she needed to work on a Saturday night. That was his bread and butter.

Actually, it was Julian who started asking questions about what she was doing. They were at the Victoria and Albert Museum for a costume exhibit that was going to be featured on the app. Nora was terrified, considering it would be the biggest write-up she'd ever done, and it had a quick turnaround time. They wanted to launch the app with fresh content about what was happening in London right at the time of launch.

Nora was standing in front of a case that held an extremely uncomfortable looking corset when she saw Julian's face in the glass. He was watching her as if looking for something.

"What is it?" she asked.

He looked a little surprised, as if he hadn't been expecting to be caught staring at her.

"I really have enjoyed coming out with you and visiting all of these places," he said.

Nora felt her nerve-endings buzz, as if jolted to life by the tone of his voice. She couldn't help but panic. What if there was a "but"? What if he didn't want to do this anymore? She couldn't write without him, and everything would fall to pieces.

"Yes?" she said, the word a little shaky on her lips.

"I was just wondering...why? Why me?"

He didn't look upset or put-off, just curious, perhaps a little confused.

Nora looked back at herself in the glass of the costume case. She didn't want to lie to him, but she didn't exactly want to tell him the truth either. She couldn't imagine making him feel as if she was just using him, as if it was all only for work, only for her writing, that she was only spending this time with him out of necessity. They were becoming real friends—not just friends of proximity like when she was Hugh's girlfriend, and not just friends of convenience because she barely knew anyone else in London. She couldn't bear for him to think that she'd just been taking advantage of him the whole time. So she told him part of the truth.

"My editor insisted that I get the perspective of some locals," she said. "Also, seeing these things with you makes it all a lot less lonely." She didn't realize how true that part was until she said it. But then her brain continued with the rest: *And because my writing is shit without you, and for some reason I can probably only manage to keep my job if you come on these outings with me. But I have no idea why it's you or how you manage to make writing about this stuff so much easier.*

He chewed his lip and looked at the corset in the costume case while she was hoping the guilt wasn't showing all over her face. How many people would take this much time helping out a random American girl as she tried to keep her job? Who else in the world could possibly be this nice? And she was the asshole who wasn't being totally honest with him.

"I'm not sure why I'm the local you picked," he said. "I can't be much help. I'm not complaining, but I just can't help wondering." He glanced back at her and shrugged.

Recently, Julian had mentioned he'd been over at James's to sell and move an old drum kit. He'd gone shopping for amps and new equipment with Hugh. He took his father grocery shopping, and he was here at the museum with her. He was always doing everything for other people, always so caring, and he didn't even seem to realize it—this was not the kind of stuff everyone just did to be nice. He was an anomaly.

"You're helping me a lot," she said. "You don't even know." She paused for a long moment, trying to find a way to put it into words. He looked over at her again, and she caught his eyes. She stared into them, trying to imbue at least some of her gratitude into the look. "You make me better, Julian."

He looked away quickly, as if unwilling to hold her gaze a second longer. He didn't believe her. He still didn't get it, and neither did she. How could she explain any of it when it truly didn't make any sense?

"Look at these pants!" she said, pointing to the next case, hoping to lighten the mood. He was still quiet, but he followed without asking again what he was doing there.

"Why do you look like that?" Darcy said when they met up at the Tube station before the show on Saturday night.

"What do you mean?" Nora asked. Yes, she may have tried on seven different outfits and three different shades of lipstick, but she thought she still looked semi-casual. Also, her leather jacket was really awesome, and she pegged it as exactly the kind of thing to wear to the show of a band called Trash Can Bunnies. Her pants were outrageously tight though. And perhaps her shirt was a little lower cut than usual...and she may have dusted a little bronzer on her cleavage, but her boobs looked amazing.

"I mean you better be careful walking around like that in this shite hole!" Darcy snarled.

"What are you talking about? I haven't had any problems around here," Nora said, looking down at her outfit again and second-guessing everything. "You don't think it's safe?"

"You haven't noticed that we're in a total dump? The company's been talking about moving the 99 Flamingo office for ages, but it's never going to happen. They're too cheap."

"I don't think it's a dump," Nora said.

Darcy stared her down. "Well, I guess you wouldn't," she said. "You're from New York. You're used to things being a bit dodgy." Nora rolled her eyes, sure that Darcy would put up a major fight if they ever decided to move the publishing office. "Anyway, how's Julian?"

"Why would you ask that?" Oh God, she was sweating already. Leather was a terrible idea.

"Just curious," Darcy said as they boarded the train and slid into plastic seats.

"He has a girlfriend, Darcy."

"And Hugh has a fiancée. What's the point?"

Nora nodded her head. "The point is that I'm in the market for a single gentleman to start courting me. And then take me home and make rough, respectful love to me."

"You're a horny bugger, aren't you?" Darcy chuckled as they made their way to the venue.

The band wasn't what she expected; the genre was different from anything The Pet Rockers played. There was more of a rockabilly, upbeat essence to their sound. Darcy bought the first round of drinks and warned Nora that the pear cider she was about to consume had an eight percent alcohol content. Nora shrugged and knocked back the sweet substance. If she was going to be showing off her dance moves to Darcy and very possibly to Hugh Jeffries as well, then she was going to need some high alcohol content. She couldn't help the way she was scanning the crowd, doing a double take every time she spotted a tall, muscular man with shaggy hair and a shadow of a beard across his face. "What are you looking for?" Darcy asked, even though Nora was sure she knew the answer. Nora gave her a small smile and poured some more cider down her throat.

The beat of the music was hypnotic—too catchy and upbeat to be unlikable. The music transported her to summers in upstate New York, going to the lake and taking out a beat-up little paddle boat with a boombox and a basket of mixed tapes, sitting in the sun until her skin was pink and her toes were wrinkled from bathing in lake water.

"They're rather good," Darcy said. *High praise from Darcy.* "Did you tell him that you would be here tonight?"

"Who?" Nora said. Darcy gave her a sour look. "Okay, fine. No, I told him I didn't think I would make it. That was before I knew I would be here with you."

"I'm surprised that you never gave him an update."

Almost the moment Darcy said it, Nora spotted him at the nearest bar.

He was wearing a nondescript black T-shirt and jeans, but even with all the hair falling in his face, she could tell it was really him. Her muscle memory seemed to be willing her to throw her arms around his shoulders, slide her fingers into his hair, and plant a kiss on him, just as she would have done if they'd met up at a show seven years ago. Quick reconnaissance revealed that there didn't seem to be any young attractive fiancées hanging around, but she saw Dev and James, and as she continued scanning the bar she spotted Julian, and she found herself smiling stupidly until she realized that there was a delicate arm looped through his, and the owner of said delicate arm was a beautiful women with a pixie haircut and a tattoo on her chest, who was talking to him animatedly.

Nora froze. It had to be Poppy. She was so freaking cool. Why did that make Nora feel a little sick to her stomach?

"What is it?" Darcy asked, starting to look in the direction that Nora was staring.

"Well, ummm—"

"Ah, I see," Darcy said. "Are you going to approach him?"

"I think that maybe I won't," Nora said, but almost at the same moment, Dev spotted her. She saw him nudge Hugh, and Hugh searched through the crowd until his eyes landed on her. A smile took over his face. Nora waved sheepishly.

When he waved her over, Nora grabbed Darcy and they moved through the crown toward the bar. She kept glancing at Julian, who was still so entirely focused on Poppy that he hadn't even noticed she was there.

"Nora," Hugh said softly. She felt like she couldn't swallow properly. "I didn't think you were coming."

"I wasn't. But then I had to for work." She gestured toward Darcy.

"Well, do you both need a drink? Cheers to a great night." Nora couldn't help noticing that he already sounded a little tipsy, and by the warm feeling in her cheeks she thought she was probably close to the same place. Still, she ordered a whiskey, unusual for her, but it seemed necessary given the circumstances. She was just taking her first sip when Julian finally realized she was there. They made eye contact, but he didn't even speak at first. He just stared at her until she felt completely exposed, like a big fraud who couldn't write without him, who also thought about him much too frequently for comfort. She couldn't seem to speak either, so for one deep breath they just stared into each other's eyes.

Darcy pinched her arm. She must have been watching them. "Um, hello?" she said.

"Hi, I'm Poppy." The woman on Julian's arm finally chimed in.

"Nice to meet you." Nora shook herself out of her reveries and took Poppy's outstretched hand. The whiskey was already kicking in. She could do this. This was totally fine.

"Yes, this is Nora," Julian said. He absently rubbed his fingers through his hair, and his eyes darted back and forth between the women. "She's writing a book about London."

Darcy snorted.

"I'm just writing little articles for an update to a book about London," Nora corrected.

"And this is Darcy," Julian said. He was often shy, but Nora thought he seemed especially nervous. He was probably trying so hard to impress Poppy, which was unbelievably adorable and also made her want to finish her drink as quickly as possible, which she did. Then she had another. She pretended to be intent on the Bunnies as she stood surrounded by Hugh's friends, but she wasn't hearing a word the band was singing. She couldn't help glancing at Julian, at the way Poppy leaned toward him to touch his arm and laughed loudly when he made faces at her.

"What?" Darcy said. "Something wrong with you?"

Nora shook her head, but she was still watching Julian and Poppy when Hugh grabbed her hand and pulled her away from the bar.

"Hey," he said.

Nora swallowed hard. Hugh tugged at her hand and led her further from the group, further from Julian and Poppy, where people were enthusiastically rocking with the music in the center of the room.

"Dance with me," Hugh whispered in her ear.

It should have been easy to demure, to laugh and shake her head while pulling away and escaping back to Darcy's side. It should have been nothing to joke that she was too clumsy, that she just wasn't up for dancing. She didn't though. Perhaps because her reaction time was slow or perhaps because she wasn't thinking straight, she allowed Hugh to spin her in a circle, to pull her toward him as she lost her balance, to breathe into her hair when she was in his arms.

In an instant, she was tense and breathless, but she could feel the warmth of Hugh's skin against her own as he wrapped his arms around her.

Fuck. It was the only thought she could make sense of in her brain. They were both drunk, and to him this was probably some meaningless dance, but the way he was looking at her and holding her...

Nora knew that she needed to get away, even if her body was already betraying her, already sinking into him, already inhaling the familiar scent of his sweat, already allowing her fingers to interlock with his. The tension in her limbs seemed to drain out of her, and for a moment, her cheek was pressed into his neck, and it felt so *nice*, so *right*, but then the song changed, and it pulled her out of her drunken haze enough to panic and try to pull away.

He spun her around again until she felt dizzy, though she couldn't be sure it was just from the dancing. As he pulled her back toward his body, she seemed to crash into his chest, and his eyes locked on her, searching her face. She remembered the look from elevators, from hotel rooms and back rooms at the pub. A look that made it hard to breathe.

"I'm going to go get a drink," she said, and he took a confused second to let go of her. His face was too close to hers. His lips were almost—

There was space between their bodies, but he was holding her hand. "It's such a good song," he said, his voice even deeper and more gravelly than normal. He had such a sexy voice.

Nora didn't move, and she didn't know if it was because she was the prey—frozen, trapped, terrified—or if it was that she was a quiet predator preparing to pounce. Hugh leaned closer again, his mouth to her ear.

"I've missed you, Nora," he said. His lips grazed her earlobe. His hand was on her hip. Something was about to happen—something awful, something wonderful. She tucked her head under his chin, letting him hold her again. She had to try to get it together.

"I'm just parched," she said, backing away awkwardly. He gave her a hurt puppy-dog look and continued to hold onto her hand, but she turned and pulled free, rushing away from the dance floor.

Darcy joined Nora at the bar immediately. "Bloody hell," Darcy said. Of course she'd been watching them. Nora felt like everyone in the whole venue must have been staring. She couldn't speak. She still felt like she was spinning. "What happened?"

"I don't know," Nora said, almost gasping. "Nothing." *Everything.*

"We decided we're mates, right?" Darcy asked. "You can tell me the truth. That was not nothing."

Nora tried to take a breath, but her head was still whirling. She shouldn't have had the whiskey. She shouldn't have danced with Hugh or let him look at her like that. It was too easy, too dangerous. She'd promised herself that nothing like this would happen, but she'd wanted it too. She'd wanted to see what it might be like, just for a second and, God, she knew that made her a horrible person, but she couldn't help it, and now it was out in the open for everyone to see.

"Nora?"

"Now you want to be my friend?" Nora said. She hated having Darcy as a witness. No one needed to know she was such an awful disaster.

Darcy stared at her, and Nora felt so exposed, like she was caught in a trap.

"I said I don't know," Nora snapped. "What do you want me to say?" She needed to get away, to have a moment alone to think.

"You made me talk to you about my *feelings...*" Darcy grumbled. "Come on, out with it."

Nora started to panic. Her cheeks felt too hot. Everything felt like it was about to boil. "I think I just need to get out of here."

Darcy shook her head. "I'll come with you. You're too drunk—"

"You're too drunk!" Nora yelled. She didn't know why she was freaking out so much. "I just need to go."

"Well, you definitely need to be away from Hugh."

"Darcy, I told you. Nothing is going on there." If she just kept saying it, it would be true. She felt like she might be sick. The leather, the tight pants. Everything was too tight and too close.

"Does he know that?" Darcy asked. "Because I've seen—"

"No. God, give it up!" Nora was shaking, and she felt like people were starting to look at them even though their voices wouldn't carry very far with the sound of the music. "You won't listen to me. We ended seven years ago. It doesn't matter anymore. And you and I—we're not real friends anyway, right? I don't know why you even care." Nora put a hand to her head and tried to take a deep breath. She'd been too close to allowing something terrible happen—something that she wouldn't be able to take back. She hated herself for getting so close to Hugh, but she couldn't shake the memories of everything they'd been to each other. Maybe she never should have seen him at all. She had no self-control and no idea what she was doing.

Darcy looked taken aback. "Just because you are trying to destroy your ex's life and crush some woman you don't even know, don't take it out on me."

Nora felt the flush in her cheeks and looked up at Darcy. *How could she think—why would she say that?* "What? I'm not trying to do anything."

"Except weasel your way into a relationship with an almost-married man. I think you should probably just leave him alone." A switch had flipped, and Darcy was frowning, no longer giving advice, no longer on her side.

Nora stood with her mouth open for a moment. How could Darcy think she was trying to destroy a relationship? That's not what she was doing. She didn't know what she was doing. She felt like she was drowning. She had trusted Darcy. She'd thought they'd come to an understanding. She thought there was a chance they cared about each other, even if she'd just stated otherwise in the heat of the moment, but now Darcy seemed to be sure that Nora was actually some homewrecker, and maybe she was, and that was even worse.

"You're the one who made me see him. You convinced me," Nora said in a broken voice. "You loved your little drama. You wanted me to..." She gulped. "Well, the drama's over now. I hope you were entertained." She didn't wait for a response before turning to go. She pushed through the crowd, knocking shoulders with people as she tried to get out, barely paying attention to where she was walking. Before she could make it out the door, she crashed right into Julian.

"Nora? What's wrong? Where are you going?" He put a hand on her shoulder, but she couldn't even look at his face.

"I just have to go," she said. *Do not start crying, you little wimp.* She was blinking wildly, trying to hold in the tears. How could Darcy think that she was purposely trying to seduce Hugh, to steal him away from his fiancée? Darcy should be on her side, helping her to figure it out, not blaming her. Or maybe she deserved all of the blame because she hadn't kept up a boundary with Hugh, and she really was the horrible person Darcy thought her to be. And she was dragging Julian into it too. Sweet, wonderful Julian.

"I'll take you," Julian said without hesitation. "Wherever you need to go. We'll fix it, whatever it is."

Nora finally managed to look at him. His blue eyes were baring down on her, filled with concern. As he slid his hand down her arm, her skin seemed to recognize every bump in the ridges of his fingers, every curve and divot of his palm pulsing through the sleeve of her jacket. Nora remembered Poppy holding onto him, the way she'd touched him so confidently, claiming him for her own. He certainly didn't need Nora dragging him all over London and using him to get ahead at work. Her head spun even faster. "No," she said. "I'm doing enough damage, and I don't need to butt into your life too."

"What are you talking about?"

"I'm sorry," she said. "I'm sorry." She broke away from him and started for the door again. She could still hear the Trash Can Bunnies playing as she burst outside onto the sidewalk.

CHAPTER EIGHTEEN

JULIAN TURNED from the doors where Nora had just fled the building, to see Hugh on the dance floor, stumbling towards him and looking for something, or someone.

"Where's Nora?" Hugh asked.

"She's gone," Julian said.

"She didn't tell me she was going," Hugh lamented. He looked like someone had just kicked his puppy. Julian had seen the two of them on the dance floor, and it was clear that Hugh wanted to continue their moment, to have Nora back in his arms.

"Why'd she leave?" Hugh continued.

Julian glanced toward the door once again and then back at Hugh. "I couldn't really make sense of it. She just said she had to go."

"I think we might be heading into dangerous territory," Hugh said.

"What do you mean?" Julian knew what Hugh meant, but he wanted to hear him say it. He wanted to be sure.

Hugh paused for a moment, like he was considering how much to reveal, but the need to talk with Julian won out. "I keep thinking about her," he coughed out. "I don't even know Nora all that well anymore, but I still keep wondering what it would be like if I was with her again. What do I do, mate?" He seemed to shake himself a bit, as if he could somehow dislodge the feelings for Nora that were inside of him until they fell right out.

Julian stood frozen, trying to figure out how out to respond. He couldn't believe Hugh was questioning his engagement. And now he was asking for Julian's help to decide what to do, when Julian was very much biased on the desired outcome. He tried to push his secret feelings for Nora aside and be the good, understanding friend Hugh needed. He could remain neutral. He had to. "If you never saw Nora again and you married Rose and went on with your life, would you regret never having tried to be with Nora?"

"I don't know."

"Alternatively, if you went and found Nora right now and told her you wanted to be with her, would you regret not marrying Rose?"

"How am I supposed to know which one of those is the better option until I've done it?" Hugh seemed to think for a moment, clearly struggling with his drunk brain.

"I want to marry Rose," Hugh declared. "Rose is ambitious and pushed me to fight for what I wanted. When a venue tried to lower the amount they were going to pay for a gig, she convinced me to stand up for myself. She pushes me every day—to get my music out there, to go on all the radio shows, to do the promos. She *knows* me. She calls me on my bullshit. If she had just seen me with Nora, she would have told me to knock it off and make up my mind about what I wanted. I couldn't stand it if I messed things up with her."

"Then what's the issue? You love Rose," Julian pointed out. That was neutral, right?

"But what if, ten years from now, we don't like each other so much anymore, and I always wonder what would've happened if I'd run away with Nora?"

Julian's forehead scrunched up as he tried to find a way to make his friend feel better. He wanted to believe this was simply a case of cold feet, and honestly, Hugh was the type for it. He'd always loved adventure and wild nights, never been the kind to settle down. But then he'd met Rose. She'd changed everything, Julian was sure of it, even if Hugh wasn't. "No one ever knows what the exact right thing is," Julian said. "You just have to trust your instincts. It's impossible to know what will happen in the future, but if you know you want to marry Rose…"

Hugh's shoulders sagged as he seemed to whisper to himself, "I just wish someone could tell me the answer. If I could just spend a day with Nora—"

"Hugh." Julian put a hand on his friend's shoulder, preparing to talk some sense into him.

"Actually, I think I better go home, sober up, and get some rest, mate." Hugh shuffled backwards, out of Julian's reach. "That's what my instincts are saying to me now."

———

Julian figured that he didn't have much reason to stick around the show after Hugh left. He was a bit devastated anyway. He'd seen the way Nora and Hugh had been dancing together, like they'd been doing it all their lives. And then Hugh had admitted it; he was actually reconsidering his relationship, that wanker. As soon as Poppy got out of the loo they were going home, and Julian was going to smile at her and hold her hand and do everything in his power not to let her know that he was thinking of another woman. He shouldn't be thinking of anyone else at all, and he was going to find a way to stop it. It couldn't be that hard. He'd even done it before. Except… Last time he'd been around Hugh and Nora, they'd been snogging all over the place, but he hadn't spent so much time alone with her then. He hadn't felt the way that her hand slipped so easily into his or the way her arms tightened around his neck when she danced with him.

"It seems the ex-lovers have abandoned us," Darcy said. She was leaning her elbows on the bar, her round face squished up into a frown. Julian hadn't realized she was still there.

"Come again?"

"They've left us—Nora and Hugh. And where's your girlfriend?"

"She's not my—she's in the loo." Julian glanced around for any sign of Poppy. The last thing he wanted was to stand around talking casually about Nora and Hugh.

"You can't handle it, can you?" Darcy said. She sounded upset, but

Julian wasn't sure what he'd done. He looked around the bar again, as if it held the key to what she was talking about.

"You're in love with Nora," Darcy said matter-of-factly. "My guess would be that this isn't exactly a new development. I don't know what it is about her, personally. I like my women a little taller and sturdier. She's a bit wobbly."

Julian was immediately defensive, even though he wasn't sure why he was entertaining this conversation with an almost-stranger. "I'm not in love with her."

"You are."

"I'm not." He knew he sounded like a child. "Did Nora say something?"

Darcy looked at him slyly—like she'd caught him red-handed.

Obviously, he had a crush on Nora, not that he was going to reveal it to this woman that he barely knew. Obviously, the crush had started the moment he met her, and it hadn't taken much to swell up inside him all over again. He could easily admit all of that to himself. It was going to take a little bit of time to get over it again. But he was not in love with her.

"Is it serious with this other woman?" Darcy asked.

"I'm not talking about this." Julian was thinking about the night at the club, about Nora twirling wildly on the dance floor, about how she'd grabbed onto him to get away from another man. He was starting to feel sick. Was he in love with her? That was an exaggeration, wasn't it? He had a harmless interest, one that he could overcome with a little willpower.

"Never mind," Darcy said. "Don't tell me anything. I've come to care about this woman over the past month, for some unknown reason because she is absolutely annoying, but she's a bit fucked up at the moment. I'm just trying to figure out what the hell's going on."

"That's because of Hugh," Julian said. "That doesn't have anything to do with me."

"I thought that at first too," Darcy said. "But now I'm not so sure."

"There you are!" Poppy said brightly, grabbing his arm. Julian slowly turned to look at her, still trying to make sense of what Darcy was insinuating. "I thought I'd lost you forever," Poppy cooed. "The toilet is a madhouse. Are you ready to leave?"

Julian nodded and glanced back at Darcy. She just shrugged.

"Nice meeting you," Poppy said to Darcy as she wrapped her arms around Julian.

Darcy simply nodded, and Julian glanced at her again. She must be quite done in if she was thinking that he...if she really believed that he could...

Pushing all thoughts of love out of his head, he turned away and let Poppy drag him toward the door without looking back again.

Julian couldn't sleep that night. He'd taken Poppy home and made up an excuse about an early morning trip with his dad, so he was alone in his room sitting in an armchair, staring out the window that overlooked the cemetery and wondering what on earth he was going to do now. He didn't know why he was letting Nora's boss get to him so much, but her words kept echoing in his head. *You're in love with her. You're in love with her. You're in love with her.*

Bloody hell.

Julian was starting to believe her. He was starting to think, besides trying to convince himself otherwise, that he was in love with Nora—that he had possibly been in love with her since that summer so long ago when she'd been dating his best mate. He'd thought it was a harmless crush on a girl he knew he could never have. She'd left, and the story was over. Then, in these past few weeks as he'd gotten to know her again, he was starting to realize he'd only ever felt this way once before, seven years ago. About her. He was putting himself in a situation where he was going to be entirely devastated and broken-hearted, and was probably already halfway there.

He knew then that he needed to make some decisions. There was no way to keep going on the way he was—watching the woman he loved fawn all over Hugh while also trying to convince himself to like Poppy instead. That wouldn't work. He either had to tell Nora and get that humiliation over with, or he had to stop seeing her altogether.

Option one was impossible though. He couldn't tell Nora, because despite the fact that Hugh was engaged, he had also just drunkenly disclosed that he still had feelings for Nora as well. That meant Julian couldn't just sweep in and tell Nora he loved her. He also didn't want to deal with the very real possibility that she would tell him that she had feelings for Hugh, and she never would have considered Julian as a possible romantic prospect. He didn't even want to imagine what that would feel like.

He came to the conclusion, around four-thirty in the morning, that he couldn't see Nora anymore. He couldn't go on her projects with her or go dancing or sit in the corners of dark bars talking for hours. There was no way he was going to stop thinking about her if he kept being her friend. It wasn't fair to Poppy either, as he had already ditched her for Nora on multiple occasions. But how could he tell Nora that he couldn't see her without giving her a reason? How could he make up excuses every time she called? He could say Poppy was jealous and he had to stay away from her. He could say he was too busy with work. He didn't know if Nora would believe any of it, but he had to tell her something, and then that would be it. He would get over her forever this time.

Before Julian knew it, sunlight was shining into his bedroom, the orangey glow of the early morning. He had been up all night agonizing about what to do, and he really was supposed to go to Stratford with his dad to meet with a new supplier for the shop; that hadn't been a lie. His father didn't *need* him, though. Julian was just going to offer a bit of company, so he canceled with his dad and buried his face in his pillow. His dad sounded hopeful on the phone, like maybe Julian was canceling to stay in bed with a woman, rather than to stay in bed pining over one.

After coming to terms with his decision and letting it sink in that he was not going to see Nora's wild hair waving in the wind or the bright lipstick stains that lingered on her drinks, he called Poppy and asked if she could pop 'round for a chat. He paced back and forth in the hallway until she got there, unsure of exactly what he was going to say. He couldn't stop running his hands back and forth through his hair as he tried to get ahold of himself.

The sound of Poppy's knock brought him to a halt, the first time in hours that he had truly been still.

"Hey," she said softly when he'd opened the door for her. He knew she could tell he was acting strange. Poppy could read people, usually guilty students, but now she was reading him, and there was no way he could act like nothing was bothering him.

"What's wrong?" she asked about ten seconds after walking into his flat.

Julian tried to smile at her, but it probably looked more like a grimace. For a moment he thought about all the things he could tell her. There were so many excuses he could make. Or maybe he could find a way to make *this* relationship work. He could stay with Poppy, this beautiful woman who enjoyed spending time with him. He could wait and see, and maybe someday he would miss her the second she left the room. Maybe one day he would stand over the stove with the tea kettle squealing, so zoned out thinking about her that he didn't even realize the water was boiling.

"I'm alright," he said.

"You were acting odd last night too, but I thought I would give you some time."

Julian still hadn't decided what or how much he was going to tell her, but as it turned out, it wasn't much of a decision at all.

"I think I'm in love with my friend," he blurted. Maybe that wasn't the best way to go about it, but he could only go with the truth. It wasn't fair to keep trying. Maybe someday he would forget about Nora, and then he could give a woman like Poppy a proper chance. It wasn't right now though. Poppy didn't deserve to wait around while he was constantly wondering about someone else.

Poppy sat down on the edge of the coach and furrowed her brow.

Julian tried again. "Uh, sorry, that came out fast and wrong. And I want you to know that nothing has happened. I don't even have a chance with her, really, but I know it isn't fair to you to keep this up when I've realized how I feel. I'm going to stop seeing her to try to get over it, but I just need some time, not that I expect you to wait for me. Sorry." *Bloody hell, I am such an idiot.* "I didn't mean for this to happen."

Poppy stared at him for a moment, and Julian held his breath.

"It's Nora, right? When did you realize you were in love with her?"

Somehow, Poppy was entirely stoic. Her voice didn't even get high or breathless the way Julian's was.

"Nora, yeah, how did you–? I realized I was in love with her..." He looked at the clock as if that might hold the answer. "This morning."

Poppy looked around the room. "Was she here?"

"What? No. I was just by myself...thinking."

"You think way too much, Julian. Probably more than anyone I know." She stood up and put a hand on his shoulder. He placed his hand over hers but didn't look up at her. "I saw how you looked at her last night. I saw it the second your eyes met hers."

"I'm sorry," Julian said again. He sighed. Apparently, everyone had known. Not Hugh, though. Not Nora. At least, he didn't think so. Or was he really so incredibly obvious?

"You have very expressive eyes," Poppy said, as if she was reading his mind. "Why are you going to stop seeing her?"

Julian finally looked up into Poppy's face. She was still completely serene, logically considering the problem as if it didn't personally affect her at all. He wished he could do the same.

"She's in love with someone else."

"She told you?"

Julian considered the question for a moment. "Practically. The way she talks about him...I just know."

Poppy nodded. "Look, we went into this thing very quickly, and maybe it was too fast. I like you, though. So if you do figure out how to get over this girl, let me know. I'm not going to wait around, but I can see that you need some time to figure this out."

"Poppy, you are far too understanding."

"I know," she said. "I will still complain about you to my girlfriends and make you look terrible. Don't worry." Julian exhaled, possibly for the first time since Poppy had arrived at his flat. "You're sure you don't have a chance? If you tell her?" Poppy asked.

"It's complicated," Julian said.

"Isn't it always?" She kissed him on the cheek and headed for the door.

"You're wonderful, Poppy," he said. "If I wasn't such a..."

"Good luck," she said, not bothering to listen to the disparaging things he was about to say about himself, and then she was gone.

Julian was stunned. As far as break-ups went, it was probably one of the best. Something for the record books. Yet he couldn't help feeling incredibly stupid. "How am I supposed to know which one is the better option until I've done it?" Hugh had said the night before. Maybe Julian was making the biggest mistake of his life. Maybe he and Poppy would have been great together and he was ending it with her for what? So he could mope around a bit, pine for something that would never happen? So he could focus all of his energy on not thinking about someone else?

Even though Poppy had been incredibly cool, as always, Julian still felt like he had a rock in his stomach. He just needed to watch *The English Patient*, wallow in his misery, and maybe have a good cry.

CHAPTER NINETEEN

NORA'S EYES were still closed, but she was smiling. The soft lips on her bare back were traveling over her shoulder, up her neck and toward her mouth in a fluid stream of kisses. Fingers traced the skin on her belly. She was half-asleep, her brain weakly trying to make sense of what was happening. *Julian is kissing me!* The hand on her stomach started to slide down between her legs and a moan escaped from her lips. She turned toward him, dying to kiss him back, her fingers searching for the firm wall of his shoulders, but at the last moment she realized she didn't know where she was. She was almost fully awake and actively trying to figure out what was going on. Why on earth would she have thought she was in bed with Julian? That didn't make any sense. *Oh my God, Hugh?!*

"Good morning," a deep voice said into her hair.

She opened her eyes and remembered. Lachlan. Somehow, she'd left the bar and found him. She must have texted him when she'd stormed out on her own. She looked up at the ceiling and realized that they were in his flat, and she'd completed her mission. She'd had sex, gotten it out of her system; all should be right with the world.

"Morning," she said, racking her brain for details from the night before. The sex hadn't been bad from what she could recall. She may not have come, but she remembered both of them enjoying it. *What on earth would have made my brain think I was in bed with Julian?* Maybe she'd had a dream about him, a dream now lost to her subconscious and buried deep inside of her.

"That was really great," Lachlan said with a bit of the fake Italian creeping into his accent. She smiled a little and thought about telling Julian about it later. Even in bed the Amazing Lorenzo couldn't stop with the act! Except, was this the kind of thing she should tell Julian about? Why was she lying in bed with a magician and wondering about what to tell Julian?!

She sank back into the pillows as Lorenzo—or Lachlan rather—tried to kiss her again. She was starting to parse out the events of the evening before she'd ended up sleeping with the illusionist—dancing with Hugh, fighting with Darcy, running off when Julian tried to talk with her because he'd been there with Poppy, and something about that made her want to melt into a puddle.

"Shall we continue where we left off last night, love?" Lachlan whispered, his fingertips pressing into her thigh.

"Ummm..." Why had she been such an idiot? She'd known it was going to be hard to be so close to Hugh for so long, especially when she was drinking, but she'd thought she could hold herself together for *one freaking night*. Just because he'd made her knees wobbly when she was a teenager didn't mean he had to have that power over her anymore. She was an adult who had slept with other men! She'd had a one-night stand with a magician!

Except, apparently, Lachlan was thinking that this was more than a one-night stand, considering the fact that his tongue was licking her earlobe, which wasn't a bad sensation, but it also didn't feel quite right.

"I really should be getting out of here," she said. She didn't know why she was trying to brush him off and get out the door. This was what she had wanted, after all, and Lachlan was objectively sexy, if sometimes also ridiculous. She should have been grateful for the distraction, but instead she couldn't wait to get home and sulk, avoiding calls from her mother, who would try to get her to talk about everything that had happened in the last twenty-four hours, which Nora really did not want to do.

"Don't go," Lachlan groaned. He pushed her hair out of her face and stroked her cheek.

Nora exhaled. Lachlan was *fine.* He'd been nothing but perfectly nice, and he'd been there for her in a moment of crisis. But her thoughts were somewhere else entirely, on Darcy and Hugh and Julian…

She needed to get out of his apartment to think. The problem was that she didn't know where her clothes were or her purse or phone or anything that would be required to get out the door and into a cab to go home and wallow. The other problem was that Lachlan was kissing her again, his body pressing into hers, his hands sliding around her waist. Maybe one more romp would get the job done…

She kissed him back, arching her body into his, enjoying the press of his palms against her skin. His mouth trailed down to her neck, and the sound of his grunt was assured and possessive. She let herself relax, let her eyes close again. Why shouldn't she enjoy it? Why not have some fun, get some pleasure that came from someone she was actually allowed to want?

But then she started thinking about Jack the Ripper and dark alleys and old-timey lanterns. She wasn't sure where that had come from. Lachlan's hand was on her breast, but she was dwelling on cobblestones, sliding across the damp ground, grasping for something, *someone*, to hold her up. She pulled away suddenly, and his mouth traveled further down her torso. "Lachlan," she said, "I really do have to go," which was perhaps emotionally true even if she didn't have any other reason to leave. She knew she would be spending the day alone, thinking about Hugh and how she'd fucked up with Darcy, who she was starting to really adore, despite her gruffness. She'd been noticing that Darcy could also be vulnerable and hilarious, and Nora loved how little she cared what anyone thought, except that she *sometimes* seemed to care what Nora thought—and Anika obviously.

Lachlan finally sighed and rolled out of bed. He tossed some of her clothes at her from across the room on his way to the bathroom. She dressed quickly, once again regretting her choice of leather as she struggled with her jacket.

When she'd collected everything and started to find her way out the door, Lachlan pulled her in to kiss her again. "Promise me you'll come back soon," he said.

Nora tried not to visibly cringe. *This is exactly what you wanted, you big dummy,* she scolded herself. She didn't know why she felt so off. "It was fun." She pulled away from him. "Thanks a lot."

"What are you thanking me for?" He was clearly flexing his muscles while hugging her, even though he was trying to seem like he wasn't flexing. She was supposed to think that this was just how he hugged.

"I don't know," she said, laughing nervously. He pulled a rose bud from behind her ear and presented it ceremoniously.

"My lady," he said with a little bow.

Nora took the flower, but she wasn't sure what else to do. There was a moment of silence as she failed to think of something more to say to him, to explain why she was so out of sorts, but she couldn't find the words. There was no good explanation to offer this stranger.

"See ya," she said finally before rushing out the door and down the stairs.

When she got out on the street, Nora realized that she didn't even know what part of the city she was in. Lachlan had met her out at some bar near the venue after she texted him, and then he'd taken her to get Belgian waffles before going back to his place, so she hadn't even paid attention to where she ended up. She was lucky that he wasn't some kind of serial killer magician that made his victims "disappear" for real, even if that would be a really good movie.

Going home with a virtual stranger wasn't the type of thing that she usually did, for that very reason. Even when she'd met Hugh as a dumb nineteen-year-old, she'd met him at the bar several times before gallivanting off to his flat or to hotel suites. Actually, they'd met at the bar for a while until Julian had suggested to Hugh that Nora deserved a proper date instead of just being forced to hang around listening to the Pet Rockers play night after night.

Nora smiled absently at the thought. Then she realized that she should probably figure out where the hell she was and how she was going to get home. She pulled up the GPS on her phone and discovered that she was in fucking Kensington, which was so fancy and also seemed very far away from the tiny flat in what Darcy called their "dodgy" part of the city. It was an especially beautiful morning, with the sun shining through the bright green trees, the classic white stucco architecture gleaming in the light. Even the people on the sidewalk looked elegant in their pastel colors and cute little handbags. She realized that she hadn't even looked at herself in the mirror before bolting out Lachlan's front door. It was going to be a long Tube ride home. She found the nearest station so she could start walking in the right direction before debating about calling Julian.

She didn't know why calling Julian was a debate, exactly, except for the weight of the guilt of using him for work. They were real friends now, she felt sure of it. He had been there for her so many times already when she had needed him.

But he also had Poppy. Nora couldn't stop thinking about the two of them the night before, how Julian hadn't even registered that Nora was there because he was so wrapped up in his girlfriend. He probably didn't care all that much about the fact that Nora was on a walk-of-shame in the middle of Kensington. He was probably having breakfast with Poppy at that very moment. And Hugh was having breakfast with Rose, and Darcy was having breakfast with herself probably, but she most likely considered that much preferable to hanging out with Nora, the homewrecker. *Stupid people and their stupid English breakfasts.* None of that stopped Nora from really wanting to have someone around while she tried to figure out her life and how she was going to make up with Darcy. It also didn't stop her from really wanting to talk to Julian.

Finally, she pulled up his contact on her phone, hit "call," and listened to the ringing on the line, but he didn't answer. Nora couldn't explain the overwhelming disappointment that she felt. For some reason, just the thought of talking to him had made her feel better, even while everything else was an utter disaster.

For days, she called and texted Julian. For days, he didn't answer and declined her invitations. Nora wasn't sure what she had done. She was just starting to panic, to wonder how she could have screwed everything up so royally, when she got the call from her mother.

Suddenly, all of Nora's little London dramas—dancing with Hugh, Darcy's cold shoulder, Julian's absence—faded to a buzzing background noise in her brain. In an instant, the world narrowed to focus on that phone call from Kathleen Shrapsan; everything revolved around the tinny voice echoing from the phone speaker. As Nora began to comprehend the full meaning of what her mother was saying, the pulse at her temple throbbed. Her blood went cold. She had fucked up the biggest thing of all, just as she'd feared, and now she needed to go home.

CHAPTER TWENTY

NORA CALLED HIM, but he didn't answer. She didn't leave a voicemail, and he never returned the call. The next day she texted, asking if he might want to go for drinks at a newly renovated hotel bar. He pondered for over an hour before he sent a response:

"Sorry, already have plans and won't make it."

It was short and sweet, and he'd put more effort into that message than any other text he'd sent in his life. He spent the evening at home, alone, watching the telly and pacing in front of his couch.

He convinced himself that it was a good start. He needed to get over her, and already he was declining plans and starting that painful process. The problem was that he didn't even feel like he could purge himself in the normal way—by going out and getting pissed with his mates—because he was also avoiding Hugh. It wasn't Hugh's fault, of course. He was completely oblivious. However, that didn't mean that Julian could just go out to the pub with him and act like he wasn't in pain—a pain that was caused, in part, by the fact that Hugh was the better, more desirable man. So he was stuck with bottled beer and streaming *Sopranos* and a short visit from his father, who asked him what was wrong but was also willing to accept Julian's lie that everything was okay for now.

Despite his mounds of "progress," when he found himself aimlessly walking the streets a day later, Julian was dangerously close to approaching Nora's flat just to pop in and see her. It seemed that he hadn't been thinking about her any less, and his muscle memory still moved him to be near her home when he wasn't concentrating on actively avoiding her altogether.

She texted again the next day:

"Want to join me at a tea house in Kensington?"

Somehow, he declined her invitation again. He didn't even give an excuse. He could not fathom why she would continue to invite him on these outings and excursions when he had nothing to offer, no meaningful insights or helpful tidbits. In the beginning, she'd pumped him for information about Hugh, but even that seemed to have fallen by the wayside while they instead spent time getting to know each other. Still, he couldn't figure out why it had been him. Surely she could have found a willing companion anywhere.

"I hope to see you soon," she sent. "And I hope you know, I'd like to see you even if we aren't out doing my research."

Julian smiled when he read it. She wanted to see him. Then he caught himself. *I'm not supposed to be happy about this. I'm supposed to move on with my life.* He was not going to see her. He didn't respond to the message, but he also couldn't stop thinking about it, sitting there in his inbox, waiting for him to say something.

It wasn't Nora's fault that he was harboring an unrequited love, and she was still obsessed with his mate. If she really cared about seeing him, in this city where she had no family and knew so few people, how could he just stop talking to her without even giving her some kind of explanation? What if she thought she'd done something wrong? How could he hurt her like that?

Over the course of the next day—day five since he had last seen her, not that he was counting—he convinced himself that he needed closure, to see her one last time before he gave her up entirely. He didn't know why, exactly, or what he was planning to say that would magically allow him to let go of her, but he felt he deserved one final encounter to say goodbye. He'd come up with something like work or whatever the lads said when they needed an excuse to get some space from their girls. He wouldn't be dramatic about it. He wouldn't even tell her that he would never see her again, but he would know the whole time that it was the last.

He didn't bother texting or calling first, just showed up at her flat and figured he would pop in. That way, she wouldn't try to convince him to go on some long, drawn-out adventure that would only make things harder.

"Hello?" she said on the intercom when he buzzed her flat. Her voice sounded strange and shaky.

"Umm, it's Julian." He didn't know what he was doing. He should have turned around and run. Instead, she let him into the building without saying anything, and he found himself walking through the entryway and up the stairs.

As soon as she opened the door, he could tell that something was very wrong. Her eyes were bare and swollen, her nose was an almost Rudolph shade of red, and her hair was crazier than Julian had ever seen before. "What's going on?" he asked before even walking through the doorway. She jumped into his arms and held onto him for a moment before pulling him into the flat. "Nora, what is it?" he said again.

He had no idea what to think. Was she giving into her despair about Hugh getting married? Was she homesick? Did she have a broken bone? Had the book's publication been canceled?

Nora sank into her sofa, and Julian realized that he was seeing the inside of her flat for the first time. Suddenly, he could observe how she lived when she was entirely alone and without any pretense; he could peek into her personal life. He noticed the thick homemade fleece blanket covered in hearts that was draped across the furniture, and Julian had a sense of someone far away who had made it for her, someone crafty who loved her immensely. He noticed the Cadbury chocolate wrappers on the side table and the overflowing bookshelf against the wall. How had she collected so many books already? Surely she hadn't brought them all with her to London.

He could tell that she was trying hard not to cry, trying so hard, in fact, that she still hadn't allowed herself to speak. He could see the pursed lips and deep breaths meant to keep the tears from escaping her eyes, and he didn't know where to move or if he should sit beside her. Then, upon closer inspection, he realized that there was a half-full suitcase in the hall that must have led into her bedroom. There were clothes on the floor around it as well. Had she been packing?

"It's my mom," she said finally, trying to keep her voice steady. "She was in remission after her breast cancer, but they found something. It looks like the cancer is back. And she's at risk for something else too. Something from the medication. I didn't even understand it all." Her last word cracked with emotion, and Julian rushed to sit beside her after all.

"I'm so sorry," he said. He wished he had something helpful to say or some way to make it the slightest bit better.

"I have to go back. I don't know how long or what will happen, but I'm trying to leave on the next plane I can get on. I haven't even talked to Darcy yet, but I can do some editing from home, I guess."

"Don't even worry about that," Julian said. He felt awful. He knew that for Nora this was possibly the very worst thing that could happen, and he wished so badly that he could make it go away, that they could laugh together over serial killers and overkill magicians. He intertwined his fingers with hers and held on tight.

She couldn't hold the tears back any longer then. "I'm glad to see you," she said through them. "Before I leave. I have to finish packing, but I..."

"What airline? I'll get you there."

She looked at him blankly, her face bright pink. "Oh, God, I don't even remember. I have to check the ticket." She fumbled around for her phone.

"And you have your passport?" he asked.

She tried to swallow a sob. "I don't know where it is."

He put a hand on her shoulder. "Don't worry," he said. "Finish packing your suitcase, and I'll help you look. Then we'll get you to the airport. Let me see your ticket."

As he scrolled through her confirmation email and flight details, then tried to help her find her passport and her backpack, he started to wonder how she was going to make it there on her own. She was pulling back her hair and stuffing more clothes into her bag when he noticed she'd only put on one shoe. After a bit of searching, they found the other one buried in her carry-on. How was she going to get safely through airport security?

Julian was repacking her carry-on bag when Nora walked into the kitchen, looking around frantically until she finally held out her hands in defeat. "I forgot what I was even looking for," she said.

Julian paced back and forth, trying not to seem too frantic while he figured out his next move. There had to be something else he could do, some other way he could help her. God, she was barely in a state to pack on her own, much less fly halfway across the world. If he could just buy a ticket to help her get back to her gate, at least he could be sure she wasn't wandering aimlessly around the airport, her eyes too blurry to even read the departures board. But it would need to be an international ticket.

He remembered Dev owed him a favor.

"It's okay." Julian took a step toward Nora but stopped short of wrapping her in his arms again. "We have time. We can make a list of what you need."

He sat Nora at her little kitchen table and got her something to drink. He made a quick call before sitting beside her with pen and paper, then wrote a checklist of everything she might need—chargers and socks and passport. He crossed off the things he knew he'd already packed, before showing her the list. She was staring into the distance without reacting to much of anything, but she silently scanned what Julian had written and nodded.

"I'll be right back." Julian touched her shoulder, and Nora looked confused but didn't say anything.

He jogged down to meet Dev right outside the door to her building. "Didn't think I'd be so happy to know you have a key to my flat," Julian said.

Dev looked baffled, but he handed over the passport. "Care to tell me what's going on here?"

"Too much to explain at the moment and might sound a bit crazy if I did."

"Which is perhaps a good reason to get a second opinion about whatever it is you're doing." Dev raised his eyebrows, waiting for an explanation.

"No need to worry." Julian slapped his friend on the back. "I'm the level-headed one, right? I wouldn't do anything that might be cause for concern."

"And yet, here I am showing up with your passport at a strange residential building in the middle of the afternoon."

Julian sighed. What reason could he possibly give for begging his mate to drop everything and retrieve a passport? What could he say that would make any of this seem unremarkable? "Uh, doing a bit of paperwork?" It didn't sound remotely true. Julian was a terrible liar.

Dev shook his head.

"Look, I'll tell you everything soon, yeah? I just need to be off right now."

Dev continued to eye him warily. "Are you in danger?"

Julian huffed out a laugh. "No, mate. Truly. Thank you for your help." He turned and rushed back inside.

Nora and Julian took a silent car ride to the airport. Nora stared out the window the whole time, and Julian wasn't sure if she even blinked. Her eyes were wide and nervous, her face splotchy from crying. She gasped when they arrived and she saw herself on an overhead security camera. "I look terrifying," she whispered.

The walk through the first stretch of airport was as silent as the car, though Julian was searching his brain for a way to talk to her. There was nothing good to say, and she was so deep in her own head, he wasn't even sure she would hear him if he tried.

Nora paused at the start of the security checkpoint, biting her lip. "Can you go through?" she asked, and it felt like the first thing she'd said to him in hours.

"If you'd like. I—uh—got a ticket. Just to see you to your gate."

Her face softened as she stared at him. He supposed she might protest for a moment, but then she turned to get in line, and he followed. He thought perhaps she couldn't imagine being alone just as much as he couldn't imagine leaving her.

After she walked through the passenger scanner, she kept right on going, not even stopping to wait for her bag to come down the conveyor belt or to put on her shoes. She wandered toward the center of the airport, clueless to the people giving her funny looks on either side, not even seeming to hear Julian call her name for the first few times.

"Your bags," he said when he finally got up to her, and she looked surprised that she even had bags to carry. "I'll get them. Just wait here."

Julian wasn't sure if it was right at that moment or when Nora started to cry at the gate or when she couldn't find her ticket on her phone again that he realized he couldn't leave her. She couldn't be on an eight-hour flight and then a three-hour bus ride alone thinking about her worst fears. She could barely even lift her bag out of the boot or locate her wallet, so how was she going to make it to a little city in New York without any support? He'd already purchased a bloody ticket. Not a cheap ticket to any international destination, but a ticket on her flight to New York. It was as if something inside of him had already known. It had never really been a choice. It didn't matter that he had gone to her flat with the intention of secretly letting go of her and never seeing her again. That had become irrelevant the moment she'd opened the door in such a state.

"Nora." He tried to get her attention as the airline made an announcement over the intercom. Her flight was boarding.

Slowly, she turned her head to look up at him, her eyes almost blank.

"I could—er. That is, I could come with you. If you wanted. I don't have to be back for a while, and you might be able to—" He was rambling. How did one handle this situation, anyway? He never would have imagined he might do this, but now it was happening. Now it seemed there was no other way.

Something that he thought might be relief flooded her face, and she took his hand in hers and squeezed.

Yes, that was all he needed. He was going with her to America.

CHAPTER TWENTY-ONE

NORA COULDN'T BE positive that she had taken a single breath since she'd left England. She felt like everything had stopped in an instant, including her basic human functions, and she wasn't entirely sure how she'd made it from London to New York City to Binghamton to room 243D at the medical center, but somehow she had. When she saw her mother lying in a bed, entranced by a page of *People* magazine, that's when she finally remembered to breathe again.

Her mother smiled when she saw Nora standing there.

"Hey, Mama," Nora exhaled.

"It's good to see your face in person," Kathleen said. "Don't look so worried. Come on, get over here."

Nora squished against her in the bed, their whole bodies aligned. "What's going on? What happened? What did the doctor say?" It felt good to feel her mother's solid form after she'd just been communicating with Kathleen's talking head on a screen for so many weeks. It made Nora feel solid too, in a way she hadn't for hours.

"Calm down. It's alright. I just should have chopped them off to begin with, I guess." Kathleen rested her head against her daughter's shoulder.

"What do you mean?" Even though her mother's tone was playful, Nora couldn't match her mood. She was still recovering from hours of traveling and panicking and not knowing what was happening back at home while she wasn't there to help.

"They're going to do a double mastectomy. I would have been able to go home until it's time for the surgery, but I had a bad reaction to something they put me on, and my blood pressure was through the roof. But hopefully this will take care of the situation, and I'll be out on the dating market again in no time."

"Mom," Nora said seriously. Her brain still felt fuzzy, and she couldn't entirely comprehend everything, despite how intensely she wanted to know every detail of her mother's current medical situation. How did people ever make sense of this stuff when they were going through it?

"I'm okay, honey. But say goodbye to the tits that fed you your first meal."

"Oh God, thanks for bringing that up."

"It needed to be said." Kathleen smiled, and Nora looked up at her. She wasn't sure how this woman that created and raised her had kept her humor and charm throughout everything. Here, in the face of another surgery, in the face of having a part of herself removed entirely, she was still joking around. "Who needs nipples anyway?" Her mother laughed.

Nora wanted to laugh along with her, and she was relieved that her mother already had a plan of action and a surgery time set, but she still felt so guilty for being gone, for not being able to take her to the hospital and hold her hand. Who was feeding Bebe? Who was bringing her non-hospital food and fresh pairs of pants and brushing her hair? How could Nora not have been there or known? If she'd been around, maybe she would have seen signs of it, maybe she would have noticed something from before, something that told her it was like last time.

"How long have you known that the cancer was back, Mom?" Nora eyed her suspiciously.

"I'm okay—"

"How long?"

"I found out at a screening a couple of weeks ago, but—"

"Oh my God."

"But I didn't want you to worry about me. I'm handling it."

"You ended up in the hospital!"

"Yes, and I only told you about it because I knew you would kill me yourself if you found out."

Nora wanted to cry again. She'd been so wrapped up in herself, so selfish, she hadn't even realized what was going on. How could she have missed this? How could she have abandoned her favorite person?

"I'm a big girl," her mother said, looking at Nora pointedly, like she knew everything she was thinking. "And I'm proud of you for getting out there and finding what you want in life. And you came right here, like the best daughter in the world, and you'll visit for a while, and then you'll go right back. That's what I want for you. Anyway, you have to update me on the drama with Hugh and all your friends in London. How is Darcy? And Julian?"

Oh shit, Julian. Nora had forgotten about him ever since they'd arrived at the medical center, and she'd run straight to her mother's bedside. She didn't even know where he was.

"What?" Kathleen asked. "What's wrong?"

"Julian," Nora said. "I guess I should find him. He's here somewhere."

Her mother's eyes went wide. "Pardon me," she said. "Could you say that again? Julian is here? In America? In New York?"

Nora sighed. She hadn't thought about how this might look or the fact that she had no explanation. She'd barely thought about the extraordinary fact that Julian had gotten on the plane with her until that moment. If she had thought on it enough to realize how much she needed him at the airport, she might have begged, might have bought his ticket herself, might have thrown herself on his mercy and pleaded for his help. But he'd just done it without her asking. "He came over to my place while I was packing, and I told him everything, and I was such a mess, and somehow he ended up on the plane."

"Nora! You're telling me you packed a young British man in your luggage? What does this mean?"

"What do you mean 'what does it mean'?" Nora watched her mom's incredulous face and knew she didn't have any kind of satisfactory account of what had occurred at the airport.

"You can't just bring strange men back home with you from another country without it meaning something!" Kathleen gasped. "Bring him in here. I want to meet him."

"Mom, it's not—he's just—" Nora stammered. "We're friends. And he knew I needed someone." That made perfect sense, right?

"Good friend," her mother said suggestively. She clearly didn't believe a word of it.

Nora hadn't had the time to wonder at all what it meant that Julian had hopped on a plane to New York with her in the middle of the day without even packing anything. She hadn't even had time to be surprised that he'd done it. *Why had he done it?* And now she'd lost him completely. "I guess I should go see where he is. You're sure you want me to bring him in? We could just hang out a while, just the two of us."

"Sorry, babe, but if this dude just flew across the country to meet me, then I would say that I'm ready for you to bring him in right now."

———

Nora found him in a waiting room in the lobby, sipping from a can of soda. He jumped out of his seat when he saw her. He looked terribly worried. Nora smiled to let him know that everything was okay, or at least, her mom was doing all right at the moment.

"Hi," she said. "Sorry about that. I kind of lost my head there." By "there" she meant for the past ten or so hours, so it was perhaps an understatement and a completely inadequate apology.

"It's not a problem. I thought I would just give you two some time." He tugged nervously at one of his shirt sleeves.

"She's okay," Nora said. "For now, I mean, she has to get her breasts cut off."

"Oh."

"Yeah, but she's awake and acting like her normal self." Nora paused for a moment. Even though he'd been in the car and the plane and the bus and the cab, she hadn't really thought about the fact that Julian was really here with her in her hometown until she saw him standing in his wrinkled clothes in the hospital lobby. He'd just been beside her the whole time, and it had made sense. In fact, it had been the only thing that made any sense at all until she really stopped to consider it the tiniest bit. "Julian?" she said.

"Yes?"

"I can't believe you're here. I mean, I don't even know how to thank you for everything." For a split second, Nora wondered what she must look like to him, after all the crying and freaking out. She was still wearing sweats, and it had been far too long since her hair had been washed. And yet, his face was warm and soft. He looked at her like there was nothing wrong, like she wasn't a mess at all, like this was all completely normal.

"After everything at your flat I just couldn't leave you like that," he said. "I couldn't let you come all this way alone."

Nora realized that she'd stopped breathing again, for a different reason this time. "Well, anyway. You can come on up now," she said. "She wants to meet you."

Nora couldn't tell if Julian was nervous as they made their way to room 243D. She supposed that he didn't really have any reason to be. He was just meeting a friend's mom for the first time. However, it was in a hospital, after he had flown across the ocean without packing, and he was in a totally new place without even having the opportunity to use a private bathroom since they'd left London. It was unusual, to say the least.

She glanced over at him in the elevator, still astounded that this was even happening, that he had been kind enough to come all this way with her. She felt exhausted and relieved and nervous and terrified. She needed a nap and food and to know that her mother was going to be okay.

"Ahhh Julian," Kathleen said when they walked into the room. It was as if she already knew a million secrets about him.

"Nice to meet you, Mrs. Shrapsan," he said.

"Oh God, call me Kathleen," she said. "Especially if you're going to do it in that British accent."

"Nice to meet you, Kathleen," Julian said, and Nora's mother looked at her sharply, like she wanted to make sure that Nora realized this guy had a mouth that made adorable sounds.

"Come, sit. Tell me everything about yourself."

"What would you like to know?" Julian asked sheepishly. He did move closer though, and he smiled as if he didn't entirely mind that he'd just flown across the world to be interrogated by a cancer patient in her hospital bed.

Nora sat on the edge of her mother's bed and watched the two of them talking. Kathleen had met all of her boyfriends, with the exception of Hugh, and Nora was always nervous because she knew her mother could find the one major flaw that'd been eating at Nora lately, or her mother would somehow unearth some terrible secret—the boyfriend loved *Nickleback* or preferred frozen yogurt to ice cream or never wore socks with his shoes, which was a particular trait of Brandon's. She would ask them question after question, and they would smile politely but eye Nora with a sense of unease, and Nora felt uneasy as well, while also secretly dying to know how they would respond to everything and silently acknowledging that they also needed to end up adoring her mother, despite the interrogation.

Except Julian wasn't her boyfriend, and there was no reason she should be nervous.

"Let's start with this," her mom said. "What kind of man jumps on a plane and flies to America with a frantic woman?"

Julian gave Nora the exact same terrified look that she'd seen so many times before, like he wasn't sure if there was a right answer to that question.

"I—uh. Well, she didn't know where her passport was," he said. "Or what airline she needed to go to." He just barely smiled at that. "I didn't think I could leave her to fend for herself. Who knows where she might have ended up?"

"She could have flown entirely the wrong direction and been in Dubai without realizing," Kathleen said.

Julian laughed. "I wouldn't have put it past her. And I'm on holiday from teaching now, anyway. I should have planned a trip myself."

Her mother smiled. "Well thank you for taking care of my girl." Nora jerked her head. That was too easy, barely an interrogation at all, except, again, Julian *wasn't* a boyfriend. It *should* be easy.

Julian looked like he didn't know what to say. "Can I ask how you're feeling?"

"I'm doing quite well, all things considered. Thank you for asking." Kathleen put her chin in her hand with a little grin. "Now, can I ask if you would please say the following words? Schedule, aluminum, and garage."

Julian laughed. "*Mother*," Nora scolded, but she was laughing again too.

Nora watched as Julian skillfully handled her mother's remaining questions, as he told her about his father and about teaching and about the time that Nora had gone with him to say goodbye to his dog. Nora hadn't even remembered that story until he started telling it. She didn't realize it was something he would think about all these years later.

"And is there someone special back in London?" Kathleen asked after she'd gotten him talking for a while. And people thought Nora was nosy!

For a second, Nora was on the edge of her seat, overly interested in how Julian would respond to the question, but then she remembered, yes, there was someone special. Poppy. Somehow, Nora had forgotten that Poppy existed, and for some reason she couldn't quite understand, the idea of Poppy made it feel like someone had dropped a stone inside her throat and it was slowly sinking to the bottom of her abdomen.

They were interrupted, however, when a nurse walked in to check Kathleen's vitals. "You need to get some rest, lady," the nurse, Georgia, said to her very disobedient patient. "It's getting late, you know."

"Sorry," Julian said. "I guess I got carried away talking about myself, but you made me do it, Kathleen."

"And I don't regret a minute of it," she said, grinning. "But I guess, just this once, I'll listen to Georgia and get some rest."

Georgia snorted. "There's a first time for everything, I guess."

"Georgia, this is my daughter, Nora, and her lovely British friend, Julian. They've just come from London to see me. Haven't even showered in ages."

"You should be very proud," Georgia said.

"Do you need anything, Mom?" Nora asked. "Do you want me to get anything from home for you? Or do you want food? Where's Bebe?"

Kathleen thought for a moment. "There's some stuff I might have you bring tomorrow, but I'm fine for now. Bebe's at the neighbor's, probably having the time of her life torturing their Pomeranian. Are you going to go home now?"

"I didn't know if we should get a hotel," Nora said, biting her lip.

Julian jumped in quickly. "If you want to stay at your house, I'm fine to get a hotel room."

"Julian, don't be ridiculous," Kathleen said. "Why would you do that? You and Nora take my car to the house and stay there. Make yourself at home. You flew across the Atlantic, for goodness sake. You need a nice rest."

Nora didn't know what to say. She didn't want to protest, and she also didn't want to bring up the idea of Poppy or the fact that it might be weird to take Julian to her childhood home. They had more than one bedroom and more than one bathroom. It would actually be more space than if they'd shared adjoining hotel rooms or something like that. Still, Julian would be in her house. He would see where she grew up. They would spend the night together, just the two of them, alone.

Julian was watching her intently, waiting to see what she would say. "Well, I guess that would be okay, if it's alright with you," she said.

"It's alright with me," Julian said, and Nora felt the stone in her stomach shift.

CHAPTER TWENTY-TWO

THROUGHOUT THE ENTIRE trip to upstate New York, Julian wasn't sure that Nora even fully realized he was there. She kept thanking him for every little thing—for carrying her bag, for buying her a bottle of water, for getting her a blanket on the plane, but she was in a trance—almost like she didn't really understand what was happening. On the flight, she'd put a movie on the little screen in front of her, but she hadn't watched it. Sometimes, he could see the tears on her cheeks, but she turned her face away from him. She held his hand, but he didn't say anything about it. He didn't even wonder what it meant, because he knew that she wasn't quite aware of anything; she could have been holding the hand of a random stranger on the plane and may not have even noticed. In fact, he was almost sure that was exactly what would have happened if he hadn't been there.

It wasn't until they were in her mother's car driving to the house that Nora seemed to become fully conscious, to be herself again. He was close to asking her if she thought that he was totally insane for hopping on a plane with her. He was desperate to know her feelings about it, but even when she thought to ask why he'd come, she had only thanked him once again without mentioning whether or not she thought he might be completely ridiculous. Despite the vast number of times he had told himself to give up all hope, there was still a glimmer of something that wouldn't die out inside of him. It was something that was catching fire since he found out he'd be going to her childhood home.

Nora's natural state was a persistent cheerfulness that Julian had never seen in anyone else before, so even though he could tell that she was still worried about her mother, she was quick to come to life again, to make jokes, and to laugh. It seemed it was impossible to keep Nora from laughing for very long; even when she was sad, she was quick to allow herself to be taken over by a happy thought, by some pop ballad on the car radio, or by the idea of Julian's embarrassment at all of her mother's questions.

"Thanks for being such a good sport," Nora said. "Though you might have turned pink during the part where she asked about your first kiss."

Julian tried not to blush again, but he wasn't sure how to control it. "I wasn't expecting that to come up," he said. "I hope I didn't disappoint her."

"Are you kidding? Your first kiss was on a balcony over a beach in Portugal! She lives for stories like that!"

"It was rather memorable," Julian said, and he looked over at Nora, watched her with her hands on the wheel, checking the mirror, driving through town on the wrong side of the street. "Who was your first kiss?" he asked. He watched the dark road spreading out in front of them, the headlights beaming as they rounded sharp curves.

"Aaron Cross in third grade," she said. "Very boring. He smacked his lips into mine right before gym class. I was so surprised I didn't even say anything, and we never talked about it again."

"He wasn't the great love of your life then?" Julian said, smirking.

Nora shrugged. "Maybe he was, and I missed my chance. I should look him up. What if he's super rich and good looking now? I wonder if he's on social media." She paused for a moment. "Are you online? Is Hugh? I tried to search for you a few years back. I remember Hugh was a total ghost when I first met him, but I thought maybe with the band…"

Julian wiggled in his seat, trying to adjust the strap of the seat belt. It was suddenly too tight, straining against his chest. "The band has a couple pages. An Instagram and that kind of thing. But Hugh doesn't have anything personal. You know how he is with technology."

As he said it, Julian realized how right he was—Nora did know. She'd known Hugh so well; she'd been in love with him. They had so much history...

"Well," Nora said, "Let's hope Aaron Cross is a lot hipper than you guys or I'll never find him."

When they pulled into the driveway of the gray Victorian home with a big yard and at least five birdfeeders and three windchimes, Julian didn't have a hard time imagining Nora or Kathleen inhabiting the place. When they walked into the foyer, he immediately inhaled the scent of pine, old books, and laundry. There were a few baskets of folded clothes next to the sofa and a stack of papers on the coffee table. There were photographs and trinkets on the mantle—young Nora in a witch costume, a porcelain bear holding a surfboard that said *Myrtle Beach 2005.*

"Welcome," Nora said. "I'll show you where you can take your, um, I guess you can call it luggage." She laughed. They'd stopped off at a Walmart, Julian's first time in the superstore, and he'd picked up a toothbrush, some underwear, a couple new shirts, and a pair of pants. He held everything in a plastic bag, a collection of every single item in America that belonged to him.

Nora took him to a little bedroom off the hall that she called the guest room. It *did* have a bed, but it looked more like an office where Kathleen had a bed dumped in the middle, just in case. There was a desk stacked with books so high, Julian thought they might topple and shelves that were full of folders and files. Julian set his plastic bag on the bed.

"Pretty fancy, huh?" Nora said.

"Quite comfortable," Julian said.

She showed him the kitchen and the dining room. He stood there trying to help while she put away some random food she'd bought at the Walmart, a place that he didn't realize held food while also stocking tires and furniture. Then they went back to the living room and sat on the sofa. Nora leaned back into the pillows looking utterly at ease. He could tell she was at home here. She *was* home.

While he waited for Nora to finish showering, he started chopping vegetables and getting ready to make pasta. When she came out to the kitchen, her hair was still wet and she was wearing *Beauty and the Beast* pajamas. "I forgot to bring anything to sleep in," she said. "These were in my room."

"You look great," he said, and she stuck out her tongue like a kid.

Instead of eating at the dining table, they sat cross-legged on the floor in the living room, slurping up noodles and telling each other stories.

"I forgot about Ralphie," Nora said. "About going to the vet when you had to put him down. I hadn't thought of that in so long until you told my mom about it."

"I remember it well," Julian replied. "You helped me quite a lot actually."

"So that's why you came with me, huh?" Nora smirked. "I went to the vet for you, you go to the hospital with me. Is that how it works?"

"I figured your mum and my dog are about equal territory," he said.

Nora was grinning, but then she stopped suddenly. She looked at him hard, without moving. Julian didn't know what to do with her gaze on him like that. He wasn't sure where to look.

"Julian," she said, and he almost closed his eyes to take in the soft sound of his name on her lips. "I don't know what I would have done without you today or yesterday or whatever day it was that we left. I really —I just—I don't know what to say."

Julian didn't know how to reply either, so he just watched her in the dim lamplight, sitting on the carpet in her *Beauty and the Beast* pajamas, her wet hair pressed against her face. He wanted to kiss her so badly. He wanted to grab onto her and hold her against his chest, to press his face into her hair until it was soaking wet as well. He wouldn't do it, though. He was an idiot who had gone to tell the woman he loved goodbye, only to make everything much, much worse.

He wanted to stay in that room forever. He did not want to go back to London, to go out for pints with Hugh on a Friday and pretend that he'd never sat on the living room floor with Nora, wanting to kiss her so badly that something hurt in his limbs because he couldn't do it.

"You have marinara sauce all over your chin," he said. She really might want to invest in some adult bibs.

She rubbed her face with the back of her hand. "You aren't going to respond to my heartfelt outpouring of gratitude?"

He rubbed his palm against the back of his neck. At least she didn't appear to believe he was ridiculous. "Um. You're welcome?" he said.

"Oh God, we haven't looked up flights or anything for you. Are you wanting to leave soon or...? When do you think you'll go back?"

Julian hadn't even considered the idea of getting back on a plane to London, of leaving without her. "I'm here now," he said. "I might as well stay for a bit if you'll have me." It was most likely another terrible, impulsive idea, but he was too tired to think of traveling again, too exhausted from fighting every part of himself that wanted to be next to her all of the time.

On the way back from brushing her teeth, Nora peeked her head into Julian's bedroom. He was sitting on the edge of the bed going through the plastic bags of things he'd bought, trying to decide what to wear to bed.

"Is there anything I can get you?" Nora asked.

"I think I'm all set," he said.

"I guess we'll finally get some rest then."

He didn't want her to go, so he tried to think up a bit of conversation. "Did you find out what your mum wants us to take her tomorrow? Does she have a favorite meal or something we can deliver?"

Nora walked into the room so she was standing right in front of him. Her hair had air-dried, and it was sprawling in curls around her face. "She'll probably be craving Dino's," she said. "That's her favorite diner."

"I'll be able to try some American cuisine then," Julian said.

Nora laughed. "I know I already told you, but thank you again, Julian. I don't know if you realize what it means to me that you came all this way..."

He was looking up at her in such a way that the light shining behind her head lit her up like a work of art. It was so much better that she was real, though, not a painting but a flesh and blood human standing in front of him. "I—uh—well there was nothing else to do. I had to make sure you were going to be okay."

She hit him playfully on the arm. "You keep saying that, but you didn't have to. It's actually kind of amazing."

Without thinking, he clasped the hand she'd pressed against his shoulder before she could draw it back entirely. She was still looking down at him with a curious look, and he felt something catch in his throat. He looked at the hand he was holding—her hand—and then back at her face. He wasn't sure what he was doing or how to explain himself, but he couldn't seem to let the hand drop back into the space between them. He couldn't open his fingers to let go, and a second, maybe two, had already passed, and she must be wondering what was wrong with him, why he was acting so strangely, what he could possibly be thinking.

But suddenly, Nora was leaning further over him rather than pulling away. Almost in slow motion, she bent her head toward his face, and then she was closing her eyes and hesitating only for a moment before putting her lips to his, her free hand pressing into his hair at the back of his head, her body leaning into him against the edge of the bed.

For a horrible second, Julian thought he must have already fallen asleep, that he was so exhausted from the past twenty-four hours that he'd already dropped into an intense REM cycle that was allowing him to have the thing he most wanted. And yet, when she grasped his hair and pressed herself into him even more, he could tell that she was solid. It was real. Nora was kissing him.

CHAPTER TWENTY-THREE

NORA PULLED AWAY QUICKLY. *Oh fuck.* She'd really screwed everything up now. What the hell had she been thinking, kissing Julian? It was possibly one of the dumbest and most impulsive things she'd done since she was nineteen and streaking through the bar in the middle of the night. But the way he'd gripped her hand and stared up at her, the way he hadn't let go, it felt...monumental. She'd been trying to fight her attraction to him for a while now, and in that instant, she just couldn't do it anymore. She didn't want to fight it. It still didn't excuse the fact that she'd just started kissing him out of the blue without any true indication that he was remotely interested in her. He'd come halfway across the world when she needed him, though, and maybe her mother was right, maybe that did mean something. Or maybe it didn't. Nora turned away and pressed her lips together, lips she had used to kiss Julian. *Like an idiot.*

But he was still holding her hand. He still hadn't let go. And when Nora got up the courage to look at his face again, he looked serious, entirely in earnest, and in an instant he pulled her back into him and started kissing her even more fiercely. The only thought in her brain wasn't really a thought at all—it was more like the sound of a blaring trumpet or a whole freaking horn section playing noisily in her head. Julian wrapped his arms around her and leaned back onto the bed, and she fell forward on top of him without breaking the kiss, without letting go for a moment. They both inched backward on the mattress, their entire bodies entangled. She couldn't breathe, but she didn't care. She didn't want to stop for a breath. She didn't want to risk a single second where they would pause to think about anything else in the world.

Slowly, she slid her hands under his shirt, wanting to feel everything, to map out every place where they were touching. He was warm and firm, and Nora realized she hadn't spent enough time thinking about what was underneath his clothing, and now she might not be able to think of anything else. His skin was so smooth, but she could feel his muscle tone too, the way the hard plane of his body pressed into hers. Perhaps what was even better than touching him, though, was the way he caressed her. His fingers moved through her hair first, before they ran down her back, and then his hands were on her waist. She shivered slightly, pleasure and excitement rolling through her. He pulled back to give her a questioning look, and she nodded. The trumpets in her head picked up the tune, even louder than before, as he deftly pulled her shirt over her head.

She remembered that it was her *Beauty and the Beast* shirt, and she was probably wearing the least sexy pajamas imaginable, or now, only half-wearing. She'd already taken off her bra earlier, sick of the wires that had been digging into her for far too long, and so she was topless. Soon she felt the soft, overwhelming touch of his thumb brushing against her nipple, and her whole body almost involuntarily arched itself toward him even further. She tugged his shirt over his head as well, and then everything seemed to take on a blurry, warm quality of skin on skin, lips all over her neck. She gasped, amazed at the feeling of it. For so long, she'd remembered her first time with Hugh, how incredible every instant had been. But the real-life Julian was so much better than anything she kept locked in her imagination about any man before him.

Weeks earlier she had wondered, just for an instant, what it would be like to kiss him. The thought hadn't entirely gone away, but instead had taken hold somewhere in her mind, waiting. Now, she could feel a hard part of him pressing between her legs, making her ache even more to know what it would be not just to kiss him, but to feel every inch of him, to have him inside of her. The shock and elation of the thought sent an excited jolt through her body, but it also cleared the haze that had made everything else go away. She broke the kiss and took a breath.

"What about Poppy?" she asked, suddenly aware that there were other people somewhere in the world, that there would be other days and nights after this one.

"What?" he said, like he'd forgotten the name entirely. "I guess I never mentioned it. It's over with Poppy."

She toppled off of him onto the other side of the bed, confused and suddenly self-conscious about the nakedness of her upper body. "What happened?"

"You really want to talk about that now?" he said with a half-smile. He sat up and looked at her. She hadn't noticed before how freaking cute that was, the way he pressed his lips together with that shy, amused look. *What the hell is happening? This is Julian! This is Hugh's sweet, quiet friend. And we are making out in my childhood home. And I want to have sex with him!* She kissed him again, moving back across the bed until she was straddling him and his fingers were pressed against her bare back, which felt so perfectly delicious...but then she pulled back again.

"What's happening?" she said out loud.

"I don't know. I'm a bit gobsmacked at the moment. You did kiss me, didn't you?" He looked rather pleased.

"Julian," she said, "have you thought about this before?"

He looked down. "Well—I—" he stammered. "Yes... Of course, I knew it was slightly outrageous, given your relationship to my best mate, but I thought it might be...good."

He'd thought about kissing her too! She wasn't totally crazy. Here they were, and it was actually happening, and they could keep going. They were adults; they could sleep together right now. Nora had never been a one-night kind of girl—with the odd exception of Lachlan—but what did it mean if it was Julian? Did they have to figure it out tonight? She held up a blanket to cover her chest, thinking hard.

"Hugh," she said, letting herself state the heart of the problem out loud. "Is it weird if we—do you think he would—"

"Mind? Possibly."

"Maybe we should just think about things before we—you know."

Julian nodded solemnly, and Nora regretted stopping them. She wanted to still be kissing him. "Right."

"Oh God," she said.

"What is it?" She could feel his soft breath. She was going to need to either make love to him right now or go get back in the shower with the water on freezing cold.

"I really want to kiss you again."

He was grinning like a schoolboy, and it made her feel giddy in a way she couldn't ever remember feeling before. She dropped the blanket she was holding, and they both lunged at the same time, groping for each other again. Why was he still wearing pants? She'd never hated pants so much in her entire life, and as she started clawing at the button and zipper at his waist, he wriggled to let himself free and put his hand in her hair, and she was gasping again. His other hand slid up her thigh, his fingers firm and desperate. They were so close, and she needed him so badly. Her body needed him. In fact, it was arching toward him, aching for him in a way that she would never have imagined.

Then he stopped again, sighing and pressing his forehead to hers. "Nora," he said. "You were right about Hugh. I think it would upset him, and it would be terrible of me to do this without talking to him about it."

Nora nodded. "Except," she said. "He is engaged to be married. And we haven't dated in seven years."

"True," Julian said. He was still holding her tightly, despite the fact that he was telling her it couldn't go any further.

Nora leaned back and smacked her hand to her head and grunted with frustration. "We can wait," she said. "You talk to Hugh, and we won't let anything else happen. I don't want to come between you two."

Julian nodded.

"Do you think he's awake now?" Nora asked, smiling. "What time is it there?"

They both laughed. He had a really wonderful laugh.

"I'll call him tomorrow," Julian said.

"Right, we need to get some sleep anyway." Nora tugged her shirt back on and got out of bed. "Or maybe you could text him?"

"Dear Hugh." Julian mimed typing on his phone. "Could I make love to your ex-girlfriend immediately? Please respond at earliest convenience."

"Okay, tomorrow," Nora said, still grinning like an idiot. Her cheeks were starting to hurt. She turned to go but then rushed back and kissed him again. Because she could do that! He was right there, and he wanted to kiss her too, and she kind of couldn't believe how much she wanted it to keep going.

"Good night then, Julian," she said when she finally broke away again and headed for the door.

"Good night, Nora," he said. His shy grin was maddening.

———

Nora walked back to her bedroom feeling a little drunk. She couldn't believe what had just happened. She covered her mouth with her hand. That mouth had just been kissing Julian. *What does that mean?* He'd thought about kissing her, but was that all? Did he just want a night together? He had come all this way for her; did that mean they could have something more? If she dated Julian, then she would see Hugh all the time. She'd still been dreaming about Hugh. She'd been lamenting his engagement, sick that she couldn't be with him, and now she was kissing his best friend. Was this some kind of senseless rebound so she could feel better about herself? Except, it couldn't be just a rebound when she enjoyed the exact taste of Julian's specific lips so immensely—when she looked forward to seeing him and talking with him, when a day without him seemed like a waste, and not just because she couldn't write. She wanted to see his smile and the way he would rub the back of his neck as he listened to her ramble, the way he would laugh so freely and tease her about making a mess of herself and the way he believed in her.

"What?!" she whispered to herself. Part of her wanted to rush right back into that room, back into Julian's arms, the rest of the world be damned. Maybe they could just sleep in the same bed. She wouldn't even have to touch him. What was her mother going to say about this?

Nora flopped onto her own bed, baffled and exhausted. She didn't know if she would be able to fall asleep after all the adrenaline and excitement, the blood still rushing to a particular place in the middle of her body. She couldn't go back into that room and keep herself from touching him. *Will power, Nora!*

A reel of wild thoughts spun through her head: her mother, Julian's body, and the loud hum of an airplane. She wanted to figure this out, but she also couldn't keep her eyes open. Somehow, it didn't take long for her to pass out entirely, all of the fog that was clouding her brain dissipating as sleep took over.

CHAPTER TWENTY-FOUR

JULIAN CALLED Hugh three times the next day without receiving any answer. In part, he was glad of it. He wasn't sure how he was going to ask him if he could sleep with Nora, especially knowing that Hugh still had feelings for her. He couldn't even tell if the nausea in his stomach was from guilt or pure elation. While Julian had spent the morning thinking about the night before, replaying the few glorious minutes he'd had with Nora in his head over and over, Hugh kept creeping into his brain. He tried to practice a speech to convey all the things he would want to say: I'm so sorry, but I think I'm in love with her, and I would really like your permission to make love to her as many times in a row as humanly possible.

That probably wouldn't be the best way to phrase it, but the problem was that there wasn't really a *good* way to go about it at all.

Julian paced in his room quietly, not wanting to wake Nora, but also desperate to see her. He wanted to jump on her bed like a kid on Christmas morning, sure that everything he'd ever wanted was right there waiting for him. And yet, he was so nervous he could hardly stand it. What if last night had just been a fleeting mistake for her? What if after a good night's sleep she had decided it was better not to bother?

He was even more worried about how honest he should be with her.

He didn't know whether to wing it and act casual or to tell her the truth—that he may have, in fact, been in love with her for quite some time. He also didn't know whether he could kiss her again or if he should keep his distance. She might pretend that nothing at all had happened. When he heard her moving down the hall past his room, he finally opened his door and went to face her.

"Hi," she said shyly when he walked into the kitchen. She was already dressed and ready for the day. She was also smiling.

"Hi," he said, sheepish. He took a deep breath, clueless about what would come next. Despite all of his planning and plotting, he had no idea what to do.

"Are you hungry?" she asked, and he exhaled and relaxed for a moment.

"Absolutely," he said.

They drove to Kathleen's favorite diner, still with the quiet between them. Nora asked if he would like to go in and eat first, then order Kathleen's food and take it to go. He shouldn't have been surprised when the diner's owner lit up when Nora walked in. He was a squat Greek man with a giant smile, and he opened his arms to hug her and then ushered them into a booth—a booth that must have belonged to her. This was her place.

"I didn't know we would be seeing you so soon, Nora," the owner said with a slight accent. "We've missed you."

"I'm back for a visit," she said, keeping her tone upbeat.

"And who is this?" the owner asked suggestively.

"This is Julian," she said. "My friend from London."

"Ah, nice to meet you, Julian. I'm excited to feed you. What would you like? Anything you want."

Julian ordered something utterly American, an egg, bacon, and cheese sandwich, and the owner shuffled off to the kitchen.

"He didn't ask for your order," Julian said.

Nora shook her head. "He knows it."

Without having another person to prompt them, silence descended over Nora and Julian again. He couldn't remember a time when they'd ever had such an awkwardness between them, but he thought she may have been blushing. Maybe that was a good sign.

He racked his brain for something to say. He finally thought to ask her whether she'd been in contact with Darcy, but then they both started speaking in a rush of words at the same time.

"Did you ever manage to—?"

"I was thinking that maybe we could—"

"Pardon?" he said with a small smile. She tucked some hair behind her ear.

"We're being weird," she said.

"I know."

"I don't want to be," Nora said. "But I'm not sure what to do."

Julian loved how she was blunt enough to acknowledge the situation, something he never would have been able to do. Already, everything felt better.

"I don't know either," he said. "I'm at a loss."

She stared at him for a moment. "Do you still want to kiss me?" she asked.

If only she knew. If only he could get the balls to tell her everything. "I certainly do," he whispered shyly.

Her smile widened. "Did you talk to Hugh?"

"I've called him but haven't been able to get in touch."

"Maybe try him again after we eat?"

Julian nodded. Was she as eager as he was?

Their meal was easy and comfortable, and it only made Julian more confident that Nora might want to explore whatever this was as much as he did. He couldn't wait to kiss her again. However, when he called Hugh after their delicious meal, there was still no answer.

"Why are you being weird?" Kathleen asked when they'd only been in her presence for about five minutes. Julian glanced at Nora.

"We're not being weird," she said.

Kathleen took a big bite of her BLT sandwich. She was in high spirits this morning, Julian thought. He was incredibly impressed with her strength of character, especially in the face of such terrible circumstances.

"So," she said. "What did the two of you do when you got to the house last night?"

Julian and Nora glanced at each other again. Kathleen looked incredibly suspicious, but she didn't comment on their strange behavior for a second time.

"We basically ate dinner, got cleaned up, and went to bed," Nora said. "We were exhausted."

"I love your house," Julian piped in, trying to sound normal. If Darcy had seen right through him, he was rather certain Kathleen would be able to read every emotion that played across his face.

"Thank you," Kathleen said. "It's basically my personality in the form of a building, so I'm going to take that to mean you like me too."

"Of course," Julian said. "From the moment we met."

"Okay, suck-up." Kathleen laughed, and Julian could see the way her smile filled up her face in the same way as Nora's. "Well, the surgery is scheduled for Friday, so here's what I think. You both should stay through the weekend—if you can—and then you should get back to your lives in London."

"Mom—" Nora began to protest immediately.

"Why don't you go ahead and book a trip for a few weeks from now so you can come check on me, Nora? But as long as the surgery goes well there's no reason for you to stay. Just come back and see me again in a while."

"I don't know," Nora said. "You'll need help during recovery, and we don't know that—"

"Julian?" Kathleen looked at him, ignoring all of Nora's protestations.

"I can stay through the weekend, and I can come back to visit you as well, if you'll have me," Julian added softly. He didn't know what would happen with Nora, but he didn't want to let Kathleen down.

"You are a sweet man," Kathleen said. "Now be quiet, please. My show's coming on."

Julian and Nora played gin rummy in the room while Kathleen watched her favorite talk show. Julian couldn't help looking up at Nora over the deck of cards, wishing he had any idea what was going to happen next.

"Deal me in for the next game," Kathleen said after a while. She looked back and forth between Julian and Nora. Julian could sense that she was trying to decipher the hidden messages going on between the two of them, and he could relate. He felt like he was trying to decipher every move Nora made, every card she discarded, every time she scrunched her nose and rearranged her hand. If Kathleen asked Nora if there was something between the two of them when they were alone, Julian had no idea what she would say.

After their third game, Kathleen decided she needed a nap, and Nora suddenly looked up at Julian with alarm. "I'm such a dummy. I'm so sorry, Julian."

"What are you talking about?"

"It only just crossed my mind that this is your first time in the United States, and you might not actually want to spend all of it in a hospital room playing gin. You can absolutely go out and see some sights. The gorges aren't far, and they're so beautiful. Or you could do a wine tour..."

Julian hesitated. Was she trying to get rid of him? Was he supposed to graciously accept a plan that meant leaving her side?

"Uh," he stuttered. "Is it odd to say that I think I'd have a lot more fun with you sitting here playing cards?"

She looked surprised for a moment and then smiled. He beamed back at her.

"You know, I've always wanted to learn how to play cribbage," she said.

"We don't have a board. Do you think they would have that around here somewhere?"

She pulled out her phone and had an answer for him within seconds. "We can pick it up today."

Julian hadn't spent so much time in a hospital since he was young. The smells and sounds still felt so familiar though; it was just like riding a terrible bike. He and Nora sat in the cafeteria for a while, drinking awful coffee and looking around at the various patrons shuffling past the tables with trays of questionable fruit, kids huddled on their mobile phones in a corner, a man in a wheelchair laughing with a teenager.

"I did this a lot when my mum was sick," Julian said. It wasn't something he ever brought up, rarely even with his father, but it had been on his mind since they'd arrived. Part of his brain was overwhelmed with lusting after Nora, the other part consumed with memories of his mother. "Not *this* like sitting in a plastic chair eating pudding from a cup, but this —hanging out in hospitals."

"I'm so sorry, Julian. I didn't even think. It must be hard to be here."

He smiled and shook his head. "I think it's part of why I felt I had to be with you," he said. "Why I had to come to the States. I know what it is to sit and watch your mum hurting and feel like you can't do anything. I did quite a lot of that as a kid."

"I bet having you around made all the difference for her," Nora said sadly. "I know it's made all the difference for me." She paused for a moment, thoughtful, as if perhaps she was just realizing the truth of her words. At least, that's what Julian was hoping.

"What was she like?" Nora asked.

He took a breath and ran a hand through his hair. "Silly. She almost never cried in front of me. She just made ridiculous faces to keep me laughing or rolling my eyes. She would be wheeling down the hall in a bed, about to go in for surgery, and asking if I'd done my maths homework."

"Which you had, of course."

"Of course. Star student, I was, in spite of it all. But I always felt like she didn't quite care. She wanted me to be smart and do well in school, but really she just wanted me to be happy. She wanted to know about every little thing, every part of my day. Like who sat where when I went to see a film or which teachers gave out the most detentions. It lit her up just to hear those tiny things."

"She sounds really lovely," Nora said.

"She was, and tough too, like your mum."

"I can't even believe my mom sometimes. I don't know how she does it."

"You're quite like her though," Julian said. "Maybe you don't see it as well from your perspective, but you did move to where you know almost no one to follow your passion. You took a chance, and even when you worried you weren't good enough, that you might get fired, you didn't give up. You're a tough one too."

Nora turned her face away, shaking her head. When she finally looked back toward him, they locked eyes and held each other's gaze for a moment, reveling in the stillness. He wanted to know her every thought. "The guy at the table next to us got the meatloaf, and it smells horrendous," she said, but he could tell that she was trying too hard to lighten the mood and brush away his compliment.

"Is it strange to think about kissing you in a hospital cafeteria that smells like meatloaf?" he joked, or rather half-joked, seeing as he really did want to kiss her again. Nora laughed, and Julian joined in as well, but he wondered if she knew that he meant it. Not just the kissing, but everything, all of it. He wanted to be with her anywhere—in a hospital in the States, at a magic show in London, in a dark alley listening to strangers spin tales about murder. It didn't matter. He wanted to be with her so badly, but he didn't know how to say any of that. At least she didn't seem to be worrying about Hugh too much. He was out of sight and out of mind, and now Julian had her all to himself at last. Or at least, he only had to share her with her delightful mother.

Later in the afternoon, Julian and Nora made it back up to Kathleen's room where *Family Feud* was on the telly. Every once in a while, Kathleen would stop talking mid-sentence and shout at the screen, randomly calling out guesses. "Toilet Paper! Doing the Laundry!"

"What's the plan for this evening?" Kathleen asked during a commercial break.

"We can do whatever you want," Nora said.

"Me? I want to sleep. What are you two going to do?"

"I don't know," Nora said. She cautiously glanced over at Julian.

"Well, may I offer a suggestion? He can't visit this town without going to the best bar in the state of New York."

"The best?" Julian raised an eyebrow. "I don't think I know anything about it."

"Well, you certainly won't forget it," Nora declared with a grin.

"In the eighties it was the best drug den in town," Kathleen informed him.

Nora sighed. "Mother."

"Ah, the good old days. I don't know if you can handle it, Julian."

"I have to admit I'm a little nervous," he said.

"Condoms!" Kathleen yelled at the TV, and he and Nora burst out laughing.

CHAPTER TWENTY-FIVE

NORA WAS ALONE with her mother for the first time in quite a while. Julian had gone for a cup of tea, and almost since the moment he'd left, Nora had been trapped in a cycle of her own thoughts, staring out the hospital window in a spiral of guilt as her mother continued to watch game shows. It hadn't been an unpleasant afternoon for being stuck in a hospital watching her favorite person in the world battle cancer. Julian taught them to play cribbage, though her mother was a hilariously lousy sport and complained about every rule of the game. They chatted about Julian's childhood—or maybe chat was the wrong word, since most of the conversation started with Kathleen's interrogations, but Julian had handled all of it with grace. Sometimes they'd sat together in companionable silence. But now that Julian was out of the room, and Kathleen was distracted by a TV rerun from 1978, Nora couldn't help the emotions that washed over her, the same belly-deep sickness that had plagued her since her mother told her the news.

"Earth to Nora," Kathleen called, waving her arms at her daughter from the hospital bed. "What are you doing?"

Nora tried to shrug herself out of her own head. "I'm going to a spectacular downtown bar with Julian. After bringing you whatever you want for dinner, of course. And a Cook's strawberry milkshake if you're allowed."

Her mother gave her a small smile and shook her head. She knew Nora was deflecting, of course. She always did. "Tell me what you're thinking about, kiddo."

Nora took a breath and then exhaled loudly. Julian had managed to keep her darkest thoughts at bay, but despite her preoccupation with him, Nora was still shrouded in a quiet panic about her mother. At the airport, on the plane, on the bus, and in every moment spent at the hospital. Maybe it could be temporarily silenced by elated trumpets and constantly obsessing over the wonderful British man she'd brought to America, but it wouldn't go away entirely.

Tears welled in her eyes as she tried to speak. "I should have been here," she choked out. "I never should have left you."

"Come here, baby," Kathleen cooed, and Nora did as she was told, moving across the room into her mother's waiting arms. Kathleen held her close and stroked her hair. "This is not something for you to feel bad about. This is not your fault, and I didn't want you here dealing with it. There's a reason I waited to tell you. I knew you'd freak out and jump on the first plane from London, and I'm so happy to see you, but the thing I really want, the thing I need from you, is for you to keep living your dream.

Nora pulled away and rubbed her eyes. "But what if it's not my dream, Mom? I'm not even good at it. What if it's all just a waste, and I could have been here taking care of you the whole time?"

"Oh, Nora." Kathleen gripper her hand. "First of all, you *are* good at it. I read your stuff, and don't even try to say it's only good because of Julian when he didn't write a damn word. You wanted this for a long time, so don't say it's a waste."

Nora hung her head.

"Secondly," Kathleen continued, "I know you. I've seen how badly you wanted to go back to London since college, and not just because of some boy. You loved it there—the history, getting to see things you'd only ever read about, meeting new people. You need to see the world, and I wouldn't keep you from that in a million years. Not for anything."

"But you're more important than that," Nora sputtered. If her mother needed her, then nothing else mattered—not her job, not the book, nothing in the whole of Great Britain.

"I know." Kathleen grinned. "But how could I let you sit around here taking care of me when I've seen that light in your eyes when you embark on a new adventure? And I can take care of myself."

Nora raised her eyebrows. Maybe Kathleen had forgotten they were currently in a hospital.

"I *can*. Impending breast-removal notwithstanding. I got to live my life how I wanted, except for during a brief period with your father, but we won't get into that. I'm not going to rob you of the same chance. You can still be here for me without always being *here* for me. And you have. Good Lord, you answer every fucking time I call. I was starting to worry that you didn't have a life."

A sudden laugh bubbled from between Nora's lips. "How can I leave you now?" she asked. "How could I possibly go back to London after this?"

"You can, and you will. I refuse to hold you back, Nora, and I promise I'll be okay." Kathleen rubbed Nora's head. "What would you even do for me if you were here? I won't eat anything you cook, and you would probably just annoy me anyway. Go back to London and keep answering the phone. Most of the time. Maybe have some fun, too."

Nora sank against her mother's shoulder. "I don't know," she said. It was hard to imagine getting on another plane, and she certainly wouldn't agree to it until after she knew the outcome of the surgery.

"Listen to your mother, Nora." Kathleen pressed a hand to her cheek and smiled. "I've never steered you wrong before."

Nora was emotionally drained after the conversation with her mother, and she knew Julian was aware of it. When he'd walked back into the hospital room, Nora and Kathleen had been snuggled against each other, and Nora was sure he would notice the ghosts of tears on her cheeks. He offered to go back to the house, have a quiet night, and get to bed early, but Nora thought some time spent out in the world might do them good.

She'd been looking forward to it actually, taking him out in her hometown. She liked playing tour guide for him.

They didn't touch in the car. In fact, Nora didn't think that they'd touched each other all day long. He'd said in the cafeteria he still wanted to kiss her, but somehow that seemed like years ago, and it had never come up again. For the past twelve hours, Julian had never even so much as patted her hand, and she didn't want to ask again whether or not he had talked to Hugh. That seemed a little desperate. *Please please please get permission for us to do it!* Maybe he'd changed his mind if he thought there was the slightest possibility that it could wreck his relationship with his best friend. Maybe he was just waiting for the right time to tell her that it had all been a stupid mistake, but he was too nice to say it right now when her mother was about to have her breasts chopped off.

He looked over and smiled at her when a Britney Spears song started playing on the radio. "Baby One More Time," just like at the dance club. That meant something, right? That was a sign? Even if the words to the song "Baby One More Time" were utterly ridiculous and meant absolutely nothing at all. The Queen of Pop was giving them her blessing. Normally, Nora would have been singing along at the top of her lungs, the sound of her voice echoing through the car and bouncing off the windshield. Instead, she was biting her lip worrying about what Julian was thinking.

She took a deep breath and tried to sound casual when they pulled into the gravel parking lot behind the bar. "Are you ready for this?" she asked.

"I thought I was, but you're making me nervous." Julian laughed, but he did actually sound a little uncomfortable. Nora wasn't sure if it was really because of the bar or because of her.

"Is everything cool?" Nora asked, because she couldn't help it and perhaps she wanted to torture herself. She needed to hear him say that they were in over their heads and shouldn't be fantasizing about having sex with each other. At least it would be better than the silent treatment.

"Y-yes," Julian said. "What do you mean?"

Nora shrugged. "You've been quiet...with me especially. I didn't know if there was something wrong."

"Sorry," Julian said. "You didn't do anything. I just feel like maybe I'm intruding. With you and your mom—you might want some time with her without having to feel like you need to entertain me. You said I should go to the gorges. And obviously you are going through a lot right now. I don't want to be in the way, and I don't want you to feel any pressure or, um, expectations from me, I guess. I don't want to make things harder for you than they already are." He ran a hand through his hair and started talking faster. "I jumped on a plane because I know what this is like, to some extent, but maybe that wasn't the right thing to do."

Nora was quiet for a moment, lips pursed, staring through the windshield into the trees beyond the parking lot. "I want you to be here," she said softly without looking at him.

Before they had kissed, she'd had no qualms about telling him how smart and sweet and funny he was, but now that there was the possibility of greater intimacy and deeper feelings, she couldn't get the words out. She was afraid to tell him just how much she wanted him there. She was still trying to work out what it meant and if he might feel the same.

He nodded. "Okay then," he said. "I'm all yours."

CHAPTER TWENTY-SIX

THE PUB—OR *bar*—was not quite like anything Julian had ever seen before. There were brightly colored Christmas lights hanging everywhere—covering up the dingy, possibly rotting wood—even though it was late summer. The patrons all looked quite scruffy and unwashed to varying degrees. Most of them were crowded around a game of shuffleboard, shouting wildly at the little puck as it slid across the sandy table. There was graffiti on everything, burn marks on the wall from where the kitchen caught fire last year, and a hole in the floor where someone had shot a gun into the ground—or so Nora informed him. He would not have pictured her in a place like this, but she seemed immediately comfortable as she greeted the bartender and sat on a stool, a stool with upholstery that looked like someone had taken a bite out of it.

"Here we are at the Rusty Tavern, my hometown hangout," Nora said before they ordered drinks. She was smiling playfully, as if she thought he'd be shocked that this was where she liked to spend her time. He adjusted his butt on his seat and kept looking around, though he tried not to make eye contact with any of the other customers. Laughter echoed from the front patio. It seemed not a soul in this place was having a bad time.

"I'm back!" Nora called to the tattooed bartender as she approached them.

"Back?" the woman said. "I didn't know you left."

"Well, either way, I'm here," Nora said.

"Don't worry, darling, I'll put on your song," the bartender said. She had a thick gold ring in her nose, and she poured out a couple shots of a mysterious liquor before even bothering to take their order.

Julian loved how everyone knew Nora and knew what she liked everywhere they went, even if the drink he let slide down his throat in one gulp was horrendous. "What is this?" he asked, coughing.

"I don't think you really want to ask that," Nora said.

In this place full of strange characters with beards and grime, the talented and beautiful Nora Shrapsan was still able to fit in and casually have a drink. He saw how lucky everyone was to be near her, himself included, when they started playing Bob Seger's "Night Moves" and she stood up and started dancing around the little bar, serenading all the patrons. Sheer joy seemed to spread throughout the room as Nora sang and shook hands with old friends. An older couple embraced her on the tiny dance floor, and Nora chatted with them before waving Julian over.

"Julian's from London," she said to them. It was his only introduction, and it skipped over any uncomfortable attempts to try to label him as a friend or romantic interest. Then she wrapped her arms around him and forced him to start dancing, and he gave in without putting up much of a fight.

"What happened with Poppy?" Nora asked as they swayed in a small circle.

He thought for a moment. He couldn't tell her the truth, obviously, that they'd broken up because of Nora. He hadn't thought about how to explain it. "We—um. We just didn't have a lot in common. It was a very civil break-up." Nora looked up at him like she was waiting for more, but he just shrugged. "We weren't dating very long."

"Oh," Nora said. Julian couldn't tell what on earth she was thinking.

"I mean, Poppy was great, but..." He trailed off, unsure of how to finish.

"She seemed like she was really into you the night that I met her."

"What ever happened with that magician?" Julian said quickly. He realized that he didn't actually want to know, but he was only trying to change the subject. Nora shifted uncomfortably.

"Forget I asked that," he said. This wasn't going well.

They went back to the bar for another round, and perhaps it was the additional alcohol or the sound of Annie Lennox playing on the jukebox that helped them to relax a bit, and Nora pulled him up to dance again. Her hair was flying back and forth, her hips shaking in time with the rhythm. When she almost tripped and ended up in his arms again, she held onto him and kept dancing.

He couldn't stop thinking about the night before, about the feeling of her on top of him, her fingers clutching his hair. He concentrated on the warm feeling of her hands around the back of his neck, and this time, when the song ended, Julian decided to take a chance. He was already in over his head anyway, and so he let himself lean in and kiss her, in front of all of those people, to let himself have this one amazing thing. It was even more incredible when her lips responded, and the people around them started hooting and cheering. He pulled back with a nervous smile. It seemed like everyone in the room was clapping.

"Sorry," he said.

Nora looked up at him. "Are you really sorry?" she asked.

"No," he admitted. "I'm not."

"Okay then," she said, and they ordered a round of waters.

They stayed at the pub, eating baskets of chips and talking for hours. People hugged Nora and told her they were sorry to hear about her mom. Nora was obviously feeling gregarious, and she talked openly about how worried she was for her mother and how she didn't know if she could go back to London. She said as much as she loved living in such a wonderful city, there were more important things, and Julian understood.

"You'll feel guilty about leaving her." Julian said matter-of-factly. Selfishly, he didn't want to think of life without her again. Days ago, he'd planned to stop seeing her entirely, but now he knew that was impossible.

"Yes, and scared and ashamed."

"But if you don't go back, imagine how your mum will feel. She'll have to handle the guilt of having you stay when she knows you have your dream job in another country."

"Mum," Nora repeated. She smiled absently. "You sound just like her, you know."

"I think everything's going to work out," Julian said.

"Are you always this positive?" she asked him.

"Probably not," he said, grinning. "Maybe it's something about this place. It just brings out my optimism."

Nora pointed to a drawing of male anatomy on the wall near their heads. "This makes you feel optimistic?" she said.

Julian laughed. "You know what? It really does."

As the night wore on, Julian couldn't believe how comfortable he felt— comfortable enough to hold Nora's hand and play the same songs over and over on the juke box, comfortable enough to talk to her about anything. He balked when he discovered she hadn't read any of his favorite science fiction novel series, and of course he couldn't stop himself from laying out the intricacies of the plot for her.

"And then in book six, the slug is reincarnated, but everyone on the planet thinks it must have been a trick, that actually the other planet sent the slug to destroy them, like a Trojan Horse situation."

"Oh no," Nora gasped, leaning in closer. "Please tell me they figured out that it was literally the answer to all of their problems."

Julian allowed himself a moment to appreciate her rapt gaze, the way she followed his every word. He was talking about the plot of this insane book, spoiling every detail too, and she was listening. More than that, she was interested, if also laughing about the most ridiculous aspects of the story.

"They're just about to kill it, but Hradji returns from the blue planet to tell them the slug is their savior. He brings one of the fortune tellers to show them a vision of the future."

"Thank goodness. Go Hradji! So what happens next?"

"Well, the people attack and kill the slug anyway."

"No!" She brought her hands to her face.

"Yes." Julian laughed. Nora's enthusiasm made his heart speed up. He hardly spoke to anyone about his mother, let alone *this*. But he was letting Nora see these parts of himself, letting her in. "Hradji escapes with a bit of the slug's slime, thinking he might be able to reincarnate it a second time…"

He could have stayed just like that—on the ripped wobbly stools with Nora holding his hand. He could have stayed like that until dawn.

Instead, they took a cab back to the house, and Nora leaned her head against Julian's shoulder in the back seat. It felt so natural and easy to him, the lavender scent of her hair right under his nose and the warmth of her body pressed against him. Part of him felt like this was always meant to happen, even when there were so many things, or really one big thing, that had kept them apart. When they arrived, Julian watched Nora rush up the driveway, her arms flapping in the moonlight and her laughter echoing in the darkness. Then she whipped around to see him watching her.

"Are you coming, slow poke?" she asked, and then she stuck the key in the lock and disappeared into the house.

CHAPTER TWENTY-SEVEN

NORA DIDN'T KNOW what would happen tomorrow or the next day, but as she walked through the dark house after getting home from the bar, she knew that she wanted to seduce Julian. Hugh was somewhere around the edges of her thoughts, but he was also an ocean away and years in the past. She was starting to realize how different it was, this thing she had with Julian. She'd been infatuated with Hugh, possibly obsessed. She loved his body and his songs, how cool he was all the time, like a rock star, even then. He was so talented. But that was all just on the surface, wasn't it? It was the kind of stuff you cared about as a teenager. Something about Julian went deeper than that—it was real and adult and…she felt so close to him. Not only was he thoughtful and kind and funny and awkward, he was caring for her mother so wonderfully, and he also just *got her*. He knew what it was like to be in that hospital room all day. He knew how worried she was and how much she needed a break from thinking about all of it. He knew what made her anxious or happy or scared or proud. He may not have known, however, that every time she took a break from freaking out about her mom, she was thinking about him.

Still, part of her had been wondering if exploring the attraction between them was really worth it. The absolute worst thing would be to destroy Hugh and Julian's relationship over one night. *But would Hugh even* care? one side of her brain asked. *No, he's engaged, so that's a moot point*, the other side of her brain had argued all day long. When Julian kissed her at the bar, that was it. She wanted him so badly. She needed to find out how the slug story ended first, obviously, but then she wanted to feel his skin again, the ridges and curves of his body, the way his fingers pressed into her thighs.

She heard Julian close the front door of the house behind him and wondered if he'd be able to find her. She hadn't turned on a light, just wandered down the hallway waiting for him. She stood outside of her bedroom in the dark, listening to his footsteps.

"Nora?" he said, but he hadn't turned on any lights either. Maybe he didn't know where to find the switches, or maybe he was anticipating what she hoped would happen in the darkness. As she heard his movement through the house, the sound of him bumping into a nearby table, her heart started beating dramatically. Soon she could make out his shadow coming toward her, and then she was able to reach out to him.

"Do you—" he started to say, but Nora had already wrapped her arms around him and started kissing him, and it took only a second for him to kiss her back the way he had the night before, like he *needed* her desperately. It was thrilling to be kissed like that.

She walked backwards into her bedroom, where he quickly pushed her up against the wall. Nora gasped audibly as he ran his hands beneath her shirt until his thumb was beneath the edge of her bra. He kissed her neck as she was undoing the buttons of his shirt, and then she heard a little chuckle escape from his lips.

"What is it?" she asked, breathless.

"I just can't believe this is happening," he said.

"Is this okay? I know we said we would wait until—"

"It's very, very acceptable to me, Nora. Extremely good."

In response, she tugged off his shirt and went back to kissing him. He lifted her T-shirt over her head and adeptly removed her bra, unlatching the clasp with one hand before cupping one of her breasts in his warm palm. Nora felt like a bird was opening its wings inside her chest and her belly. Her skin seemed to be tingling inside and out. Soon it was as if every part of him was pressing into her—his tongue pushing against hers, his fingertips on her back, then his nose against her neck, his lips against her nipple, and all the while, the press of something firm between her legs where she was throbbing.

She couldn't stop herself from reaching for that firm length, and she was ecstatic at the soft groan that escaped Julian's lips at her touch. He grabbed for the button of her jeans, and they both shimmied out of their pants before landing on the bed in only their underwear. Julian's mouth found hers again as he pressed a hand between her thighs, moving up between her legs until his fingers slipped underneath the last remaining piece of fabric on her body. She let out a gasp when he touched her there, and if he was surprised to find how ready she was, how easily his finger slipped inside her, he didn't let on. She arched her back and pressed her pelvis against him, aching for that last remaining unseen part of him to be exposed.

His body was solid against her, and she clung to him hungrily, holding his warm, flushed skin against her own as he maneuvered to delicately slide the fabric down her legs. She tugged at the cotton around his thighs less kindly and pulled him toward her again, spreading her legs and reaching to guide him to the part of her that was dying to be filled with him.

"Do you have something?" he said breathlessly, and she nodded, scrambling to reach her arm over her head for the drawer in her nightstand, then ripping open the little foil wrapper with her teeth. This hadn't ever happened in her childhood bedroom before, even when she and Brandon had come for a visit. However, her mother was Kathleen Shrapsan, and Kathleen Shrapsan made sure her daughter was always prepared for a sexual encounter.

Nora had been sorely mistaken when she thought her desire could be quenched by a night with a silly magician or even some stranger at a club. How could she have failed to realize that it was Julian who could set her on fire so exquisitely, who could make her burn with desperation at the touch of his fingers in her hair or his tongue against her nipples?

He groaned again as he eased inside of her, his breathing sharp and rapid. She thought she might explode at the sound of her name, at the way he said it so greedily and unwavering.

She moved her body with his, grasping his hair and biting at his mouth as pleasure built up inside of her. She couldn't help the moan that vibrated between her lips as he rocked with her in his arms, his lips against her ear and his hand sliding up her thigh. He met her gaze before letting out a heavy breath and pressing his face into her neck again.

She gasped when he placed a hand on each of her hips and then arched her body toward him as he found a way to fill her even more completely. He kissed her harder, his tongue unyielding in her mouth, and she didn't know how much longer she could hold out, but she knew he must be close as well, from the movement in his limbs and the way he said her name again as if he could hardly last another second.

She seemed to feel it everywhere as she tumbled over the edge, and her fingers clung to Julian even tighter, pressing hard into his skin. She felt him following soon after and delighted in how his body shuddered so completely. He sank onto her after that, as if he was coming home, and she welcomed the weight of him as he fell against her, his arm draped across her middle.

She could barely think after that point, except to realize that her body was humming everywhere, like a bell that had just been rung, and Julian was breathing heavily, a sheer layer of sweat gleaming all over his skin.

He smiled at her then, an unabashed, triumphant look that she'd never seen him wear. She sighed happily as he laced his fingers with hers and leaned in to kiss her hair. After a few minutes, he pulled away briefly to throw out the condom, but when he returned to bed he was grinning.

"What?" she asked.

He leaned into her arms and nuzzled her collarbone. "I don't know," he said. "I'm speechless."

Nora smiled and knew what he meant. Even as she drifted to sleep beside him, she could feel it too, something she couldn't quite name, like a firecracker in her chest.

They made breakfast at the house the next morning. Every time their eyes met, Nora and Julian smiled, like they were keeping a juicy secret. They were, Nora supposed. As she sliced into her runny egg yolk, she kept remembering the feeling of Julian holding her throughout the night. How was it so nice simply to be next to him? Even with the weight of her mother's impending surgery, she was lighter somehow. She had someone to lean on.

"I've been thinking a lot about this," she started, trying to wipe off the yolk running across her hand.

Julian's head jerked up, and he gave her a questioning look.

"If Hradji mixed the slug DNA with his own, would it pollute the royal slug bloodline? Or would the worker slugs still accept the new slug incarnation as king?"

Julian's posture relaxed, and he broke into a grin. "You're so into this."

Nora tried to remain serious, like the future lineage of slug kind was a devastatingly important topic. "There's a lot to unpack here." She couldn't hold out for long and stifled her laugh into her hand.

"If my students knew this is what I was reading on the weekends while making them slog through *Paradise Lost*, they'd never let me hear the end of it."

"Oh, so if someone left an anonymous note in your classroom, that wouldn't be helpful?"

Julian narrowed his eyes. "Don't even think about it. They have so much respect for me. I'm the ultimate authority figure."

"I'm sure you are. Very stern all the time." Nora pulled a face. "But with a heart of gold."

"Very stern," Julian repeated sarcastically, and they went back to giving each other dopey smiles again.

They listened to the radio and played cards while they waited until it was time to go to the hospital. Neither of them were focused on the card game, and they both made silly mistakes, eventually forfeiting before a winner had been determined. Nora kept looking at the clock. She was under strict orders not to arrive at the hospital before ten a.m. because if she was hanging around worrying for too long, she would make her mother anxious before the surgery.

Julian wasn't overly affectionate, but Nora noticed every time they touched. Before, if he had squeezed her shoulder or placed a hand on the small of her back, she wouldn't have thought of it as anything more than a natural gesture of friendship. But now her body seemed to spark when his fingers brushed her forearm. She didn't know how to begin talking about last night, but she didn't feel like they needed to quite yet. It was nice to have these moments of comfort and ease between them without questioning what would happen next. So they went to wish her mother luck and they worried in the waiting room. Eventually, they were told that the surgery was over and Kathleen was okay, but there were no other updates. Nora went in to watch her mother sleeping before she and Julian drove back to the house.

He held her in the soft lamplight of the living room but didn't try to do anything else, and Nora was grateful. She didn't want to reject him even the tiniest bit, but she also didn't feel like she could make love properly when she was tense with worry.

Instead, they made TV dinners and watched *Golden Girls* reruns on cable. Julian kept glancing over at her to ensure that she was okay. She could see the worry in his eyes. Kathleen eventually texted that she was fine—just tired—and would see them in the morning.

"Will you stay with me tonight?" Nora asked. "Just to hold me?" She didn't know if she was asking too much, if perhaps that kind of intimacy was too different or would go beyond the kind they'd agreed to share. He said yes without hesitation, though, and held her in her bed, stroking her hair softly.

"You slept with him, didn't you?" Kathleen said from her hospital bed. She looked the same as always in her paper gown, despite the new absence from her chest.

Nora looked down at her in surprise. "What? You just had your breasts removed, and this is what you want to talk about?!"

"I knew it! I could tell by that sheepish glow on your face. You can't hide anything from me, Nora. I thought you learned that when you were eight and tried to steal my lipstick."

"Okay, fine," Nora sighed. "You're right." There really was no way to lie to her mother.

Kathleen squealed like a teenager. "How did this happen? I mean, I knew you were both acting weird the other day. Are you in a relationship now?"

"I don't know. He was just so nice, and we were having so much fun together."

"And he's clearly in love with you," Nora's mother stated matter-of-factly.

Nora snorted. "You think everyone's in love with me, Mom. Just because you want to spend the rest of your life with me doesn't mean that every man on the planet is jumping for the chance as well."

"This is different, Nora. He flew across the world to be with you."

"He flew across the world because I was freaking out about your health. Have you forgotten that we're in a hospital right now?" Nora didn't know why she was fighting it. Her mother could think whatever she wanted, and she would, no matter what Nora said about it. But *love* was too big of a word, wasn't it? She couldn't contemplate that now. She just needed to be sure her mom was okay.

"Yeah, sure, you were freaking out and having a hard time. A good friend would help you pack, take you to the airport. Only someone who is completely in love with you would go so far as to fly to your hometown and stay there." Despite the fact that she was lecturing and arguing with her daughter, Kathleen was smiling.

Nora was quiet for a moment. Her brain didn't seem to be working properly. Julian was clearly attracted to her, and they were great in bed together; in fact, they were kind of magical in bed together, but he couldn't be in love with her. He was Hugh's best friend since childhood, and until recently, their whole relationship was only because of Hugh. What did that mean for their future?

"Julian is just a really great guy," she said. "Anyway, could we talk about your health now? What did the doctor say? How are you feeling?"

"I'm feeling good," Kathleen said. "Just waiting for some test results, but I have a sense that everything will be fine. Which will mean that you need to get your butt back to London and finish that book."

"I don't know if I can—"

"Yes, you can. We've been over this. You'll come back and see me while I'm still recovering, and once they say it's okay, I'll fly out to visit you. Your aunt is coming to stay with me for a month, so don't worry. I mean, we might kill each other, but she'll make sure nothing else kills me."

Nora knew how strong and stubborn her mother was and that going against her wishes would be inadvisable. Kathleen managed her daughter just like she managed the water treatment initiative on city council, and she was going to get her way. Nora decided not to fight it. She would come back as often as she wanted to, no matter how much her mother protested, but she wanted to be writing, she wanted to be in the office with Darcy, and despite everything, something inside her was dying to get back to London.

"Mom?" Nora said after a moment.

"Yeah?"

"I missed you."

CHAPTER TWENTY-EIGHT

JULIAN AWOKE with Nora in his arms, her back against his chest. He was already used to it. In fact, he was already certain that he wouldn't mind waking up that way every day of his life.

Kathleen was doing well, thankfully. Her scans all looked positive, and she was as bright and snarky as ever. Nora was already calmer and less frazzled, and Julian was so thankful for all of it. He'd spent weeks at the hospital in the past and seen it turn out a different way. He knew what it was like with the opposite outcome, and he didn't want to witness it again. He didn't think he could have borne it to see Nora go through something like that.

Instead, everyone was happy. Nora's aunt had brought dinner to the hospital the night before, and they'd all eaten together in the little hospital chairs. Nora sat cross-legged on the linoleum floor and sucked up her spaghetti, and her aunt kept looking at Julian as if she could possibly, just by staring, piece out his whole back story and how he'd ended up in the States with Nora.

Nora had finally agreed to book their flights back to London, and they were leaving in the afternoon. It seemed too soon. A part of Julian wanted to live in Nora's mother's house forever, waking up in Nora's childhood bedroom, ignoring the fact that he would have to talk to Hugh, who still had feelings for Nora. He never wanted to face the shock and jokes from all of his mates about going after Hugh's American love.

But that wasn't what she was to him anymore. She wasn't Hugh's bird or the one that got away. She wasn't even Julian's great unrequited love of a lifetime any longer. She was a real person in his arms, a person with overwhelming passion and loyalty who loved to laugh and couldn't walk properly on cobblestones. She'd chosen him, if only for a day or two.

Not that he'd managed to tell her about his feelings yet, but he was sure that she had to know; she had to feel it every time he looked at her or held the door for her or put his lips to hers. You didn't kiss like that when you were only sleeping with someone. It had to be more.

Nora stretched and rolled to face him, looking up at him with a gleam in her eyes. *And you didn't smile like that when you were only sleeping with someone, did you?*

"Morning," she said.

"I've been waiting for you to wake up," he said.

"Oh yeah?"

"Not for very long."

"Well, what are you waiting for?" Nora asked with a sly grin.

He leaned in and kissed her, still a bit flabbergasted that he could do that now without any hesitation and that she would happily kiss him back. With everything that was going on, though, they'd only kissed since that night they'd made love for the first time, and he didn't want to put any pressure on her or try to do anything she wasn't ready for.

But when her hand slid down his stomach and into the band on his pants, it seemed that she was ready for something. She giggled and wrapped her leg over his body. He *definitely* wouldn't mind waking up this way every day of his life. He put his hand on her hip, spreading his fingers open to grasp as much of her as he could, the heat from her skin seeming to radiate through the thin fabric of her shorts.

He was already done for by the time she straddled him, swiftly sweeping her shirt over her head and leaning toward him until her small breasts pressed against the bare skin of his chest. He sighed with pleasure, and she pressed her mouth to his neck, her teeth grazing him playfully.

He was on the verge of saying it, of whispering that he loved her, but he didn't want her to think it was a lustful, heat-of-the-moment, false admission. He wanted to do it when he could stare into her eyes, serious and completely sober, when she would know that it was entirely real and true.

It wasn't long before he lost all sense of the world. All it took was the small moan from her lips as he took her nipple in between his teeth, then the only thing he could think of was the movement of her body against him, her hips grinding into him until he could hardly breathe, until he could only focus on getting more of her, of touching every part of her body. He wanted to be lost there forever. He already couldn't imagine sitting next to her for so many hours on a plane without being able to hold onto her like this.

After, he kissed all over her face before resting his forehead against the nape of her neck, breathing her in.

"Well, Julian, what a pleasant surprise it was to have you here." Kathleen was wearing a smile that reminded him of Darcy, as if she could see into his brain, the way his synapses fired in a very specific way every time he looked at Nora, the dopamine that his body released at the sight of her.

He cleared his throat. "I'm so happy I got to meet you," he said. "I wish the circumstances were different."

"But we still had a good bit of fun, boobs or no boobs," Kathleen finished with a smile.

"Mother," Nora said, but she was laughing. Julian couldn't quite catch his breath when she laughed like that.

When he looked back toward Kathleen, he realized she was grinning at him. She gave a little wink when Nora wasn't looking, as if they were in on some private conspiracy. *Had Nora told her what had happened between them?*

He kissed her on the cheek and said goodbye again before leaving the room to allow the mother and daughter some time to say their farewells in private. Then he sat down in the waiting room with a coffee, replaying the events of that morning in his head over and over again and smiling to himself.

CHAPTER TWENTY-NINE

ON THE PLANE, Nora kept thinking about what her mother said. Of course she knew it was ridiculous; there was no way Julian was *in love* with her.

"Are you relieved?" Julian asked from the seat beside her. The test results were good so far, and her mother was feeling strong. The surgery had gone according to plan, and sometimes when Nora thought of it, she sighed involuntarily, a result of feeling like she could finally take a full breath again.

"Much better than on the way here," Nora said. "When I was a total zombie freak."

"You were," Julian teased. "But it was understandable." He took her hand in his, and Nora froze. *Were they dating?* Neither of them had mentioned Hugh since they'd slept together the first time. The second time had been just as delicious. So it wasn't technically a one-night-stand, but Nora didn't want to bring up Hugh or what was going to happen once they were back in London and back around the whole gang, who might lose their shit if they saw the two of them holding hands.

Nora liked holding Julian's hand though, so she decided that for the next few hours when they were alone, except for all of the strangers on the plane and the guy coughing up snot in the row next to them, she wouldn't think about the future. She wouldn't worry or wonder about their relationship status or what was going to happen when the plane hit the ground; she would only focus on this moment in the air above the vast blue sea.

"What did you think of New York?" she asked him.

"Not at all what I was picturing."

"There's a lot more to New York than the little island at the bottom."

"And yet," Julian teased, "I'm still disappointed that I didn't see a single celebrity or even go up in a skyscraper!"

"I guess you'll have to get your skyscraper fix in London. Sorry to bum you out."

Julian rocked in his seat, almost like a kid. Nora couldn't help thinking that he looked happy. "The weather reminded me of London, though. Don't you think?"

She laughed. "Because it rained?"

"That's pretty much the only criteria for London weather," Julian said.

"Well, you should see it in the winter when there's two feet of snow covering everything," Nora said. *Does that seem too much like an invitation?*

"I bet it's beautiful," he said, locking eyes with her.

Something wriggled in her chest when he did that, though she couldn't quite explain it.

When they landed, they shared a car back to Nora's apartment. Julian had the driver wait while he walked her up to her door.

"Thank you again for everything," she said.

He was quiet, watching her, waiting for something maybe. Should she ask him to come up? Were they still going to make love? "Nora?" he said.

"Yes?'

"Would you be able to have dinner with me tomorrow night?"

A stone in her throat seemed to dissolve, and her body unclenched. She'd been so worried that everything would change in an instant in London, and maybe it still would, but thank goodness he had finally asked her on a date. "Yes," she said.

"Good. I am still going to talk to Hugh about all of this."

She wanted to ask him what he was going to say exactly. What was all of *this*? What were they doing? What if Hugh was furious with him, and it broke up their friendship? What if Hugh didn't care at all—how would she feel about that? But the car was waiting, and Nora didn't want to stifle a nice moment with all of her questions and uncertainty. It was much easier to smile and nod and press her lips against his as he leaned in to kiss her. Everything else could be sorted out later.

CHAPTER THIRTY

HUGH KNEW he shouldn't have written another verse to the song. But when he spoke to the record producer, an actual professional in the business, he had said that the new song needed something more. More emotion, more truth. Hugh was desperately trying to deliver, and that meant more specifics about Nora.

He was missing her all over again, just like he had when she'd gone back to America years before. He wanted to call her and hear her voice, but at least he still had enough sense to know that was a terrible idea. He turned off his phone so he wouldn't even try.

He focused his energy on the music instead, but that was still a thing that could manage to get him in trouble. He hadn't even heard Rose walk in the room while he was writing the new lyrics; he was so wrapped up in his own creative energy that her footsteps hadn't registered. He was singing a new phrase, playing with the sound of it in his mouth: *a down-home American / can't bear to lose you again / your eyes blue like the sea / another sea away from me.*

"American?" Rose asked tersely.

Hugh jumped and dropped his guitar pick. "Hello love," he said.

"Hi. Who are you writing about?" Rose wouldn't stop until she received a full explanation. It was one of the things that he loved about her, that she was so fierce and open. She didn't play games; she wasn't passive aggressive or even just passive about anything.

"Just this girl I used to know. I was thinking about her for some reason. It's nothing. Just a fiction for the record company, you know." A white lie, sort of. It *was* dramatized, Hugh told himself. It *was* just something to make this big shot producer guy happy. And the thing with Nora *was*...nothing.

"You can't bear to lose her again?"

"It just works there for the line, Rose." Hugh tried to keep his voice casual. "You know how it goes. It's nothing." Perhaps repeating that had been a bit too much.

"In all the time I've known you, your songs have been about real, meaningful things. So now you're either lying to me, or you're completely changing yourself and your art for a record company. Knowing you, I highly doubt it's the latter, so you might as well tell me the truth now."

The funny thing about Rose was that she didn't even *sound* angry. She was so logical—she just wanted a full and complete explanation so that she could pass some kind of reasonable judgment.

"Is it that girl? The one from 'Lift?'"

In other words, the only American woman he knew. Hugh wasn't sure what to say. Of course he didn't want to upset Rose, but he thought the relief of telling her the truth might be worth it. He'd been thinking about Nora too much lately, and he wanted to get that off his chest, although he also didn't want to hurt his fiancée. The guilt was weighing on him; maybe if he could just come clean, his feelings would dissipate.

"That was a long time ago," he replied finally.

"Of course," she said. "I know it was a long time ago. Or, at least, I thought it was."

"It was," he said. "You know it was about a girl I knew years ago. She was important to me, but then she left, and that was it."

"What does that mean?" Rose asked. "Are you trying to tell me you're just coming up with songs about the same girl that you haven't seen in years?"

"It is about the same girl." Hugh paused, his thoughts bouncing around his head, never aligning themselves into anything coherent. "Except I've seen her."

Rose stared at him without responding, just waiting for him to keep going. Something in his throat felt thick and hard. He coughed once. "She came back to London for work, and I saw her again at a show."

Rose started walking out of the room without waiting to hear the rest of the explanation. It was rare that she got emotional, but when she did, she hated to be around anyone, hated for them to see her like that. Hugh chased after her. "Nothing happened, Rose. Nothing, nothing, I swear."

This was what he'd been fearing for so long—letting her down like this, revealing who he truly was, someone who didn't have his shit together, someone who didn't deserve her. She was so bloody perfect, just the right measure of caring and tough, too smart for him by far. He loved her. So why would he do this?

Rose whipped around violently to face him. "You're writing a song about how you can't bear to lose her again," she spat. "That's not nothing."

Hugh tried to take her hand, but she yanked it away. "It's just a song. Seeing her made me remember some things, but that's all."

Rose's eyes were starting to water. She *never* cried, and Hugh hated himself for causing this.

"I don't want to talk to you," Rose said quietly. He couldn't bear it.

"Just listen for one minute." His voice was firmer now, though he also wasn't quite sure how he would explain it all given the chance. Rose liked logic and reason, and there was no logic and reason in this. There were no pieces for her to put together and make sense of when it didn't make sense. The past just had a hold on you sometimes.

"I don't want to listen. I don't have to listen to you, Hugh. I need to get out of here."

This was awful. He'd been so bloody worried about disappointing her, so sure he would ruin everything. Self-fucking-sabotage. Why couldn't he just be happy? He took a breath. "Rose, I love you. Just come to the show tonight, yeah? It's all right."

"That's not true!" she yelled, finally breaking. Hugh took a step back without realizing. He'd never seen her this way. He'd never hurt her, never imagined how much he could.

"No matter what did or didn't happen, don't tell me whether I can be upset or not," she said, and her voice was level again, almost eerily so.

Hugh backed off then because he didn't want to say something he would regret. Instead, he let her walk out the door, unsure of when he would see her again.

CHAPTER THIRTY-ONE

NORA HADN'T SPOKEN to Darcy since the night out when they'd fought. They'd been out of the office for the weekend and then Nora had been out on assignments, and then she'd suddenly been in America without a chance to make things right between them. They'd communicated only in brief, professional emails—Darcy telling Nora to spend the week with her mum without worries, Nora thanking her for understanding, but that was all. So on her first day back at work, Nora was fidgety and paranoid, waiting for Darcy to march in.

Darcy did indeed march in, barking orders from the second she made it through the door as usual. When she spoke to Timothy, he spun in his chair and saluted, "You got it, boss." When Darcy saw Nora, she paused. Then she said gruffly, "Shrapsan, in my office."

Nora got up to the sound of Timothy making an "ooooo" noise like she was going to speak to the principal. She could not believe that she considered going on a date with him even for a second.

"Close the door," Darcy said. Nora bit her lip and did as she was told. "Sit down," Darcy said, and Nora sat. Then Darcy's tone softened slightly. "How's your mother?" she asked. Nora hoped this was a Scrooge-on-Christmas-morning situation where Darcy was faking her out with sternness but actually had a turkey and a raise behind her back.

"They think she's going to be okay," Nora stammered. She had never been that intimidated by the Darcy who was her boss, at least not in the same way as everyone else seemed to be, but she was afraid of the opinion of the Darcy who was kind of her friend.

"Good."

"Sorry I took off like that so quickly," Nora said.

"You did what you had to do."

Nora nodded. "Do I have a lot of projects waiting?"

"Of course, we're behind all of our deadlines, as usual, but that's not your fault. I know you'll finish this thing."

"I definitely will."

"There's a museum exhibit, another hotel, another historic tour, another pub. It's all on the docket for you this week. Then we'll have to decide what to cut."

"What to cut?"

"It won't all make the book. It's just too much information. But at least we'll get to choose what works best."

Nora nodded again.

"Well, that's it then, I guess." Darcy said.

Nora took a breath and started to get up. She wanted to say that she was sorry for the night at the Trash Can Bunnies show, that she'd been drunk and foolish and insecure. The only reason that Darcy saying she was a homewrecker had affected her so much was because she was so worried that it was true.

She paused in the doorway and looked back at Darcy again. Darcy was staring at her computer, already typing at record speeds, and didn't seem to have any interest in having a more personal conversation. Perhaps that was for the best, after all.

Then the sound of Darcy's raspy voice made her stop again. "Are you going tonight?" she asked.

"What?" Nora asked, turning. Darcy hadn't even looked up from her computer.

"The show. The Pet Rockers. They're doing another special event for the Goose and Cobbler. Some fundraising or charity thing, I think. I have tickets, but…" Darcy finally paused and looked up at Nora's face. "I didn't know if that was… Or if you'd…"

Nora didn't think she'd ever heard Darcy have such a hard time forming a sentence, even in front of Anika. "Tonight?" she asked.

Darcy nodded but didn't bother trying to say anything else.

"I have a thing," Nora said. Just at the vague mention of her plans with Julian, she seemed to be able to feel him touching her again. Her cheeks flushed. "I don't think it would be a great idea."

"Don't blame you," Darcy said. "Word is, they're debuting a new song though, so I don't want to miss that."

"You'll have to let me know how it is."

"Could be about you for all we know."

Nora remembered the shock of hearing Hugh sing "Lift" in front of a huge crowd, of hearing the words that were written about her being shouted by everyone in the pub at the same time.

She thought that Darcy might ask more about why Nora was missing the show, that this might spark an interest in the little drama of Nora's life, but Darcy only shrugged. "Well…" she said, and Nora almost couldn't bear her hesitation. Nora had been wrong all along, she supposed. They really hadn't been friends or anything close to it if it could all disappear so easily, and Darcy must have wanted it that way, or she would have said *something*. She would have told Nora off for being a prick, or she would have teased her about getting too drunk. If she truly cared about Nora, she would have yelled or rolled her eyes or kicked Nora in the shin.

Instead, she sat there in silence. Mercifully, she'd finally stopped typing, but that didn't really make anything better. It somehow made things even more silent and awkward.

Darcy cleared her throat at last. "They're renovating a hotel on Blackfriars Road," she said. "Might be worth checking out."

"Right," Nora replied before finally walking out of the office.

Blackfriars. A big hotel. Something about that rang a bell. She decided to go over to check it out immediately so that she could avoid being in the office any longer and try to start catching up on work. Everything just felt so weird. Nora was checking in with her mom every hour, but it still didn't feel like enough, and Darcy had seemed like she really didn't want to talk to her for longer than necessary. Maybe she should have made Darcy talk to her and hash it out. She should have laid it all out on the table.

Nora rushed down the sidewalk and turned a corner, only to see a massive building down the road. She had a feeling like déjà vu. As she got closer, she noticed the large sculpture in front of big glass windows and the small, carefully curated garden on the side of the building. It was more than familiar.

Nora stared, her jaw actually dropping. Of course Darcy couldn't have known, but she had sent Nora to the very place where sweet little baby Nora had lost her virginity. Her life was so freaking ridiculous.

The lobby was different, and it had certainly been renovated and updated, but she could still remember everything. Giggling at the front desk with Hugh's arm around her, watching their skinny house-of-mirrors reflections in the doors while they waited for the elevator, feeling overwhelmed as they crossed the threshold into their room, where Nora knew that everything was about to change.

She would never understand how in one whole ginormous city she'd ended up in a place where everything reminded her of Hugh. Perhaps it was a sign. Perhaps it meant nothing, and she shouldn't read into weird coincidences. Perhaps she should stop thinking about lying on the bed while Hugh undressed in front of her, looking nervous even though he was the experienced one.

Everything was so white in her memory, even Hugh's T-shirt. The curtains had been drawn, and the way the light reflected off them made it seem like the whole hotel room was aglow.

"Are you okay?" Hugh asked before joining her on the comforter.

She smiled and nodded, surprisingly sure and calm. She knew she would never regret it, no matter what happened later.

"This is a lot more romantic than fooling around in my flat to the sounds of Dev snoring."

"You mean you don't find Dev's snores romantic?" she asked. "I'm going to miss it. It soothes me."

"Jesus, I'm sorry I brought it up. You're sure you're alright?"

She nodded again and leaned in to kiss him, but he stopped her and stared into her eyes. "I love you, you know that?" he said.

"Now, don't get all mushy on me." Nora smiled.

"Never," Hugh said, but then he kissed her in a way that was very mushy.

"Wait, aren't you going to serenade me first?" She pressed a hand against his chest.

"Nora."

"You want it to be perfect, don't you?"

Hugh shook his head. "What am I going to do with you?"

Nora laughed and then kissed him again.

It had been so perfect, truly. There was a reason she'd compared everything else to that night, compared everyone else to Hugh Jeffries. That didn't mean they were supposed to end up together or she was still in love with him. It meant that the past would always be a part of who she was, even if it wasn't *all* of who she was. She was a different person now, and even though she'd been so ridiculously happy and carefree when she was a teenager, she was starting to think she might like the person she was becoming. And she was starting to think there might be a little bit more to falling in love, more than kissing and romantic songs and sex. There was trust, too. And companionship and commitment. God, real love seemed kind of terrifying.

"Can I help you with something?" A woman in a slimming black suit and a clipboard approached Nora while she was staring out the window that overlooked the side garden.

"Yes, I wanted to see if I could talk to someone about the renovations. Sorry I didn't make an appointment."

"Of course. Right this way," the woman said, and Nora followed.

CHAPTER THIRTY-TWO

THOUGH JULIAN HAD BEEN to dinner with Nora several times before, this occasion already felt different. He'd even put on a tie, though he'd also abandoned it before walking out the door of his flat. He'd bought flowers, though he wasn't sure what she would think. Flowers seemed so serious, like a real gesture, and he had no clue what she was expecting from this evening.

Julian's breath caught when Nora opened the door to her flat. She was wearing a light pink dress with matching lipstick, and her curls fell down her back in a way that made him want to run his hands through them. Nora smiled and took the flowers into her arms, sniffing them dramatically. "They're beautiful," she said. Of course Julian should have realized she was unlikely to have worried about packing something like a flower vase to move to another country. She scrambled around the kitchen, looking for something that would work. They still looked nice in the plastic food storage container that was able to hold them.

At dinner, they were both smiling and energetic. Julian poured out the wine, and Nora kept happily shoving bread into her mouth, then talking a mile a minute when she wasn't chewing.

"It's a shame you didn't get to meet Mom's dog. She has a thing for men, actually. She's way friendlier with random guys than she is with me.

We should have walked over to the neighbor's house just so Bebe could give your face a good lick."

"I didn't realize you were holding out on me." Julian leaned his head in his hand, watching Nora break off another piece of bread. "I could have been a random guy your mum's dog would lick."

"Well," Nora continued. "We did have a lot of other stuff going on." Her face was slightly flushed, making her look even lovelier.

"That's true." He let out a long breath, eyes locked on hers. "Maybe next time."

Nora didn't stop looking at him, and they stayed like that for a moment until she picked up the thread of conversation again.

"Speaking of dogs..." she started, waving around a butter knife. She wanted to know if Julian ever thought about getting a new dog, which he did occasionally, but it would make it harder to travel. Then she asked about his teaching curriculum and the books his students read for class "since they aren't allowed to read slug tales apparently," as Nora put it. Julian hadn't talked this much about his process for planning class with anyone, probably not even his fellow teachers, but Nora wanted to know all the little details. When she found out he also sometimes directed the fall play, she suddenly had a million more questions, and Julian delighted in answering all of them.

It wasn't until dessert when she asked him if he'd spoken to Hugh since they'd been back.

"Well, I did," Julian said. "But he was in a big rush and said he didn't have time to talk. He told me to come see him at the show tonight."

"I heard they were doing another one at the pub," Nora said.

"Yeah, he said there was a list or something, and my name is on it so I can get in."

"Oh." Nora bit her lip. "Are you planning to go?"

Julian cleared his throat. He'd been constantly debating the best way to talk to Hugh about this ever since they'd gotten back from London and still hadn't figured out what to say. "I don't know," he said. "Do you think we should go and tell him together?"

Nora was quiet for a moment, the cute little wrinkle between her eyebrows scrunched on her face. "That might be better, both of us together. We could tell him almost casually, like he shouldn't even think it is a big deal."

That gave Julian misgivings about the whole thing. First of all, he didn't know if he would be able to act casually, and secondly, it was a very big deal. He wasn't sure if Nora knew what a big deal it was for him, but he also wasn't quite ready to tell her.

"So, then we can leave the show to have some guilt-free sex?" he said, trying to laugh away his nerves.

Nora didn't crack a smile. She was clearly still concentrating on how to tell Hugh the truth. "I guess we have to tell him now, right? I think he'll be happy for us. Except, if he's mad at you, Julian, I'll feel terrible."

"Don't worry," he said, though he wasn't sure if he sounded at all convincing. He knew that Hugh wasn't going to like this, but it didn't matter. He was in love with Nora, and he couldn't turn that off or hide it any longer. He hadn't told the truth for seven years, and it was finally time. Not to mention, Hugh was engaged, and Nora was in his past. Hugh had no right to hold a claim on her.

The pub was already packed by the time they arrived, which only heightened Julian's anxiety. He and Nora gave each other a *here it goes* look, before they dove into the massive crowd. It was a miracle when they found Darcy, who was pounding a drink by the bar. She whispered something to Nora, but Julian couldn't make out what they were saying over the sound of the band. He gave Darcy a little wave and watched Hugh belting out one of his new songs.

Hugh seemed different on stage than how he usually was, like he was stumbling a bit and the words weren't quite as clear. Julian wasn't sure if anyone who hadn't seen him perform one thousand times would notice, but he was almost positive that he was drunk. Hugh often had a couple of drinks when he was playing in pubs, but not to that degree where it changed him. He took the music and the performance so seriously.

Julian's shoulders relaxed a bit when Nora grabbed his arm and leaned her mouth to his ear. "Do you want a drink?" she asked.

"I could kiss you," he said, and he meant it.

Nora grinned. "I think we could both use something."

They awkwardly toasted with Darcy and went back to watching the show. Julian remembered the look on Nora's face when she'd seen Hugh up there a month ago, the first time she'd laid eyes on him since being back in London. Julian had watched her so longingly, so jealously then. Everything was different now, and Hugh had to come 'round; it had to all work out, because love conquered all, right? Julian didn't even care if Hugh sang "Lift" with all the emotion he'd had when he wrote it or if he flirted with Nora or if he blew her a kiss in the crowd like in the old days. None of that mattered anymore. Julian had just gone on a real date with her. He'd kissed her in the cab. He'd loved her for so long. It felt so good to be able to admit, even to say it to himself in his head.

His ears perked up when the band started to play a song he didn't recognize. Nora glanced over at him, and he shrugged. Then Hugh started to sing.

It's like I haven't seen you for one hundred years.
But now that you're beside me, no one else is here.
I could have gone without you for the rest of my life, but not
*   tonight, not tonight...*
It's like I haven't held you for one hundred years.
But now that I can touch you, the past is all right here.
I could have gone without you for the rest of my life, but it
*   wouldn't be right...*

Hugh's voice almost broke on the last word, from emotion or alcohol, Julian couldn't tell. It almost sounded like he was playing too fast as well, like the tempo was just slightly off.

Nora was staring at the stage with her mouth open. Julian couldn't believe it. Hugh was performing another song about her in the same bar, but this one wasn't years old. This was fresh. Julian glanced at Nora when Hugh got to the part about the "American girl," hoping she'd be shaking her head in disbelief and embarrassment. But she was transfixed, her eyes following Hugh as he crossed the stage with his guitar. All the elation and certainty he'd felt only moments before was draining out of him.

"What the fuck?" Darcy yelled. Julian had no trouble hearing *that* over the music and the crowd.

When the song ended, Nora finally tore her eyes away and turned toward him.

"Ummm," she said.

"That was unexpected," Julian replied.

"Yeah, something doesn't seem right. That song was…odd. I'm wondering if we should still tell him tonight. Maybe it's not the right time."

Julian deflated. Then he started to wonder about Rose. Wasn't she supposed to be here tonight listening to this? "What should we do?"

"I don't know. That was really weird though, right? I mean, maybe it wasn't, or maybe—"

"That guy just can't let you alone, Nora!" Darcy yelled, clearly as annoyed with Hugh as Julian was, though he wasn't going to shout about it in the same way. He loved Hugh, but why did he have to do this? Why did he have to ruin everything when Julian was so close to having what he wanted?

After the set, Marty told them all they were free to pop backstage to the VIP closet. Julian would have been much more inclined to run home and bury his head between the couch cushions before figuring out how to interact with his best mate, but there didn't seem to be a way to avoid it. He held Nora's hand until the last minute, but as they rounded the corner, she pulled away.

"You're here!" Hugh shouted with his arms open, clearly already drunker than he had been on stage. "Nora, I'm so glad to see you." He wrapped her up in his limbs, and every muscle in Julian's body stiffened. Darcy was glancing at him with sympathy, or possibly as if he was the most pathetic creature in the world.

"I really, really wanted you to be here," Hugh said, and he planted a kiss on Nora's cheek.

CHAPTER THIRTY-THREE

IT HAD BEEN strange to hear a song about her sung in front of a huge crowd. It was even stranger for Nora to hear a song that her ex-boyfriend had recently written about her, a song about how he couldn't let her go. Some deep part of her had been hoping that this exact thing would happen, that she and Hugh would find a way to fall in love with each other all over again. But she'd just started sleeping with his best friend. She'd been on a date with his best friend, and if she and Julian weren't at pub trying to sort things out with Hugh, it might have been the kind of date that lasts all night, the kind where you stay up late talking for hours because you can't wait to learn everything about the other person.

When Hugh kissed her cheek after the show, Nora allowed it. It was a harmless greeting, and he was British after all. There seemed to be a lot more cheek-kissing in the UK. She decided to just power through this encounter before she could run home and freak out about everything while pacing back and forth across her flat and eating all the Cadbury chocolate she could find. Julian would tease her when he saw how quickly she could devour it, how she would moan as the chocolate hit her tongue when she was trying to make him laugh. *Julian would be there*. She couldn't believe how easily she could imagine having him around all the time, how good it would feel.

"It's nice to see you," she said to Hugh. She glanced at Julian, but he wasn't looking, even though she was sure that he was aware of everything —every word she said, every movement.

"We just keep meeting like this," Hugh said loudly.

"It was a great set," Nora said. Julian still wasn't looking at her. Darcy, however, wasn't looking away.

"Nora, could we talk about something?" Hugh asked.

Nora nodded, but she was especially relieved when her phone started vibrating, and she excused herself so she could slip outside to talk to her mom. "I'll be right back," she said.

The fresh air outside was a lifesaver.

"So what's the verdict?" Kathleen asked as soon as Nora said hello.

"What do you mean?"

"How was the date with Julian?"

It seemed like a million years ago, and Nora's thoughts jumbled together. The restaurant with Julian. Hugh singing that song. The look in Hugh's eyes when he saw her. She couldn't seem to find a response.

"The date was...nice. I'm still out..."

"You're still out? Well, that's a good sign, right? What are you two up to now? I won't keep you."

Nora watched as Hugh walked out of the pub, swaying slightly, making his way toward her. *What is he doing?*

"Ummm," she said. She'd forgotten the question. "How are you feeling, mom? Are you doing okay?"

"What? Why are you changing the subject?"

"I better go," Nora said. "Can I call you when I get home?"

"You better fucking call me when you get home so you can tell me what the hell is going on."

Hugh had made his way to Nora, and he was standing quietly, staring her in the eyes.

"OK, love you," Nora said into the phone, but she was watching the man right in front of her.

"Hi," Hugh said when she hung up.

"Hi."

"How's your mum? I was sorry to hear that she was sick." His hair was doing that drift-in-his-face thing again, and there was something about his beard that made her keep staring at it.

"She's alright. Doing a lot better now.'"

"That's brilliant," he sighed.

Nora wasn't quite sure what was happening, but she didn't move.

"Did you like the song?" Hugh asked.

She might have been starting to sweat; her armpits felt precarious, but she couldn't tell if her shirt was wet yet. "It was a good set." Had she said that already? Her brain was turning into applesauce.

"But the song," Hugh said. "About you. It's true. I keep thinking about you, Nora."

Fuck! her head screamed. But also, *Wow! What? This is just what you imagined!*

"I know that I shouldn't, but seeing you again, it's made me remember how perfect we were, the two of us."

Nora tried to remember to breathe. It was just like the things he said in her dreams. It was almost exactly how every single one of her fantasies had played out. Except, in her fantasies, she'd welcomed it. She'd been elated and excited and a lot of other things that were nothing like this. This was awful in real life.

Nora hesitated, chewing her lip for a moment and trying to figure out how to respond. "Do you think that maybe you're just a little nervous about getting married, and this is an excuse?" she asked, because she figured it was a time to be honest about exactly what she was thinking. She needed to be careful to get the facts straight here, but she wasn't sure if mostly-intoxicated Hugh would have the real answers.

"No," he said firmly, but then she saw him waver. "It wasn't until you came back, Nora. I just can't stop thinking about the past."

"But you love Rose," she said. She couldn't believe she was having this conversation on the sidewalk outside of the pub, with warm streetlamps glowing and people around them smoking cigarettes and laughing, oblivious to the weird thing that was happening right before their very eyes. She also couldn't believe that she was trying to discourage her first love from admitting he still cared about her when that was exactly what she'd been wanting for months. She thought she felt a raindrop, and she assumed that, in fact, it must actually be that the heavens were cracking open and about to unleash the apocalypse.

"I do love Rose," he said. "I do, but—"

"But?"

He leaned in and kissed her then, and it was warm and overwhelming and shocking and terrible. She'd imagined kissing him now would be just like when she was nineteen years old, when the whole earth had seemed to spin faster on its axis and gravity had seemed to lose a little of its pull, allowing her to float right off the ground. But it wasn't like that, she realized, as he pressed himself against her. In fact, it didn't remotely compare to anything in her memory.

He tasted like smoke and whiskey and a hint of peppermint and rosewood. Goosebumps were erupting all over her skin, and her heart was a bass drum, but it wasn't right. Her brain yelled at her to make it stop, and she listened, pulling away quickly. She wiped her mouth with her hand and stared at the ground, scared to look up into his face.

"We shouldn't," she said.

"Rose knows," he said. "She's furious with me, but I had to tell her."

"Tell her what?" Nora asked, suddenly terrified at how far this had gone for Hugh already, that she may have inadvertently broken up their relationship without even knowing.

"About you. That I still have feelings for you. I just want a chance for us to see…"

Nora nodded. She knew exactly what he meant. If only they could take a pause from real life, if only they could put on virtual reality headsets and see what might happen if they were to get back together again without any consequences. That's what she'd thought she wanted when she first set foot in London again. But they were such different people now. Perhaps they had always been too different, but Nora had lived in New York and Hugh in London, so it had never really mattered. "We can't," she said finally. "There's Julian…and you would lose Rose for good."

"Julian? What about Julian?"

"There wouldn't be a way to rewind and take it back," Nora continued, realizing her slip and ignoring the question. "It would be forever, and I don't think that's what you want." It wasn't what *she* wanted.

Hugh seemed to sober a bit. He put his hands on the top of his head and exhaled. "Nora," he said. Then again, more slowly, as if just taking it all in. "Nora."

Nora felt like crying. Or perhaps breaking out into a run. This was real. It had completely diverged from the ending in her fantasies where he swept her away and they lived happily ever after. Real people would get hurt. And her fantasies weren't the same anymore. She was aware of that now, or maybe she had been for a while. She thought of Julian and wanted to see him so badly. If she could just talk to Julian, everything would feel right again.

"I know," she said to Hugh. "I know."

He nodded. "I do want to marry Rose," he affirmed. "You just confused me."

"Can't say that I blame you," Nora said. She smirked just a little. "I think it's just that we had something great once. Something we'll always remember. But I don't know if we could ever have that again. You and Rose. You really know each other." She couldn't believe that this was what was coming out of her mouth and that she sounded so calm, but it felt right. At the hotel earlier, she'd remembered how perfect their first time had been, but that was all in the past. As much as she could imagine so vividly how he'd once made her chest swell with happiness, she knew he couldn't make her feel that way anymore. But someone could.

"It's scary sometimes," he said. "When someone understands you so well, and they can change your whole day or your whole mood with a word, when you'd do anything for them, until suddenly everything is moving so quickly, and you don't even have control anymore. I do love her so much. I think I'm just so terrified of disappointing her I was trying to get it over with. She's going to kill me."

Nora squeezed his hand. "You should find her."

He nodded and ran his fingers through his hair. "Thanks for not letting me be an idiot."

"I may have let you for like two seconds," she said.

"It may have already started before I kissed you. I've been a complete bugger. I just felt like there was something unanswered, something I wanted to find out."

"Me too," Nora said. "But I think you really already knew the answer."

"It broke my heart when you left, though, Nora. It really did. I guess part of me thought that someday…"

"I know. But…" The raindrops were falling a bit harder now; her wet eyelids were heavy and tired.

"There's always a but," he said.

"It's different now. Everything is different, including us."

"Right."

"You want to marry Rose?"

"More than anything," he said, as if he had just realized it was true.

"Go." Nora smiled. If you would have told nineteen-year-old Nora that she would be standing in a summer drizzle telling Hugh Jeffries to run off and marry another woman, she never would have believed it. Past Nora would have fought tooth and nail for the romanticized version of her and Hugh, the one she built up in her mind for so many years. But finally, the image was shattered. She wasn't supposed to end up with Hugh. It was perhaps the first time she'd truly realized or believed that since she'd met him.

"Thanks, Nora," he said. "I'm sorry for kissing you like that. Except maybe we needed it, ya know? Just once more."

Nora nodded, but her throat felt thick. "Go on," she said quietly.

Nora rushed back inside, weaving through the crowd that was still gathered, still listening to rock music from the speakers and clinking beer glasses together. The band was drinking by the stage, chatting with fans, but there was no sign of Julian. She rushed over to Marty, and he let her go to the back room behind the stage, but it was empty.

She finally found Darcy, in line for the women's restroom. "What's a girl gotta do to take a wee around here?" she was yelling to a queue of disgruntled ladies.

"Darcy!"

Darcy shook her head. "Don't come too close, I'm about to pee my pants. Where in the hell did you run off to? You've been talking to your mum for a bloody week. I know she has cancer, but Christ."

"Where's Julian?" Nora asked.

"I thought he was with you. He went out to look for ya." Darcy's accent was becoming even more pronounced with the alcohol.

"He was looking for me?" Nora glanced over to the bar again, as if maybe she'd missed him the first time, maybe he was still sitting there with a drink.

"He was all in a flurry, looking around, then he rushed out the back, never to return. Why? What's going on?"

"Hugh kissed me."

"What!" Darcy yelled. "You can't just make out with the lead singer of the Pet Rockers!" Everyone in the line turned to stare, craning their necks to get a good look at Nora.

"You're sure Julian went out the back?"

"What do you need him for? This is too bloody insane."

Nora was panicked, but she knew Darcy was right. Everything seemed to be spinning out of control, but it was time to own up to her shit, and some of that shit started with Darcy. "Hey, I'm sorry, you know. About that night. I was so stupid."

Darcy tried to frown, but she couldn't help the playfulness that crept into her eyes. "It's about time you said so."

Nora exhaled. "I didn't think you wanted to talk to me. I shouldn't have stormed out."

Darcy sighed. "I know that you needed some help and support, not a lecture. I'm just only good at lecturing. I don't know why you want to be friends with me. I'm terrible at it."

"Sometimes." Nora smiled. "But you were right. I needed a lecture."

"Wait, did he really just kiss you?"

"Yes, but I told him we shouldn't. It was a terrible mistake."

"God, your life is so dramatic. So why are you looking for Julian?"

"We kind of have a thing," Nora said. "I was in a state before I went to the airport, and he came over and saw me that way, and I—" Nora paused. "He ended up going home with me."

"Home to your flat?" Darcy gasped.

"Home to New York."

"I'm seriously going to pee my pants right now."

"I don't know what happened. He's just really wonderful."

"I knew it," Darcy said smugly.

"Knew what?"

"That he was completely in love with you. Are you in love with him?" Darcy asked.

Nora shook her head. "I don't know, I... We haven't even talked about the relationship or what we are."

"I don't care if you've talked about it," Darcy said. She was back to her usual, pushy self. "You don't have to have a serious discussion to know how you feel about him. Are you over Hugh now? He's that bad of a kisser? You've been pining for him for ages."

Nora blushed. She wasn't sure how to explain it, even to herself. She just needed to find Julian.

"Ah, finally." Darcy rushed to the open bathroom stall. "Go find him!" she called behind her. "Tell me what happens!"

Nora glanced around the bar again, trying to decide which way to go.

She buzzed at Julian's flat over and over, but no one was answering. When an older gentleman walked out the front door of the building, she slipped in and rushed up to his floor, but still no one responded when she pounded on the door. "Julian?" she called. There was only silence.

She wondered if he had gone to another bar or to his dad's house or to wander the streets of London. She walked back out into the night and checked her phone, but he hadn't responded to any of her messages. She tried calling again, but he didn't pick up. She started walking down the sidewalk, the phone still ringing in her ear.

Then, a distant sound caught her attention, the tinkling ringtone of a phone unanswered. It was coming from what Julian sometimes called "the park" but what was actually a cemetery outside of his building. As she crept closer to the sound of the ringing cell, her eyes adjusted to take in a shadow in the distance.

"Julian?" she called. She did not want to go into the cemetery at what must be after midnight, but he didn't turn around or respond, so she barged through the gate. Suddenly, she hoped it really was him and not some serial killer lingering in the cemetery after dark, waiting for weird girls to waltz right up to him.

When she got nearer to the figure, though, Nora recognized the tall, thin frame, the wavy fluff of hair on his head, and the strong outline of his jaw. She wiped her sweaty hands on her jeans and walked toward him.

"Julian." She breathed a sigh of relief.

CHAPTER THIRTY-FOUR

THOUGH THEY'D ATTENDED the same school, Julian and Hugh hadn't met until they went to camp together. Hugh was a year ahead, so they'd never had the same class, but at camp they were placed into the young adolescent group, and they lived, for those weeks of summer, in the same cabin. Julian was a quiet twelve-year-old who kept to himself a lot. He liked to find different bugs and examine their daily lives—ants building their hills, pill bugs dragging found bits of food toward the grass. Sometimes at night, when other boys were playing cards before bed or wrestling too near the fire, Julian would find a quiet place to listen to the crickets, to inspect any large spiders that came his way, and to read with a flashlight.

That's what he was doing when he really spoke to Hugh for the first time, outside of the icebreakers and group activities they'd done together. Hugh was sneaking back to the cabin in the dark, and Julian was outside with a book and a flashlight.

"You caught me," Hugh said.

Julian recognized him at once. He was the boy with the guitar, obsessed with music, always practicing at the campfire. And Julian was just the sad boy with a sick mom.

"Caught you what?" Julian asked.

"Out after dark," Hugh said. "Though I guess you can't rat me out since you're out here too. I was with a girl," he said proudly.

This was not even on the radar to Julian. Sure, Hugh was a year older, but a single year of maturity didn't seem like quite enough to be sneaking around the campgrounds with someone of the opposite sex. "Oh," Julian said, because there was really no other way to reply.

Without invitation, Hugh sat down next to Julian, and as he got closer to the beam of light shining across the book, Julian could just make out the pinkish glittering lip gloss around the edges of Hugh's mouth. "What are you reading?" Hugh asked.

It was another of the science fiction novels that Julian had been devouring all summer, but he didn't want to say it out loud, so he just flipped the book so his interloper could see the cover.

"I like that one," Hugh said.

"Yeah?" Julian couldn't disguise his shock.

"I just read it. Have you gotten to the part where they find the other planet?"

"They just found it!" Julian said, astonished that the guitar boy with lip gloss on his face had a common interest. "They're deciding to land or if they want to turn around. They're running out of fuel though."

"I won't spoil it," Hugh said, grinning. "Have you read his other book? That one's my favorite. I have it here at camp, if you want."

Somehow, in spite of everything, Julian had found someone to talk with, and it changed things for him. He wasn't just the kid with the sick mom to Hugh. They had other things to discuss—Hugh's grand plans for becoming a musician and Julian's favorite episodes of *Dr. Who*. They would become almost inseparable, and Julian couldn't help thinking of this moment, of meeting his friend with the smudged lip gloss on his face, when he saw Hugh kissing Nora.

Julian was well aware, as he rushed out of the bar, there was absolutely no way he was going to be able to go home and lie in bed without his thoughts completely devouring him and turning him into a madman. He wasn't sure, however, where else he should go. His father was sleeping. The taco truck around the corner would still be open, but the thought of eating made him want to vomit, and it wasn't like he could go off to his best mate's house and receive some comfort there. He walked to his flat, but he couldn't bear the thought of going in and sitting there alone. He kept walking and found himself in the graveyard, which also wasn't really the most comforting place in the world, but at least it was calm. It felt, in some morbid way, like it was setting the perfect mood for his wallowing.

He was surprised when he heard Nora's voice calling over the headstones. He was so surprised that he wasn't sure it was real, but he was unwilling to turn to see for himself. She'd phoned him, but he hadn't been able to bring himself to answer. It wasn't that he was refusing to speak to her, exactly, but he didn't even feel like himself. Even as she walked across the cemetery and grasped his arm, he didn't feel like he was present in the moment. Perhaps he'd instead joined all the lost souls of the cemetery, floating over everything, watching the scene play out below from a great distance.

"Julian," Nora said. "I've been looking all over for you."

"Yeah," the Julian who still had a body and was somehow standing on the earth replied. He knew what she was going to say, but he didn't want to hear it. They could just skip this part, he thought. The part where she let him down easy, made her apologies. They didn't need to have the conversation.

Except, apparently Nora thought they did.

"I need to tell you something," she blurted in a rush. She moved her head toward him, trying to get him to look at her.

"No you don't," he said. "I get it."

He could see the confusion on her face even though he was trying not to look.

"You get what?"

Julian shook his head. This was so much worse than when he had decided to stop seeing her. He'd let it go too far, and now it was going to hurt even more.

When he didn't respond, Nora took it as an opportunity to go back to her original speech. "Hugh kissed me," she said. "Outside the pub. It all happened so fast, and I kissed him too, just for a moment. I'm so sorry, Julian, but—"

"You really don't have to do this," Julian reiterated, staring at the ground.

"I do," Nora said. "I have to tell you about it. Hugh and I talked things over, and I told him he should marry Rose."

Julian still seemed to be listening to the words as if from far away. He paused to try to see if he could make sense of them. *She told him to marry Rose?* It didn't matter anymore, really. He'd had his shot. He'd gotten to spend several days loving her openly—well, almost openly—and he shouldn't have hoped for more than that.

Nora was still talking, but only the last bit of what she said came through. "We agreed that whatever we had is long over."

"Except it's not," Julian said. "You just kissed. He wrote that song about you."

Nora held up a hand toward him but didn't touch him again. "It was just a stupid mistake. I want to be with you, though, Julian." Her hair was still damp from when it had been raining, and her curls sprung wildly from her face. Her eyes were big and glossed with water, her nose slightly pink from the chill of the evening. She was so close he could barely make her face out in the dim light, but he could also remember. He knew the color of her cheeks when she was sad. His brain could fill in the bright blue of her eyes even when he couldn't fully see them. He was familiar with the creases around her mouth when she frowned.

He hadn't expected this—for her to say she wanted him instead. He'd been so busy preparing for the pain of Nora choosing Hugh, so sure he would be forced to let her go. But the kiss kept playing in his mind, and even though she was saying she wanted him now, the kiss said something else.

"I don't think I can do that," he whispered, but it didn't feel like his voice.

"Julian." She sounded strange. "Couldn't we just try? I swear that was just a weird thing with Hugh. I don't want to be with him."

He hesitated. He wanted to say yes, of course. Everything was okay, and they could just pretend that it was still last week, and they were isolated in New York, taking care of her mother. "The problem," he said, "is that I know you have feelings for him, and obviously he still loves you. I can't compete with your first love, Nora. I don't want to have to keep feeling like I'm in competition with him, always a centimeter from losing."

"That's not what it is, though. Really."

"Then why did you kiss him back?" He had rushed away quickly, unwilling to watch what was happening with Nora and Hugh for any longer than necessary to get the picture, but it had been long enough to see she hadn't pulled away immediately. If only for a moment, she'd lingered.

Nora was silent, and Julian started walking toward his building. She followed without saying anything. Finally, when he got to the gate of the cemetery, he turned back to face her.

"Please," she said.

"I don't understand why you invited me along with you in the first place. Why even bother asking me to tour London with you? What was the purpose of that?"

Her eyebrows drew together. "You made me better somehow," she murmured. "I don't know how to explain it."

He took a deep breath. This was not how it was supposed to go. He'd thought there would be candlelight, and they'd be holding each other, that he'd be able to trace his lips across her neck. He'd been waiting to say it, waiting for the perfect moment to finally tell her, but he realized it was never going to come. Better to get it off his chest and never speak of it again.

"I'm in love with you, Nora," he said finally. "I think I have been for a long time. This isn't just a 'try it out and see how it goes' kind of thing for me. This is a serious, maybe-forever kind of thing. I know that what you have with Hugh is confusing, and you're still figuring it out. But I don't want to wait, hoping that you start to love me more than him someday. It's too hard. I should've realized that already I guess, but I thought—"

"Julian," she said, her voice breaking. "You know I care about you." She still looked lovely, but he could only imagine Hugh's arms around her, the way he pulled her in, and she'd relaxed into that kiss as if she'd been waiting for it.

"I know," he said. "I know. I'm just not sure it's enough. I can't be a back-up option for you."

He started walking again, and this time he could feel she wasn't following. She was still standing by the cemetery, stunned and immobile. He forced himself not to look back at her. *Just keep going, you idiot.* It would have been so easy to turn around. To go back and kiss her and take her upstairs. Now he knew, though, that he would always be wondering if she loved him as much as she loved Hugh, if she had really chosen him or if it was just the safest and most convenient option, if she'd really wanted him or if she just hadn't wanted to hurt anyone.

He walked upstairs and thought about texting her immediately, but he didn't. Instead, he collapsed on his bed and wished that he could sleep for days on end.

CHAPTER THIRTY-FIVE

HUGH WAS desperate to talk to his wise, level-headed friend. It had been days since the fiasco with Rose and Nora, and he needed to sit down with someone and have a chat, and honestly, since he'd been a teenager, that someone had always been Julian.

Julian was logical, patient, and supportive. Even when Hugh had fucked about royally, Julian was always able to see the way through it all somehow, to see how to get to the other side of the mess without causing any more damage. Since Rose still wasn't speaking to him and he thought it a bad idea to call Nora, Hugh had been waiting to sort it all out over a pint and some pub cheese with his best mate.

The only problem was that he hadn't been able to get hold of Julian since the night of his show—the night when he foolishly kissed Nora—and he was starting to wonder what the hell was going on. Sure, sometimes Hugh lost his phone or locked himself into a musical retreat or went on a bender and didn't call anyone back for days, but in all the time he'd known him, Julian had never done such a thing. He'd always been prompt and responsible. And so Hugh was on the verge of marching over to Julian's flat and breaking down the door, when the dingus finally texted him back.

They met at a pub in Covent Garden, and because of all of his worrying and stress, Hugh knew that he must look awful. He'd been surviving on coffee and cigarettes, even though he had severely cut back on his smoking since meeting Rose. It was a time of crisis, though, and all his willpower had depleted. What really surprised him was that Julian was in much the same state. Julian didn't smoke, but he looked like shit. His hair was a disaster, and he had bags under his eyes; instead of sitting down properly, he just kind of fell into the chair as if he couldn't bother to offer any more effort.

"What the bloody hell happened to you?" Hugh asked, still looking him over.

Julian leaned forward, his face in his hands.

Hugh kept prodding, worrying even more the longer he looked at his friend. "Have you been sick, mate? What's going on? I really needed you."

Julian finally managed to lift his head and look at Hugh. His eyes were bloodshot and a bit frightening. "I have to tell you something," he said.

Hugh hesitated. In all the years they'd known each other, he'd never seen Julian like this before. "Right. Okay, what is it?"

Julian sighed, and it was like all the strength drained out of him, like a deflated balloon. "You're not going to like it," he said.

Hugh raised his eyebrows and waited. He didn't understand what could possibly be going on. They were supposed to be fixing *his* life.

"Well, I—I don't know what she might have told you—" Julian began.

He couldn't take the pauses. Something serious was going on, and Julian was taking all fucking millennium to spill it. "What who told me? What is it, mate? We better talk about it, 'cause we've a lot of ground to cover today. I'm a disaster, and I need—"

"I'm in love with Nora," Julian said.

Hugh froze. He thought this must be some kind of odd joke. Then he thought about who he was talking to and the terrible state he was in. Julian was too kind and honest to joke about something like this, but it still didn't make any sense. "What?" he said through his teeth.

"I've been wanting to tell you for a while, but the timing's been off."

"The timing?" Hugh said, his voice a bit louder. People at the tables around them glanced in his direction. "What do you mean the bloody timing? I told you I still had feelings for her, and you couldn't bother to share with me that you happen to be in love with her? How long has this been happening?"

"I didn't realize then." Julian looked a little ashamed, but still more exhausted, like perhaps he didn't have all that much left in him that could care about what Hugh was going to say next. It was something else that Hugh had never seen in him before.

"You didn't realize? Okay, so when? How long have you been in love with her?"

Julian paused. "I don't know. I figured it out...that night maybe. The night you told me you still had feelings for her. Or maybe a long time ago, but I just didn't want to believe it. Listen, let me just get it all out."

"You of all people," Hugh scoffed.

"What does that mean?" Julian asked. His voice was getting louder as well. Hugh couldn't believe his wild look or the harsh creases around his eyes. "I tried so hard not to do anything. I never thought I would have had a chance anyway, and it seemed pointless to even mention it. I tried so hard not to be with her, even though you were engaged anyway."

Hugh was quiet. He opened his mouth to respond, but he didn't even know what to say. It was like he'd entered some parallel dimension where his friend had turned out to be a robot the whole time, and he'd never suspected. They were supposed to be talking about *his* problems, figuring out *his* love life, not raking through the details of Julian's pining for Nora. It had to be one-sided, after all. But then Hugh remembered something Nora had said after they'd kissed. Something about Julian.

"Does she—?"

"There's more," Julian said.

"More what?"

"Just let me get it all out. I hope you'll forgive me someday, but also, you should forgive me because you're fucking engaged, Hugh. You haven't been with Nora for years."

Hugh's mouth was hanging open again. "Go on then," he said gruffly.

"I took her to see her mother when she had the surgery. That's where I was that week, not that you really noticed. I tried to call you a million times before it happened, to tell you the truth before it got out of control."

"Before what got out of control?"

"We slept together."

Hugh stood up, his chair scraping behind him loudly. He looked around the pub, trying to decide what he was even doing, but people were looking at him again and he sat back down. "She has feelings for you too?" he whispered. Then he said it again, a statement this time, not a question. "She has feelings for you too. The other night, when she was saying that we couldn't be together, she said your name. I didn't realize she wanted to be with you instead. I really was just an idiot pining after something that had disappeared a long time ago."

Julian sat back and didn't look at him for a long moment. "It hadn't disappeared though. She still felt it too, and you know it. She kissed you."

"I kissed her, like a bloody fool."

"She kissed you back, because somewhere she still feels it. She's not over it either, even after—even after me."

"So are the two of you dating now?" Hugh was still trying to make sense of everything in his head. He'd been writing songs about her and fighting with Rose, while Nora had been falling for Julian.

"No."

Hugh sighed. "You went to the States together, you shagged, she turned me down, and yet you aren't together now?" It was odd that he felt like the logical one for a change. He was still in a state of disbelief, but this was Julian. Shy, calm Julian, who had made himself sick over a girl. Hugh still felt the nudge to act like his friend, even if he was confused and angry.

"I can't compete with you, mate," Julian said darkly. "I don't want to."

"Hmmm," Hugh grumbled. "Setting aside the fact that I'm still right on the verge of starting a barney with you in the middle of this place, did you forget the part where I said she turned me down? We didn't run off into the sunset. You've won."

"Maybe she wanted to run off into the sunset with you," Julian said glumly. Neither of them were shouting any longer. "But she's too responsible now. She didn't want to be the cause of breaking up your marriage. She didn't want to hurt Rose."

"She didn't want to hurt *you*."

"Yeah? Maybe she didn't want to hurt me, but that's different from being in love with me."

"She knows that you're in love with her?"

"I told her, yes."

"And she said she didn't feel the same way?"

"Well, basically. She didn't say anything. She'd just been kissing you."

Hugh smacked the table. "Julian, if Nora wanted to be with me, she would be with me. I would have gone off with her that night, which would have been a giant mistake. I haven't spoken to her since, and she hasn't tried to talk to me. Where did she go after we kissed?"

"What? I don't know."

"No, you saw her. You said you told her then that you were in love with her. Where was it? Did you show up at her door?"

"No—I—it was outside of my flat." Julian's face was red, and Hugh couldn't tell if it was from embarrassment or pure despair. Sometimes Julian just went red in the face without warning when he was slowly building up a wall of sadness inside himself.

"I kissed her, and she rushed to your flat? It's not sounding like a competition at all, mate."

"Well, it doesn't matter," Julian exploded. "I don't want to do that to you anyway. I knew you wouldn't like it. I didn't mean for it to happen; I just couldn't stop it. I didn't want to stop it."

They were both silent for a long time. Hugh chugged a pint and waved his finger to request another. Julian watched him but didn't say anything else. This hadn't been what Hugh was expecting at all when he went out to get comfort and advice from his oldest friend. He put a finger to his lip and tapped it, thinking hard. He really had stepped into a parallel universe somehow. He never would have imagined anything like this, but he was almost afraid of Julian—not *of* him, but of how upset he was. It was completely unusual, and that must have meant something important. *Jesus*, he still couldn't believe it.

"I want to marry Rose," he said.

Julian looked up and gave a small shrug.

"I guess it would be rather ridiculous of me to go off and marry another woman that I love and forbid you from seeing Nora. It'd be childish, and I'm trying to be more mature here. Everything Nora said to me was right, anyway. We don't belong together. I was excited by the past coming up and remembering all that passion, but we're different people now. I'm in love with someone else. Hurting Rose like this, not being able to see her every day. I'm more gutted than I've ever been in my life. Even if I was scared before, well, this is much worse. And Nora's in love with you. I don't want to get in the way of that."

"I don't know what you're even saying."

Hugh took a dramatic breath and placed a hand on Julian's shoulder. "I guess I'm saying that I give you my blessing."

Julian scoffed. "Come off it," he said.

"I'm serious."

"Well, it doesn't matter."

"What do you mean? Stop moping and let yourself be happy about this, man. I'm telling you it's okay. I'd be a total prick to stay mad at you, though I wish I'd known sooner."

"She's not in love with me. And I don't want to be her second choice, so your blessing is irrelevant. Thanks anyway."

"You're not her second choice, you idiot. I kissed her, and she said no. Why aren't you getting this?"

"She said no for a million reasons. The first is that you were probably being a drunk arsehole to begin with."

"No, take that back," Hugh said in his *Real Housewives* accent, and Julian smiled for the first time. Hugh breathed a sigh of relief. They could fix this somehow. "Maybe you're right. Maybe she's not in love with you. But did you even give her a chance to tell you if she was? Or did you storm off in a huff like you do when you lose at *Warcraft*, which is the maddest I've seen you until now, by the way."

Julian didn't answer, he just pursed his lips and looked away.

"That's what I thought," Hugh said. "You and Nora. Fuck. Did not see that coming at all to tell you the truth."

"Sorry," Julian said, a bit of his usual self coming back again. "I didn't mean—"

Hugh waved him off. "We'll figure it out," he said. "Just please tell me you aren't going to ruin this for yourself."

Julian didn't answer. He took a drink of his tea, his eyes cold and distant.

"Come on, mate. I need you. That's the whole point of why I brought you here this morning. I need to get Rose to speak to me again. I need your good sense of romance. Don't go trying to turn it off now."

CHAPTER THIRTY-SIX

NORA HADN'T WRITTEN anything good about London without Julian. Any solid blurb or article she'd created had been about a place that they'd been to together. Every piece that Darcy had praised was full of Julian, even though he wasn't explicitly mentioned. He'd been there for all of it, for every good sentence. She'd only been able to really experience each place, to really understand it and let it become part of her, if he was there too. She'd needed him from the beginning, and she wasn't sure how to keep going, how to pretend that London wasn't a vast empty wasteland and that Shakespeare wasn't a stupid git and that even the murders weren't incredibly boring without Julian.

She spent half of the time she was "writing" with her head on her desk in despair. Sometimes, she even moaned, to which Timothy would respond by shouting, "Tell me about it, sister!" across the room.

Not only had she let Hugh kiss her, which was a ridiculous mistake, she had also let Julian walk away without really having a conversation—without telling him that she had some kind of feelings inside of her, and they were probably important, even if she didn't know how to explain or make sense of what was happening.

She tried calling him a couple of times, but he didn't answer. She texted that she was sorry, that she really wanted to talk to him, that she could explain everything, but she wasn't sure that was true. How could she explain that she'd fantasized about Hugh as the perfect man for years and years, but that suddenly everything was different now and nothing from the past mattered? She wasn't even thinking about Hugh, except to hope that he was able to get his engagement back on track. She was thinking about Julian every moment, in every word that she wrote about London, in every line that she edited to try to make the guide book a little less personal and a little less obvious that she was crying over the person that had spent time taking her through the city.

"In my office," Darcy said to her just as Nora was staring blankly at her computer screen. It was the same every time. Darcy crooked a finger and Nora followed behind her without question. She slumped into a chair as Darcy closed the door. Darcy sat across from her, an expectant look on her face.

"Well?" she said. "How long are you going to continue moping?"

Nora stared at the ugly brown and yellow patterned carpet beneath her feet. "I don't know," she said quietly.

"I can't complain," Darcy said. "You've been meeting your deadlines, and the writing isn't horrible, but I'm worried about you..." She sighed. "As a friend, I guess."

Nora couldn't help the little smirk that crept onto her face. "I'm your friend," she said, not letting Darcy get away with the use of the word without any comment.

"Don't get all fat headed. You're a mess, and I'm trying to help here. So what are you going to do?"

"You don't think the writing is horrible?" Nora asked, a little amazed.

"It's not. You never needed him for the writing, Nora. You just needed to get over yourself and actually have some fun and feel something."

"That's why I needed him. I always had fun with Julian. I always felt...something."

"Which brings me back to my question. What are you going to do?"

"There's nothing I can do," Nora said. "I've called him. I've tried. He won't talk to me."

"Well maybe you haven't tried hard enough."

"Darcy..."

"What? Do you remember what a pain in the arse you were about Anika? Always bugging me to do something about it. And look at you now."

"If I remember correctly, you never really did anything about the Anika situation. One measly text. I've tried way more than that," Nora said. "So you really have no place to be offering advice here."

"Don't start with me," Darcy said.

"What? Why?"

"Because you aren't the only one allowed to be confused about a relationship and your feelings, and my fears and insecurities about Anika shouldn't just be a convenient topic of interest when you don't want to talk about your own problems."

"You're right," Nora said. "But I care, Darcy. It's not just a distraction from my own mess. I'm not just teasing you."

"I know," Darcy said. "It's frustrating. I've seen her here, but it's the same as always, like nothing happened. I don't have the balls to do anything, Nora. I need to just move on. I've got a date with a girl from the internet."

"Please let me see your online dating profile," Nora laughed.

"Now you are teasing me," Darcy said, but she was almost smiling. She handed over her phone, with the profile on the screen.

"Enjoys reading, eating food, and watching the telly," Nora read aloud. "Very specific, Darce."

"I figured I would start by casting a wide net."

"Well, apparently it worked."

"Is he as shy and polite in bed as he is in real life?" Darcy asked suddenly. "I just imagine him, like 'ah, pardon, how can I move my penis to your exact preference? Would you like a drink of water before I orgasm?'"

Nora couldn't stop herself from laughing. "Actually," she said. "He kind of takes charge in the bedroom. I didn't expect it, but he is super passionate. It's really hot."

"Oh, Christ, I'm sorry I asked." Darcy laughed.

Nora groaned. "I totally screwed this up."

"Like I said, fix it."

"I'm sorry, but again, I must refer to the Anika situation. It's not that easy to do something to make it better."

"Well, what if I did?" Darcy asked.

"What?"

"What if I finally made some grand gesture with Anika, like you're always on about, then would you do something to get Julian back?"

"Yes," Nora said quickly, but then she bit her lip and shook her head. "I don't know what I would do though. He doesn't want to talk to me. I'm going to respect that."

"Tell him that your mom isn't doing well. He'll have to speak to you then."

"Darcy!"

"Okay, a bit manipulative, maybe. How is she, by the by?"

"She's doing great, *by the by*," Nora teased. "Thank you for asking. She's in remission."

"Well that certainly is good. But I guess that strategy won't work out for your love life."

"Back to square one," Nora said.

As if on cue, the front door of the building opened at that moment, and Darcy and Nora both turned to look through the glass wall of Darcy's office. Anika was heaving a box of mail in the entryway, where she set it down at the front desk and began to sort through various large envelopes.

Nora decided not to say anything about it and continue with their conversation, but Darcy started to rise from her chair.

"What are you doing?"

"Going to have a word with Anika," Darcy said, a look of resolve on her face.

"What word?" Nora sat stunned as Darcy marched out of her office and headed toward the mail carrier. She couldn't hear what they were saying to each other, but it didn't take long until they were laughing. Then Darcy held the front door open and led Anika out.

Everyone in the office seemed to turn toward them, straining their eyes and ears to figure out what was going on and why their uptight boss had just exited the building with the hot mail lady. Tim was leaning awkwardly out of his chair to try to get a view of the sidewalk. He almost lost his balance and tumbled to the floor. Nora was a little disappointed he caught himself.

After what seemed like ages, Darcy strutted back into the office alone, snapped at Tim to get back to work, and appeared back at her desk across from Nora once again.

"What the hell just happened?" Nora asked.

Darcy smirked. "Game on, Nora," she said.

"Pardon me?"

"I just asked her out. We're getting drinks after work. She seemed into it, like she was happy that I'd asked."

"After all this time, it was that simple? Why had she never asked you before? You two made out, and it's taken this long to go on one lousy date?"

Darcy was beaming in a way that Nora found unbelievably odd. Darcy had never been so happy before. And Nora had never been the downer, especially compared to her grumpy boss. It was supposed to be "Doom and Gloom Darcy," not "Negative Nora."

"She was nervous about it too. Didn't know if it was just a one-night, out-of-the-ordinary encounter. She said she's had a crush on me." Darcy was actually blushing.

"You just did it," Nora said. "How did you do that?"

"You were right, I guess. I didn't want to give up on that yet...not without even trying."

"But you were so nervous! I mean, I am so happy for you Darcy, but I never expected you to do that."

Darcy smiled brighter than Nora had even seen. "I don't know why I was such a twat. She never even saw the text. Maybe it was a wrong number. She had no idea what I was talking about."

"But you made it look easy, Darcy!" Nora almost shouted, then managed to calm herself down again. After all this time, Darcy had made up her mind in an instant, and she'd gone for it. She'd completely put herself out there in a way that Nora had never thought possible.

"So, it should be really easy for you and Julian, then," she said.

Nora raised her eyebrows, baffled.

"You two have had sex. Multiple times. Should be no problem to go out on a date and talk things through."

Nora dropped her head in her hands. She wanted to go back to her desk and wallow in peace. She was thrilled that things had gone well with Anika, that her friend had finally found the courage to make a move. But she was still miserable, and Darcy's success didn't change anything. "Things are so complicated with Julian. It's not that easy."

"But what if it is?" Darcy asked, still smiling from ear to ear. "What if it is that easy after all?"

When Nora finally managed to change the subject from Julian, Darcy admitted that they had plenty to discuss about the book. The deadline for a draft was quickly approaching before a graphic designer and photographer would start to put the disparate pieces of London's story together for a Millennial and Gen Z audience. And they would need to heavily revise and edit all of those pieces.

But the company was already looking ahead and thinking about future projects where they might apply this same tactic, which would also include the online material and a funky travel app. They also still wanted additional London content to be written for the app, so there would still be some kind of narrative and interactive maps with reviews. Bulking up the technology and online content was next on the list. And if all went well, they wanted to do the same thing in Barcelona.

"The project would still technically be based out of the London office, but you would do research in Spain for a few months at a time to come up with the content," Darcy said.

"What do you mean *I would?*" Nora asked. She leaned closer to her boss, as if she wasn't hearing her correctly.

"I mean, I'm not going to Barcelona. I won't even be writing, but I'll coordinate projects and assign locations. You'll take a team and work as the lead writer over there."

Nora stared in disbelief.

"Oh, I'll still be your editor. You will report back and send everything to me, but you'll have a bit more independence to shape the app. A bit less oversight."

Without realizing what was happening, Nora literally fell out of her chair and plopped on the floor. She'd been so concentrated on Darcy's words, inching closer to make sure that she was understanding, that she hadn't realized where the chair ended, and found it disappearing right out from under her. If Timothy were to walk in he might die of laughter. Darcy stood up and looked over the desk.

"Are you comfortable down there?"

Nora gaped up at her. "What about Timothy?" she asked.

"I don't trust Timothy in Spain. You might have fallen in love with your London guide, but I imagine that Timothy might spend most of his time focused on threesomes in sex clubs in Barcelona. And you're a better writer. You have more of a sense of the vision of this whole undertaking. There's a piece of you in it. Please do get up off the floor, though, and don't make me question this."

Nora clawed against the desk and struggled to pull herself into a standing position. "Thank you, Darcy," she stuttered. "I don't know what to say."

"They hope to start next year before the London project is even finished. I suggested getting initial numbers on the app first, but we'll see. There's a lot to do before then, so don't zone out on me now."

"This is kind of exactly what I want," Nora said. "I mean what I've wanted for a long time. You don't even know…"

"Nora," Darcy admonished. "This isn't something I'm giving to you. I'm not being nice here. You worked really hard and did a good job. You earned this. And I'm not complimenting you again, so don't ask. This is your one moment with me to treasure forever, so don't go expecting anything else."

Nora refrained from wrapping her boss up in a giant hug, but she couldn't help grabbing Darcy's hand and squeezing it enthusiastically, if also a little too hard. She didn't want to say thank you, because as Darcy said, this wasn't a gift. She didn't want to say, "I won't let you down," because Darcy would have laughed in her face and probably reminded her about what a dufus she had been for ages. Instead, she just smiled and didn't let go of Darcy's hand.

"Bloody hell, you really are such a sap," Darcy said.

Though Darcy had warned her not to "zone out," Nora couldn't concentrate on anything else the rest of the day. Instead of going home after work to sit alone in her empty flat, she decided to take a walk and release some of the pent-up energy from her "promotion" and her heartache. Without really having any idea where she was going exactly, she found herself walking toward the Thames, and before long she was on Tower Bridge, looking out over the water while boats were drifting lazily down the river.

At sunset, she couldn't take her eyes from the pink and purple celestial light that gleamed around the London skyline. She was simultaneously both thrilled with herself and devastated. She was going to be the lead writer on the Barcelona book, which was probably one of the best things that had ever happened in her whole life. She had a stream of texts in all caps from her mother, who was out at a movie with her aunt and probably texting through the whole thing, annoying everyone nearby with the glow of her phone. Her mother's latest text read:

> "YOU ARE A GENIUS MAGNIFICENT
> PUMPKIN!!!!!!! IM SOOOOOOO PROUD!!!!!"

Her mother was already making plans to visit Barcelona and was probably Googling tourist attractions right there in the middle of the film as well. But Nora kept thinking about Darcy's face when she'd come back into the office after asking Anika out. She'd finally had the courage to ask this woman for the thing she'd wanted for so long, and it had paid off. Even if it wouldn't have paid off, she'd finally had the ovaries to go for it.

Nora had been brave in her life too, hadn't she? She'd moved to London by herself, after all, which not only took bravery, but also a lot of grueling paperwork. Even though she was the freaking *lead writer* for the Barcelona book, she still wanted to call Julian and tell him all about it more than she could have put into words. She wanted to hear how thrilled he would be about her success, how much it would mean to him, even though he wasn't getting anything out of it. He would just be happy for her without any other interest or agenda. She wanted to hear his voice so badly. She wanted to tell him that she was an idiot for ever kissing Hugh back, for ever having feelings for him again, when Julian had been there the whole time. She wanted to tell him that she had quite possibly fallen in love with him, even though she hadn't remotely expected it, and she was kind of freaking out.

She took out her phone and rubbed her thumb against the screen. She really had tried calling him. She didn't know what else Darcy expected her to do. Hugh had texted to let her know that Rose was coming around, or rather, Rose was talking to him at least, after a very thorough analysis of why he'd kissed Nora in the first place; that was good. But what the hell was Julian doing? Where was he? Hugh told her they'd had drinks in Covent Garden, but that was about all she could get out of him.

Nora wandered off the bridge and walked past the Tower of London. She thought of Anne Boleyn, of Richard III's little nephews who had been trapped there. Then she thought of Julian. He kept popping up no matter what she did.

Nora's mind drifted back to the day that they'd all gone together when she was nineteen, how Dev had teased the Beefeater, and Hugh had begged her to get a touristy Tower of London T-shirt and wear it all over the city, announcing her American citizenship wherever she went.

Before they'd left, she'd found Julian standing alone in a brick corridor, listening to some audio guide, taking it all in. He beamed when he saw her.

"Can you believe I've never been here?" he said. "Five hundred years of history, and I never bothered."

Nora grinned up at him. "It's very cool. I'm glad you all came with me."

"We never would have if it weren't for you. I mean, maybe I would go on a school field trip sometime, but I don't think I'd appreciate it like this. You're good for us, Nora."

"You're good for me," she said. "I would've gotten lost on the Tube five times getting here if I didn't have you."

He had been blushing a little, and he turned his face slightly away from her. Nora hadn't noticed his eyes before that, how they glimmered in the dim light. He was still smiling, but he looked nervous. She wasn't sure what she had done to make him feel weird. She was probably embarrassing him again somehow, but this time there wasn't anyone else around.

Then the rest of the gang caught up to them, their voices echoing through the hallways, and Julian turned back toward the stones until she couldn't see his face at all.

Did he care about me, even then? Nora hadn't wondered about it at the time; she never would have believed it. But now he'd said that he was in love with her, that this could never just be a fling. It was a terrifying thing to say that she was ready, that she could handle it—to take on the weight of his heart and have the power to hurt him. To give him the power to hurt her. But what if it was something that could make her truly happy? What if it was easy after all?

CHAPTER THIRTY-SEVEN

JULIAN DIDN'T WANT to speak to anyone, but his father didn't care. Every day, he showed up at Julian's flat, banging on the door, and he wouldn't leave until Julian had at least eaten something and smiled once. When Julian started fake smiling, his father shook his head.

"Not genuine," he said. "I can tell. You aren't that good at acting, despite all those Shakespeare plays you did in high school."

"You could leave me alone for one day, Father," Julian said.

And yet, the next day at 19:00, there would be pounding on the door again, and Julian would roll himself off the couch and open it.

He did go out for drinks one night but left early when Dev brought a couple of girls to the table to chat, or to flirt, really. And he also went to the cinema once, alone, to watch a showing of *Monty Python and the Holy Grail.* He ended up wondering what he was doing there and left early to grab a street sausage and sit in silence on a park bench. The rest of his days were spent on the sofa, reading the sad poetry he was making his students read so he could thoroughly teach them about the pain of life.

He held his mobile in his hand whenever Nora called. He felt it vibrate against his fingers and stared at her contact photo on the screen. He thought about answering, but he didn't. When she texted:

"Please can we talk?"

He typed "I want to," but never hit send. The draft message was still waiting there, taunting him.

He taught an abbreviated night course at a writing program. He played video games with Hugh—who was growing more confident that Rose would marry him again—in the late evenings. He answered the door when his father tried to pound it down.

"The way I see it," his father told him, "you're just delaying your own happiness. Imagine if you were to call her tomorrow, to go meet up with her so that she can tell you that she feels the same way about you. Why are you putting that off with your wallowing?"

Julian was hanging upside down from the sofa, blood rushing to his head. It had taken weeks, but his father had finally pried most of the details out of him. "Because I know that's not what's going to happen. She was in love with my best mate, and I don't think it changed overnight."

"It may have, if it was a really amazing night." His Dad snickered. "Just call her, and stop being so pathetic."

"That's exactly why I can't call her," Julian argued. He flipped himself right-side-up so he could really drive home his point. "Because it would be so pathetic. I need to stop pining for this woman and move on with my life."

"What happened to all of your confidence, man? Get it together." His father handed him a bottle of beer and sat beside him.

"What would you have me do then?"

"Show up with roses and kiss her. Bloody hell, it's not that hard."

"It *is* that hard when I'm not the one she wants."

"Oh Christ, will you come off it already? There's not a timeline in this story where she wasn't in love with Hugh first. That will never change. What you can change, though, is what you do about it now, when she wants to be with you and you're hiding away from her, drenched in your own tears."

"Those aren't tears. I spilled my tea."

"Julian..."

"You don't even know her, Dad. Why are you fighting so hard for this?"

His father scratched his chin and didn't speak for a moment. "I know you," he said finally. "And I know you deserve to be happy."

It's a special kind of sorrow—loving the woman who was in love with your best friend. Seven years ago, Julian never had any hope with Nora. Even if she would have come on to him, he would certainly have never done anything when Hugh was her boyfriend. He would have thought less of her for trying, despite the fact that he was absolutely mad about her and still hoping every day that she would notice him. It was an impossible situation.

Things were different now, but Julian wasn't sure of how much they could have changed after all. Hugh was engaged to someone else this time around, but as his dad had pointed out, the past could never be erased. She would always have loved Hugh first, in every version of the story. Julian didn't know how to forget that fact, especially when he had found them kissing so recently.

A large part of the problem, he knew, was his own lack of confidence. He had enough self-awareness to realize that if Hugh hadn't always been the popular one with a girlfriend—the cool guy that everyone wanted to talk to at parties—then perhaps he wouldn't have had such an inferiority complex. If he could just truly believe for a moment that Nora might actually be in love with him instead, then perhaps he could have shown up with flowers and kissed her as his father had suggested. But there was no evidence of this. As he always told his students, there needed to be factual evidence in the argument, not just emotional appeals. He and Nora had a good time together, sure. They'd walked the streets of London and made love in her childhood bedroom. They'd talked for hours in low restaurant lighting, where she'd discovered that he couldn't whistle, and he'd found out that she looked terrifying when she tried to roll her tongue. But a large portion of their time had also been spent talking about Hugh, as she had conducted an investigation into his engagement and tried to sort out her own feelings. Julian couldn't ignore that part.

"You're miserable," Hugh said, which was a nice way to be greeted when Julian reluctantly arrived at a pub to see him. For the first time, their friendship had been awkward and strange that first week after all was revealed, but it hadn't taken long for them to arrive back on normal ground, giving each other shite and bickering like brothers.

"You're annoyingly chipper," Julian replied.

Hugh grinned. "Rose is moving back in tonight. Finally."

"I'm glad for you, mate," Julian said. "I hoped you two would work it out soon."

"It was a struggle," Hugh said through a mouth of doughy bread. "I just about entirely fucked that up. But now I feel surer than ever that this is the right thing."

Julian smiled and popped a piece of bread into his mouth as well.

"Have you talked to her?" Hugh asked with a meaningful look.

Julian couldn't pretend he didn't know what he meant. He shook his head.

"I'm not going to give you another lecture about what a thick-headed idiot you are," Hugh said. "I'm just going to remind you one last time that she had a chance to have me. It wouldn't have worked out, and it would have been a terrible mistake for both of us, but whatever the case, she said no. She wants you."

"I'm trying to believe that." Julian coughed.

"Don't be daft, Julian. Don't you remember Marnie Wilde?"

"Yeah, you broke up with her at the end of sixth year. Why?"

"I didn't break up with her because I didn't like her. It was because she would moon all over you every time you were around. 'Julian, can you help with my literature assignment? Julian, come have a dance with me. Julian, you look so good in those slacks.'"

"You're full of it. She was just being friendly." He ripped a piece of bread in half and twisted it in his hands.

"I can't say I know what it was. Maybe she mistook your whole awkward bit for aloofness. She was trying to get to you though, and the only reason she didn't break it off with me was because you never looked twice at her."

"Marnie Wilde?" Julian said, astounded.

"The only reason why I had girlfriends is because I flirted shamelessly and asked out a lot of women. It was a numbers game, really." He was talking with his mouth completely full, and Julian smirked at the thought of his heartthrob best mate flirting with loads of women while anyone could see all the food on his tongue.

"So you're telling me you aren't actually cooler or better looking than me?" Julian laughed. He appreciated Hugh's effort to cheer him up.

"The jury's still out on that," Hugh said. "But I'm telling you that if you want to get the girl, you have to ask."

Julian shook his head and ran a hand through his hair. Then he put a hand on Hugh's shoulder. "Rose is a lucky woman," he said.

"She will be. I'm going to do everything in my power to make her feel lucky every day." Hugh finally swallowed, the look on his face full of utter determination.

"Wouldn't it be strange for you if Nora and I..." Julian trailed off, only just daring to allow himself to think of what could happen. "What if she was going to be my date to your wedding?"

"Things might be a bit off at first, especially with her and Rose, but I think they'll come around to each other. Look, if you're really in love with her, you have to give it a chance."

Julian shrugged.

"You're terrible," Hugh said, laughing. "You're buying the next round."

Julian returned to his flat slightly tipsy and feeling better than he had in weeks. That wasn't saying much, since he'd been a regular Scrooge, stalking the streets of London without a kind word for anyone, but an improvement was something anyway. For a quick moment, he'd let himself imagine that he could end up with Nora after all. It was perhaps ridiculous to cling to that one tiny hope so fiercely, but it made him feel like he could survive.

When he'd finally trudged up four flights of stairs in his complex and made it to his front door, he found that something was taped there, right below the peep hole. An envelope. His name was written on the front in cursive—only his first name—in large sweeping letters that he recognized immediately.

Nora had been here. Somehow, she'd made her way into the building and put something on his door. He sat at the kitchen table and turned it over in his hands for at least ten minutes without opening the seal. He hadn't spoken to her in weeks and had no idea what this letter would say. When he finally tore the envelope open, he nearly ripped the paper in half, but then he slowed to be more careful, gently unfolding the several pages that were written in her neat handwriting.

"Julian," it began at the top of the first page without any other kind of greeting. When he had only read the first few lines, Julian was already sure that this was a letter that he would read over and over again many times.

CHAPTER THIRTY-EIGHT

NORA HADN'T MEANT to write a letter. She'd been writing for the book, talking about adventures across the city, about the best places to eat and drink in London, but suddenly she was describing the graveyard where Julian had told her that he loved her and the look on his face before he turned and walked away. She wasn't sure the CEO of 99 Flamingo would want to put that part in the travel book, but without thinking she grabbed a notebook and started scrawling across a blank page, filling it with all of the things she wanted to say.

She wrote about the moment in the nineties club when they were dancing, the first time she imagined kissing him. She rambled in several incoherent sentences about sitting with him in the hospital as they kept vigil over her sick mother. Then she talked about Hugh, about the kiss, about how much she wished she could take that moment back forever, but —at the same time—it had helped her to realize what she really wanted.

When she was finished, she folded the pages and put them in the bottom of her purse. Sometimes, over the next several days, she would take them out and read them over again, scratching some things out and changing the wording, revising all the time, even though she never expected anyone to read it.

"You don't seem as ecstatic as I thought you would be about

Barcelona," her mother said over video chat, raising and lowering her eyebrows dramatically. Kathleen was clearly spending most of the conversation staring at herself in the little box to see how good she looked, but Nora was okay with that. She did look good, after all. She deserved to admire herself in the video chat box.

"I'm thrilled about it," she said.

"But there's still something wrong," her mother replied, because she always knew, and also it was probably obvious to anyone who was looking. "Something by the name of Julian?"

"I don't want to talk about it," Nora said.

"You also don't want to wonder for the rest of your life what would have happened if you would have told him how you feel."

"He won't talk to me."

"I think you don't even know what you want to say."

Nora rolled her eyes at the little camera over the screen. "I know what I want to say, Mom. I wrote him a letter."

"And?"

"And what?"

Kathleen sighed heavily. "And what happened after you gave him the letter? He had to have had some response. You're a writer, after all, so I hope it was good."

Nora looked off into the distance. "I didn't give it to him," she said quietly.

"Oh, God, Nora!" Her mother's voice boomed out of the speakers. "Give him the letter. If it doesn't make any difference—well, what have you got to lose at this point? You might as well just try."

Everyone always talked about it so nonchalantly, as if it were easy to pour your heart out to someone and finally be honest with them and with yourself. But what if she gave him the letter and Julian still never spoke to her again? It might be even more devastating that way.

"I see your mind working," her mother said. "I can always tell when you're thinking really hard, usually about some snarky comeback you want to say to me. But whatever you're going to say, don't bother with it. Just give him the letter, for God's sake, Nora."

And so she did. She read it one last time, stuck it in an envelope, and let her thoughts and feelings out into the world for another person to know and hopefully understand. Then she sat around restless and sleepless for twelve hours until she had to go to work. After that, she sat at work without doing anything except imagining him opening the letter and reading her words. She tried to picture his reaction. In her worst fantasies, she imagined him angrily tearing it into pieces and abandoning the scattered bits on the ground. In another scenario, the letter fell off the door of his flat and was swept into the trash, never to be seen or read at all, without Julian ever even knowing it had existed. She wouldn't hear from him again and would have no idea that he'd never read it. In another fantasy, he held the pages to his chest and almost cried before rushing to call her and tell her that he needed to see her right away and then taking off her clothing, piece by piece, and kissing all over her body until it tingled...

That was her favorite one to imagine.

She sat at her desk, desperate and devastated, waiting for something to happen, waiting to hear something from Julian. Surely he had read the letter by now, but still not a word from him. *What could he possibly be thinking?*

"You doing alright over there, Buttercup?" Tim asked, rolling his office chair toward her.

"I'm fine," she said.

"Americans always say that when everything's awful." He laughed. "*I'm fine. I'm fine.* But usually the world is falling apart."

"I think I just need some air," she said, standing up from her chair. She walked outside robotically, unsure what she was going to do. Her feet carried her to the Tube station, and on the way she realized that she might be marching off to see Julian, to ask him how he could decide not to respond to her letter, not to offer the slightest courtesy of what he was feeling so that she could have just a little closure or something.

She sent him a message, and she told herself that this would be the last.

This was it. If he wasn't going to talk to her after she had poured her damn heart out, then screw him anyway.

Talk to me, she wrote.

After almost a month of nothing from him, she was ready to hash this out, to demand that he speak to her, if only to say he really would never see her again. *But how could he say that?* She was speed-walking to the Elephant and Castle Station, so angry and hurt and confused and tired of feeling this way, even if much of it was her fault.

She paced back and forth outside the station, trying to decide where she would go if she were to get on a train. She wouldn't show up at his flat again. She'd already tried that, and look how well it had worked out. She didn't even know where he was, and he still hadn't responded to her message. She'd never imagined that he could possibly be so cold after everything—after the way he'd held her and stroked her hair, the way he'd put his hot mouth against her thigh.

Then she thought of how much she'd hurt him and felt like she couldn't breathe. Why had she let him think for a moment that Hugh was more important? How could she let him believe she didn't feel the same thing he did? Why had it taken her so much to be able to admit it?

She was still pacing in front of the station, digging her fingernails into her palms. She had to go somewhere. She had to do something, to wait outside his flat all night if that's what it would take. She rushed into the station, her eyes wild. She was never going to be able to find him in the whole of London, but maybe Hugh could help her. There had to be some way...

But somehow, as if by magic, Julian was there. He was getting off the escalator wearing a light blue button-down shirt, which only made her remember tearing a similar item of clothing from his chest the first night they had kissed. And he was carrying a bouquet of flowers, just like the ones he'd brought on their first date, the ones she kept for too long as they started to keel over in her plastic food container. He didn't see her yet, but still she could barely move or speak, utterly breathless as she watched him moving through the crowded station.

In a moment, she realized that he might walk out the door and miss her altogether if she didn't do something, so she shouted his name and moved toward him, all of her anger and pain seeming to melt as he saw her and changed the trajectory of his path.

It was actually him. He was coming toward her. She was still trying to make sure it wasn't just some mirage from her desperate heart. *How could he be here?*

"Nora," he said, stopping right before her.

"When I saw you in the crowd, I couldn't believe you were real," she said.

He smiled. "I've had that same feeling before."

He's smiling at me! She thought she might faint like some lovesick debutante in a Victorian novel. "Julian, I—" Nora began, but she didn't know how to continue. He'd read it all. Surely he knew. "How are you here right now?" she asked, wanting to break into sobs at the relief of seeing him, of having him speak to her.

"Well, I thought I would go to your office to find you, but then you started calling to me through the station."

"Like a total stalker," she said, and he smiled again. It was so beautiful.

"I read your letter," he said. "You're a pretty good writer. You should work on a book or something."

She bit her lip and waited for what he would say next.

"You meant it?" he asked. "You're in love with me?"

She nodded shyly, still holding back tears. "I am very much in love with you," she said. "I should have just said it outright sooner but, well, I'm an idiot."

He shook his head and looked down, finding her hand and taking it in his. "I've missed you so much."

Nora smiled, though she felt like she might be having a heart attack. "I'm sorry," she started, but she was interrupted by a very pleasant sensation. Julian took her in his arms, wrapping himself around her until the flowers were pressed against the back of her hair, and he kissed her hard on the mouth, somehow unlike any time before and somehow also so comfortable and perfect.

People rushed past the station, on the way to whatever important place they were going—to work, to the pub, to school. Nora let the rush of bodies blow right past her, up and down the escalators, in and out of the doors. She didn't need to move at all, because for the moment she was sure that she was right where she was supposed to be.

When they broke away from the kiss, a rush of words came out of her mouth. She still wanted to explain, to let him know that he wasn't just second-best, like he'd said at the cemetery. "I'm so sorry for everything. Being with you has meant so much to me. More than anything you're my friend, and you—"

"I know," he said. "I know. Like I said, you're a great writer." He kissed her again.

"By the way," he asked. "Are we going to Barcelona?"

"I was hoping you might be able to join me there for a while. And in New York. And in London. And basically anywhere we want to go, forever." Nora could feel the heat rising up her neck and into her cheeks.

He gave her a mischievous look. "You don't need me around to write though," he said. "I can't believe you thought you did." She'd explained that part too, all of it, how she'd only been able to write about London if he was there.

"I want you around," she said. She should really write more letters. They were such a great way to clarify everything. Now he knew it all. And he had come.

"I'll be there," he said. "And for the sake of honesty and getting everything out in the open... Since you were so forthright with me..."

"Yeah?" She couldn't imagine what he would say. Her stomach dropped for a moment.

"I've loved you for a very, very long time, Nora Shrapsan. Since the first time you were in London. You thought I was embarrassed by you, but I was embarrassed by how much I wanted you."

"What?" She wrapped her arms around him, amazed that she could hold him, shocked that he'd cared for her so long ago. "I had no idea. You never..." She trailed off, trying to find any sign of his feelings in memories from seven years earlier.

"Maybe we won't ever mention that part to Hugh." He smirked, raising an eyebrow.

She shook her head in disbelief before grabbing his face and pressing her lips to his again.

EPILOGUE

NINE MONTHS LATER

NORA WOULDN'T HAVE EXPECTED that one of her first stops after she landed in London would be a double date with Darcy, but Anika was so freaking cool, and whether or not she would ever admit it (she would not) she had missed Darcy. A lot.

She was thrilled to see them there waiting at the pub; Nora had picked the Goose and Cobbler, for old time's sake, and they were already at the bar. Darcy looked happy, her round cheeks even fuller when she smiled, her eyes sparkling when they landed on her girlfriend. Anika absolutely brought out the best in her. She'd even taken Darcy out to her family farm several times to get away from the city. Nora would have paid to see Darcy on a farm with pigs and overalls.

"Hello," a voice said from behind her. Suddenly Nora felt like she'd just stepped off a Tilt-a-Whirl, dizzy and delighted. She thought it would wear off after a while, but that still happened every time Julian was near her—when he stepped out of a cab outside her place in Barcelona, when he opened the door to his flat in a wrinkled tee. It gave her carnival ride insides every time.

She turned and kissed him on the mouth before nuzzling her head up under his neck and letting herself breathe in his perfect scent. He kissed the top of her hair.

"Yes, we get it. You're mad about each other," Darcy grumbled, but her complaints were hollow, and her smile was quick to reappear when she looked at Anika. "By the way, the app update seems to be going well. They fixed that thing where the pop-ups keep blocking the maps."

"Thank goodness," Nora said. "That was so frustrating. I mean, I love having my content all over the page, but not if you can't even see where you're going."

Julian and Nora slid onto stools at the bar and gave Marty a wave.

"I can imagine you would relate to that since you often don't know where you're going."

Julian laughed. "She's getting better with directions, Darcy. She really is."

"Hey, don't talk about that in front of Anika; it's humiliating. She has the best sense of direction of anyone in the entire world," Nora said.

"GPS is actually my best friend," Anika chimed in.

"You know your way around London better than any person in this city."

Anika shrugged. "You can't help it after a while. It just becomes ingrained in you."

"And gives you a great ass," Darcy said matter-of-factly. "All that cycling."

Nora made eye contact with Julian and grinned. Barcelona was absolutely one of the most amazing places in the world, and she'd been loving it. Even Kathleen Shrapsan had made the trek to visit, though she did question why she'd traveled all that way to look at some unfinished church. But nothing could beat sitting in the back of the little pub that felt like home, the place where Nora had found Julian again.

"Are you two prepared for the festivities this weekend?" Darcy asked.

"You should see me in my tux," Julian said. "I basically look like James Bond."

Nora squeezed his leg. "I can confirm that."

Darcy rolled her eyes. "And you're sure the bride doesn't mind that you've slept with her groom?"

"Darcy!" Anika said.

"What? I'm asking this to the nosiest person in the world. If the roles were reversed, she would absolutely be questioning me as well."

Nora shrugged. "She's not wrong."

"Rose insisted that I bring her," Julian said. "They get on quite well, actually. Better than I would have ever imagined, considering, you know."

"Rose is even cooler than I pictured her," Nora said. "I'm kind of surprised how not-weird things are with us. Especially since Hugh was so jittery the first time we met."

Julian smiled. "She's certainly more easy-going than I will be in that situation. Even if Hugh is my best mate."

"In what situation?" Nora asked.

Julian blushed a bit. Anika and Darcy smiled at him and then at each other.

"Well, um—"

"I think he means when *you* are the bride and your ex-boyfriend is a guest at the wedding," Darcy said.

Julian coughed and took a gulp of water.

"Oh, is that what you mean, Julian?' Nora asked, teasing him. She batted her eyelashes. "You're thinking about when you marry me?"

Julian tugged at his shirt collar. "Well, I'm not proposing...right now," he said. "Anyway, you know your mother would kill me if I didn't tell her first."

Nora blinked. She'd only been joking because she liked to make him blush, but he *was* thinking about marrying her. They'd talked about their future together, but no one had said the word *marriage*. She looked over at Julian, and his attention was focused on her, waiting for her response. A wide smile spread across her face, and he relaxed, his expression matching her own. "That's a good point." She brushed her hair behind her ear and let herself stare at him with dopey eyes for a second longer. It was amazing how much she didn't care about the fact that she would soon be attending Hugh Jeffries' wedding. If anyone had told her a year ago that she would become platonic friends with Hugh, that her heart wouldn't even register that he was going to be saying his vows to someone else, she would never have believed it.

Somehow, she was instead head-over-heels about Hugh's best friend in the world, and he was even thinking about marrying her. She took Julian's hand in hers and squeezed, trying to keep herself steady, even though she felt like she was on the Scrambler this time, or maybe the Spinning Swings.

Nora hadn't kept a diary since she was nineteen, but she'd started a new one to keep track of her adventures with Julian. They were soon going back to New York again for another visit with her mother. Then she'd be in Barcelona for a while, and they would do long distance again until she finished that project and was able to get back to London. Julian's students were doing a production of *As You Like It* in the fall, and she would be there, cheering them on from the front row. Then they would go wherever they wanted when Julian was able to travel. She would go anywhere and everywhere with him and never for a second let him feel like he was second-best again. She would always choose him, no matter what, and she'd make sure he knew it.

"I love you," she whispered while Anika and Darcy were ordering another round.

He grinned. "You're not afraid about the head-getting-chopped-off thing? I seem to recall that you had a rather grim view of marriage."

"You're no Henry VIII." She smiled. "I think my head is feeling quite secure where it is."

Thank you for reading! Did you enjoy? Please add your review because nothing helps an author more and encourages readers to take a chance on a book than a review.

And don't miss more from Hannah Ledford coming soon. Until then, discover ROCK BOTTOM ROMANCE, by City Owl Author, Diane Holiday. Turn the page for a sneak peek!

You can also sign up for the City Owl Press newsletter to receive notice of all book releases!

SNEAK PEEK OF ROCK BOTTOM ROMANCE

BY DIANE HOLIDAY

Crystal Lovechild would rather be caught without makeup by paparazzi than scout another wretched location for a campground-set reality show. From the passenger seat of a dented SUV, she tugged at the seatbelt, chafing her neck. She checked her fresh manicure and let out a breath. All good. The tips and polish would have to last throughout filming. How she longed for the days when she arrived at a gig in a chauffeured limo with her own hair, makeup, and wardrobe team.

"You gotta be shitting me. More wild turkeys?" Sydney, her field producer, leaned on the horn. She blew her purple-streaked bangs up and slapped the steering wheel. The flock jerked, separated, and trotted off the road.

"Are we almost there?" Crystal gazed out the window. They sure as hell weren't in Hollywood anymore. Cows grazed behind miles of fences. This spot in the Midlands of South Carolina took the prize for the most remote of the four locations they'd scouted and showed the least promise. Nothing but farms, fruit stands, and blood-thirsty mosquitos. She shuddered and scratched her now itchy arm.

"We're close." Sydney's pierced lips twisted. "Not exactly what you're used to, is it?"

"I'll be fine." Crystal hoped.

Sydney was a real pain in the ass with a chip on her shoulder a mile high, knowing the star of the show would be a fallen celebrity. From the moment they'd met, the woman had doled out one backhanded insult after another. People loved to see a famous person out of their element. The concept of a celebrity learning to rough it camping had thrilled test audiences, but Sydney's production company couldn't afford an A-list actor. She'd made sure Crystal knew she'd been their *last* choice in the low-budget production.

Since subletting her Hollywood penthouse wasn't enough to put a dent in Crystal's bills, it was the reality show or wait tables. So not happening. She cringed at the mere thought.

She glanced at her silent phone, and a pit formed in her stomach. No texts, messages, or calls, aside from Jenna, Crystal's long-time friend, the one person who hadn't ghosted her.

Sydney slowed for yet another turn in the road. "I hope you like hot dogs and beans because there's no caviar on the island."

"It's two months. I'll survive." A bead of sweat trickled down Crystal's back. Her agent had made it clear it was this gig or nothing. Crystal needed a spark to get people talking about her again, and any screen time counted. Besides, how hard could camping be?

At last, they reached the gate. A sign that read "Stone Island Park" marked the entrance. Sydney stopped at the admissions booth and opened the window.

Hot humid air rushed in. The temperature topped ninety and it was only the first week of June.

A short, stout woman, wearing a khaki safari shirt and shorts, stepped out of the booth.

Sydney handed her a business card. "We're with the production company for *Celebrity Trials*."

"Yeah, I heard y'all were coming to check out the island. You're gonna love it." The park attendant bent and peered at Crystal's glittery halter tank, miniskirt, and stilettos. Her lips twitched and her eyebrows knitted. "That's…quite the outfit."

"Thank you." Crystal's chest inflated and rose like a hot-air balloon. She'd glammed up for scouting the sites. In the end, she might decide she didn't want them to use any of the footage, but if she did, she'd give her fans a glimpse of the star they knew and loved. Couldn't hurt to start off with some confidence, and it might be a while before she could dress in her fashion line of clothes again.

The attendant straightened, scratched her head, and checked the road behind them. "I expected a row of cars. You know, full of bodyguards and reporters."

"I don't think she has to worry about paparazzi anymore." Sydney smirked.

Crystal's blood heated. The truth stung. Even if she had the money to pay for a bodyguard, she wouldn't need one. She'd lost mega followers and subscribers on social media. No one tried to sneak candid shots anymore.

The park attendant grabbed a pamphlet from the booth and handed it to Sydney with a big smile. "Here's a map. Feel free to stop back and ask any questions. We're excited for y'all to be here."

Sydney thanked the woman and pulled forward. "Trevor is meeting us at the campsite for the opening shoot. I hope the cameras are all set up because I need him to capture your arrival. If not, I'll have to help him again like the last time when he was running behind."

"Don't look at me," Crystal replied. "I only know one side of the lens."

"I wasn't holding my breath, hoping for your assistance." Sydney's cheeks puffed.

They crossed a long bridge over the lake with water rippling on both sides. Random small boats peppered the shoreline as fishermen cast near the rocks. What fish was worth baking in the sun and bouncing around in the water all day? No thanks. Plated and served was more Crystal's style.

She gazed at the woods on either side of the single-lane road beyond the bridge and shook her head. "Why don't we save us all some time and turn around? This is too remote."

"You haven't even seen the camp yet."

"I've seen enough." Crystal dusted her hands of the place. "Go back. We're done here."

Sydney hit the brakes and turned to Crystal, her face bright red. "I've had it with you. I busted my ass for four years to work my way up to producer, and this is my big chance. I'm not about to let some washed-up child star living off her past celebrity status blow it. The contract says the company picks the site, not you. Got it?"

Crystal's throat constricted. Damn. She hadn't read the contract.

That's why she had an agent, who should have told her about the stipulation.

She huffed. "Fine. Let's get it over with then."

Sydney pulled into a shady parking spot on a campsite loop. "Looks like Trevor is ready for us."

He stood by a cement slab surrounded by woods with a trail that led to the lake. Just like at the other locations, people pitched tents on concrete here. Crystal's hips and elbows ached at the thought. She'd hoped for a more comfortable arrangement. Maybe she'd buy a foam pad like the one she had for her bed. The thicker, the better. As soon as she had money for one, she'd order it.

With her well-practiced, red-carpet smile pasted on, she opened the car door. She pushed out of the SUV, making sure to pause as her heels hit the ground for the best toned-legs shot. Not that it mattered, because she had no intention of working on this island.

For now, she'd play along.

She crinkled her nose and shrugged. "I think my viewers will be bored with this remote place. The other sites had way more campers and action."

The roar of an engine cut through the silence. She spun around as some sort of jeep or four-wheeler thingy came to a halt next to them.

A mountain of a man jumped off the vehicle wearing camo pants and an olive T-shirt stretched to the max over his broad shoulders. The fabric clung to the rippled muscles of his stomach. He radiated pure strength with corded veins in his neck and not an ounce of fat on him. She judged him to be about her age, late twenties.

He had a buzz cut and a couple of days of stubble on a chiseled face. His prominent, strong jawline clenched as he strode toward them. This guy moved with purpose and power, like a big black bear on its hind legs defending his territory.

Crystal swallowed and tried to ignore the fluttering under her ribs. The unfamiliar feeling caught her off guard. Sure, she'd worked with macho types in the movies, but Hollywood used special effects and cosmetics to make them appear larger than life.

Aviator glasses hid his eyes, yet she sensed anger emanating from him. What was his problem?

Sydney made a keep-the-cameras-rolling hand gesture to Trevor.

Great. Sydney and Trevor couldn't be on film, so it was up to Crystal to deal with the man.

He stopped in front of her, planting his feet in a wide stance. "I'm Zach Stone. Obviously, you are the celebrity whatever crew." The sides of his mouth turned down. "I run this campground."

Not the most welcoming hello. And either he didn't care enough to know the name of the production company, or he'd dissed it on purpose. She smoothed back her hair and shrugged. "Doesn't look like much to manage. A bunch of woods and tents. What's the worst problem? Sunburn?"

He snorted and his chest expanded.

She tore her gaze from his pecs to his face, and her own reflected in his mirrored sunglasses. Her cheeks heated, and they turned pink before her eyes. What the hell? She didn't blush. Then again, she'd never been this close to someone so…daunting.

"What's this getup?" He waved a hand from her head to her feet. "You plan to camp in that?"

Her skin prickled. Getup? He should be thrilled she'd even considered wearing one of her designer outfits to his Podunk grounds. From the corner of her eye, she noted Trevor had moved closer, zooming in on them.

"I'll have you know this is the latest in my line." She smoothed a hand down her side and squared her shoulders. "It's so popular I can't even keep up with the orders." If only that were true.

Zach's head dipped and snapped back up. Was he checking her out?

"Cut." Trevor lowered the camera. "This thing's on the fritz again. I have to get the other one from the villa."

"That's fine. I need more coffee anyway." Sydney checked her watch. "We'll grab some at the general store and meet again in half an hour?"

Trevor nodded.

"I'll make sure I'm here," Zach said.

Crystal raised her chin. "We don't need you to be. Why don't you do whatever you do while we check out the place?"

"Keeping people like you from getting hurt while stomping around my territory unsupervised *is* what I do. I'll be back."

Crystal glared at him as he stalked to his vehicle. Her face burned. The guy had a bad attitude and a load of arrogance to go with it.

Just another reason to make sure they chose a different location.

Like hell he'd have the last word. She had a thing or two to say to him before she left him in the dust.

———

Don't stop now. Keep reading with your copy of ROCK BOTTOM ROMANCE, by City Owl Author, Diane Holiday.

Don't miss more from Hannah Ledford, coming soon, and keep up-to-date at www.hannahledford.com

Until then, discover ROCK BOTTOM ROMANCE, by City Owl Author, Diane Holiday!

———

A grumpy outdoorsman tempts a spoiled celebrity to trade the red carpet for roughing-it.

Bankruptcy can drive a girl to drastic measures, like leaving Hollywood to star in a low-budget camping reality show. Crystal Lovechild despises the grouchy man who runs the campgrounds. He's condescending, arrogant, and...hot. One glare from him and she sizzles like butter on a skillet. Doesn't matter because they are complete opposites. All she has to do is survive two months, revive her career, and get back her life.

Zach Stone has nothing in common with the pampered diva, who shows up and brings chaos to his camp. He wants her gone and has a scheme to make her high-tail it back to California.

As Crystal and Zach spend more time together, each grasps that the other isn't what they thought. Crystal realizes Zach hides a soft side under his gruff exterior. He's nothing like her pretentious Hollywood boyfriends. Before she knows it, she's questioning how much she really wants to go back to her fake world. And Zach sees that she's spunky, determined, and has deeper layers beneath her glamorous façade. He's in trouble because if she doesn't leave soon, he's in danger of falling for this fallen star.

———

Please sign up for the City Owl Press newsletter for chances to win special subscriber-only contests and giveaways as well as receiving information on upcoming releases and special excerpts.

All reviews are **welcome** and **appreciated**. Please consider leaving one on your favorite social media and book buying sites.

Escape Your World. Get Lost in Ours! City Owl Press at www.cityowlpress.com.

ACKNOWLEDGMENTS

For so long I didn't know if this novel or anything I'd written would make its way out into the world, but here it is, and I have so many people to thank for their help along the way. Huge thanks to Jessica Shearer for working with me to make this book so much better than it was. Yelena Casale, Marianne Hull, Tina Moss (I still swoon when I look at the cover), and everyone at City Owl Press—I am forever grateful.

Thanks to the many writing students and instructors I have worked with over the years, and a special thanks to the Plaza Writing Team, which is great for writing but even better for idle chit chat. Sarah Bull, thank you for being one of the first people to read this and texting me out-of-context comments in the middle of the afternoon. I seriously don't know where I'd be without you. And Joshua Wallenstein, thanks for your support and writing advice, but most of all, thanks for being a lovely human and making me laugh.

Jaimee Wriston Colbert and Jen Bokal, thank you for talking me through high anxiety moments when I knew absolutely nothing about publishing. I'm also so grateful to the people who were early champions of this book—Lisa Peterson, Amanda Johnston, Lauren Becker, Dyane Foltz (world's best photographer), Olga Valdivia, everyone in office book club, and my awesome family.

I think my parents must be the most supportive people in the entire world. Mom, thank you for being the first person to read everything, and Dad, thank you for always believing in me without question. I cannot express how much you both mean to me.

One gigantic thank you to John, who just kept telling me to "publish the book already" and never doubted I would. And thanks to my boys. You guys are too amazing for words, and I can't believe I'm lucky enough to call you mine.

ABOUT THE AUTHOR

HANNAH LEDFORD is a romance novelist with a PhD in English. She loves travel, giant sweaters, and making up bedtime stories about Bigfoot in space. She's lived many different places, including a tiny flat on Tower Bridge Road. *Elephant and Castle* is her first novel.

Follow her across social media and find out more on her website at www. hannahledford.com

Photo by Dyane Foltz

instagram.com/hannahledfordwrites

tiktok.com/@hannahledfordwrites

facebook.com/hannahledfordwrites

ABOUT THE PUBLISHER

City Owl Press is a cutting edge indie publishing company, bringing the world of romance and speculative fiction to discerning readers.

Escape Your World. Get Lost in Ours!

www.cityowlpress.com

f facebook.com/CityOwlPress
X x.com/cityowlpress
instagram.com/cityowlbooks
pinterest.com/cityowlpress
tiktok.com/@cityowlpress